THE LIBRARY

First published in the UK in 2021 by Head of Zeus Ltd
This paperback edition first published in the UK in 2022 by Head of Zeus Ltd,
part of Bloomsbury Publishing Plc

9 7 5 3 2 4 6 8

A CIP catalogue record for this book is available from the British Library.

ISBN (E): 9781801100465
ISBN (PB): 9781801100489

Typeset by Siliconchips Services Ltd UK

Printed and bound in Great Britain by
CPI Group (UK) Ltd, Croydon CR0 4YY

Head of Zeus
5–8 Hardwick Street
London EC1R 4RG

www.headofzeus.com

For The Shed Gang:
Anne, Carol, Charlotte, Emma, Heather,
Jane and Riannah

– I love you guys!

I

TOM

My name is Tom Harris and I am invisible.

Not actually invisible – that would make me interesting and I'm not. I'm the person others find easy to forget. The one who is lost in the crowd. To be honest it suits me to be invisible. I hate it when I get noticed and I'm thrown into the spotlight, I'd rather be lost in the white noise of life. My neck goes red and blotchy at all sorts of unhelpful moments, like if a teacher asks me a question. 'Thomas Harris, what do you think the author meant by "We are responsible for each other"?' How would I know? I'm always Thomas Harris at school or Tom H. Never just Tom or Thomas. It's a really common name at my school. There are five Thomases in my year. There's a confident one, a sporty one, a loud and funny one, a stroppy one that the girls seem to like and then there's me, the other one.

My skin heats up if I make eye contact with a girl. I think it might be something in my DNA that's trying to stop me breeding another generation of invisible people. So far it's working. It's easier if I avoid girls. But there's one girl that I wish I could look at without doing an impression of a tomato. She's Farah Shah. Farah is perfect; from her black, straight-as-a-ruler hair to her bubbles of laughter. She's smart too. She asks the sorts of questions that make the teachers think. I know she's completely out of my league but that's okay; most people are.

'Tom!' said Dad loudly, his ruddy face looming around my bedroom door. He waved the fish and chip bag at me. I pointed at my noise-cancelling headphones by way of reply.

He wasn't cross but he'd probably been calling me. He's all right is my dad. He's a bit invisible like me. I followed him downstairs. We don't talk much. He works nights and I'm at school all day. He dished out the food, I grabbed the tomato ketchup and we ate it on our laps in front of the TV. We always have our meals like this. It's just me, Dad and the TV. Mum died when I was in year four.

I unwrapped my dinner. 'Saveloy?' I pointed at the alarmingly red item peering at me from under the chips.

'Yeah, sorry. They'd run out of battered sausages.' He went back to eating his.

'But I hate them.' I gave it a prod with my fork.

'Do you?' He seemed surprised. 'My mistake. It was your mum who loved the things. First meal I bought her was saveloy and chips.'

I was a bit surprised at that. Not that my mum like saveloys but that my dad had mentioned her. He doesn't talk much anyway but he never talks about Mum. I guess I'd got used to not trying to chat about her because it was pointless. He'd always change the subject or simply walk away. But now I saw my chance to ask about her. It was a good opportunity because it was a workday so he'd not been at the whisky. But what did I want to know?

I ignored the offensive saveloy and mopped up some ketchup with a giant chip. A thought struck me. 'How did you and Mum first meet?' I asked, turning on the old brown sofa so I could see my dad's reaction. There was patchy stubble on his chin; he'd not shaved properly.

He put down his cutlery and blew out a sigh. 'Blimey, that's made me think.' He seemed to drift off. His eyes rested on the photograph of Mum on the mantelpiece. It's one taken on our last holiday when we rented a caravan in Hunstanton. I love that picture of her. She's laughing. She used to laugh a lot. We all did. I can hear her laugh if I concentrate hard but I worry that one day I won't be able to remember what she sounded like. It's like she's slowly being rubbed out. Dad blinked and gave me a sorrowful look. He always looked like that if I tried to talk about Mum. I was ready for him to change the subject. 'We met in Plummers,' he said at last.

'At a plumber's?' I laughed at the thought of them surrounded by toilets.

'No, you goon. Plummers was the little bookshop in the high street. I was picking up the latest Stephen King novel. I made out I'd ordered it but really it was my dad's.' He chuckled at the memory. 'Your mum was with her friends giggling in the romance section. We got chatting and I asked her if she wanted to go for a Coke float. I loved a Coke float, me. Why don't we have those anymore?'

I rolled my eyes at his nostalgic view of the old days. I knew they were my age when they got together. Soul mates he called it when he'd said a few words at her funeral. I don't know exactly what he meant but I do know they were happy. Not perfect. There were arguments, sometimes, but nothing to spoil my memories. Dad said they didn't have much money and that's the only thing they rowed about.

'She loved to read, did your mum.' He looked at the photograph again.

'I remember her sitting on my bed reading me bedtime stories.'

He gave me a watery look. 'Books never interested me. Do you read much?'

I shrugged but he expected more of a response. 'Just the stuff school makes us read.'

He looked around the small dim living room. It had hardly changed since Mum died. Just that it was a bit neglected and more of a mess.

What he'd said gave me something to think about. Girls liked romance novels. I wondered if that was still true?

'Right.' Dad checked his watch. He needed to leave for work. 'You going out?' He always asked me this and I always shook my head. I never go anywhere in the evenings. I have a couple of mates but we play FIFA on the Xbox. We can do it from the comfort of our beds so why would we go out? Playing Xbox with my mates makes me feel less of a sad case stuck here on my own. 'Okay, then. I need to be making tracks. Lock up and I'll see you in the morning.' He gave my shoulder a squeeze as he passed and took my dinner plate out. I'll do the washing up before I go to bed. It's how we do things: Dad gets tea; I wash up. I put the washing on; Dad does the ironing.

My mates moan about their parents all the time. How they want to control their lives, never let them out of their sight and get on their case. I always agree and say my dad's the same but he's not. He is annoying when he goes on about bills, politics and the state of the roads but I guess I do stuff that annoys him too. I could go out tonight and he'd not know where I was or what I was doing and he'd be okay with that. But I've no reason to go out. I'm invisible.

I was woken by the toilet flush. Dad was home from work. I cast a blurry eye at my alarm clock: 6.37am. I pulled the covers over my head. It was Saturday so I went back to sleep. Dad would go to bed soon. It must be well weird to have to work at night and try to sleep in the day, like being forced to be nocturnal. Although I'm getting a taste of it thanks to some bloke in America challenging me on *Call of Duty* and keeping me up until 3am. I settled back down and tried to go back to my dream about Ariana Grande.

I rolled over and checked the clock again: 11.58am. That's more like it. Dad's alarm would go off in two minutes. He only grabs a few hours on a Saturday morning so that he can sleep on a Saturday night. I heard his alarm start. That was my cue to get in the shower before he did.

Dad was getting coffee when I came into the kitchen. 'Afternoon, son.' He tried to mess up my hair but I dodged out of the way. I finished off the half bottle of apple juice from the fridge and dropped the bottle in the recycling. 'I'm walking into the village. Do we need anything?' I asked.

'Magic beans,' said Dad, looking at a bank statement.

'What like those half sugar ones?' I hate those reduced sugar baked beans. They taste like crap. 'Oh, right.' I got the pantomime reference a little too late.

'Never mind,' he said, then he opened a cupboard and shook his head. 'Crisps and biscuits but only the cheap ones. Okay?' He handed me five pounds.

I grabbed my rucksack, earbuds and coat and I left. I'm glad he didn't ask me why I was going into the village. I'm not sure it's my best idea but it's worth checking out. A few kids from my school live in the village but nobody I'm friends with. Farah Shah lives between my village and town. I don't know how I know that. I'm not a stalker; it's just something I heard and chose to remember. Farah is in some of my lessons but we don't speak. She's the popular girl. All the boys want to go out with her and all the girls want to be her. I'd like to be able to say hello without turning into something that resembles an overripe vegetable.

I kept an eye out for her, just in case, as I walked past the row of shops: a barber's, a hairdresser's – of the old lady variety – post office, art gallery (go figure) and corner shop. On the other side of the road there's the pub – the Limping Fox, where Dad used to go – an Indian restaurant, which is apparently well nice, a florist and a printer's that was almost never open. There were a few people about but I kept my head down and nobody noticed me. It was February and it was cold so no one was hanging about.

It was a short walk past the village green and its olde worlde stocks that the tourists loved and the giant cedar tree that everyone fretted over when we had high winds. Tucked behind a row of terraced cottages was the village library. It had been years since I came here. I must have been at primary school. It looked exactly as I remembered it and there was something reassuring about that.

According to the fancy stone over the door the library had once been the old schoolhouse and was built in 1837. It had automatic door buttons, which weren't here the last time I visited. I stepped inside and the warmth overpowered me. There was a blow heater above the door and I moved quickly out of the way. Coming in from the cold the blast of heat was nice at first but if I overheated I'd sweat and I hate that. Inside it had barely changed. It still had the high ceiling with its wooden-beamed roof trusses, arched windows, rows and rows of books and that aroma that only libraries have.

Maybe it was the smell but something made my eyes go all watery. I don't know if I would ever be able to explain the feeling – like a giant wave of muddled emotions crashing over me. I always felt happy when I came to the library. It was a time I had Mum to myself. It was the thing we always did together. No matter how busy she was we always went to the library and I loved it. I loved her. All those feelings had come back in a rush. A part of me wanted to run for the door but something inside me wanted to stay. Wanted to turn back time and be that little kid again. Safe and happy.

I remembered the last time I was here with Mum. I could almost picture her scanning the shelves for her favourite authors. I'd chosen a book about dinosaurs along with some others and I wanted to sit down and read them all. I used to read a lot back then. I blinked to clear my eyes and began checking the place out.

A few older women who were sitting around a table paused to see who had come in. I pulled my rucksack off my back and headed for a seat in the far corner, undoing my coat as I went. I sat down and surveyed the library. It was a big space. I remember the layout being different. There was more shelving in the middle to make lots of sections; now it was all open-plan. It was quiet. There was a children's area where a mother and a little girl were sitting next to each other. They had two piles of books in front of them. The little girl pouted. I could guess what was going on. I was like that when I used to come here with Mum. I wanted to take home all the books, not just what my library card would allow.

I realised I was smiling at the memory and I stopped. I flicked my hair over my eyes and from the safety of my fringe I carried on looking about. The ladies at the table all had copies of the same book in front of them and they were deep in discussion. There used to be an extra high desk where you checked your items in and out. But I had been smaller then so maybe it hadn't been that high. It had gone, replaced by a wooden podium with a screen on the top. A woman with a blue lanyard was standing there tapping away at a keyboard. I guessed she was the librarian.

I started feeling a bit more comfortable but it was still uncomfortably warm. If Farah came in I didn't want to be sweating. I took the bottom of my T-shirt in my fingers and gave it a waft to get some air to my armpits. Such a relief. I kept my earbuds in so hopefully nobody would come and speak to me.

I scanned the shelves nearest to me. K to O. A sign above said "Fiction". I craned my neck. Was that it? Fiction, Non-Fiction and Children's? No crime section, no biographies and, most importantly, no romance? I could have asked the librarian, only I couldn't. Not without going all radish-like and triggering Olympic-level sweating. I guessed the romance novels were mixed in. That changed my cleverly thought through plan a bit. Although looking around the library, the distinct lack of anybody else my age was also an issue.

It was weird being back here. Apart from the overenthusiastic heater there was something nice about it. I know nice is a rubbish word – my English teacher tells me that all the time. But that's how it felt. Nice. It was familiar even though I'd not been inside for years. The smell of books lingered in the air. I'd forgotten that. As a kid I used to breathe it in. The library had been somewhere really special and I guess it still was – it was me who'd changed.

I got that prickly feeling that someone was watching me. I instinctively turned my head and one of the ladies at the table was scrutinising me. She had wild grey hair and a colourful swirly top. We eyeballed each other and the introvert trapped inside me screamed. I looked away. My neck started to feel warm again and I gave my T-shirt another waft. I guess I looked a bit suspicious. I'm more conscious than most that people get twitchy around teenage boys. They think we're all either on drugs or about to nick stuff. I glanced behind me. There was a book with a pink swirly spine. That was probably romance. I pulled it out and had a look. *I Owe You One* by Sophie Kinsella. Yep, that looked like the sort of thing my mum would have read. I read the blurb on the back cover.

I glanced up. The woman at the table was still staring at me but now looked intrigued. That wasn't good. I looked down at the book. Studying a romance book made me look suspicious. I swallowed hard, twisted around and returned the book carefully to the shelf. When I turned back someone was leaning over me.

'Can I help you?' asked the librarian. Crap!

I was no longer invisible and I didn't like it. 'Err, err. Umm.' Usually I could form words. The woman was waiting, her eyebrows slowly rising in question. *Pull yourself together, Tom.*

I took a breath. 'I um. I…' Deep breath. 'I'm looking for books.' Well that sentence was the work of a complete genius. I tried a brief smile. 'Didn't you used to have sections? Like crime and romance?' I couldn't keep eye contact any longer. It was exhausting.

'Yes, we did but this seems to work quite well. We have sections for new releases by genre over there.' She indicated the shelves by the door. 'And there's quick reads, large print and audio next to them.' I'd completely missed those.

'Right, thanks.' I glanced up briefly and hoped she'd see me as a lost cause and give up.

'I saw you looking at the Sophie Kinsella.'

'What?' I remembered the pink book on the shelf behind me. Kill me now. If spontaneous combustion is real let it happen to me this instant. My head was definitely hot enough to explode.

'If you're looking for romance books…' I was already shaking my overheating head. 'Say, for someone else…' Why didn't I think of that? 'We've a Mills and Boon stand.' She pointed to a carousel nearby. 'And all other romance, like historical and contemporary, is filed in with general fiction but I could suggest some authors if you like?' She was keen – this was beyond bad.

What do I do? I opened my mouth and did an excellent

goldfish impression. The librarian leaned a little closer with a conspiratorial look in her eyes. 'Did your mum send you to get her a book?'

I nodded like a car's nodding dog racing over speed bumps. 'Yeah, my mum, she's...' Think of something plausible. Dead is not a good reason to need a library book. 'At work.' My eyes pinged wide with the revelation that I had given a good answer. I repeated my lie for good measure. 'She's at work.' At last the sweating reduced.

The librarian looked rather proud of herself. She rolled her eyes. 'What are mums like, eh?' I shrugged as I joined her in collusion. This was great. 'What's her name? I'll pull up her records just so I can see what sort of thing she usually takes out.'

Argh! This couldn't be happening. The sweating returned like a tsunami. Think of something. She was giving me an odd look. I'd left it too long for what should have been quite an easy question for a sixteen-year-old to answer. THINK. I glanced around for inspiration. There was a sign on the wall about borrowing e-books. 'Kindle!' I almost shouted making the woman jolt away from me slightly. I swallowed and tried to compose my lie. 'She usually reads e-books but her Kindle died.'

The librarian smiled again. I wasn't smiling. I could probably have wrung my T-shirt out. 'Ah, I see. Have you got a library card?'

'No, I had one as a kid but I don't know where it is.'

'No problem. Are you over sixteen?' I nodded. 'You'll need an adult card now anyway. I can either input your details to our library management system or you can use the computer over there and join online.'

'I'll do it myself, thanks.'

'Lovely. While you sign up would you like me to get your mum a selection of novels?'

'Yes, thanks.' No! I don't need romance novels. Thankfully I'd got my bag with me or I'd be leaving with armfuls of chick lit. How did I even get in this mess? Oh, yeah, it was my loser's approach to meeting girls. So much for that venture. Not quite the genius plan I had hoped.

I slunk over to the computer and followed the instructions, which were taped to the table. As I clicked the last button a pile of eight books appeared next to me. Eight! 'Thanks. Err, Mum will be pleased.' The librarian looked chuffed and I wanted to dissolve in a puddle, which could well have been possible given how much I was sweating. I wiped my palms on my jeans before I touched the books and quickly committed them to my bag and zipped it up. The librarian hadn't taken her eyes off me. Why was she still staring?

'Was there anything else I could help you with? We have a Young Adults book section.' I said nothing – I'd not be able to get any more books in my bag. 'Or you can book internet time on our computers.'

It was clear I couldn't just sit there and wait for girls to appear and I'd run out of convincing lies. It was rubbish because I was quite liking being back in the library. 'I'm all set, thanks.' I patted my bag and stood up.

'She can keep them for three weeks and you can renew online if she needs them for longer. Okay?'

No, I had rarely been less okay. 'Yep, great.' I grabbed my coat, put my head down and at last escaped into the blissful cool air outside. I scanned the green for anyone I knew. All clear. I pulled my heavy rucksack onto my shoulder and headed home with my embarrassing haul.

2

MAGGIE

Maggie hadn't enjoyed this week's book club read. She was getting sick of psychological thrillers that told you you'd never see the big twist coming when invariably she could spot it like a pink striped cow in a field of sheep. She also found some of the stories played on her mind, which wasn't good for a seventy-two-year-old living on her own. Not that living alone bothered her; it didn't. She'd been on her own for almost ten years. Maggie liked her own company and her own space but she forced herself to make the trip into the village every week. Without it she would likely not see or speak to anyone unless the postman had something she needed to sign for, in which case those interactions usually consisted of him moaning excessively about the number of potholes on her drive and the permanent damage they had likely done to his coccyx.

The book club discussion came to a natural conclusion and the group started to disperse. Maggie took the copy of *The Pickwick Papers*, which was the next read. They liked to do a classic every so often, which was good because unlike most of the group Maggie wasn't widely read and there were many times she felt she should have got around to reading more but once upon a time hers had been a full life – overflowing. Only recently had she found she had to hunt down things to do rather than it coming to her freely.

'Did you see that boy?' Betty asked her while pulling on her coat. Her eyebrows heavy with questions.

Maggie had noticed him. 'He seemed a bit flustered.' Anyone male and under sixty was a rare sight in the library, or the village come to that.

'Do you think he was casing the joint?' asked Betty, leaning in closely.

Maggie hooted a laugh. 'The joint? It's a library, Betty. There's very little here worth stealing. Nobody's ever late returning their books so there's not even any pennies in the tin.'

'Still,' said Betty, straightening out her hunched spine before returning it to its curved position. 'You read about these things. Drugs, muggings, murders!' She seemed to surprise herself with the last suggestion and hastily buttoned up her coat.

'He looked more scared of us, if you ask me. Terrified, in fact. I doubt he'll be back.'

Betty appeared relieved. 'Well, that's good then. See you next week,' she added in a cheery tone and left to meet her husband who would be parked dutifully outside in his freshly polished Škoda.

Maggie had spotted the boy as soon as he walked in. She'd recognised the look of terror most creatures displayed when placed in an unnatural environment. He had seemed less fish out of water and more alien on wrong planet. She'd seen similar expressions when she'd transported her sheep. But this one didn't have the safety of the herd. He'd come alone and that intrigued her.

Maggie decided to catch up on world events via the newspapers while she was there. February was chilly and the longer she stayed the later she would need to light a fire back at home.

Maggie liked it at the library; she always had. Books provided a secret door to escape through – something she had often been grateful for in her life. She'd been grateful of the library too. Many a time she'd needed somewhere safe and quiet to run to and the library had never let her down. These days she came for slightly different reasons. It was warm and most of the book group attendees were friendly people. She liked to be around people. Even if they weren't the most exciting bunch they still had something to say, as did she, but Maggie had found she increasingly had no one to say it to. She chatted to the other lingerers until they too ebbed away and she settled herself down with the selection of newspapers and some magazines. She went to the headlines first to catch up on what was happening in the world. She'd save the gossipy magazine stuff until after the news had depressed her; it usually served to cheer her up.

After a while she'd become so engrossed in the latest scandals she'd almost forgotten where she was. She read about an actor getting locked out of a hotel room with only a sock to cover his manhood and she hooted a laugh.

'Are you okay, Maggie?' asked Christine the librarian, straightening an already perfectly neat pile of books.

'I'm fine.' Maggie quickly closed the magazine.

'Nice to see youngsters using the library. That teenage lad signed up earlier. I'll be able to report back to the council that my poster campaign has been a success.' Christine pointed to the noticeboard where a sad picture of a teddy bear informed kids that reading was fun.

'I thought I heard him say the books were for his mother?'

Christine bristled. 'Technically, yes. But getting kids in here is the first hurdle.'

Maggie wasn't going to argue. It was pointless. 'Let's hope we didn't scare him off.' She saw the time and began packing up. She had a while before her bus but Christine didn't like people lingering when it was nearing closing time. Maggie said goodbye and made her way outside.

It was dark and raining. Maggie zipped up her floral mac, slung her bag onto one shoulder and stepped out. The village was quiet now. It had been quite busy first thing when she'd arrived. Well, not exactly *busy* but there had been a few people milling around, which for Compton Mallow was positively teeming. She strode down the little cut-through between two cottages with her head down against the rain. Her thoughts were on what to cook for tea. She had some leftover cottage pie but she didn't fancy that. Maybe she'd have cheese on toast. She liked cheese on toast. The only downside was that it was quick and what Maggie needed was things that filled up her time.

She heard footsteps up ahead and glanced in that direction. A hunched figure was coming her way. They looked up and she recognised him as the young man who'd visited the library earlier. She smiled as they skirted to the sides to make enough room to pass each other comfortably. The boy gave her a fleeting glance before returning his concentration to the ground. Maggie wondered what he'd come back for.

Another person was following him a little distance behind. They were of a similar size and build with their head bent and covered by a black hood but they didn't move to the side as he had done, instead bumping her arm and dislodging her bag from her shoulder. Before she could right it her handbag was being tugged away. She reacted immediately by dropping her weight to the ground. She wasn't going to get pulled over. The bag snatcher was wrong-footed by the deadweight of the woman attached to the bag.

'Hey!' She hollered hanging on tight to the strap and finding herself being propelled along by the hooded figure. Anger coursed through her. She loved that bag and she wasn't going to lose it.

'Let go!' shouted the hooded figure playing tug of war with her.

'Piss off!' yelled Maggie. She was losing her hold. Her fingers didn't grip like they used to. She was in a bad position. She couldn't do anything from down here. She heard someone running towards them. Maybe an accomplice? On his next tug she went with the bag and let him haul her to her feet, surprising him and giving her a second to lash out.

'Ow. Shit!' yelled the second person, taking the brunt of Maggie's punch. As she only had one hand on the bag the snatcher whipped it free and fled. Their pounding steps echoing down the alley back the way they had come.

Maggie turned on the second person, her fists held aloft. She was prepared to fight this time.

The other person quickly held up their hands in defeat. 'I was trying to help,' he said, his voice distorted.

Maggie peered closer. It was the boy from the library. And he had blood pouring from his nose. 'I thought you were with him.' She pointed up the alleyway but the bag snatcher was long gone.

'No, I heard you sw... shout so I came back.'

'Here,' she said, pulling a wad of tissues from her pocket. 'You're hurt.'

'Yeah, someone thumped me,' he said, rolling his eyes.

Maggie grimaced. 'Sorry about that. Tilt your head forward.'

He did as he was told and she reached up and pinched his nose. 'Ow. That hurts.'

'Don't be a baby. It'll stop the bleeding. Come on, let's have a look in the light.' She guided him back to the library.

Christine was tidying a stack of newspapers and putting the one with the headline about library closures to the bottom. 'Christine, have you got a first aid box in there?' called Maggie, steering the youth in her general direction.

'Oh my goodness. Whatever's happened?'

'She pun—'

'I had my bag snatched and he came to my rescue but took a punch in the process,' said Maggie, giving the lad a wink, which seemed to alarm him.

'Oh, Maggie, are you all right?'

'I'm fine. He took the worst of it.'

'What a hero you are,' said Christine, ushering the boy inside. 'Sit there. I'll get the first aid kit. Please try not to bleed on the carpet.' Christine disappeared into a small back room.

Maggie and the youth exchanged looks.

'I'm Maggie,' she said. 'And I am very sorry about punching you.' She held out a hand for him to shake. He hesitated before shaking it.

'Tom. I'm not going to report you for assault. If that's what you're worried about.'

That actually hadn't crossed her mind. What a litigious society they lived in. 'I was thinking more that you'd be embarrassed about getting whacked by a pensioner.'

Tom seemed to consider this. 'Fair point.'

'I won't tell anyone. I promise.'

'Thanks. I think,' he said, returning his neck to a more normal position.

Christine returned in a flurry of gauze pads and bandages. 'Has it stopped bleeding?' She asked scanning the carpet.

'Yeah. He's all right. Aren't you?' asked Maggie.

Tom took the wad of blood-soaked tissues from his nose and baulked at the sight. 'I guess.'

'We should call the police,' said Christine, her hand already on the telephone.

'No, it's fine. There was nothing of value in my bag. I've lost my bus pass, my glasses, oh and the buggery book club book for next week. Sorry.'

'That's all right,' said Christine, although her face said something quite different. 'Anything else?'

Maggie had a think. 'A new pack of chewing gum and a purse with about forty pence in it.'

'What about credit cards?' asked Christine, lifting the telephone receiver a fraction.

'Don't have any.' Maggie took a sterile wipe from the first aid box and like a mum washing a reluctant toddler's face she started to clean away the blood around Tom's nose. He snatched the wipe from her and gingerly dabbed at his face.

Christine hovered by the phone looking disappointed. 'But he's hurt.'

'He's fine,' said Maggie.

'I'm fine *apparently*,' said Tom, marvelling at the blood-soaked tissues.

'What about you, Maggie?' asked Christine, her voice hopeful.

Maggie paused for a moment to scan her body and make an assessment. 'I've bruised my bum and my clothes are soaked but no injuries.'

'Oh.' Christine was further deflated. She checked her watch. 'If we're not getting the police involved then I should be getting home. Alf will worry where I am.'

'Yes, I need to get going too,' said Maggie, realising she'd be walking home now she didn't have her bus pass.

'Okay then,' said Christine, merrily putting everything back in the first aid box.

'Could I have another copy of the book club read?' asked Maggie.

Christine's smile was a little forced as she found a copy, handed it over and hurried them out the door. 'See you next week, Maggie. Hope to see you again soon too.' She waved at Tom and he recoiled.

Tom and Maggie were left standing outside the library. They watched Christine get in her oversized mini and drive off.

'Alf's her cat,' said Maggie. Tom beamed a grin. It was the first time he'd smiled and it changed his features a great deal, revealing another version of him hiding inside like it had been waiting for a safe moment to venture out. Maggie smiled too. 'Well. Sorry again. Bye.' She turned to head towards home.

'Weren't you walking that way?' asked Tom, his eyebrows puckered.

'I was but that swine stole my bus pass so now I'm walking home.' She put up her hood as the rain picked up its pace.

'Where do you live?' he asked.

'Out by Furrow's Cross.'

His eyes widened. 'That's miles.' Tom dug a hand in his pocket and pulled out a five-pound note. 'Here.' He shoved it at Maggie. 'And I'll walk you to the bus stop.'

'No, I can't take this.'

Tom stepped away so she couldn't return the money. 'You need to watch out. There's thugs out there…' he paused and she nodded '…who punch people in the face when they come to their rescue.'

'Again, very sorry.' There was something about this lad that she liked.

They exchanged smiles and started back down the alleyway, Tom leading the way and Maggie a pace behind. They walked in time. Their steps making a steady rhythm.

They reached the bus stop and nipped into the shelter and out of the worst of the weather.

'Thanks for this.' Maggie held up the five-pound note. 'I'll pay you back.'

'No rush.'

The rain made a noise like gentle applause on the shelter roof. There was an awkward silence where they looked at each other and neither knew what to say. The sound of the bus approaching saved them.

'Bye then,' said Tom, turning to leave.

'Will I see you at the library next week?'

'I dunno. Maybe.'

'If you come I can give you this money back.'

He appeared to consider this. 'It doesn't matter.'

She got on the bus, paid the driver and took a seat on the side closest to the kerb. She watched Tom trudging up the hill. As the bus drew level he looked up. She lifted her hand and he gave her a brief nod of recognition. Well, what a Saturday that had been. She'd been mugged. It was the most exciting thing that had happened to her in years.

3

TOM

'Have we got anything to eat?' I shouted, with my head still inside the cupboard. I was seriously hungry but then I'm starving most of the time. I'd already checked the fridge but all that was in there was milk, salad cream, beer and some dodgy-looking cheese. It's not like when Mum was alive when there was always food. I wish we had cake in the house or at least something decent to eat.

My dad appeared in the doorway. 'You went out earlier. Where's the stuff you bought?'

I guessed Dad would be pissed if I told him I gave the cash away, even if it was to an old lady. I did some quick thinking. 'I ate it.'

'Bloody hell, Tom. You're like a bottomless pit. It's not normal.'

'Yeah it is.' I know this to be fact as the few friends I have say their parents are always moaning about how much they eat and that it's like a swarm of locusts descending as soon as they unpack the shopping. 'What can I eat?' I scanned the tins of tomatoes in the cupboard. We never ate tinned tomatoes. What were they even for? They were probably out of date.

'Bread and butter.' Dad almost threw the loaf at me. It would have to do. I stuck two slices in the toaster. 'You need to realise how much stuff costs.' Dad was shaking his head. He does that a lot. 'I'll be glad when you're working,' he said.

I snorted. 'That's not for years yet.'

Dad looked like he'd sat on something sharp. 'I was working full-time at your age.' He likes to talk about the good old days which, to be honest, sound rubbish – no internet, no mobile phones and only four TV channels is not my idea of good.

'I've got a paper round.'

It was Dad's turn to snort. 'It's a couple of days a week. That's not work. But when you leave school you need to have something lined up.'

I stared at him not quite believing he wasn't joking. The toast popped up and broke the freeze frame. 'But I'm going to do A levels and go to university.' I knew I needed to work hard, but still, everyone went to university these days. Didn't they?

Dad continued to shake his head. 'I can't afford that.'

'I'll get student loans.'

'Tom, have you any idea how much this place costs to run?'

For some reason I took a fresh look at our murky little kitchen. 'Dunno. But if I'm not here eating stuff you'll save loads of money.'

'Don't try and be clever. I work my arse off to put a roof over your head.'

'Some roof,' I muttered. I knew as soon as I'd said it that it was the conversational equivalent of lighting the end of a firework.

Dad took a moment to build his anger before going off on an epic rant. I kind of switched off. A bit like putting on imaginary headphones. I've heard it all before – it's really boring. And I don't like rowing with Dad.

I buttered and ate my toast, hoping he'd soon stop shouting.

'Are you even listening to me?' He was going an unhealthy shade of scarlet, not that any shade of red is healthy.

'Yep. I'm ungrateful. You do everything. I do nothing. We have no money.' A fair summary, I thought.

Stand back; rocket number two ready for launch. 'Don't get smart with me!' He wagged a finger in my general direction. 'You're going to get an almighty shock, Tom. I don't know how much longer I can keep juggling all the bills. You need to wise up.' He pulled a whisky bottle out of the cupboard, scowled at the small amount of liquid in the bottom and tipped it into a glass. I tried some of it once when he was at work. It was disgusting.

He scowled at me while he drank his whisky. 'Have you been fighting?'

'No,' I said it like a reflex and then realised he was studying my eyes.

'You've got a black eye.' He raised an eyebrow.

'I fell over.' I don't know why I lied. I was getting the feeling I couldn't do anything right. He made a lot of tutting sounds and shook his head.

Dad finished his drink and stormed out. I made more toast and took it to my room. I guess a few hours passed while I was on my Xbox but I'm not sure. Dad made me jump when the bedroom door banged open. He almost fell inside. His face was red and sweaty and he was shouting but I couldn't make out exactly what the words were. He looked furious. I pulled my headphones off one ear.

'You okay?' I asked.

'No, I'm not bloody okay.' His words were slurred. I hate it when he drinks. He jabbed his finger at the television screen where I'd paused my game. 'This! This is the problem.' He stumbled forward and I laughed. I couldn't help it. It was a proper comedy stumble and it was funny. 'You could be out working but oh, no! You're too bloody lazy. You sit on your arse, wasting your life away on this... this...' He struggled to find the word he wanted and I had to bite my lip not to crack up. It wasn't that funny this time but I think it's a nervous reaction that I sometimes snigger when it's not appropriate. He stared at me almost daring me to laugh. 'You think this is funny. Do you?'

'No.'

'No... Because it's not funny.' I think he was hoping I was going to say yes. 'And I'll show you what else isn't funny.' He staggered over to the games console. Ripped out the cables and picked the box up.

'Hey! What are you doing?' I hadn't saved my progress.

'It's time you grew up. Stopped playing games and found out what the real world is like.'

'What, am I meant to get a job now? At...' I scanned my alarm clock '...almost midnight on a Saturday?'

'It's up to you. But I'm keeping this until you do,' he said with a classic bad-guy sneer. He gave a Disney villain sort of sneer.

My Xbox is my life. 'Seriously? Don't be a dick.'

His expression changed to one I hadn't witnessed before. It kinda scared me. 'What did you call me!' he bellowed.

'I didn't call you anything.' For the second time that day I held my palms up, to show I wasn't after a fight.

'I. Said. What. Did. You. Call. Me.' He stepped closer clutching the console so tight his knuckles were white. A stark contrast to the dark red of his face.

'It was more advice. I said, "*Don't* be a dick."'

He turned and left and I breathed a sigh of relief. It was short-lived as I heard the sound of something crashing down the stairs. I leaped from the bed and took the two strides onto the landing. Dad was standing at the top of the stairs leaning against the banister for support. He was no longer holding my Xbox.

I don't think I've ever been as cross as I was at that moment. I could have happily thrown him down the stairs after it. I'd saved my paper round money, birthday and Christmas money to buy that. I was shaking with anger but I wasn't going to give him the satisfaction of seeing he'd got to me. I shrugged, walked back to my room and shut the door. For a while I waited, expecting him to come back shouting and goading me into a reaction but he didn't.

I thumped out my frustration on my pillows. My Xbox. MY PISSING XBOX! What was he thinking? And more importantly what the hell was I going to do with my life now?

I was up early on Sunday for my paper round – I did the minimum number of rounds to be able to do the weekend one, which paid better. There was no sign of Dad. Only an empty bottle in the living room and the shattered plastic of my life at the bottom of the stairs. I ignored them both and went out. The chill of the early air did nothing to improve my mood, nor did the extra supplements with the papers weighing me down.

When I got back the house was silent. For a moment I was worried that he might be dead. You heard of it happening. People getting so drunk they choked on their own vomit. I dashed upstairs and opened his bedroom door – my hand was shaking. The smell was rank. I remember when this had been Mum and Dad's bedroom. I used to run in there and jump on the bed. I liked to snuggle down in the middle between both of them. Back then it smelled good. Sort of a fabric softener flowery kind of smell, like Mum. It smelled of home. But that was all gone now. Everything was stagnant. There was a mound of my father in the bed. Still and silent. I waited in the doorway, not sure what to do. At last he let out a heavy breath – he was alive. I closed the door and retreated to my room.

I stared at the blank screen of the television for a long time before switching it on and realising there was nothing I'd want to watch anyway. We couldn't afford Sky or Netflix or anything interesting. Without my console I couldn't even watch clips of *Game of Thrones* on YouTube. I switched it off and dropped the controller on to the bed. I looked around my room. Bed, wardrobe, shelf and TV. Not much. My rucksack was on the floor and I heaved it onto the bed. It was seriously heavy. I tipped out all the library books. All the stupid romance novels. Where was I meant to keep these until I could return them? If Dad saw them he'd rip it out of me.

I stacked them into a pile at the far side of my bed. The one on the top had an interesting cover. *Sense & Sensibility*. I picked it up, turned it over and read the back cover. It sounded vaguely interesting. I opened it up and had a quick read of the first page – I literally had nothing better to do.

A few hours later I heard Dad put the shower on. If I wanted feeding today I'd be doing it myself. And if I was going to avoid Dad I needed to eat now. Reluctantly I put the book down. I hid it under my pillow and went to the kitchen.

I found a tin of spaghetti hoops, microwaved the contents and dumped them on some toast.

Dad looked rough when he came into the kitchen. He put the kettle on and then exited quickly to avoid the noise of it. It was a sign he had a raging hangover. He crept back in after it had boiled and made himself a coffee. I finished eating and dumped the plate and cutlery in the sink.

'You not washing those up?'

I always do the washing up but today I wasn't in the mood. 'Later.' I tried to push past him but he grabbed my arm. I didn't look up.

'Tom, I did it for your own good.'

Those words sparked my annoyance. 'How is trashing the only good thing in my life for my own good?' He always had an excuse. Always a reason to justify what he did. If it had been me he would have said I wasn't taking responsibility for my own actions but when it's him he's doing it for my own good. It's seriously annoying. He looked startled by my tone. I don't usually engage.

'It's just a game.' He shrugged and let me go.

My Xbox is not just a games console to me – it's my social life and my escape, but there's no point trying to explain that to him. He doesn't care, not anymore. Since Mum died he doesn't care about anything much at all.

4

MAGGIE

Maggie brushed out her hair, marvelling at how bushy it had become. It had always been thick and curly but the advent of turning grey had brought a new dimension to what had always been 'difficult' locks. She snatched it all up into a messy bun and stuck a clip in it to keep it in place. It wouldn't stay that way but it didn't matter; nobody would see her today.

Looking at the day ahead, Wednesday had the potential to be a good day. She had things to do. There were the daily tasks of attending to the chickens and the sheep but some fencing needed some attention and she had her mind on making a rhubarb crumble, if she had any of last year's crop left in the freezer.

Maggie made herself scrambled eggs for breakfast, courtesy of her chickens or 'The Girls' as she liked to call them. Tidied up. Put her coat and wellies on and headed outside after a brief quarrel with the back door. Like a lot of the old farmhouse it was tired and in need of a little TLC.

Outside it was windy and it shook the budding apple trees with force. It whipped around the yard and dismantled the bun in Maggie's hair. Maggie filled an old metal bucket with water from the outside tap and marched down to the top field, with the wind whistling in her ears. She was glad of the noise. Most of the time life was quiet.

Midweek was always the worst. By that point she'd not seen anyone for a few days and Saturday was a long way off. This week she had had the advantage of Saturday's adventure to mull over. And it had been such an adventure. Revisiting what had happened in the alleyway had given her brain something to chew over and she was grateful for it. She knew she'd got off lightly. Everything still ached but not as bad as on Sunday morning when she'd had to roll out of bed because every muscle had seized up in protest. The bruise on her bum was colourful but she knew she could have been seriously hurt. She'd never been one for thinking through the consequences of her actions. Always a jump and then work out where to land sort of person. Impulsive her mother had said. Stubborn as a mule her husband had called her. Maggie was cross about losing her bag and it had made her realise how out of condition she was. She was flexible – the daily yoga saw to that – but her strength was lacking and her reflexes were diminished. The latter surprised her because she had to deal with Colin on a daily basis.

Maggie braced herself and knocked on the gate. Colin was a young Jacob ram. Colin's head shot up and he eyed her with disdain. Maggie always let him know she was there because he was even more aggressive when startled. He waggled his head as if limbering up for a fight. The ram tilted his head forward presenting his heavy horns in challenge.

She lifted the fraying rope from the post, opened the gate and dashed in with the bucket. She sloshed the water into his trough and turned to face him. Colin came thundering across the field and she held the bucket in front of her for protection. Colin glanced off it and retreated in preparation for a second attack.

He'd been hand-reared by a farmer she knew and she had jumped at the chance to borrow him to service her ewes. That had been back in August and some eight months later she now understood why the owners were in no hurry to have him back. Colin was permanently angry and slightly unhinged. Maggie hurried out of the field and shut the gate behind her as Colin charged at it, making it rattle. It was the same every morning.

This time of year, Maggie had to check the ewes carefully. She bred Jacobs with Poll Dorsets to get lavenders, which had the most beautiful colour fleece. Of her flock she was hoping quite a few were pregnant and due to lamb shortly. That was assuming Colin had managed to put aside his hostile nature long enough but she wasn't convinced he'd got the hang of it. She didn't mind how many lambs – any would be a bonus as long as they arrived safely. The weather was mild, which was a blessing for lambing season. She'd spent too many nights in the cold and a couple of years ago she'd had two ewes deliver in the snow. The sheep all grazed naturally on the grass and wild herbs that grew in the pastures.

She whistled and they all looked up, took a moment to register who it was and then her three favourites sauntered over. They were called Barbara, Nancy and Dolly. They didn't know their names – sheep were fairly stupid and not capable of responding to individual naming conventions – but that hadn't stopped Maggie taking a great deal of time over choosing their monikers.

Since Saturday she'd been thinking about her son. She missed him all the time but he was right at the front of her thoughts now. She tried to picture what he might look like but despite her best efforts she couldn't. Maggie wondered what sort of person he might have become. Would he have done what that young lad, Tom, had done and come to a stranger's aid? She didn't know. She'd thought Tom had been brave and not typical of what society would have her believe of youths his age. The newspapers in the library told of impending doom on most fronts – environmentally, socially and economically. A society unsatisfied with its lot but not prepared to make the effort to fix it. Snowflakes, knife-wielding thugs and the government were all to blame depending on which paper you read.

Her memories of her son were like frayed newspaper cuttings from a long-forgotten scrapbook. It was the most unusual things that would trigger a train of thought that put him central in her mind. Sometimes she might go a while without thinking of him. Those days brought retrospective guilt but they were still the better days. It was selfish but it was the truth. Her memories of him inflicted deep wounds upon her peace of mind.

Maggie fed the ewes some sheep nuts and checked them over. Nancy continued to bleat for more, which gave Maggie an opportunity to give her a once-over. She was pretty sure she was pregnant but there were no tell-tale signs of imminent birth. They had a small lean-to for shelter if they needed it but generally they preferred to mooch around the field. They spent most of their day grazing. Not the most demanding of lives. She gave Barbara a fuss. Maggie had hand-reared Barbara two years ago but unlike Colin she was a gentle soul and enjoyed having her ears scratched. She'd check on them again later. Her little flock of lavenders in the next field were all doing fine. Their pretty coats would need shearing soon but for now they provided the perfect protection against the elements.

Maggie let the chickens out, fed them and collected the eggs. The Girls were a mixed bunch. Some were rescue birds, some she'd raised from chicks and five she'd got from the free noticeboard at the library because someone had been keeping them in the back garden of a rental property and were utterly surprised that the landlord was none too pleased when he'd found out. They were a motley bunch and Joan was the ringleader. She wasn't the biggest hen but she was the quickest and she'd fought her way to be top of the pecking order.

It was a harsh thing to witness when the chickens went at each other, but it was nature's way. It was how they agreed who went first at feeding time and who got which roost. Things were fairly civilised now and to see them when they settled in for the night you would have thought they were all the best of friends, huddled together. Maggie had gone to a lot of trouble to make their hut and run fox-proof and, so far, it was working.

At one time this had been a thriving farm, so other people had told her. They had bought it shortly before her husband died. She'd sold off most of the usable land to surrounding farms since then, leaving her with about twenty acres of mixed woodland and hilly pasture. Her nearest neighbour was about a mile away, slightly less if she braved the field occupied by a large bull owned by the next farm. The smallholding was her island of distraction in a sea of boredom.

All was well so she made her way back to the farmhouse. Maggie put her boots next to her husband's and went into the kitchen. She wasn't sure why she'd kept his wellies. Most things had gone to charity, but she couldn't part with his old boots. Daft really, but it made her feel less alone to see the wellingtons of years gone by all rowed up. She had a rummage in the freezer and found the last of the rhubarb. She liked crumble but unfortunately it was quick and easy to make. She set about making lasagne. That would kill some time.

Loneliness had crept up on her like damp seeping into her soul. She often thought about all the times in her life when she had wished for more time and now here she was with oodles of the stuff stretching out before her like it had all been saved up and paid with interest when she needed it least.

After dinner Maggie, wearing a kaftan teamed with her stretchiest leggings, made herself comfortable on the sitting room floor. She knelt down and moved easily into the Balasana or child's yoga pose with her arms stretched out in front of her, her forehead resting on the rug. She let her mind wash freely with thoughts and focused on her breathing before moving onto a Shirshasana headstand.

She'd been doing yoga since her teens when she'd briefly lived on a commune and fully embraced the hippie way of life. Yoga helped her to clear her mind and focus on her body. Her body had done her proud. She'd not always looked after it over the years and yet it didn't seem to hold a grudge. She'd favoured Maharishi yoga before the Beatles made it and its Yogi popular. A phase of being vegetarian and taking up yoga had almost tipped her mother over the edge. They had seemed like such radical life changes at the time and yet now they were commonplace. For many it was part of their journey to spiritual enlightenment; for Maggie it was about breaking away from the confines of her parents and their safe little lives.

Over the years her yoga had evolved as she had pushed herself and explored the limits of her body. Now she had a few solid routines she returned to that kept her mind and body healthy. Although after Saturday's revelation she had decided to focus on building her strength. Maggie eased herself down into a comfortable sitting position to begin her silent mantra meditation but her mind was distracted.

Maggie loved her home. It was all hers. She didn't owe anyone a penny, so as long as she paid the bills she had a roof over her head for life. Not something she had always been fortunate enough to enjoy but something she was desperate to maintain. It was far from perfect. This was most notable during the winter months when she was constantly patching the place up and heating it was more than a challenge. She focused her warming efforts on the kitchen, small sitting room and her bedroom. They were the rooms she used, and therefore all that needed to be liveable.

It was an old property but it was a sturdy one. What it

lacked in modern conveniences it made up for in character. Its stone floors would chill you to the bone if you were fool enough to walk on them barefoot in winter. But in summer they were a joy to lie on. They had also been a boon when Maggie had gone through the menopause and hot flushes had driven her to lying on the flagstones naked. She only ever met the posh people from the Hall that one time; they never called by again.

Nobody visited now so there was no call for ceremony, not that she'd ever been one for that. But she did miss the parties. Oh the parties she'd held when she was younger and married. She'd been happy and she'd been loved by a good man. She'd lived a life. All very long ago now though. All that was left were shadows of happiness that had lingered briefly before disappearing like smoke in the breeze.

Maggie gave up on the meditation and went to sit in her chair. She picked up her current read. Reading was her other escape. Another world she could step into and be surrounded by characters brought to life on the page. She could meet untold people and live a thousand exciting lives through the pages. It was her solace and always had been ever since she was a child. It had helped her in difficult times – of which she had experienced many. And now reading helped ease the lack of human contact.

Most of all Maggie missed the hugs. It was a peculiar quirk of polite modern society that without a partner or offspring in your life you were denied that one key comfort that humans require – the need for physical contact. An embrace can be on many different levels but the basic sensation of emotional and physical warmth given freely by another is most noticeable when it is no longer there. If she'd realised

5

TOM

I had rehearsed my speech a thousand times in my head. Each time it went slightly differently, which wasn't a good thing. It was Saturday and I needed to return the eight romance novels. I had read them all, but only because I'd been *that* bored. My goal was to be as quick as possible in the library without drawing attention to myself. My invisibility shield was in place.

I hurried towards Christine the librarian who was standing at the podium, giving the briefest of acknowledgements to Maggie as I passed. I tugged my bag off my shoulder but I did it too quickly and the weight of it swung into the computer monitor. Christine gasped. I tried to grab the monitor but it skidded off the podium. It hung for a second by the cable before the connector let go and the monitor crashed to the floor. She gasped again. I could feel everyone watching me. It was all the ladies from around the big table. Their eyes were boring holes in my skull and it prickled.

Christine was wildly waving her arms about but apart from more gasps she said nothing.

'I'm really sorry,' I said, my voice sounding strange even to my own ears. I went to help pick up the monitor but my precariously balanced bag fell over, spilling out most of its contents onto the floor: some of the books, half a pack of gaming cards and some chewing gum wrappers. We almost bumped heads as we bent down at the same time. 'Sorry,' I said, lurching out of the way, the familiar rush of heat spreading up my neck like spilled tomato soup.

Christine picked up the monitor and scanned it closely from many different angles. 'I think it's broken.' She showed it to me but from a distance to avoid me doing any further damage.

'Looks okay to me,' I said. There were no cracks on the screen, which was a huge relief. Dad would freak if he had to pay for a new one.

'It can't have survived that drop,' said Christine, turning it in my direction again.

'Let's plug it back in and see,' said Maggie, taking it from her and returning it to the podium while I shoved everything back in my bag. 'I'm sure it's fine, Christine. It landed on carpet. How much damage can it have done?' Maggie reattached the cable and she and the librarian watched the screen intently. I joined them. My pulse beating frantically but my breathing momentarily paused as I waited for the monitor to show some signs of life.

The screen flickered and I took in a deep breath. 'See,' said Maggie. 'No harm done.'

'Thanks,' I said, leaving my rucksack on the floor and decanting the books from it one by one. Everyone continued to watch. So much for not drawing attention to myself. Invisible people like me don't usually break cover unless it's a life or death situation.

'Here,' said Maggie, passing me a five-pound note. 'Thanks again for the loan. And for stepping in.' I glanced at the table and all the women were silently watching our exchange. I expect she'll have told them what happened last week.

''S all right.'

'How's the nose?' asked Maggie.

'Fine. You okay?' I felt I had to ask and I kind of wanted to know she was all right too.

'Fine. Annoyed about losing the bag and it's a pain trying to get a new bus pass.'

She was still looking at me as if waiting for something else. I didn't know what to say so I nodded.

'Which books did your mum like the best?' asked Christine.

This was not a question I had prepared for. I had responses planned for "Did she enjoy them?" and "Does she want any more?" But not this. The unexpected question made me stare at the pile of books now stacked on the podium. I scanned their spines trying to pick one. *Pick one!* my brain yelled.

'*Frederica*...'

'Oh, the Georgette Heyer,' said Christine. 'It is a classic of hers. If history's her thing then let me see.' She darted from behind the podium before I could speak.

'I loved this one,' said Maggie tapping the book on the top of the pile, *Staying at Daisy's* by Jill Mansell, and drawing my attention away from Christine who was collecting books from the shelves like a library version of a trolley dash.

I was already nodding. 'I…' I nearly said, "I liked that one too." Shit. That was close. I was in dangerous territory and I was afraid of dropping myself into more trouble. 'I think my mum liked that one too.'

'Has she read *Me Before You*?' asked Maggie. It was likely the fear was now clearly visible in my eyes. 'It's okay. I'll dig it out and you can take it home and ask her.'

'If she's not read it I'm sure she'll love that one,' said a tiny lady from the table. I nodded and tried to swallow. It was quite difficult because I appeared to have stopped producing saliva.

'She's probably read it,' said a gruff woman.

'Or most likely she's seen the film,' added another.

'The film wasn't as good as the book,' said the tiny lady, half to me and half to the group.

'They never are,' said Christine, adding books to a very tall pile that teetered in her arms.

'I liked the film better,' said one of them and a heated discussion ensued. I envied the humble hedgehog its ability to hide within itself. My invisibility cloak didn't seem to work at the library.

'Here,' said Maggie, handing me the book they were discussing. 'It's one of my favourites. Funny and poignant is tricky to pull off.'

Its cover didn't give much away but I was intrigued by the thirteen million copies sold sticker – that's a lot of romance books. 'Thanks.' It was an automatic response.

'I hope she enjoys it.' Maggie returned to the table.

'Right,' said Christine, puffing out a breath. 'I feel like Amazon.' She snorted a laugh. 'If you liked that, you may also like this.' She held up the books in turn and grinned wildly. She checked them all out for me, including the one Maggie had recommended. Christine patted the books into a neat pile and slid them towards me. I took a hasty glance at the door. Thankfully there was no sign of anyone I knew. I plunged the books into my rucksack and pulled the drawstring tight shut.

This wasn't how this was meant to go. I was meant to return the romance novels and that would be the end of it. I'd brought some homework to do because I was still avoiding Dad and thought the library might help me keep focused and for some reason I'd quite liked being there. Also I didn't have anywhere to work at home. The kitchen and living room were a mess and it just didn't work lying on my bed. 'Do you have any books on the history of medicine?' I asked. Christine froze like someone had hit a pause button.

'But you wanted romance books?'

'No. Not me. My mum wants those. I've got homework and I thought I'd work on it here.'

'Oh, I see.' She seemed to relax a bit. 'Let me check if we have anything on the history of medicine.' She tapped a few things into the computer and beckoned me to follow her to the back of the library to search out some relevant books.

My afternoon in the library was all right. There's a smell – a good one. Something you only get at the library. And it was quiet. At home the TV is always on. Since Mum died Dad doesn't do silence. I usually have my music on but the peacefulness was better. I actually got some decent work done. A few people came and went. Everyone left me alone. I liked it.

I'm not usually great when it comes to homework. Shoddy is the word my maths teacher likes to use and I think most of my other teachers would agree. I don't find it easy so I do what I have to, just enough to avoid anything being sent home. But we had our GCSE mock results this week and basically I'm okay in English but pretty much everything else is barely above rubbish. I'd said I wasn't bothered to my mates, because that's what you do, but really I was. It might sound dumb but I've just realised getting good results is my ticket out of here. Good GCSEs means I get to do A levels, which could get me a place at university. I wish I'd worked this out sooner. All my mates assumed they'd go to university apart from one who wants to sell cars like his dad. Now we've got our mock results it's looking a lot less likely. That scares me because there's no jobs around here – only rubbish ones.

When I packed up my things there was just Christine and Maggie left in the library. I'd been focused on my essay and not noticed the other people drift away. I put my coat on at the same time as Maggie and found we were walking out together. She held the door for me.

'New bag?' I asked noticing the brightly patterned shopper she had slung on her shoulder.

'Not new. One I've dug out of the cupboard. I don't care if I lose this one.'

It dawned on me that she was anticipating being attacked again. Although she hadn't seemed it last week Maggie must have been shaken by the experience. She was probably terrified of walking back down the alleyway. She wasn't very big and she was pretty old. 'I'll walk you to the bus stop. You know? If you like.'

Maggie turned. She was frowning hard at me. 'That's kind but I will be all right on my own.'

'I know.' I pointed at my nose. But we both knew that was a lucky punch and she could have ended up in hospital. 'I'm going that way anyway. I don't want you thinking I'm following you.'

Her frown softened. 'As long as you don't think I'm some little old lady who needs looking after.'

'Err. No. Obviously not.' That was *exactly* what I was thinking because she was a little old lady. I don't think my thoughts were unreasonable.

'I saw you studying. Did you get much done?' she asked.

'Yeah.'

'What subject?'

'History.'

'Because you like history or because you need to do better?'

'I got bad results in my mocks.' Why was I telling her that? I've not even told Dad. I'm waiting for the school to do that. Everyone else has a computer so their parents already know. It's the first time I've been pleased about not having one.

'Bit of a wake-up call, was it?' she asked.

'Yeah. Fail now and it's the dog food factory for me.'

Maggie spun around to face me, making me stop suddenly to avoid knocking her over. 'What?' She gave me the same concerned look she did last week when there was blood pouring from my nose. But this time she looked more alarmed. 'Is someone threatening you?'

'Yeah.' Her concerned expression intensified. 'My dad wants me to work at the factory.'

Maggie dissolved into peals of laughter. 'Goodness, you had me worried there. I thought someone was threatening to turn *you* into dog food.'

'It's not a Mafia thing. They're not going to feed me to the fishes.' She was still laughing. It wasn't that funny. 'Although, that would be better than working at the factory. It stinks.'

She renewed her cackle of a laugh and it set me off too. We'd stopped by the time we reached the bus shelter. It was dark and there was nobody else waiting.

'When's your bus?' I asked.

'Twenty minutes. Go on, you get off. I'm fine.' She did a shooing motion with her hand.

'Nah, you're okay.' I didn't like the thought of her sitting there on her own. It didn't seem right to walk off and leave her, not after what had happened.

There was silence while we both took it in turns to look at our feet and smile at each other. It seems she wasn't great at conversation either. She got a book out of her bag and I thought of the many that were weighing mine down and put it on the ground. 'What's your book?' I asked.

'Book club read. It's what I come here for each week. And to read the papers.' She turned the book to show me and I read the title. *Dark Matter* by Michelle Paver. 'It's a ghost story. It's not really my thing but that's why you join a book club. Do you read much?'

'No, not at all.' I shook my head firmly and then thought maybe that was a bit extreme. 'I do read a bit. You know. What they make me read at school.' I tried to look bored.

Maggie's eyes looked sad. 'I used to love reading when I was young. I'd spend hours escaping into a book. Rather be reading than studying – that was always my problem. Until I discovered boys then... well... Here's my bus.'

'See ya then.'

'Next week?' She held my gaze. Usually this made me feel uncomfortable, like seriously uncomfortable, as if I wanted to unzip my own skin and take it off like a onesie, but for some reason this time I was okay.

'Yeah. See ya next week.'

She got on the bus and I watched it go.

6

MAGGIE

She wasn't sure if it was her but the week was dragging. She longed for Saturday more than she usually did. Meeting Tom had added a whole new dimension to her trip to the village library. She could strike up a conversation with the others in book group but for some reason when people reached a certain age they seemed fascinated with their ailing health and their misguided belief that others were equally as interested.

She didn't want to be reminded of her advancing years; she wanted to rewind. Actually that wasn't it at all. Her youth had not been a happy one, she certainly didn't want to relive that. But she did like talking to Tom. She was stretching things by describing it as talking. He wasn't chatty at all but at least any conversation, however brief, wasn't focused on his bowels or medication, which was a relief.

Her midweek highlight had been one of The Girls getting egg-bound. She'd brought her into the farmhouse, given her a dose of extra vitamins and subjected her to a warm bath, which she seemed to quite enjoy. Maggie had cuddled her gently and massaged her abdomen and after an hour in front of the cooker she had happily laid the offending egg. Such a simple thing and yet if left unattended she would most likely have died. Maggie liked caring for things; it gave her a sense of purpose.

Saturday finally rolled around and Maggie was like a kid about to go on a school trip. Would Tom be there three weeks in a row? What would happen when his mother's Kindle was fixed? All sorts flashed through her mind on the bus on the way there.

She'd read the book club novel and then immediately wished that she hadn't because it had put the willies up her. She hadn't actually had any nightmares, but it was definitely playing on her mind. It had been a story about people who were in a remote place being haunted in their dreams. It was too close a comparison to her own life for Maggie's liking. Although her little farm wasn't in the Arctic it felt almost as cold sometimes. At least the library was warm. She loved the heater that hit you with a blast of hot air as you walked in. Like a warm hug – or at least the closest Maggie got to one.

She was early and there was no sign of Tom. Christine was switching on the computers. 'Morning, Maggie, how are you?'

'Good thanks.'

'All recovered from being attacked?' She seemed to be scanning her.

'Yes, thanks. It wasn't that dramatic, Christine.' Maggie claimed her place at the table.

'You're not the only one. There's been a spate of attacks in the local area.' Christine rushed over with a few-days-old local paper and shoved it under her nose. 'See.' She tapped the page.

Maggie read the article. It was fairly similar to what had happened to her but this poor woman had come off worse, having fallen and broken her hip, landing herself in hospital. She shuddered. 'Doesn't say anything about anyone else. Just this one incident,' said Maggie, folding it up. 'Not really a spate.'

'Don't forget yours. That makes it a crime wave. It's rife!' Her voice went up at the end.

'Not exactly a rampant scourge though.' Christine was prone to being overdramatic.

She enjoyed having the place to herself but it wasn't good for the library; she knew that. Christine was always banging on about them drumming up more people. *Use it or lose it* was her favourite phrase. But Maggie liked the peacefulness. Which was odd because she wasn't a fan of being alone at home. Maybe it was the happy memories she had of the library that kept her company. The times she'd gone there when she literally had nowhere else to go. Living in a hostel in her twenties had been her real low point. Despite all the people and noise in the hostel she'd never felt as alone as she had done at that point in her life.

She'd sought peace at the library, and it had given her exactly that along with multiple worlds to hide herself in. She could disappear into a book and be gone from the harsh reality of the real world for hours. That had saved her. Saved her from herself and most likely a much shorter life.

The door opened and few others came in already mid-conversation about Betty's constipation. Maggie rolled her eyes. There were a few fleeting greetings before they all took off layers and settled themselves down around the table. The conversation moved on to Audrey's swollen ankles and her husband's cholesterol level. Maggie sighed.

The door opened again and in crept Tom, and Maggie's day brightened immeasurably. For the first time she hoped book club didn't go on too long.

7

TOM

I was better prepared the next time I went to the library. I knew to keep away from the computer and anything else I could break, and I had what I hoped were believable mum-type responses for which of the books I'd liked and wanted more of. I needed to renew the JoJo Moyes one because I'd not finished it thanks to a load of revision my chemistry teacher had dropped on me. I was enjoying the book too. That was both good and bad. It was great disappearing into a story but the shame of anyone discovering I was reading romance books was nagging away at me like toothache. Just the thought of it made me nauseous but the truth was I loved them. I was probably a bit addicted. Mainly because they were basically self-help guides for useless men. They were exactly what I needed. Simple lessons in how not to behave around females. I was learning way more from them than I did from my schoolbooks. Maybe there was a market for turning GCSE textbooks into stories.

Christine looked pleased to see me, which was a bit of a

new concept for me. I don't usually get that reaction from anyone else. 'Hello again. It's Tom, isn't it?' She grinned and I could see she had lipstick on her teeth.

'Yep. Bringing these back for my *mum*.' I pronounced mum like I was talking to a kid – I'm not sure why. 'And I… er… *she* needs the JoJo… um… that one renewed.' Well, that went well, not. I was such a bad actor even when I'd practised my lines.

'No problem at all,' said Christine efficiently tapping them into the computer. 'Shall I choose her some more?'

'Please.' I was too quick with that response. 'Yeah, you know, if you like.' I shrugged. 'I've got work to do so I'll be…' I pointed to the back of the library.

'Okay. I'll bring them down in a bit.'

'Cool.' I picked up my bag and headed to my usual corner. I saw Maggie looking at me as I passed the book club table and she nodded. I did the same in response. That was far easier. Why wasn't that level of communication acceptable all the time? I could cope with a nod.

I got quite a bit of work done. I've been a bit of an idiot. Dad doesn't seem to care much about what I do at school as long as I don't get into any sort of trouble that means he has to go down there and talk to teachers. I've sort of been coasting for a bit. And I know I shouldn't have done but if nobody else was bothered then why should I be?

In my defence I did go along to an after-school revision group. It sounded like it would help me catch up, which was what I knew I needed to do. And as no one was forcing me to go I was all right about it. That was until I walked into the classroom. There was one boy leaving as I went in. He was making some excuse to the teacher that he'd remembered he'd got football practice and when I checked out the room I got why he was making a run for it. It was full of girls. I'm not even exaggerating. There must have been about forty of them because they'd run out of desks and there wasn't another boy in sight.

There was no way I was staying there on my own, even if Farah Shah was one of the girls. I piggybacked on the other boy's lie and said I had to go to football too and got out of there as quick as I could. I didn't bother going to revision classes anymore; they defo aren't for me.

Mum used to spend a lot of time with me and my schoolwork. It was only primary school stuff but she took time to sit down with me and practise my spellings and reading. I made out I hated doing it but really I liked having time with my mum. Sometimes I pretended to keep getting the word wrong so I could have a few more minutes with her all to myself.

'Here you are,' said Christine brightly plonking down a tower of romance novels.

I quickly chucked them in my backpack. 'Thanks. Oh and Mum says thanks too.'

That seemed to make her happy. She flicked her hair off her shoulder and showed me her lipstick teeth again. 'Tell her it's my absolute pleasure to help a reader.'

'Okay.' I looked back at my schoolwork and hoped she'd go away. After a moment she did and I could relax again.

I finished the chemistry revision and checked my watch. There was nothing to go home for. Dad and I were still ignoring each other. He was either at work or wasted, which suited me fine. I couldn't even look at him right now. I decided to stay at the library. It was kind of an all right place to be. The old ladies had stopped staring at me. I was becoming invisible here too and that helped. I was dying to finish off the JoJo Moyes book but I couldn't. Looking around me I decided there had to be another more acceptable book I could read in public.

I got up and started to peruse the shelves. I'm not sure how long I was there but it was good to check out all the covers and read the blurbs. I found *A Game of Thrones* and was made up. I didn't even know it was a book series. Nobody at school had mentioned that. This was awesome. I took the first book and went to head back to my spot. But as I turned I saw Maggie was now sitting in the seat next to mine.

'Is it okay if I sit here?' she asked.

'It's a free country.' I hated myself a little bit for my reply.

'True but if you want some space I can clear off.'

'No, you're all right.' I sat back down and opened my book. Maggie was reading the newspapers and then she moved on to a magazine.

We stayed like that for ages. Both of us just reading. She occasionally chuckled at something. I didn't ask what.

'Do you want a water?' she asked getting to her feet. There was a dispenser in the corner.

'Er. Yeah. Please.'

She brought two paper cups back. 'Is that any good?' she asked nodding at my new find.

'Awesome.' I'd already read forty-something pages.

'Have you tried Terry Pratchett?' she asked.

'No. Any good?'

'The best. Start with *Good Omens* – it's funny.' I

nodded and made a note to check it out. 'You finished your homework?'

'Yeah.'

'Are you doing O levels or A levels?' she asked nodding at my textbook.

'GCSEs then A levels if I get good enough grades, which I probably won't.'

'Ah.' She nodded wisely. 'Is that you being realistic or modest?'

'Realistic.'

'Not everyone is academic,' she said kindly. 'I wasn't. It doesn't mean you can't get a decent job. They seem to be going in for apprenticeships again. They were a big thing in my day. Good way to get experience.'

'Yeah but if I stand a chance of getting out of the village I need to get into university and that means decent results.' Why was I telling her all this?

'What makes you think you need to get out of the village?'

I shrugged. I wasn't about to tell her my whole life story. But she'd made me think. Why was I so set on university? Simple answer – because the worst thing that could happen to me was if I ended up like my dad.

8

MAGGIE

Saturdays had been Maggie's favourite day of the week for a long time but they'd just got even better. Tom intrigued her. He was ordinary and yet he wasn't. They didn't often see teenagers in the library and if they did come in it was only to use the computers and when they discovered the dodgy sites were blocked they usually didn't return. There was something going on with Tom; she was sure of it. She was a keeper of secrets and she recognised the same in others.

Of course it had crossed her mind that there was no mystery at all, that he was simply a teenager using the library but that was dull and didn't fill her time nearly as well. No, she much preferred the conspiracy theory idea – it had far more potential.

Maggie was keen to get to the library, even more so than her usual desire to check there were still other human beings on the planet. But first she had to check on the animals. She strode down to Colin and completed their well-choregraphed routine before heading over to the ewes. She could see something was amiss and quickened her pace.

Barbara was cast. The other ewes were in a corner together eating. At some point in the night Barbara had managed to flip herself onto her back, probably owing to the uneven ground and trying to have a scratch. Until she'd seen it Maggie had often been entertained by the thought of gymnast sheep but once she'd witnessed the devastating results it had lost its humour instantly. A cast sheep would eventually die. Maggie checked Barbara over. Thankfully she was okay and the crows hadn't found her. If they'd got there first, they would have pecked at her like she were a live buffet.

Maggie bent her knees, took firm hold of two of Barbara's legs and heaved her up onto her feet. Barbara wobbled and Maggie held her steady. The ewe did a record-breaking wee before tottering off across the field with not so much as a bleat of thanks.

Maggie hung around to check Barbara was okay, meaning she missed the early bus she usually caught, leaving no time for her customary trip to the village shop and the post office. Even if she had had time she probably would have skipped them because today she was keen to get to the library and see if Tom showed up again.

Maggie was the last of the book club group to arrive. She took her seat, pulled the book from her bag and looked about. The usual suspects were assembled but there was no sign of Tom. As if on cue he slunk in. This week he carefully placed his bag down and gave his usual shifty glance around. He handed over the books to Christine and went to study the shelves.

Maggie tried to keep her mind on the book club discussion but it was difficult with her concentration elsewhere and the novel hadn't gripped her anyway. She chipped in occasionally but her attention was on Tom. She was relieved when they reached the end of the set questions and opened it up for general conversation about the book.

Maggie pushed back her chair and sidled over to Christine.

'Does his mum not want any more?' she asked, tilting her head at Tom who was engrossed in selecting books.

'He says he's going to choose them himself.' Christine's shoulder twitched in a half shrug but she did look a bit put out. Christine liked to think she knew all there was to know about books. It was true that she was the librarian; however, she did have a tendency to recommend the same tried and trusted novels.

Maggie kept watch on Tom until she could wait no more and went to peruse the shelves near to where he was. 'Hello,' she said.

'All right?' he asked, although it was doubtful he wanted a full and considered response.

'Good thank you. What did your mum think of *Me Before You*? Did she say anything? I talked about it to everyone when I finished it.' Maggie tried not to scrutinise him while she waited for his response.

'Um. Yeah. She liked it.' He gave a considered nod.

'That's great. I'm pleased. It's always hard when you recommend a book and the person hates it. The heroine is my favourite character. I like quirky.' Maggie splayed out her long colourful cardigan.

'I see that,' said Tom.

'Hey. Don't judge a book by its cover or a lady by her cardigan.'

'It makes a change from beige.' Tom nodded at the ladies around the table displaying all shades of the colour with a few pastels thrown in.

'Matches their hearing aids,' said Maggie.

Tom chuckled but stared hard at the bookshelf.

Perhaps she was getting too chatty for him. Maggie went back to the book chat. 'She's one of those characters who gets under your skin and doesn't leave you. You know?'

'Yeah.'

'I liked how the story made you think. Made you put yourself in their situation.'

'Uh-huh,' said Tom, focusing on the book in his hand.

'I didn't like Will's mother, but then mothers are controlling by nature.'

'Maybe she was trying to help,' said Tom. 'Probably. I dunno.'

'And I'm a sucker for a love story. Will truly loved Louise and that was so real.'

'Louisa,' said Tom. He put the book he was holding on his pile and stepped sideways.

'Yes. You're right, it was Louisa,' said Maggie. Tom was turning pink. Maggie moved away. She had uncovered what she needed to.

When it reached shutting-up time Tom appeared at Maggie's shoulder. 'You getting the bus?'

'Are you asking?' She pushed her chair back.

'What?' He frowned at her. The generation divide was cavernous.

'Nothing. Yes, I'm getting the bus.'

'Come on then,' said Tom, leading the way, his head down.

Maggie pulled on her coat like an excited teenager and followed him out. 'How was your chemistry test?'

'Huh?'

'Last week you were working on chemistry revision. Did you get a good mark?'

'It was okay.'

'Right.' He wasn't as talkative this week and it was disappointing. 'What did you work on today?' She didn't like to interrogate him but needs must.

'English literature. We're doing *Animal Farm*.'

'Do you like it?'

'Yeah. I liked the story but I'm not sure I understand all the analysis we have to do for the exam.'

'Does it spoil the enjoyment of the story?'

'Yeah. It does.' He put his head down and walked in front of her down the alleyway.

Perhaps she'd get to natter to him again when they reached the bus stop. She was pleased to see there was nobody else waiting. She feared if anyone arrived he'd be off. They sat side by side on the cool metal seats and waited for the bus. 'I think this week's book club read will be more up my street.'

He was looking about. He seemed to have lost interest in her. She got the book out anyway and showed it to him.

'*The Fault in Our Stars*.' He nodded. 'You might like it,' she said. He nodded again before realising his mistake.

'Nah. Doubt it.' Tom looked away.

'It's okay, Tom. The others don't know and I won't be telling them.'

'Know what?' He pulled his shoulders back and stared her down.

'That it's you reading the books and not your mum.'

His shoulders sagged with every word, until he was back to his rounded-shoulder posture. 'How'd you know?'

'The way you read the blurbs before choosing the books. The conversation about *Me Before You*.' She gave a shrug. 'I'm a bit like a dog with a bone when something doesn't add up.'

He turned to look up the road for the bus, as if willing it to arrive, but there was ages yet. 'Well done, Miss Marple.'

'Hey, I have better footwear than her.' She waggled her red Doc Marten boots at him. 'Reading isn't something to be ashamed of.'

'Err, yes it is. Especially when it's romance.' He turned back to face her. 'I'd get slaughtered for this.'

'At school?'

'At school, at home, everywhere!' He threw his arms up.

'At home. Surely your mum wouldn't...' Tom's face changed. It was his eyes mainly. Like a light going out. His expression broke Maggie's heart just a fraction. She lowered her voice. 'You don't have a mum around, do you, Tom?'

'Miss Marple strikes again.' He swallowed hard and shook his head. 'She died when I was eight.'

'I'm so sorry,' she said reaching out a hand and squeezing

his shoulder. He gave a weak smile at the gesture. 'It's crap isn't it?'

Tom laughed and looked at her through his fringe. 'Yeah. It is total crap. You're funny…'

'For an old woman?'

'Nah, you're just funny.'

'So come on. What did you really think of the ending of *Me Before You*?' she asked, leaning forward and resting her forearms on her thighs.

'Bloody hell. That was a shock, wasn't it? I can't stop thinking about it. It was different to all the other books I've read and those last few pages… Whoa.'

Maggie loved to hear the indignation and excitement in his voice. She'd not heard him speak for so long in all the weeks he'd been coming to the library. She'd found a kindred spirit in the most unlikely place and she was going to hang on to him as if her life depended on it.

9

TOM

I thought about Maggie a lot that evening. I didn't like how she'd got the truth out of me. I thought I was smarter than that. My big secret was out and weirdly it was a huge relief. More than that it felt good to talk about the books with another reader. It was like reliving them. I had been reading every night since Dad killed my Xbox.

The books opened a door for me to escape into a different world. One where I was the hero. I could also convince myself that it was research. Research into a life I wanted to lead, people I wanted to be like. I had even made some notes. These heroes had some great lines. They were mostly aloof or idiots at the start of the stories but they learned along the way and came good in the end. They were arrogant rather than shy like me but still awkward in their own way with the ability to push women away. But what I was learning was that this situation wasn't irretrievable. There was hope. Not a lot of it, but it was enough to make me want to know more.

I finished the last page of *The Notebook* by Nicholas Sparks and put the book down. It was one I didn't want to end. The couple had been through loads to get to the happily ever after. I think I've been through quite a bit but there's no sign of my happy ending.

A clattering sound came from downstairs. I checked the clock. Dad and I had kept our distance since the night of the Xbox murder. My anger had gone but the resentment was strong and stood on firm foundations and was unlikely to fade without some effort on his part. The house was silent again apart from the rumble of my stomach. I went downstairs to get something to eat. I'd finished the Marmite earlier so it would have to be plain toast with a bit of marg.

I found the five-pound note in my pocket that Maggie had returned a few weeks ago. It wasn't much good to me there. I should have spent it on food but I'd got too caught up in talking to Maggie and then I'd forgotten all about it again. I thought about giving it back to Dad but he'd only spend it on beer or whisky.

Something made me stick my head around the living room door. Dad was lying on the floor. Sometimes I like to lie on the floor; I'm too long for our sofa now. But the way Dad was lying didn't look like he'd chosen that position. His glass and some beer cans were scattered on the carpet – that must have been the clatter I heard.

'Dad?' He didn't move. I stepped into the room and nudged him with my toe. His leg rocked but he didn't stir. I walked around the sofa to get a better look. He didn't look good. 'Dad!' I raised my voice and gave him a shake. No response. Shit. Was he unconscious? I knelt down next to him. My stomach tightened as fear gripped it like an icy hand. I couldn't lose my dad. He was all I had. I grabbed him by the shoulders and shook him – harder this time. His head bounced off the leg of the table.

'Bloody hell, Tom!' Dad was suddenly conscious. His red face scowling as he rubbed the back of his head.

I let his shoulders go and leaned back on my haunches. 'I thought you'd…' I drew in a deep breath to steady my shaking limbs. There was something about his expression that made me question what had just happened. 'Were you faking?'

'Can't you take a joke?' He shuffled himself upright.

What sort of sick person does that? My fear morphed into anger. 'What's wrong with you? I thought you were… hurt.'

'I did hurt myself.' His voice was slurred. 'That bloody table is trying to kill me. I twisted my ankle.'

He rolled up his trouser leg but I didn't care. I stood up. 'You're an idiot.'

He looked up at me in an exaggerated movement. 'Lighten up, Tom. It was a joke.'

'Not funny.'

'Life isn't,' said Dad. 'You'll find that out when you get a job.'

'I'm going to university.' I'd got my mind set on it now. An apprenticeship might have been more my level but it would be local and I needed to get away.

'Not this again.' His voice was rising. 'You're acting like a child.' He reached for his glass and I kicked it away.

'You're acting like a drunk.' I walked out so I didn't have to listen to him. I wished I'd gone via the kitchen because, with a loud rumble, my stomach reminded me I was still hungry.

I went to my bedroom but it was the wrong place to go. I was like a dog at the rescue, pacing up and down. I could cover the small room in three paces. I'd outgrown this space. It was starting to feel like I'd outgrown a lot of things.

On Monday I walked into my history class and they'd moved the desks around. I hate it when they do that. I paused in the doorway, scanning the faces and working out my best odds of making it through the lesson unnoticed.

'Ah, Tom Harris,' said Mr Thackery, the teacher. 'I'm introducing a buddy system.' I scratched my head. He consulted a list on his desk. 'Can you sit next to Farah please?'

Instant overheating mode engaged. 'Uh, well...' I frantically looked about. Farah had her back to me and was chatting to her friend.

'Move along. Over there.' He shooed me away as more people clogged the doorway.

Had I remembered to put on deodorant today? I had but was it up to this kind of extreme test? I tried to tilt my nose towards my armpit and have a sniff as I walked. Not great but not enough to scorch her eyeballs. At least I hadn't had PE today. Farah swivelled around and her eyebrows registered alarm at my strange underarm-sniffing behaviour. Bad start.

'All right?' I mumbled but didn't make eye contact, dropped my bag to the floor and slid onto the chair, being careful not to sit centrally for fear of looking like I was getting too close to her.

'You're Thomas Harris right?' She said it like a question.

But the fact was she knew who I was. Farah Shah knew who I was! It was like a metal rod being inserted in my spine.

I looked at her for a moment. 'Yeah. It's just Tom.'

'I'm Farah.' She smiled. A sweet delicate smile. Her face bright and her voice confident but warm. My life was turning a corner and this was it. I was buddied with Farah Shah. I wanted to punch the air but I was rooted to my chair as my thoughts drifted to what this could mean. A legitimate reason to spend time with her. The discussions we could have about history. Revision schedules from now until the end of term. Images of me doing my homework with her in her bedroom loomed large and unfortunately triggered some excessive sweating. It was like a single ray of sunshine warming me until someone bumped me in the back.

'Shift, Harris.' Joshua Kemp was standing over me. Kemp who thought he was big time because his dad was a school governor and he was captain of the rugby team. He was more big time than me, though.

'Ah, Joshua,' said Mr Thackery. 'We have a new seating arrangement, which I will explain now everyone has deigned to join us. You'll be sitting next to Amy and she will be your buddy.'

'Sorry, sir. I won't be able to see the board from there,' said Kemp, brightly. 'It's okay. I'll swap with Harris. You don't mind. Do you?' It wasn't a question. My time with Farah had been short and beautiful.

'Er,' I said, but Kemp was already leaning over me. 'I guess not.' I gave Farah a wan smile. Oh, what might have been. I went to lift my bag but Farah's chair leg was on it. 'Sorry…' I pointed at the chair leg.

'Piss off, Harris,' whispered Kemp in my ear. His menace lost a little something as I smelled Hubba Bubba on his breath.

'Bag. Stuck.' Suddenly forming a sentence was a struggle.

'Here.' Kemp pulled it hard, making Farah topple and ripping my bag. Farah scowled at us both. My heart clenched. Moments ago her look had been so inviting. Joshua slammed my bag into my chest and propelled me out of the way. I left with a heavy heart and my rucksack in tatters.

Amy shook her head as I sat down. A little unnecessary I thought. She'd had a lucky escape from Kemp. He was a bully and he believed he was untouchable. He took pleasure in tripping up year sevens and it was common knowledge that he paid Nicholas Burns to do his maths homework for him. Oddly, though, some of the girls seemed to fancy him. Life was unfair.

Mr Thackery returned our history essays. 'Eight, Farah, very good. Five, Joshua, needs a lot of work. Nine, Amy, excellent but expected…' Amy preened herself as she took the essay back from Mr Thackery. 'Eight, Tom, very good and unexpected.' His voice was full of suspicion. I took the essay and glanced at Farah. I longed to be back sitting next to her. We had the same score. We were so compatible. We could have discussed our essays, shared what we needed to do to inch our scores up. I sighed at my lost opportunity.

'Did you cheat?' asked Amy, scowling hard at my essay.

'No. Did you?'

She huffed a response and was so affronted she moved her desk a few centimetres away from mine.

At the end of class I gathered my things slowly. I was in

no rush to get home. I'd spent half the lesson rehearsing a conversation with Farah just in case she too had noticed that we'd got matching scores and had spotted the enormous similarity. But when I looked across she had already left. I hauled my ripped bag into my arms as I could no longer carry it on my shoulder. This was a disaster. Dad was going to flip and he wasn't going to pay for a new one this close to the end of term. He was the same with school uniforms, which was why I always looked like my clothes had shrunk in the wash.

Joshua and his mate Kyle Fletcher were loitering in the corridor. I ignored them and walked past.

'Oi, Harris.'

Piss it. I paused but didn't turn around. I didn't expect the shove that sent me to the floor and my backpack contents spewing across the dusty lino.

'Don't you dare even look at Farah. You got that?' Kemp snarled while Fletcher nodded like a car insurance dog. He bore an uncanny resemblance to the advert, which distracted me for a moment. 'Got it?' repeated Kemp. He kicked me and gave me a dead thigh.

'Yeah. Got it,' I said, rubbing my leg. 'I didn't know you and her were...'

'They're not,' said Fletcher.

'Shut up, Fletcher.' Joshua turned his aggression on him. 'We've virtually hooked up.'

The laugh that came was involuntary. I doubted I was on Farah's radar but the thought that she would be attracted to this thug was laughable.

'You got something to say, Harris?'

'No. Bit of a cough coming I think,' I said, rubbing my

throat for effect before gathering up my well-distributed bag contents.

Kemp loomed over me and I covered my groin.

'Kemp, Fletcher and Harris. Don't you have homes to go to?' called Mr Thackery from the other end of the corridor. My groin was spared for another day.

10

MAGGIE

Maggie was now in possession of a new bus pass and had celebrated on Tuesday by taking the bus into Leamington Spa. She had treated herself to a cappuccino and a chocolate twist. It had been good to be out and surrounded by people but the brief exchange over what size drink she wanted and whether she was eating in or out couldn't be classed as a significant human interaction. There was something oddly isolating about being surrounded by people and yet completely alone.

It was such a faff to get the bus though, as she had to first go in to Compton Mallow, which was in the opposite direction, to then swap buses to Leamington. It was far from ideal and meant it took her almost two hours to get there. She had been pleased to have a brief discussion with a woman on the bus about how manoeuvrable pushchairs were these days. Sadly the woman got off one stop afterwards and that was the last time Maggie spoke to anyone.

All was quiet with the animals. Still no sign of lambs

although there had been an alarming drop in egg production, which indicated that Mr Fox may be doing the rounds again. She had time to kill and she needed to set up some pens for the pregnant sheep for when they gave birth. Assuming any of them were pregnant. With the amount of land Maggie had and the undulating nature of most of it, moving things around was a challenge. Providence Farm had once been a thriving sheep farm. On the farmer's passing the family had been keen to sell and were happy for most of the farm equipment to be included, mainly because they didn't want the hassle, or cost, of disposing of it. Most of what was left was past its best but at that stage Maggie and her husband had wanted to keep their options open so had inherited the little old grey Ferguson tractor and trailer along with a variety of other farm paraphernalia.

Maggie didn't own a car. She wasn't entirely against them but having been a vehement campaigner for saving the planet, long before it was a popular pastime, she was aware of the environmental damage.

It took a few goes to get the tractor started but eventually it chugged into life. Maggie reversed, hitched up the trailer and drove it out of the barn and round to the side of the house. She took a sharp turn to miss one pothole only to hit another bigger one with the trailer, she felt it list dramatically to one side. She switched off the engine and climbed down.

The trailer tyre was punctured and almost pulled off the wheel. 'Bugger it,' she said. With her hands on her hips she surveyed the situation. The ancient trailer was leaning over and with its tyre almost off it was stranded. She needed to lift the trailer up in order to get the tyre off, but looking at the rusted nuts it was going to be a struggle. But Maggie was nothing if not tenacious. A few hours later she reluctantly accepted this wasn't something she was going to be able to fix on her own.

Maggie's mind was elsewhere during the deep questions about this week's book club read – *The Fault in Our Stars*. She'd thoroughly enjoyed the story and she was sure Tom would too. Most of the group had liked it meaning there wasn't much of a discussion.

Tom was beavering away in his usual corner. Christine was busying herself with putting up new posters. Maggie was preoccupied by her tyre problems. She could see little choice but to ask a neighbouring farmer for help but as he had pointed out before it wasn't like she could return the favour so he would expect to be paid for his trouble.

Betty waved a bony hand in front of Maggie's eyes. 'I said are you coming to the cake sale?'

Maggie had been miles away. 'Sorry. Where is this now?'

'In the church hall. It's all for charity. Children or cancer or some such thing. Anyway it's a good cause,' said Betty.

'Err.' Maggie was torn. She'd found she was looking forward to her weekly chats with Tom. Despite being surrounded by women her age it was him she felt most at ease with. If she left now, she couldn't come back merely for Tom to walk her to the bus stop; that would look ridiculous. She was watching Tom. He had his head down and was studying in the corner. She didn't like to disturb him but he seemed to sense her gaze and he looked up, giving her a warm smile.

'Well?' said Betty growing impatient.

'I'll see you down there,' said Maggie.

She joined Tom at the small table at the back of the library. 'Hello, you look busy.'

'Trying to get my head around cumulative frequency polygons.'

She had no idea what they were. 'I'm going to a cake sale.' An idea struck her. 'And I wondered if you'd like me to bring you some back. It's important to feed the brain when you're studying.'

Tom pursed his lips. 'I never say no to cake.'

'Excellent.' The joy she felt was ridiculous. 'What's your favourite? I can't promise anything mind.'

Tom seemed thoughtful. 'I dunno. We don't have proper cake much. Once Dad bought those cake bar things.' They both screwed their noses up at the same time. 'What cake are *you* getting?'

Now it was her turn to have a think. 'I'm a big lemon drizzle fan...'

'Awww.' Tom looked like he was going to dribble. 'My mum...' He glanced about before continuing. 'She used to make that. It was amazing.'

'Although Victoria sandwich is a classic that's hard to beat. But I'm a sucker for a scone with jam and cream. But it has to be clotted cream mind.'

He shook his head. 'Don't think I've ever had a scone.'

'Well, knock me down with a feather. You poor lamb. You've not lived until you've had a scone.' Tom started packing his books into a torn bag. 'What are you doing?'

'I'm coming with you. I can't concentrate on this now. All I can think about is cake.'

*

The church hall was cavernous. At one end there was an open gap through to the kitchen, in front of which were three tables, one of them was occupied by a couple of the other book club regulars. Betty beckoned them over.

Maggie gave them a brief greeting. There was little else to say when you'd just spent two hours together. Tom followed her to the counter where three eager-looking women hovered in matching aprons.

'What can I get you,' trilled one of them. 'Tea or coffee and a slice of cake for two pounds. It all goes to charity.'

'After we've taken out the money for the tea, coffee and milk,' muttered the lady to her left. She reminded Maggie of the person delivering the terms and conditions on the radio.

'What cakes have you got?' Maggie asked. She could sense Tom peering over her shoulder.

'Chocolate, coffee and walnut, carrot cake, which I made fresh last night, or blueberry muffins.' It was a sorry offering to Maggie's mind.

'A tea and a piece of carrot cake for me then,' said Maggie, getting out her purse. 'Tom?'

He was studying the cakes intensely. 'Chocolate cake please.'

'And what would you like to drink? We have squash,' said the woman behind the counter.

Maggie felt a little insulted on Tom's behalf.

'No thanks. Just the cake please.'

'I don't know that we can do cake without a drink.' A lot of muttering between the three women ensued.

'It's fine,' said Maggie, handing over four pounds. 'It's all for charity.'

'That's lovely, thank you,' said the woman looking

mightily relieved as she passed over a tray. Tom put his bag on a chair and came back for the tray. It was a nice gesture. Maggie could have managed but she wasn't going to go on a feminist rant about equality because he'd been thoughtful. They sat at the third table away from Betty and the others.

They both tucked into their cakes in silence. The carrot cake was good but it would never have been Maggie's first choice. 'How is the cake?' asked Maggie realising too late that she should have been using the past tense as there was no sign that there had ever been any cake on Tom's plate. 'Did you inhale it?'

'Sorry.' He looked awkward and she regretted her comment.

'No, it's nice to see someone enjoy their food. My husband wasn't a foodie. He would have been happy with a pill instead of a meal.' Why she was telling him that she had no idea but he was politely nodding.

'Dad says I'm a bottomless pit.'

'I'd rather that than a picky eater.' She paused to drink her tea. It was stewed.

'The cake was great. Thanks, Maggie.'

'You're welcome. I feel guilty that I'm stopping you studying.' She wanted to give him a get-out option.

'Nah. It's okay. I think cumulative frequency polygons are beyond me to be honest.'

'Maths is it?' She ventured a guess.

'Yeah. Not my strong subject.'

'Nor mine. Although, I was pretty rubbish at everything at school. I once drew an apple and my teacher asked me what it was.'

Tom laughed. 'I'm all right at art. Not many jobs you can do with that though.'

'Yes there are,' said Maggie, her indignation strong. 'Sign writer, architect, art teacher…' She was starting to run out of examples; perhaps he was right. She looked around for inspiration. 'Cake decorator.'

'I don't think that's the career for me. I'd love to illustrate graphic novels or work on anime films.'

Maggie nodded, not entirely sure what he'd said but she wanted to show him some encouragement. 'I was a holistic therapist. Thank goodness I didn't need any exams for that.'

Tom now had an expression that most likely mirrored her own thirty seconds ago. 'What do you do now?' he asked.

Oh what a question that was. If she were to answer it honestly would he be shocked? I spend my time desperately trying to fill my day until one morning I don't wake up.

She gave herself a mental shake. 'Well, this morning I was trying to get a wheel off a trailer,' she said.

Tom was grinning. 'What, like nicking one?'

'No. The other day I was moving hurdles with my tractor and I got a puncture.'

Tom laughed. Maggie wasn't seeing what was funny. 'You're joking right?'

'No. Honestly. I've got a bit of land so it's the only way to move large things about. And Tuesday morning I got a puncture and the wheel won't come off. It's a right pain because I can't free it without some help.'

'I'll help you,' said Tom. He was picking up non-existent cake crumbs with his finger.

'That's kind but I live a way out.'

Tom shrugged. 'Sundays are dull as… anything. Furrow's

Cross wasn't it?' She nodded. 'I can get a bus over.' He looked up and she could see that the offer was genuine.

'Okay but on one condition.'

'Name it.'

'You stay for Sunday roast.'

His face lit up like a toddler on Christmas morning. 'You're on.'

11

TOM

I checked Maggie got her bus and set off home. As I turned the corner to go up the hill I saw Joshua Kemp coming the other way. What was he doing in the village? I had a split second to make a decision about whether to turn around or not but I was too slow. He saw me and his lip curled into a sneer.

I put my head down, hugged my broken bag and kept going.

'Harris! What are you doing around here? Don't you live on the council estate with the other losers?' Kemp laughed at his own joke.

'Josh,' I said as if greeting a friend but kept going.

'Hey. I asked you a question.' He held his palm out like a traffic cop to stop me. I had no choice.

'I'm going home.'

'Do you know where Farah lives?' he asked.

'Err…' Again far too slow.

'You do. Are you some sort of stalker?'

'No. I don't know *exactly* where she lives. I think it's on the way into town.'

He gave me a shove. 'You can do better than that.'

'Off the London Road, I think. But I don't know.' If I had known where she lived I would have been taking regular walks up that way like a right saddo. It was better all round that I didn't have her address.

'If I find out you're lying.' He puffed his chest up like a pigeon.

'I'm not.'

I began walking again and Kemp must have tripped me up because my foot caught on something. I fell to the pavement like a brick. I clutched my bag for fear of its contents falling out. My romance book addiction remained strong. Thank goodness I didn't drop any but I landed hard on my wrist and it bloody hurt. Kemp chuckled to himself like a third-rate Disney villain as he walked away.

I did my Sunday paper round in double quick time despite the ache in my wrist and was showered and dressed before Dad had surfaced. I left a note to say I'd be out all day at a friend's. I figured it wasn't that far from the truth.

The bus dropped me near the crossroads that gave Furrow's Cross its name and Maggie's instructions were to walk back from there and take the dirt track on the same side of the road that the bus had dropped me off.

The track was narrow with grass growing in the centre and plenty of craters. There were fields on either side but not a lot else. I walked on and just when I thought I'd somehow gone the wrong way I saw a roof. The house was in a dip off to the right, hidden by a row of tall trees where the track dropped down to it. An old wooden gate looked like it hadn't been closed in a while and a well-worn sign read *Providence Farm*. The house was a bit like how a child would draw a farmhouse; all symmetrical, with a central door, a large window either side and three above, each one split into tiny panes.

There was an arched portico and a white-painted front door. I knocked on the door while trying to take in my surroundings. This wasn't what I'd expected at all.

'You found it,' said Maggie, opening the door. She looked red in the face and the sleeves on her oversized swirly-patterned shirt were rolled up. 'Come in.' She disappeared inside leaving me to shut the door. The hall was about the same size as my bedroom. I took my jacket off. It was chilly but I couldn't put my jacket back on without appearing rude. There were a series of coat hooks or at least I guessed there were but they were hidden under a lifetime's collection of coats and cardigans. I placed my jacket on top of another coat and hoped it stayed there.

'Come through,' came Maggie's disembodied voice. I followed the shiny pavement-style flooring through to the kitchen where it was far warmer. Maggie was draining something at the sink. 'I got some Coke.' She nodded at a large bottle on the table. 'Is that okay?'

'Yeah. Thanks.' It was proper branded Coke. We always had the cheap stuff at home. Dad said it wasn't worth it because when I chugged it I never tasted it anyway.

'Glasses are in the end cupboard.' She tilted her head to guide me. I chose a large glass, poured a drink and sat and watched while she scurried about. Something smelled good but I couldn't work out exactly what it was.

Eventually she clapped her hands together and spun in my direction. 'We have an hour before dinner. So drink up and I'll show you the problem.'

I'd only had a few sips but I downed the rest, carefully managed a burp and followed her out of the kitchen and into a tiny room full of buckets, brooms and footwear.

'What size are you?' she asked as she rooted through a selection of wellington boots.

'Nine, I think. Maybe a ten.' My school shoes were tight again.

'Try those.' She handed me some dark green boots and I did as I was told. They were a bit tight but they fitted and I followed her out of the back door. I tried to shut it but it needed a good tug to do so. At the side of the house was a concrete yard with a little tractor and a rusty old wooden trailer stuck in the middle. I'd been expecting the tractor to be much bigger. It was a bit of a let-down.

Maggie explained what had happened, showed me the punctured tyre and the rusted nuts. 'I need you to jack it up.' She pointed at a rusty-looking contraption. 'And you'll probably have to do the nuts on the wheel too.' She rubbed her hands over themselves like a miser in a movie. 'My grip's not what it once was.'

I had no idea what I was doing but with Maggie's instructions and help we managed to change the tyre. Although the one she put on looked in almost as bad a state as the one we'd taken off, she said it would be fine until she got the other one repaired.

She slapped me on the back with more force than I'd expected she was capable of. 'You've earned your lunch,' she said, striding back to the farmhouse.

*

I drank more Coke and watched Maggie serve up a full roast dinner. The last time I ate a roast dinner was when my grandparents last visited and took us to the pub. That was four years ago.

When Maggie was putting some stuff in the sink to soak I took a quick photo on my phone. I wasn't the sort of person who posted pictures of their food on Instagram but I wanted to capture this. It looked so good.

'It's like Christmas dinner,' I said when she sat down to join me.

She chuckled a gentle tinkle of a laugh. 'There's no cranberry or pigs in blankets. You can't have Christmas dinner without those.'

'We usually have steak and chips at Christmas.'

'Oh, well that's nice too.' She gave me a tight smile. I got the feeling it was nothing less than turkey and all the trimmings for Maggie.

She was right. Steak was always good but it wasn't a proper Christmas dinner like this. Christmas in March.

There was a pile of something colourful on my plate. Yellow, pink and purple slices of something familiar. 'Umm, what is that?' I asked.

'Carrots. They come in other colours than orange you know.' I did not know that. Everything on my plate tasted good. The chicken was full of flavour, not like a KFC bucket, but still good. The roast potatoes were crispy like Mum used to do them, and although the carrots were in all these weird colours they tasted amazing. I was sad when I'd eaten it all. I sipped my Coke and waited for Maggie to finish. She was smiling the whole time she was eating.

She placed her knife and fork together on her plate and leaned back into her chair.

'Thanks. That was great,' I said.

'Crumble?'

'Yeah. Please.'

At the end of the crumble I was full up. I wasn't sure it would last long but it was a good feeling.

'Do you have plans for this afternoon?' she asked.

'Nope.'

'You're welcome to stay here. I need to check on the sheep but otherwise I've no plans.'

'Sheep? Cool.' I hadn't realised she had animals. It got better and better. I had nothing to rush home for.

When she got up I followed her to the sink with my plate. I was hoping she had a dishwasher but I couldn't see one so I picked up a tea towel to show willing.

'I'll wash up but there's no need to dry. They'll drain on the board. Life's too short for drying up.'

We were soon tugging the wellies back on and heading outside. It wasn't warm but it wasn't raining, not that I think that would have bothered Maggie. 'Wait there,' she said forcefully. She strode off at the pace of someone younger. A few moments later she reappeared riding a quad bike. I must have looked surprised, mainly because I was. It wasn't the sight you expected to see – an old lady revving up a quad bike. The sound rippled through me.

'Well, get on,' she said, indicating behind her with a thumb.

'Err, yeah. Okay.'

I didn't need asking twice.

'There's a bar on the rack behind you. Hold on.'

I had moments to grab it before she revved the engine and the quad bike scooted out of the yard. She had a bucket hooked over one of the handlebars and it swung about violently. A sharp left turn and we were heading away from the farm. The dirt track gave way to soft ground and the quad made easy work of it, racing along a ridge with fields rising to the left and dropping away to our right. I stuck my head to one side to get a better view.

Maggie took a quick look behind her. 'Stop grinning. You'll get flies in your teeth or worse still a wasp.' I hadn't realised I was grinning until she said but how could I not? This was completely brilliant – the wind hitting me in the face, the smell of grass filling my nostrils and all the time I was bouncing about on the back of a quad bike.

She stopped and pointed up to the left. 'That woodland marks the boundary. It supplies all my wood for my wood burner and I plant new trees every year. The bloody muntjacs nibble them but more survive than don't.'

'You've got deer?'

'Not mine. They just pop in to eat stuff. It's like a deer buffet up there. Lots of rabbits too. Do you like rabbit?'

'Yeah, they're cute. I guess.'

Maggie laughed. 'Not to cuddle. To eat.'

'Dunno, never had it.' I wasn't squeamish but I wasn't sure about eating rabbits. They were a bit too close to pets but I didn't want Maggie to think I was a wimp.

'Right. Hold on.'

Thankfully I hadn't let go because she set off again. This

time taking a sharp right and skittering us down the field at a serious angle. It was terrifying and awesome in equal measure. 'Woo hoo!' I yelled as we hit a bump and the wheels left the grass. I couldn't help it. At the bottom was a rickety-looking fence and Maggie shouted that it marked the edge of her land. There were more fields on the other side. We bounced further along and I could see the sheep – some white and others sort of greyish in colour. They paused with mouths full of grass to watch us dismount.

'I'll move them down to the bottom field soon and they can give that one a trim.' She marched off and I had to lengthen my stride to catch her. 'Here's the ewes I'm hoping are going to lamb soon,' she said, pointing. She took the bucket from the handlebar of the quad bike and slipped into the field. The fat sheep ran over to her and hoovered up the contents as she was tipping it into a trough.

Nearby was what Maggie introduced as her vegetable patch but as it was about the size of a football pitch it was more like a whole allotment. She rattled off what was planted there but I kind of zoned out after carrots and potatoes.

Next were the chickens. I wasn't sure about these. Maggie invited me to join her in their enclosure and I did but they all flocked around my ankles and a couple had a good peck at the wellies. I could feel it through the rubber and was glad I wasn't wearing my pumps.

'Do you eat eggs?'

'Yeah.' We bought them when we were having a fry-up.

'Help yourself. I've not collected today.' She handed me a proper old-fashioned wicker basket and lifted up a hatch on the side of the wooden chicken house. Inside, resting on straw, like they'd been placed there for me, were three eggs. I put them carefully in the basket, danced around a couple of chickens and followed Maggie. The other chicken house just had two eggs but I was pleased with my haul. As we left the hens I heard a thud. Like someone slamming a gate. Maggie saw me turn.

'Ah, now, you'll need to leave your eggs here if you don't want them scrambled. It's time to meet Colin.'

Was this the part where it all went a bit horror movie? Did she have a husband locked up somewhere? Or perhaps it was the last person who had wandered by to help? Maybe I'd been reading too much.

We neared the next field and she waved her arm like a royal courtier for me to go ahead. As I neared the gate, which appeared to be held together with string, a sheep with too many horns ran at it full pelt and hit it so hard I thought it was going to splinter into a thousand pieces. 'Whoa!' I leaped out of the way, stumbled and landed on my bum.

Maggie laughed. I mean she laughed hard. Proper holding her sides belly laughs. I guess it was pretty funny. Eventually she pulled herself together. 'Tom meet Colin. He's a ram on loan but for some reason his farm isn't in a rush to have him back.'

'He's nuts,' I said watching the animal reverse back and aim his head at the gate ready for another attack.

'Yep. That's cade lambs for you.'

'What's that mean?' I asked, getting to my feet.

'Means he was bottle fed.'

'Would that not make him more like a pet?' Colin hurtled towards the gate, hitting it hard and making it shudder.

'You'd think so, wouldn't you? But not with Colin here. It means he has absolutely no fear of humans. Contempt, yes, but fear, not a drop. Anyway, that's the grand tour. I need tea.' She made for the quad bike.

We headed back towards the house, which was closer than I realised as we'd come a seriously long way round to get there. I was glad she lived in the middle of nowhere because I really didn't want anyone seeing me with a wicker basket over my arm, sitting on the back of a quad bike, driven by a little old lady.

She stopped in the yard near the back door. 'I'll put this away.' She patted the bike. 'You could make us drinks. I'll have a tea please. Tea caddy is near the kettle. Cupboard above it for mugs.'

I liked how she gave out instructions. It didn't feel like she was telling me what to do, although she was. There was something reassuring about how she commanded things. I was starting to learn there was more to her than I had ever imagined, plus her quad bike was awesome.

12

MAGGIE

For once the week had flown by. Having Tom over on Sunday was like having her batteries recharged. She'd had a purpose. It had been a while since she'd bothered with a roast dinner. It never seemed worth the effort for one. On the rare occasions she did cook a Sunday lunch she struggled to only cook sufficient for her and ended up feeding roast potatoes to the chickens, not that they minded. But when there was someone else who was going to tuck in with you it made all the difference. And tuck in he had. It was a pleasure to see him eat and a challenge to fill him up.

Tom had waxed lyrical about the quad bike. It was something of a necessity for her and she took it for granted. Seeing it through Tom's eyes had given her morning rounds a new perspective. Living alone had rubbed some of the fun out of her way of life and she needed to find it again. She'd found herself letting out a holler when she went down the steep slope into the bottom field – it was fun.

However, there was a downside. Being with Tom had sent

her mind off troubling about her son again. She thought of him often but having Tom in the house made her try to contrast and compare. None of which was healthy. Every thought was another scratch across her already damaged heart.

Maggie had a root around the other end of her wardrobe. She usually chose things from the right-hand side. The same things got a lot of wear and were on a constant loop – wear, wash, dry. She wasn't one for ironing – there was no point. She liked to fill her time but even she couldn't be doing with pointless tasks like ironing, drying up and polishing – they were a last resort.

She pulled out a long-forgotten kaftan. They were wonderfully comfy. This one was a riot of colour and merely pulling it free of the confines of the wardrobe made her smile. She gave it a sniff. She made a conscious effort that she wouldn't have that distinct old person pong. She could smell it on a couple of people who came to book club. It was an unpleasant musty scent and she feared the day she couldn't notice it was the day she smelled like it too. She always added vinegar and bicarbonate of soda to her wash, dried her clothes on the line whenever she could and used little bags of thyme, rosemary, and cloves instead of mothballs. Although she feared that made her smell like a casserole but it was still better than fusty old person.

She couldn't remember the last time she'd been shopping for clothes. She had no need to, but looking at them now, many she had were threadbare and most were shockingly outdated. Maggie had always bucked the trend but it was time she gave her wardrobe a little shake-up. She added sorting out her clothes to her growing list of tasks for the week ahead. She felt a trip to the charity shops was a good opportunity for out with the old and in with the not quite so old.

Saturday morning came around quicker than usual. Maggie walked into the library and noted the heads that cocked at her outfit. It felt good. She'd missed that sensation. She'd have to dig out her old afghan coat that had been a real head-turner in its day – now they'd call it vintage. She guessed they'd say the same about her.

Book club went well. It was always best when the viewpoints were opposing. It generated a good discussion. When everyone agreed with each other it was a much quieter and shorter session. Maggie liked a good debate, something she could get her teeth into. A load of nodding dogs wasn't nearly as much fun. The door opened and in walked Tom. His smile for her was brief but it was there and it warmed her soul.

She'd planned to keep her distance. She didn't want to push him away by coming across as needy. But she'd left him with the offer of calling in anytime, so now it was up to him. Although she had already planned out what she'd feed him next time he visited.

A few other people came in. The library was almost busy. Maggie watched Tom out of the corner of her eye. He was choosing books. He had a pile on the back table and he was lingering over *Polo* by Jilly Cooper. Maggie remembered being exactly the same. She'd always loved Jilly Cooper although she feared they may be a little racy for Tom.

A lean girl with straight black hair was hovering behind

the Mills and Boon carousel but on seeing Tom she made a beeline for him. Maggie was intrigued and also thrilled to be within listening distance.

'Hi, Tom.'

Tom shut the Jilly Cooper with a snap and almost threw it at the shelf. It hit another book, pinged out and landed on the floor with a light thud. Tom had the look of someone pulled from another galaxy. The girl crouched and picked the book up. Crimson spread quickly up his neck and his mouth opened and closed rapidly before he managed to reply.

'Farah. Hi.'

'I don't think this is on the GCSE reading list.' She held out the book.

He took it from her, shoved it in a gap on the shelf and turned his back on it. 'No, ha-ha.' His fake laugh was pitiful and Maggie was fascinated by the effect this girl had on him. He had turned into a gibbering idiot.

'I've not seen you in the library before,' she said. 'I sometimes do my homework here on a Tuesday instead of going back to an empty house. Mum and Dad are late home on Tuesdays and my brother has piano lessons.'

'Right,' said Tom.

'What you doing here?' She glanced at the pile of romance books stacked neatly next to his rucksack.

Tom followed her gaze. 'I work here,' said Tom. Farah's expression was questioning. 'Help out. Just sometimes. When it's busy.' They both looked around. There were far more people in the library than Maggie had seen there in a while.

'Great. Mum says I have to stop downloading books to

my Kindle. I've got a bit of a habit. So here I am.' She almost curtseyed and Maggie thought Tom was going to faint.

'Right. That's good. The library is… um… full of books,' he said. Maggie shook her head at his ineptitude.

'What would you recommend?' asked the girl.

'For you?' Tom pointed at her and she laughed.

'Yes, for me.'

'Err, yeah. Of course. Duh. What do you usually read?'

'Teen stuff mainly but I'm struggling to find new authors.'

'Okay… You like history, right?'

'I do.'

'Do you like romance?'

'I liked *The Fault in Our Stars* by—'

'John Green. Terrific. Stay there.' He moved quickly and returned with a book and presented it to her. '*Frederica* by Georgette Heyer.'

She read the back and gave a thoughtful pout. 'I'll give it a go.'

'Brilliant.' Tom ran his fingers through his hair. They eyed each other awkwardly and Tom's cheeks inched up the colour chart. 'You need to take it to the lady over there. She'll check it out for you.'

'Right. Okay. I might sit here and have a quick read. You know to check if it's my thing or not.'

'Sure. Of course.' Tom moved his bag to the floor and began returning his carefully selected pile of books to the shelves.

The post lady came in and handed over a pile of letters and something Christine had to sign for. Christine let out a gasp worthy of anyone winning a TV prize jackpot but her face told a different story. Maggie went to see what had caused it but Betty was quicker off the mark.

'Something wrong?' asked Betty, her face laden with glee.

'They're closing us down,' said Christine, followed by a dramatic sob as she clutched the podium for support.

Betty was quick with the tissues, which gave Maggie a chance to swivel around the offending letter and have a quick read for herself. She wasn't surprised to see that Christine had made a mansion out of a Lego brick. 'It's inviting you to a meeting about the future of the library, Christine.' It wasn't exactly an eviction notice. Maggie had seen plenty of those in her time.

Christine looked affronted. 'That's what it means.' She stabbed the letter with a neat fingernail. 'It came by recorded delivery. They call you to a meeting and that's when they tell you. They're closing you down...' She did add something on the end but it was inaudible and lost in the sniffing.

But if Christine was right, this would be the end of the book club and most likely the end of Maggie's contact with Tom.

13

TOM

School was all right today. I've been replaying my conversation with Farah a lot. It's like having my own Farah YouTube channel in my head. I was smiling to myself as I let myself in. The house was in darkness. Usually Dad would be up, maybe not up but at least dressed and the curtains drawn but not today. It felt odd to walk out of daylight and into the gloomy hallway. It was silent too. Imaginary fingertips crept up my spine making me shiver. I needed to get a grip. I wasn't alone because Dad was here – somewhere. We had an uneasy truce. Dad kept asking me if I was talking to him. I wasn't *not* talking to him; it was basically because I didn't have anything to say to him.

I checked the living room and dropped my bag on the sofa. I so needed a new bag but Dad said I had to wait until my birthday. Sporty Tom at school got a moped for his birthday. After the other Sunday at Maggie's I'd like a quad bike but that's not going to happen.

The living room is a tip. I'm no neat freak but it's starting to get to me. The whole place is a mess. I've not put any washing on this week because we've run out of washing powder. I had to get a shirt out of the laundry bin this morning. It was hard to choose which one smelled the best. Best is the wrong word to use. They all smelled bad but the one I put on didn't make my eyes water. I sprayed it and me with the last of my deodorant and nobody recoiled although a dinner lady did say she thought she could smell toilet freshener.

I looked around the room. If she was here to see the state of it Mum would have had a blue hairy fit. That's what she used to call my giant paddies I used to have. I can't think what I had to get cross about back then. I picked up the empty beer cans and carried them to the recycling bin in the kitchen but that was overflowing. He'd not put the bins out. I moved some paper off the counter and dropped the armful of cans with a clatter.

The kitchen was probably in a worse state than the living room. I didn't want to clear it up but it was that or a row with Dad about it. Not great choices. I emptied the kitchen bin and the recycling crate into the already full wheelie bins outside. We'd missed bin day this week. I put a reminder on my phone to put them out next time even though it wasn't my job. With the cans gone things looked a little better. It wasn't much but it was a start.

I decided I'd have a snack and then I'd clean up a bit. The fridge was empty again. Dad came into the kitchen looking a lot like one of the undead. 'When are you going shopping?' I asked.

'Don't start,' he said, switching on the kettle. He smelled like my shirt before the deodorant assault.

'I'm not having a go. I'm just saying we need stuff. Do you want me to go?' I hoped he'd say no because it was a long walk and those carrier bags really dig into my fingers.

He scratched his head. 'Need to wait until Friday when I get paid.'

'You have to be joking. We literally have nothing to eat.'

He blinked a few times. 'What's in the freezer?'

I opened it. It was slightly more inhabited than the fridge. Two sausages that were completely encased in ice like they had been in there a while. A large box of fish fingers but there was only one left in there. And half a bag of mixed veg.

He yawned as he leaned over my shoulder. 'There you go and there's cereal in the cupboard.'

'But there's no milk.'

'Then get some,' he snapped.

I held my hand out for some cash. Dad pointed at the few coins on the counter. 'That's all there is. You must have some from your paper round.'

'I'm saving for a new Xbox. Remember?' I clenched my teeth together so I didn't rant.

He looked away. 'I'll pay you back.'

This wasn't how it was meant to be. He wouldn't pay me back. How could he?

'Can you get some more fish fingers as well?' he asked. 'That should see us all right until Friday.'

'Right.' It was hard to speak, my jaw was so tight.

He grabbed my arm as I went to leave the room. 'Look I know it's not ideal. We've had a few bills all come in at once. That's all. But at least you get a meal at school and thank heavens that's free.'

'Can we pay for those?' I nodded at the red bills on the counter. I wasn't great at maths but I knew they added up to more than Dad's weekly wage.

'We'll be okay after Friday, Tom. I promise.' He tried to smile and it came out more like a twitch.

'Don't promise me, Dad.' I pulled my arm free. I could cope with the mess, with the lack of money and shoddy financial management but not with broken promises.

I went to the corner shop because it was nearest. Seeing as I was paying I decided I'd face the extra cost that the little village stores charged versus the long walk to the supermarket. I remembered to take a carrier bag with me. I wasn't stretching to ten pence for one of their flimsy ones. It was such a rip-off. Some younger kids from my school were standing outside drinking bottles of Coke and sharing out a multi pack of chocolate bars.

The sight of the Coke made me think about Maggie. Pictures of her kitchen filled my mind. Did these kids have a roast dinner every Sunday? Probably. They had no idea how lucky they were. I could easily have swiped something from them but I never would. It didn't mean I didn't want to.

Inside I found the few things I needed while avoiding eye contact with Mr Gill because otherwise he'd try to have a conversation with me. A couple of ladies were at the till chatting.

'I can't believe they're closing the library,' said one wearing a headscarf.

'They never are,' replied the other who was sorting through the going-out-of-date section.

'My neighbour lives two up from Christine who runs it. She says they're knocking it down for flats.'

I snorted at the story. Our village was first class for dramatising events. Once when someone lit the Guy Fawkes bonfire early half the village turned out because the rumour was that the pub was on fire and the whole place would be ash by morning.

'That's shocking,' said the other. 'I'll have to go into town to get my books renewed.'

'Exactly. I mean, I don't use the library but I wouldn't want to see it close.'

I shook my head. People were only interested in themselves. No thought for the impact on others. Lots of people used our little library. But most importantly what about me? All because of our village library Farah had spoken to me. I had done a first-rate impression of a salad vegetable but at least we had spoken – I called that serious progress. The library was also my link to Maggie. I had to keep going because I was hoping she was going to ask me over for Sunday dinner again. And I liked being in the library – there was something familiar and safe about it. And maybe I felt closer to Mum there – I dunno.

Mr Gill was stacking up some empty boxes. One of those would be an excellent place to hide my romance books at home. 'Could I have one of those please?' I asked.

'Instead of a carrier bag?' he replied.

'Yeah. If that's okay?'

'Five pence,' he said. This guy was never going to have financial problems.

I added a small bottle of Coke and a large Mars bar to the other shopping. Why shouldn't I? My Xbox flashed into my mind. I'd sold off my games and accessories already because I figured they were useless without the actual console and as it was going to take ages to save up there might be a new version out by then. Even if I went for a second-hand one it was going to take a while to save up for it. Probably years. Maybe never. I knew what I needed to do.

I left Dad a note with the sixty-eight pounds I'd got for selling all my Xbox gear and games minus today's shop and enough for a new rucksack. I knew he'd found the money when I heard him sobbing at the kitchen table but I didn't go down. Neither of us would have been comfortable with that.

Maggie was waiting for me on Saturday morning. 'Good you're here, Tom. We're having a meeting after book club – the more the merrier. Can you call up some friends, like that nice girl who was here last week?'

'What? No. I don't have her number.' I liked Maggie's optimism that I might have had Farah's phone number. I'd love to have her phone number.

She waved a hand in front of my eyes. 'We need as many people as possible.'

'Why? What's the meeting about?'

She looked at me like I'd turned into a fish finger, which would not have surprised me given how many of the things I'd eaten recently. 'The council trying to close the library of course.'

Christine scurried over. 'I went to a meeting. We're on

the list of the next round of closures. We have twelve weeks before they shut us down. That's not long to gather support. It's all down to us. We have to come up with something or that's it.' She ran a finger across her throat. I tried not to smile. I was pretty sure they didn't cull the librarians when they closed down the facilities.

'We need to act and act fast!' said Maggie, doing something of an old person version of a fist pump.

'Yeah but this afternoon. It's a bit short notice,' I said.

Maggie and Christine looked at each other. I felt like I'd said something useful. 'Maybe next week would be better,' said Christine.

Maggie seemed to consider this. 'It would give us a chance to rally people.'

'I could make some posters,' said Christine, visibly brightening up.

'That's good,' said Maggie. 'We could lobby the Women's Institute and the church.' She looked quite excited.

'I belong to Slimming World. I could lobby them,' added Christine.

'Excellent. You can put a poster up at school, Tom,' said Maggie.

'I guess.' I was *definitely* not doing that. I'd be labelled one of the Nerd Herd before the last drawing pin was in.

'You do realise how important the library is, don't you?' said Maggie giving me a stare to rival Medusa.

'Sure. I just don't know if the council will listen. That's all.' I scratched my head. Both women were looking displeased.

The door opened and in came Farah. I wasn't sure if that made things better or worse. I straightened my T-shirt and wished I'd worn my better one.

'You'll miss the library if it closes, won't you?' Christine asked Farah and I tried to hide under my fringe.

'It isn't going to close, is it?' she asked and on the last word she turned to look at me for a response.

'It's looking that way but we're going to complain...' I said. Farah was nodding. This was good. 'Well, protest, actually.' I was buoyed by her nods of encouragement. 'Fight.' My hands clenched into fists. 'We're going to fight them every step of the way!' Now Farah looked slightly alarmed. I unclenched my fists. 'You know. As much as we can.' I studied my trainers and concentrated on the warm sensation that had reached my ears.

'Exactly!' said Maggie. 'And we need all the help we can get. Are you in?' she asked Farah.

'Definitely,' Farah replied and a happy feeling rippled through me.

Maggie and Christine started making a list and I tried to look anywhere instead of directly at Farah. I didn't want to weird her out. She waved a book under my nose and got my attention.

'Sorry, I was thinking about ideas to save the library.' Strictly speaking I was imagining making a protest banner with Farah but that would have sounded creepy.

'I just wanted to say thank you for recommending this book.' She held up the Georgette Heyer.

'Did you like it?'

'I loved it. I'm going to take out some more of hers. What else do you recommend?'

My life had peaked.

14

MAGGIE

When Farah left the library Tom pulled out a chair and joined Maggie and Christine at the table. They had been in deep conversation for the last thirty minutes.

'Do we have a plan?' he asked, looking slightly hyper, his fingers thrumming on the table.

'Yes,' said Maggie, straightening her back and tapping the list in front of her.

Christine was chewing her lip. 'I'm not entirely sure all of that is legal.'

'We have to take a stand, Christine. Show them we mean business. That we won't be crushed by the establishment,' said Maggie, thumping a fist on the table and making Christine jump.

'Great,' said Tom. 'What's on the list?'

Maggie cleared her throat. 'Barricade ourselves in the library...'

'I was thinking more of a read-in.' Christine dabbed at

her lip with a tissue where she'd made it bleed – most likely from angst-ridden chewing.

'It's a peaceful protest but it would get the papers interested more than a readathon would,' said Maggie.

'What about placards?' asked Tom.

'Yes, we need those,' said Maggie, pleased with his suggestion. 'I think a protest march from here to the council offices would draw some attention.'

'Or some posters might be nice,' said Christine.

'We need to get as many people to sign a petition as possible and we need to lobby our MP.' Maggie was sounding more forceful.

'I can set up an online petition. If we share that on social media you'll get loads of randos sign up,' said Tom.

'Randos?' asked Christine.

'Random people,' explained Tom.

'Brilliant,' said Maggie. 'But most importantly we need support from the village and surrounding area. I say we invite people to a meeting here to get everyone fired up.'

'I'm in,' said Tom.

Maggie and Tom looked at Christine. 'Well, obviously you can count me in but I don't want to get arrested.'

'Why not? It would make for good newspaper headlines,' said Maggie. Christine looked startled.

'Anyway, I'll be here and I'll support any drive to get more people in the library but I can't be seen to be involved in any protests or the council will sack me. On the spot. They said that at the meeting.' Christine visibly shuddered.

Maggie and Tom continued to bounce ideas around while Christine tidied up. When Christine jangled the keys they knew it was time to leave.

'Do you want to carry on this chat at mine, tomorrow?' asked Maggie. 'I'll do dinner.'

'Yeah. Great,' said Tom, holding the door open for her.

Maggie had expected Tom to arrive close to dinnertime but he arrived on the first bus.

'You're keen,' she said, letting him in.

'Am I too early?' He paused with his jacket zip half unfastened.

She regretted her comment – she didn't want him to feel unwelcome. 'No. You would have been welcome for breakfast.' His eyes lit up at this. 'I don't like stealing your time that's all,' she explained.

'Honestly, Maggie. After my paper round I have nothing else to do on a Sunday.' He hung up his coat.

'Aren't you meant to be revising?' She led the way through to the kitchen.

'Yeah. And I am.' He didn't look too sure about it. 'It's just that the library is more important.'

She turned to face him square on. 'No, it's not, Tom. Your future should be your top priority. It's nobody else's.'

He seemed to pause for a second to take her words in. 'I guess.'

Maggie passed him a new bottle of Coke and a glass. 'I've a few things you could give me a hand with before dinner if you don't mind.'

'Sure.' He looked keen but that might have been the Coke. She'd never been one for fizzy drinks but Tom seemed to like it.

'Dinner is on but there's a cake in there that needs to come out in ten minutes.'

'What sort?' Tom was leaning towards the oven trying to get a glimpse.

'Lemon drizzle,' she said and Tom licked his lips.

Outside spring was preparing for summer. The trees and hedges spanned all shades of the green colour chart. Inside the barn Maggie pulled a large plank from a small pile of oddly shaped wood. She passed it to Tom, picked up a battered-looking toolbox and walked past the quad bike and back outside. She could see Tom's disappointment at not taking the quad bike out.

They walked down to where the chickens were busily scratching and pecking at the ground. The sun darted in and out of the clouds as if to tease them. Once they entered the pen the hens gathered around but soon lost interest when there were no treats forthcoming. One had a tentative peck at Tom's laces before scurrying away.

'The bottom of that henhouse has a hole in it. Now I don't mind the mice getting in as the chickens usually take care of them.' Tom was pulling a face. 'They're almost as good as a cat for killing mice but rats are an issue. They eat the eggs, and sometimes go for the birds so it needs boarding up.' She went inside the henhouse and plonked down the toolbox.

They worked together. Maggie marked the size of the piece of wood needed and Tom sawed it under instruction. Maggie held the wood in place and Tom picked up the hammer and a nail. His brow was furrowed as he held the nail in place, brought down the hammer and missed, whacking his thumb in the process.

'Ow, sh… sugar,' he said with a yelp and Maggie hid her amusement.

'You'd do better if you held the hammer nearer the head. You'll have more control,' she advised.

Tom adjusted his grip, narrowed his eyes in concentration and recommenced tapping at the nail head.

'You can hit it a bit harder. Imagine you're not stopping at the head but hammering to the wood.'

'Okay,' he said, but didn't look convinced. He brought down the hammer as instructed and in three hits it was secured. A few more nails and the repair was complete.

'You've done a fine job there,' said Maggie and Tom pulled back his shoulders, almost radiating pride. 'You've earned yourself some eggs. Basket's over there.'

As he stood up he caught the sleeve of his top on the latch and they both heard something rip.

'Let's have a look,' said Maggie.

'Don't worry. This top is knackered anyway.' Tom inspected the tear.

'I could fix that.' She ran an eye over the worn fabric. 'You'll need to take it off, mind. I've probably got a plain T-shirt you can pop on while I stitch it up.'

'No, really. It's not worth it. But thanks.' He gave her a wan smile.

'Right. As a kid were you any good at building things like Lego or Meccano?'

'I was all right,' said Tom.

'Excellent.' Maggie rubbed her hands together. 'Then I've got another job that's right up your alley.'

Maggie showed Tom how to put sheep hurdles together to make pens for when the lambs arrived. Tom was a quick learner and made light work of the cumbersome metal hurdles. Back at the house Maggie served up stew, dumplings and a mountain of vegetables. She caught sight of Tom's disappointed face. 'Sorry it's not a roast but I can't spare any more hens at the moment.'

'Okay,' said Tom, his frown tightening. 'Was the chicken... was it one of yours?'

'Of course it was. You don't go to the shop for a frozen one if you've got fresh at home.'

'I guess not.' He looked shocked.

'You did know that was where they came from?' Maggie seemed amused.

'Yeah. It just seems... brutal.'

'Life is.' She picked up her cutlery and began eating. Tom did the same. She tried not to watch him eat. It was still a novelty to have company and it warmed her soul to see him enjoying the food she'd prepared. She'd spent a whole evening mulling over what to serve. When they'd finished he sat back.

'Did you like that?' she asked.

'Yes. It was lovely. Thank you.' His words came out in a childlike rush, as if he'd been reprimanded for not using his manners.

'Do you know what it was?' A hint of a smile teased at Maggie's lips.

Tom scrunched up his shoulders. 'Dunno. Pork maybe?'

'Rabbit,' she said and she waited for his response.

He blinked a couple of times and completed his shrug. 'I liked it.'

'Have you got room for some cake?'

'Definitely.' He stacked his plate on Maggie's, took them to the sink and rushed back to sit at the table.

Maggie cut him a large slice of cake and a smaller piece for herself. Tom picked it up quickly and bit into it but then seemed to almost go into slow motion.

'Good?' asked Maggie, watching him closely.

'That's amazing.' He ate slowly savouring every bite, very different to how he'd eaten his main meal. When he'd finished he meticulously picked up every crumb from the plate. 'That was exactly like my mum's cake,' he said, melancholy tingeing his words.

'Then she was a fine cook,' said Maggie, with a wink.

As if already in a routine, Maggie washed up and Tom made her a cup of tea and poured another Coke for himself. This time they took their drinks through to the small sitting room. A large fireplace took centre stage and Maggie lit the prepared firewood and kindling nest she'd made in the wood burner before he arrived.

Tom set the drinks down on floral coasters, pausing to study a couple of photographs on the low coffee table.

'Is that your husband?'

'It is.' She stopped herself from gushing about him. The man who had brought her back from the brink. The person she had expected to spend her twilight years with.

'That you?' he asked, taking in the second photograph of a young woman in patchwork flares cradling a baby.

Maggie glanced over her shoulder. 'Yep.'

'Who's the baby?'

Maggie hesitated. 'My son.'

'Were you a hippie?'

She could feel the smile in his voice without looking. 'I always preferred the term flower child.'

Tom snorted a laugh and sat down on the sofa. 'Aren't hippies all vegetarians?' he asked.

'Aren't teenagers all lazy delinquents?' said Maggie with a knowing look.

Tom laughed. 'Good point. Sorry.'

'People make wrong assumptions. We're not all drug users either.' Maggie stood up and felt the pain of arthritis blossom in her knee. A bit of weed would have helped to ease that.

'I bet you did demos and stuff.' He was leaning forward.

Maggie tried to look nonchalant. 'I might have led a few peaceful protests…'

'Cool,' said Tom, his head bobbing to an unheard rhythm of respect.

'Bared my breasts at Greenham Common.' Tom broke eye contact.

Maggie was sitting in her usual chair. Her book was on one chair arm and a blanket over the other for when she couldn't be bothered to light a fire. It wasn't particularly cold but she preferred to heat individual rooms she used rather than put the central heating on and heat a whole house. There was something about the fire that made the room more homely. Perhaps it was the soft glow it added to the walls or the gentle crackle of the wood; she wasn't sure but having a fire on often made her feel like she had company.

Maggie leaned down to the side of her chair and picked up a notepad and pen and placed them on the table between her and Tom. 'Here's the list I started for saving the library but we need to build on it.'

Making the list had brought home to Maggie how much the library meant to her. She could remember going there as a child, all bundled up in winter clothes and having to blow on her fingers to warm them before she could turn the pages. It had been a regular weekly outing – as sacrosanct as going to church. She had spent many hours doing homework within its walls and stolen the odd kiss in the map section as a teenager. There were fewer nooks and crannies for that now they favoured the more open-plan design.

She remembered missing the familiarity of the Compton Mallow library when she'd left home, finding solace in other libraries to feed her reading habit, which had never waned. It had been like coming home when she had moved back to the area and stepped inside. The people had changed but the building had been reassuringly familiar. In recent years it had been her escape from loneliness. Her weekly opportunity to connect with others. Her lifeline. The thought of it closing was almost inconceivable.

Tom picked up the pen and began writing on the front of the notepad. 'That's my mobile number. I'm not great at keeping it charged but if you ever get stuck again – like with the tyre – call me and I'll get the bus over.'

Maggie had to swallow her feelings down hard. The kind gesture had taken her by surprise. The fact that someone genuinely cared had caught her off guard. Of course she had a local farmer, Fraser Savage, who was only three fields away if she ever got desperate but it was heart-warming to think she now had someone else if she really needed them.

'Thank you,' said Maggie. Tom did his usual nonchalant shrug. She wouldn't embarrass him. She rubbed her hands together. 'Right. Let's hatch a plan of attack.'

15

TOM

I was starting to like Sundays. Usually they sucked. We never did anything. It was a nothing day. One of my mates always went out for a meal on a Sunday, usually had a carvery with his folks, lucky bastard, and then visited his gran for tea. I thought that sounded good but he always moaned about it because I was playing on the Xbox most of the day and he thought that was way better. Now my mates play it without me. I told them my Xbox was glitching. I could hardly tell them my drunk of an old man had chucked it down the stairs. I say *mates* but all we had in common was gaming and now it's gone so have they.

Mum used to hoover and clean on Sundays in between making a roast dinner. But Dad and I don't bother with either. He did used to clean but I can't remember the last time I heard the hoover going. Mum used to send me outside to play football. Sometimes me and Dad would go to the park to get out of her hair. I used to like those times with me and Dad. He was happy back then.

I'd had a good time at Maggie's. I guessed it was a bit like visiting grandparents. I can't really remember mine. Dad's mum is in a home somewhere. We used to visit when Mum was alive but not anymore. I get a birthday card and twenty pounds from Nan and Granddad, my mum's parents, but otherwise we don't keep in touch. Dad doesn't like to talk about them. I think there's some beef there.

I hoped I'd been of use to Maggie so she'd invite me again. It was good having things to do and her cooking was ace. And I liked the idea of me being useful – it was a new concept. Most of the time I feel like a waste of space – like I'm something else draining Dad of money. Maggie'd even sent me off with most of the lemon drizzle cake, four fresh eggs and half a bag of cucumbers. I'd refused the cauliflowers because I had no idea what to do with those and I knew Dad wouldn't know either.

The bus ride home was torture. I kept getting delicious wafts of the cake. She'd wrapped it up in greaseproof paper and tied it with string, like in the olden days, but the smell was escaping and tormenting me. I'd promised myself another slice when I got in. At least Dad and I could have scrambled eggs on toast and some cake for tea. I wondered briefly what he would have eaten for dinner. A picture of the meal Maggie had made popped into my head. Rabbit. I'd eaten a rabbit and I'd liked it. Who knew?

A few metres before the bus pulled into the bus stop I saw Joshua Kemp and one of his minions hanging around near the garage. It snapped me back to the present. What was he doing hanging around Compton Mallow again? There wasn't much here and even less on a Sunday afternoon. Maybe he was still stalking Farah. I hoped Kemp didn't work out Farah's connection to the library. The last thing I needed was him showing up there. I got off the bus and hurried home.

The curtains hadn't been opened – that was never a good sign. I stepped inside and for the first time I noticed the smell. It wasn't like majorly disgusting but it did make me sniff. It was somewhere between my PE bag and the kitchen bin when it needs emptying. It wasn't nice. Maggie's house had a completely different smell. And it wasn't just the scent of cooking that seeped from her kitchen. There was an earthiness about the hallway, like nature shared the space. But that could have been the draughty front door. Maybe if I opened all the windows it would make our place stink a bit less?

I looked into the living room. Dad was crashed out on the sofa and the TV was on. The smell was worse in there. I switched the TV off, drew the curtains and after a bit of a struggle with the latch, pushed the windows wide open. There was an empty whisky bottle on the floor but no sign of any plate. That was his dinner then.

I picked up the bottle and he stirred, shielding his eyes from the light coming in through the window. 'Bloody hell, Tom,' he croaked. 'Switch the light off!'

I laughed. 'It's the sun, Dad. No off switch.'

'Where've you been?'

'At my friend's.' I scratched my head and wondered how I'd explain the bag of food I'd come home with. I wasn't ready to share my friendship with Maggie. He wouldn't understand.

'I called you.' He took three attempts to sit upright, still shielding his screwed-up eyes with his arm.

I checked my phone. 'Nope. No missed calls today. You rang yesterday when I was leaving the library.'

'Yeah. Right. You okay? You're okay aren't you?'

'Yeah.' I was a bit suspicious of the questioning. Dad wasn't the gushy sort. I knew he cared but he wasn't big on showing it. 'I'm fine.'

'That's good.' He held his head in his hands.

'Are *you* okay?' He didn't look well. His skin was an odd colour and he'd not shaved. I also figured some of the smell was coming from him.

'Err. Yeah.' He lifted his head to look at me and blinked a few times.

'Good. Did you want some tea? Mag… My friend's mum gave me some eggs and cucumbers.'

Dad snorted a laugh. 'Bloody hell, what can you make from that?'

'We've got bread, so I was thinking either scrambled eggs on toast or cucumber sandwiches.'

'Proper little Gordon Ramsay.' He rubbed his stomach and belched. 'I think I'll pass.' He glanced up. 'But thanks for offering.'

I opened the bag to remind myself of what else was in there and got a waft of lemon drizzle cake. 'And there's this awesome cake she made. You have to try it. It's like—'

'Maybe later.' He lay back down on the sofa and closed his eyes.

I finished reading *The Rosie Project* and placed it in the box, which I was keeping in the bottom of my wardrobe. It had been different to anything else I'd read. It was funny and my takeaway from the story was that there was someone for everyone out there, even the really quirky people – you just had to work out the best way to track each other down.

It was getting late and the house was silent. I went downstairs. It did smell a bit better. Dad was asleep on the sofa. There was yet another whisky bottle on the table. I gave it another look. This one was half full. I'd already put an empty one in the recycling. I needed to remember to put the bin out on Tuesday. We couldn't go another week.

The room had grown cold. I shut the windows and drew the curtains. I stared at Dad. He was curled up on his side with his head on a cushion and his lips vibrating as he breathed. He looked quite peaceful. It seemed odd to wake him up to go to bed but I figured that I should. 'Dad.' There was no response. 'Dad, I'm going to bed.' I jostled his arm and he jerked awake.

His eyes stared through me in alarm, as if for a moment he didn't recognise me. 'Was wrong?' His voice wasn't his own, distorted by the alcohol, something that was happening so often I barely noticed.

'I'm going to bed. Night.' I turned to go.

'Where's my tea?'

'You didn't want any.'

'You do nuffin for me.' I hated that he got like this when he'd been drinking. It wasn't him. He wasn't this bad when he was sober. He wasn't even that bad on beer but there was something about whisky that brought out the worst in him.

I wasn't going to argue; it was pointless. 'Right. Night then.' He turned his body in an exaggerated movement almost swinging himself off the sofa. It was a good job he didn't work Mondays – he was going to have an epic hangover tomorrow.

'Don't you walk away from me!' His voice rose quickly. I paused in the doorway and watched him stagger to his feet like an old man. Maggie could move way quicker than him.

'I'm going to bed and you should too.' I kept my tone level so I didn't annoy him further. 'Night.'

'No!' He swung an arm as if trying to punch my words out of the room. Instead his fist made contact with Mum's photograph and I watched it fall like it was in slow motion. It spun briefly, landed corner down and the glass shattered. Splinters flew across the floor.

'Dad!' Something inside me snapped. I shouted at him but there were no actual words. It was a primal cry, like an injured animal, and I wondered that I could make such a noise. I dropped to my knees and carefully picked up the frame. The photograph inside was scratched. A scar across Mum's face. 'What's wrong with you?' I yelled but my voice was full of tears.

He reversed away and landed so hard on the sofa it jumped backwards into the wall. 'You blame me. Don't you?' I knew what he meant and he wasn't talking about the picture frame.

'It *is* all your fault!' I tried to control the sobs but they weren't mine to own.

'I'm sorry, Tom.' His hooded eyes watched me. I took the photograph from the frame and stood up.

I rubbed my eyes with my torn sleeve. 'I'm going to bed.'

I didn't sleep much. I swung between being furious enough

to batter something and crying like some little kid. I cried when Mum died. Not at first. I guess I was in shock. Those first few days I watched a lot of TV. I thought that was good because Mum didn't let me watch too much TV. I remember Dad crying and wondering why and then it would pop back into my head and I'd remember that Mum had gone.

I was eight when it happened. It didn't seem real to start with and then it hit me. Like someone had kicked a football at my guts. That hollow feeling that eats you from the inside. A despair that only sorrow brings. It felt like that now. Not just because of the photograph but because Dad was leaving me too. Not the same way Mum had done; his was a slow painful way to go. The alcohol was chipping pieces of him away. Rubbing him out.

I placed Mum's photograph inside the front cover of my next book. It would be safe there until I got a new frame for it. Then I'd keep it in my room. I couldn't trust Dad anymore.

16

MAGGIE

Maggie leaned back into the garden bench and hugged her mug of tea. She loved this time of the morning when the world was drifting awake. It was chilly but spring was very much in full swing. The fresh canvas of sky like an ever-changing picture and the sound of the birds hiding in the trees. If she closed her eyes she could pick out the different birdsongs. The blackbirds were always dominant first thing with the thrushes adding in their tune soon after. When the wrens joined in she knew it was time to get moving. Getting mobile seemed to take her longer these days. Once she got going she was fine; it was merely first thing when everything seemed to have seized up overnight.

She had a fine view from the bench. Looking out across the patchwork of fields that gently tumbled away from the house she lacked a great incentive to stir; however, today she had a long list of things she wanted to achieve and first up was getting the trailer tyre repaired.

The quad bike wasn't insured for the road but the tractor

was. She hadn't had the tractor serviced for a good few years but after a bit of TLC and a few plumes of black smoke out the back end it started. She filled it up with the red diesel she'd bought from Savage. She had quite a journey planned. The little grey Fergie was ancient and she wondered if it would see her through another year without any repairs. She sent up a silent prayer to whichever god was responsible for farm machinery and reversed it out of the barn. It had virtually no suspension and it was like sitting in a bucket, only less comfortable, but there was something exhilarating about taking it out on the road.

It did a steady pace for a vehicle of its age, having been made shortly after the war. Around Furrow's Cross tractors were a common sight so any approaching cars waited patiently until there was plenty of space to overtake. As she neared the town that was a different story, but she didn't care about being hooted at because she was having fun. The air was warm and the wind in her face made her feel like a film star in an open-top sports car, simply travelling at a far safer speed.

Even with a stop en route to drop off her trailer tyre for mending, it still took less than an hour for Maggie to bump her way to Leamington Spa, half the time it would have taken on the bus. It was only when she arrived that she considered that parking the tractor may be an issue. She turned a few heads as she chugged down the Parade. Her rusty old tractor was a stark contrast to the majestic white facades of the Regency spa town. She turned in to a side street and was pleased to find a nice wide parking bay. She popped a pound in the meter, shoved the ticket it spewed out into her pocket, pulled her bag from under the seat and set off on her mission.

When she returned some time later a traffic warden was looking the vehicle over and scratching his head. Thankfully the lack of windscreen seemed to be foxing him as to how he could issue a ticket. Maggie strode up to the tractor, slung her bags under the seat and got on board.

'Er, excuse me, madam,' said the traffic warden. 'Is this your vehicle?'

'No. I'm stealing it.' She turned the ignition and was beyond grateful that it spluttered into life on her first attempt. She dropped the ticket she'd got from the machine at his feet and waved as she pulled away, safe in the knowledge that the little tractor's number plate was obscured with mud so the chances of him tracking her down were minimal. Anyway what offence had she committed? None as far as she could work out.

While the trip home was quicker than the bus it was far less comfortable and the rain that started a couple of miles from Furrow's Cross was an unwelcome accompaniment. She was glad to finally turn into her drive and trundle over the potholes. Even if it was a little like negotiating the surface of the moon, it meant she was home. Her bum was numb, she was soggy and her back felt like she'd been kicked all the way to Leamington Spa and back by an angry mule. Still, it had been a worthwhile trip. She parked the tractor in the barn and then climbed down, relishing the feeling of straightening out her spine. She took her bags inside and made herself a well-earned cup of tea.

She must have dozed off in the armchair after her lunch because something pulled her from her dream about Elvis Presley changing a washer on her outside tap. She sat for a moment and listened. The noise was faint but it was there –

a distant rhythmic banging. At first she thought of Colin but he wasn't that musically equipped. Maggie eased herself to her feet and did some stretching exercises to loosen up her limbs.

She put her cup and saucer in the sink and made her way outside, taking her air rifle from the utility on the way – it was a handy deterrent if there was anyone lurking about. The banging was more obvious here. She squinted down to the animals but it was too far and the land sloped away, making it difficult to see. Maggie was quite tired now. She'd had a busy day. She clambered onto the quad bike and set off down to the animal pens.

The ewes all paused to watch her approach and Barbara trotted to the gate when she stopped. They all seemed fine. The banging started again and Maggie looked straight at where the sound was coming from. The gate to Colin's field was swinging in the breeze and there was no sign of Colin.

Maggie left a message for Savage but she knew he was in the thick of the lambing season and would be up to his ears in ewes so it was more of an awareness message that Colin was on the loose. She puzzled long and hard over whether or not to make the next phone call. It wasn't exactly an emergency but even if she did track Colin down it was most definitely not a one-man job to get him securely returned to his field.

She dialled the number and waited, half expecting it to go to an answerphone like Savage's had done.

''Allo?' came a wary voice.

'Tom? It's Maggie.'

'Hiya, Maggie.' His voice changed in an instant to something bright. 'Are you okay?' And then switched again to a tone with an air of concern.

'Yes. I'm fine but bloody Colin's escaped. I know you're busy but—'

'No. I'm not busy. I'm just doing my homework—'

It was her turn to butt in. 'Then you are busy. I'm sorry to have interrupted you. Don't you worry. The daft beggar will come home when he's hungry.'

'I've nearly finished. I'm still at school using the computer. I can get a bus from here to Furrow's Cross…' He paused and she waited. 'In like ten minutes. I'll see you in a bit. All right?'

'I'm a bit worried about your homework.'

'I promise I'll finish it on the bus. Okay?' She could sense the smile in his voice.

'That would make me feel better. See you soon, Tom. Bye.'

'Bye, Maggie.'

Tom's timing was perfect. She was taking a hastily whipped up Victoria sponge out of the oven when he knocked at the door. 'Come in, it's open!' she called while transferring the sponges to cooling racks.

'Mmm, something smells good,' said Tom, coming into the kitchen, his nostrils flaring and his eyes wide.

'It needs to cool and we need to track down Colin.' Maggie swapped her oven mitts for some heavy-duty gardening gloves. She passed another pair to Tom. 'You might need these. Come on.'

The quad bike was right outside. Maggie got on, being careful not to dislodge the air rifle.

'What's the shotgun for?' asked Tom, his eyebrows registering alarm.

Maggie hooted a laugh. 'It's an air rifle. I use it for rabbits and in case I need to scare off a fox or something. I grabbed it because it might come in handy for shooing Colin back towards home.'

Tom looked even more confused. 'Should you have a gun?' His words were carefully placed.

'I don't need a licence for it if that's what you're asking.' Tom pursed his lips but he didn't respond. 'Are you coming?' she asked and he quickly got on board. Maggie set off along the route they'd taken before.

'Keep your eyes peeled, he might be foraging in the woods.' She'd already done one sweep of the farm with no luck but there was every possibility she'd missed him. His brown and white colouring was actually quite good camouflage.

Maggie switched off the engine near the main wooded region and stood up on the bike for a better view. She swivelled around to scan the area. They only had a couple of hours before the light would start to fade.

'Has he done this before?' asked Tom, himself twisting around.

'No. It's my fault. I should have renewed the binder twine on the gate.' You were always wise after the event.

'Don't worry. We'll find him,' said Tom.

Maggie sat back down, restarted the engine and carried on the circuit. But there was no sign of Colin. It appeared he had literally made for pastures new. Maggie drove back to the driveway and turned right where the track got narrower and more grassy. They bumped along, drawing the attention of the sheep on either side. They were dotted liberally across the green fields, like a cotton wool picture a child might make.

Maggie slowed the bike as they neared someone walking across the field towards the track. The man couldn't have looked more like a farmer if he'd tried. Flat cap, dark green coat and wellies. Something was swinging in his hand.

'Fraser,' said Maggie in greeting as she cut the engine. 'Tom, this is Mr Savage. He runs the farm that backs onto my land. Tom here is helping me out.'

Savage made a gruff noise.

'I left a message. Colin's gone walkabout. I'm going to sweep up to your place and round. Have you seen him?'

'No. I've been out here most of the day. I'll keep an eye out for him.'

'Thank you,' said Maggie, becoming aware that Tom was staring at what Savage was carrying. 'Ah, poor little soul didn't make it.' She nodded at the dead lamb carried loosely in his large hand.

'Lost four today. They're birthing too quick. And I'll be damned if the fox is having them,' said Savage.

'I hope you have a better day tomorrow.' Maggie restarted the bike.

'Aye.' He gave a brisk nod. 'I might need a hand with feeding the cades. If I get any more multiples I'll be overrun.'

'Of course. Just bring them down.'

He nodded again and strode off. Tom was still watching Savage intently. 'You okay?' Maggie asked him.

'Yeah, fine,' he said, but he'd gone a little pale.

They set off again. Savage's farmhouse was a grander affair than Maggie's, set over three storeys with multiple barns and outbuildings. Maggie drove all around the yard area at the back as if she owned it too. A couple of dogs ran up to the bike barking. Maggie stopped and Tom hitched up his feet out of biting range.

'It's okay.' She pointed at the black and white collie. 'This is Mac and this is Rusty.' The second dog was a similar size but a completely different colour.

'He's a nice colour,' said Tom, tentatively pointing at Rusty. The dog came forward to sniff him and Tom snatched back his hand.

'Red merle and it's a bitch.'

Tom flinched at the word and Maggie chuckled to herself. 'As in female dog. She won't hurt you. She's very gentle and very pregnant.' Tom tentatively let Rusty sniff his fingers until Maggie fired up the quad bike again and the dogs retreated.

They seemed to follow a tree line from Savage's farm for ages until they popped out near a pub garden. 'Wait there,' said Maggie, getting off. 'I'd best warn them about Colin.'

When she returned Tom was off the bike and standing on the pub's low wall. 'Is everything all right?' she asked.

'I've seen him,' said Tom, pointing up the lane. 'He crossed the road, right up there. He was just a dot but I swear it's him.'

'Brilliant!' They both jumped back on the bike like a pair of budget superheroes and set off across the grass verge.

'Slow down,' called Tom. 'It was around here I think.'

Maggie did as he asked. 'Which way was he going?'

'That way,' said Tom, pointing to the right. They were nearing the bus stop. 'There!' He shouted.

Maggie saw him too. Colin was munching away at the bottom of a hedgerow. She checked the road was clear and drove across to the other side. She revved the engine and Colin looked up. He was momentarily startled and he dashed off following the line of the hedgerow with Maggie and Tom in hot pursuit. As they neared the end of Maggie's drive she turned the bike quickly making it skid on the gravel and block Colin's exit to the road. Instinctively Colin dashed up the driveway.

'Yes!' said Tom with a fist pump.

'Don't you go celebrating too soon,' advised Maggie and she set off at a snail's pace behind the ram. Colin wasn't going to be rushed and he took a full fifteen minutes to walk to the farmhouse. The ram got distracted by some dandelions on the front grass and Maggie stopped the bike and jumped off.

'You take over,' she called to Tom.

'What? Okay but I don't know how to drive it,' he said but he was already sliding into the vacated seat.

'Turn the key, press the start button.' She pointed to them in turn and gave him a quick run-down of the other controls. 'Got it?'

'Er, yeah. I think so.' Tom blinked a few times. He turned the key, pressed the button and seemed to swell with pride as the bike started.

'Keep roadside of Lord Lucan over here,' said Maggie, pointing at Colin.

'Who?'

'Never mind. Low revs,' she said walking towards the barn.

Tom kept the bike purring gently and edged it forward a fraction each time Colin moved onto a new patch of grass. Tom revved the engine a little and Colin turned to eyeball him. Maggie was coming back carrying a large piece of board. Colin started to reverse away from Tom.

'Watch out!' yelled Maggie. 'He's going to butt the bike.'

'Shiiiiiit!' said Tom, as Colin charged towards him.

Maggie banged on the wooden sheet but it didn't put Colin off his target. He hit the front of the bike hard making it shudder. Maggie continued to bang on the board and at last Colin took notice and hurried off towards the back of the farmhouse.

'Well go after him!' shouted Maggie.

Tom panicked and the bike kangarooed forward a few times before he finally had control and trundled off after the recalcitrant ram.

'Crikey, I can *walk* faster than that,' said Maggie following them.

She hadn't needed the board because Colin had decided he was going back to his field anyway. She watched him barge the gate open. Once he was inside Maggie tied up the gate with binder twine – properly this time. She leaned against the fence and let out a sigh. Tom cut the engine on the bike but showed no sign of getting off.

'Thanks, Tom. You did well,' she said. 'Dinner on Sunday to say thank you?'

'Yeah. Great.'

'Roast lamb,' she said.

'Um. Okay,' he said, his forehead puckering.

'What?' asked Maggie sensing something was amiss.

'I honestly daren't ask,' replied Tom, with a nod in Colin's direction.

17

TOM

Sitting in Maggie's kitchen I was kind of hoping she was going to invite me to dinner that night. All that was waiting for me at home was fish fingers. I'd had pizza at school, which I had most days, but it never filled me up. I was pleased when she offered me some cake though, and it was a large slice filled with thick buttercream and home-made raspberry jam. It was very nearly as good as the lemon drizzle.

'Bus goes at quarter past,' she said, nodding at the kitchen clock. I felt my body sag at the thought of going home and of the state Dad had been in yesterday. He'd been home all day and I had no idea what he'd been doing. He used to do the shopping, ironing and cleaning on a Monday but not anymore; he doesn't seem to do much of anything these days. At least I wouldn't see him for long tonight though because he had to be at work for half eight. I felt bad for thinking it but it was just easier when he was out. He had to keep it together for his job.

Maggie was giving me an odd look. 'Is everything all right?' she asked. I paused to have a think about what I should say. Part of me wanted to spill my guts but I'd look pathetic if I did that. I didn't really have much to complain about. It wasn't like he was beating me or about to chuck me out. 'I don't mean to pry,' she added.

'No, you're not. My dad and me…' I stopped. Why had I started like that? I stared at the plate and tried to think of how to say it.

'Ah, parents and children. It's all extremely tricky. Especially around the teenage years.' She nodded wisely.

'Yeah. It is.'

'He knows you're here though?'

'Yeah. I messaged him.' I didn't like lying to Maggie but it didn't seem right to say, "He wouldn't care." That was a bit unfair. Dad did care but he had no clue about how I spent my time. He knew I had to stay at school to do my homework, because for most of it I need a PC, but otherwise he let me do what I liked. It was getting dark now, which might make Dad wonder where I'd got to. I'd text him from the bus.

'Maggie?'

'Yes.' She put down her cup and waited like I was going to say something important. Resting her forearms on the kitchen table and letting the long flowy sleeves of her top puddle on the surface. She had some well weird clothes.

'That lamb. The one the farmer had…'

'Ah. Pitiful little mite. Sometimes they get stuck and you can't save them. Other times they're already dead. Given how many his flock will produce this season the number he'll lose will be very low.'

'It's sad though. Isn't it?' I said. It had looked like a child's toy hanging at his side. All perfect and yet lifeless.

'That's nature I'm afraid, Tom. It's neither cruel nor kind just pitilessly indifferent.'

Maggie was well wise.

Dad didn't reply to my text from the bus but at least he was up and dressed when I got in. He was having an argument with someone on the phone. He waved hello to me but then shut himself in the kitchen. That meant it was most likely about money. Did he think I was blind or stupid? The red bills had been coming in for months now and I knew things weren't getting any better. If he stopped spending so much on alcohol we'd be better off although I'd never tell him that. But then he doesn't spend it on anything else for himself. My mate's dad goes to the football every week and his season ticket costs, like, a thousand pounds. At least Dad wasn't spending that sort of money.

I heard him raise his voice. He wasn't happy. And then it went quiet. He opened the door. 'There's fish fingers for tea and I've left you some beans in the saucepan,' he said.

'Thanks. Is everything okay?' I felt I should ask.

'Not really. No. I missed a mortgage payment. I've had that mortgage for well over ten years but the bank got all arsey about it.' His face looked more tired than I remembered. He looked older too somehow. It was like I hadn't had a good look at him for a few years.

'What happens now?'

He sniffed. 'Not much. I have to pay a bit extra each month to catch up the payments I've missed.'

He said payments plural. That couldn't be good. I know he said the only times he and Mum argued were about money so things have never been great on that score but now he's drinking more and more we have even less. 'How many payments have you missed?'

He took a while to answer. 'Three in the last year.' He could see I was alarmed because he held his hands up. 'Which is fine. As long as I don't miss any more.'

'Are we going to lose the house?' I didn't like the tight feeling in my chest. It was hard to breathe.

'No. No, of course not.' He shook his head but his expression didn't make me feel any better. 'I won't let that happen. I'll sort it.' He rubbed his palm across his chin. He'd cut himself shaving and there was a fresh scab.

I didn't know what to say. I wanted to ask what he was going to do, how he was going to make sure we didn't lose our home but I was afraid he wouldn't have an answer, so I didn't ask.

He seemed to jolt to life. He looked at the clock. 'I'd better go. Are you going out, Tom?'

'Nope.'

'Then lock up behind me… and take care.' He gave me a slap on the back, which ended with a squeeze of my shoulder. He meant well.

Wednesday was never a great day at school. I was useless at French and biology but at least I got to see Farah in English, although I had to make sure Kemp didn't see me. I sort of nodded at her and she smiled back at me. It was the highlight of my day – other than that it had been the usual dullness. After the lesson I was packing my bag and she was talking to a friend but looking at me. I put my head down but she came over anyway. Joy, embarrassment and fear wrestled inside me. Embarrassment won and the heat rose steadily from my collar.

She'd only come over to ask me about the library so I relaxed a fraction until I saw Kemp standing behind her running his finger across his throat. I gathered all my stuff in a rush and told Farah I couldn't talk. In my haste to escape I tripped over my desk and sent it flying. It narrowly missed hitting the teacher. He thought I was kicking off and gave me an instant detention. Utter disaster.

I went to the library and picked up a load of Save The Library flyers to deliver with my paper round at the weekend. When I finally got in Dad was whistling. Instead of feeling good about him sounding upbeat I was suspicious. It had been a long time since I'd heard him whistle. What had happened to make him sound so happy? Lottery win perhaps? He was stirring beans on the stove.

'All right?' I said dropping my bag on the floor.

He did a double take. 'Is that a new bag?'

'Mine broke. I used some of the Xbox game money.' I'd kept a bit back.

'Oh, yeah. I meant to say thanks.' He looked embarrassed. You could tell we shared the same gene pool. 'Grab a tray and I'll dish up.' I looked around. The kitchen wasn't exactly clean but the bin wasn't overflowing anymore.

There was clattering behind me and he swore when he burned himself on the oven tray. At last he put the fish fingers and beans on a plate and handed it to me. 'Thanks,' I said, hearing the suspicion in my own voice. What was going on?

We took our meals through to the lounge and ate in silence for a bit. Dad paused to drink some water. 'I've got some good news.'

'Awesome.' He did look happier. I was pleased something had cheered him up; we needed some good news. I hoped he'd won the lottery because I really missed my Xbox.

'Now don't get your hopes up because nothing's guaranteed…' He had my interest now and I put down my knife and fork. 'They're running an apprentice scheme at work and you might be able to get a place on it.' He was grinning. He looked thrilled. 'You'll have to get through an interview but they'll take you as soon as you've finished school at the end of June.'

I wondered what I looked like. I knew what I felt like. I'd gone kind of rigid. The dog food factory. An apprenticeship at the pissing dog food factory! Did the disgust at what he was suggesting show on my face? He looked so pleased with himself I almost felt sorry for him but right at that moment I could only feel sorry for me.

'At the factory?' I needed to clarify the full horror of the situation. He nodded. 'For how long?' My mouth was dry.

'Three years but if you work hard you stand a good chance of getting a permanent job. And it's only four days a week because you get a day at college. You wanted to go to college. This is the best of both worlds.'

My eyes felt so wide I thought they might pop out. 'University. I want to go to *university*.'

'Uni, college, same thing. And get this.' He leaned forward. 'You'll get paid nine grand a year! University would cost you that.' He flopped back against the sofa in an olds' equivalent of a mic drop.

I put my tray on the floor. I couldn't eat anymore. I was sick of fish fingers. I was fed up with everything. My sucky life had reached a whole new sucking level.

Dad's happy expression was melting away. 'I've gone to a lot of trouble to find all this out.' I looked up but I couldn't say anything that wouldn't cause him to rant. 'Well, say something.'

'Um. Thanks.' He beamed a self-satisfied smile and picked his cutlery back up. I was feeling brave. Like it was now or never. I drew in a breath and spoke. 'But it's not what I want. Being an apprentice at the factory – it's not what I want to do.'

He looked up midchew. 'You wouldn't be an apprentice forever – it's a rung on the ladder. It'll get you started. Get you earning.'

And there it was – the real reason for all this. Money. None of this was about what was best for me or what I wanted. It was all about him. All about the great pile of crap he'd got himself into. 'So I can pay the bills?'

His shoulders tensed and I waited for the backlash, but he relaxed and forked up some more beans. 'It's about time you paid your way. I was working full-time at sixteen. It didn't do me any harm.'

I glanced around the room, the smell of overcooked fish fingers hanging in the air. If this was the prize you got for working forty-hour weeks for years and years I didn't want it.

18

MAGGIE

Maggie was looking a little more conventional; her wild mane of hair was wrestled into a neat bun and she was wearing a long dark cardigan and jeans. Although the flared bottoms were a little out of sync with other ladies her age they showed off her red Doc Martens every time she strode about the library giving out instructions, which was every few seconds. The book club regulars had stayed on to help set up for the inaugural Save the Library meeting and Christine was like a caged bird being circled by a ravenous cat and seemed to jump at every order.

'Christine? Are you all right?' asked Maggie, her voice gentle.

Christine breathed in deeply. 'No. I'm not all right. We've got umpteen people arriving for a meeting. I've not told the council that we're holding it here and I don't think any of it will really do any good and…'

'Christine. Breathe,' instructed Maggie, taking her by the forearms and breathing slowly with her. 'Breathe in peace and tranquillity. Hold it. Breathe out negativity and stress.'

Tom continued to put the returns back in the right places on the shelves, giving only a cursory glance at the two women and their mutual breathing exercises. The door opened and he spun around. Seeing who it was he almost tripped over his feet in haste.

'Hiya,' said Farah. 'I brought my friend, Amy. Is that okay?'

'Yeah. Come in.' Amy and Tom exchanged taut expressions.

'Hiya,' repeated Farah in Maggie and Christine's direction.

'Christine's a bit stressed,' explained Tom in a whisper because Amy was looking slightly alarmed by the synchronised puffing that was going on.

After a few breaths Christine seemed to be calmer. She gave a series of hurried nods. 'I'm fine. It's just that everything hinges on this.'

'I know,' said Maggie. 'That's why we're here.' Christine gave her a weak smile. 'Right, Tom, are you sure you'll be all right doing refreshments?' asked Maggie.

'Yep. We've got it all covered,' he said tilting his head at the two girls already setting out paper cups.

Before long they had a throng of people. Christine's poster campaign and Tom's door-to-door flyer drop had clearly stirred up the locals. Within ten minutes it was standing room only and Tom, Farah and Amy had a smooth system going on the drinks. The noise in the room was quite something and multiple conversations all on the same subject competed for air space.

Maggie brought the meeting to order. 'I'd like to introduce Christine, who is our resident librarian.'

Christine got to her feet and as all eyes fixed on her she instantly challenged Tom in the *who can turn red the quickest* competition. 'Err. Oh. Well. Thanks, everyone, for coming. Um. Yes. Well. I'm Christine and I'm the librarian here,' she repeated. 'But I'm not actually allowed to be at the meeting.' She looked to Maggie, her eyes pleading.

'Shall I say a few words?' said Maggie.

Christine's bum hit her seat so fast she almost bounced back up again.

'Right,' said Maggie, clapping her hands together. 'The purpose of this meeting is to make sure everyone has the facts about the library's situation, share our plan of action and seek your input and support to save our library!' Her voice rose at the end and there was a ripple of applause. 'This is how it is. Compton Mallow library is earmarked for closure in ten weeks' time. This means if we do nothing we lose this fabulous community asset along with this delightful building and the ripples of what this means for our community will affect countless generations to come.'

Maggie explained that the council's reasoning for the plan to close the facility was based entirely on usage numbers, she highlighted all the library's current facilities and went through the plan she had agreed with Christine, one she had only had to make a couple of compromises on. 'What else can we do to utilise this amazing facility?'

Farah had moved from the tea-making station and was poised to make notes. Tom was rationing the biscuits as they were disappearing fast.

A middle-aged mum put her hand up to speak. 'I used to bring my eldest daughter here to reading time when she was a toddler but you don't have it anymore.'

'Great suggestion,' said Maggie. 'We'll add it to the list.'

'Hi, I'm Lorna Booth and I run the Cedars nursing home,' said a suited woman with a shock of neat grey hair. 'I'm interested—'

'I'm Alice,' said a wizened lady sitting next to her.

Lorna didn't look like she welcomed being interrupted. 'I brought Alice in for a haircut. Anyway, the council have offered to provide a mobile library for us, which would be far better because we can't bring our residents in here.'

There was a ripple of dissent. Lorna had not judged her audience very well. Maggie calmed the masses with a wave of her hand. 'Hi, Lorna and Alice, thanks for coming. The mobile library has not been confirmed so I would not put any store by that ever materialising. It's simply the council trying to fob you off. Now, I'm sure your more mobile residents would enjoy a trip to the library and I'm certain we can rally support to get them ferried in. We also have online ordering and if you let us know we can easily get the books brought out to you. Your residents are part of the community and we are keen that they receive the same service as everyone else.'

Farah frantically scribbled notes while Lorna's eyebrows appeared to be impressed with Maggie's response.

Alice put her hand up and Lorna glared at her but Alice carried on undeterred. 'I want to use the t'interweb,' said Alice.

'We would love to show you how, Alice. Maybe a special session for you and some fellow residents so we can go at a pace that's right for you,' said Maggie. 'And that's a lovely hairdo, by the way.' Alice beamed at her.

'I'm Bill,' said a rotund man. 'Landlord at the Limping

Fox. Pensioners Tuesdays two meals for ten pounds. Anyway.' He took a breath. 'I want to help, I really do, but if this place is on a list to be closed then it's a done deal. An old building like this has huge potential. Most worryingly it could reopen as a restaurant or worse still a bar, which would hit my business, so I genuinely want it to stay as a library, but the decision is made and no amount of reading is going to change it.' The room was deathly silent. 'Sorry. Oh...' His tone brightened. 'Don't forget curry night on Thursdays. You get free naan bread and a small drink of your choice. Excludes real ales and spirits.'

Eyes shifted from Bill back to Maggie who drew in a long slow breath. 'You could be right, Bill. And you are most likely voicing what some people here are thinking and what a lot of others who didn't bother to come tonight believe too. But if we do nothing then it definitely will close and once it closes it's gone forever, for this generation and all the others to come. But,' said Maggie raising a slightly bent index finger, 'if we stand up to the council and if we come together as a community to use and cherish this beautiful building and all that it represents, then we might stand a chance of saving it. And I for one want to be able to say that at least I tried.' There was a brief silence and then a wave of "hear, hears" and clapping. Farah even put down her pen to applaud. She was looking at Maggie like she was a film star.

After that there were lots of other positive suggestions. Tom's old primary school teacher was keen to bring a class in, the postmaster wanted to return the support he'd received when the post office had been under threat and the florist offered to give out flyers but what Bill had said hung heavy in the room. One lady said the city libraries hosted author events, which she often wanted to attend but couldn't due to transport issues.

'Yeah,' said Tom. Eyes shifted in his direction and his colour deepened. 'I like that idea. I'd love to meet authors.' His voice tailed off to a mumble. Farah gave him an indulgent smile and he retreated under his fringe. There was a muttering of agreement that this would be something lots of people would like.

'Excellent!' said Maggie. 'We will look into all of those things. Now in return we need you to support whatever we put on, we need you to use your library and we need your attendance at further meetings. Are you with us?'

There was a positive response of mumbles and a hearty round of applause. Tom looked at Maggie with renewed respect.

Once the stragglers had departed Christine, Maggie, Tom and Farah were having a debrief over a round of tea and the last few Hobnobs Tom had managed to hold in reserve.

'Four new people signed up for book club,' said Farah. 'And three people showed interest in reading time for toddlers.'

'We used to do that but people didn't come regularly,' said Christine.

'Looks to me like if you offer them a biscuit they turn out,' said Tom, taking the last Hobnob and screwing up the empty packet.

'We could do squash quite cheaply,' added Farah. 'And I'd like to read to the children.'

'You'd be great at that,' said Tom.

'Usually it's midweek daytime but maybe we could do

midweek four o'clock and mums could bring primary age children too,' suggested Christine.

'That would work for me,' said Farah, looking delighted at the prospect. 'I'm here on a Tuesday straight from school anyway. I could also do one on a Saturday.'

Tom cleared his throat. 'I could run the silver surfers internet class if you like,' he said, sounding unsure.

'Top job, Tom. I'm sure you'll charm all the oldies,' said Maggie.

They ticked off the last few points and a few sniffs from Christine made the others look her way. She buried her face in a tissue. 'I'm sorry,' she said. 'You've all been brilliant today. I don't know what I'd have done without you. Actually I think I'd have probably curled up in a corner and accepted my fate.'

'You're stronger than you think, Christine,' said Maggie, patting her arm.

Christine shook her head. 'I don't know what I'd do if I lost this job.' She blew her nose again. Tom busied himself with clearing away cups.

'You'd bounce back,' said Maggie and Christine looked alarmed that Maggie wasn't offering her a guarantee. 'But let's hope it doesn't come to that,' Maggie added. She wasn't one for offering false hope, only practical solutions.

19

TOM

There was no answer from Maggie's when I knocked. I peered through the living room window and was relieved that she wasn't sitting dead in the chair as that horror had suddenly charged into my mind. Although there was still the thought that she could be lying somewhere else in the house. I tried the door but it was locked. I had got the earlier bus so perhaps I was too early. Maybe she was having a Sunday lie-in after her rousing speech at the library yesterday?

I was looking forward to having a chat to her because I'd finished *Pride and Prejudice*, which she'd recommended, and I'd loved it. The whole time I was reading it I kept thinking about Farah. Partly because I kept picturing her as Elizabeth Bennet but mainly because I knew she'd love it too. I could also see myself as Darcy but nobody needed to know that.

I wandered around the side of the house and stuck my head in the barn on the way. The tractor was there but the quad bike wasn't. A sigh of relief escaped. She was most likely somewhere on the farm. I tried the back door, which was open and I swapped my tatty trainers for the wellies I'd borrowed before. I put my hands in my pockets and strode off towards the animals. The sun was barely starting to warm things up and I breathed in the fresh air. Here it was easy to understand why it was called fresh air. It was different – like it was purer, filtered somehow. There was a scent about it, sort of grassy with a hint of earth. I sounded like the bloke off the wine programme Dad used to like to watch.

'Tom!' The shout was distant.

I turned my head in the direction of Maggie's voice. She was down in the field with the ewes and she was waving. I waved back and pointed myself in her direction. As I got closer I could see she was still waving. For a moment I was chuffed by how pleased she was to see me. Then I realised it was more of a hurry-up wave.

'Come on!' she shouted and I started to run.

I halted at the fence and took in the scene. Maggie was next to one of the ewes, which was lying on its side. Maggie was kneeling on one of those green pad things that gardeners use and she appeared to have her hand stuck up the sheep's arse.

'What the...?' was all I could think to say.

Now I took a proper look at Maggie I could see she was wearing a dressing gown with what looked like checked pyjamas underneath. Maggie and the sheep puffed out a breath at the same time. 'The lamb's stuck. She's been in labour for almost three hours. If we don't shift it we'll lose them both. She's exhausted.'

Maggie looked more tired than the sheep. How did you tell if a sheep was exhausted? It looked the same as the others that were walking about. Apart from the other one on its side. 'Is that one okay?' I asked nodding at the far corner of the field.

Maggie twisted to look. 'Flaming Nora! She's in labour too. Can you go and check on her?'

'Err, yeah... What am I checking for exactly?' I climbed over the fence.

'Under her tail. How far into labour is she?' I must have looked blankly at her so she elaborated. 'Check her fanny!'

'No way.' I held up my hands like a spy about to be shot. I would have preferred to have been shot rather than look up a sheep's vag.

Maggie fixed me with a stern look. 'Barbara here is about to die. Nancy, over there, had trouble last year. I don't want to lose them both.'

'No, but...' I pointed at Nancy. The sheep responded on cue with frantic bleating.

'Please,' said Maggie, her eyes looking up at me big and round like Barbara's but lighter in colour.

Bloody hell, emotional blackmail was all around me. 'Right. If I look...' Maggie beamed a victorious smile at me. '*If* I look. What am I looking for again?' I didn't know why I was asking because I really didn't want to hear the instructions repeated but I was definitely only doing it once and I didn't want to get it wrong.

'Check the opening. See if you can get a hand in there.'

I retched at the thought of it and Maggie chuckled. 'Cheers,' I said but I could see the funny side too.

'Quickly. Because I need your strength to get this lamb out of Barbara.'

'Right.' I jogged down the field to Nancy. The sheep had her head up at an awkward angle and eyed me suspiciously as I neared her. I gave myself a firm talking-to. *Maggie has her hand up the other sheep. She's not asking you to do that. You only need to have a look under its tail and...* Eurgh, the thought of it made my stomach churn. Maybe it was best if I didn't think about it.

'Right, Nancy. Are you ready?' I asked. Nancy flicked a back leg, which I took as a positive response. I took a deep breath, and gripped her tail. It was wet and gross and there was something under it.

'Shiiiiiit!' I didn't need to lift her tail up because I could see a giant bubble coming out of her. It was revolting. I dropped the tail and fled back to Maggie.

'There's this gross bubble thing coming out of her.'

'Bloody hell, Nancy! Right. She's got a few minutes. Can you get hold of this and when I tell you to, you need to pull as hard as you can.' She handed me two bloodied pieces of binder twine. My hand didn't want to take it. Maggie offered it again. 'Oh, come on.' She was losing her patience.

I did as I was told. It was cold and wet and disgusting. I tried to focus on the lamb.

'See here,' said Maggie pointing at the ewe's nether regions. 'The lamb has got his leg stuck.'

'You know it's a boy?' I was amazed. I could only see a small patch of white.

'He's lazy and he's got a big head, so it's just a guess at this stage,' she said, cocking her head on one side.

'Funny.'

'On three. Slow and steady but with force. Got it?'

'Yeah.' I had no idea what I was doing. Nancy bleated from the other end of the field and I felt like she was calling me back. I needed to help Barbara and then get back to Nancy. I'd never been so much in demand.

'One, two, three. Pull. Keep it steady. Here he comes...' Maggie gave a running commentary. The twine was digging into my fingers like cheap carrier bags do when they're full of shopping. It was tough to keep the pressure on and it felt like nothing was happening. A bit like a tug of war against a brick wall. 'Don't let it go slack. Come on, Tom. Pull.' It was an odd angle to pull at as I was on my knees and it was like pulling a dead weight. A picture of the little lamb the farmer had been carrying last week shot into my mind and I started to fight for this one. I wanted to save him.

'That's it. Keep it coming.' All of a sudden Barbara's legs started kicking about and I lost my grip on the slippery twine.

'Ah.' I made a grab for it as Barbara stood up.

'It's okay. She's got it now,' said Maggie, giving my shoulder a pat. I watched as the lamb slid out and landed with a cushioned thump on the grass. Some gunk came out too but I kept my focus on the tiny perfect lamb. Perfect apart from the blood, which I was trying my hardest to pretend wasn't there. He was a beautiful colour – grey and white.

Maggie wiped the gunk off his face and stuck her fingers in his mouth. 'Clearing his airway,' she explained. She then appeared to be sticking straw up his nose. 'Come on,' she said. I could tell from her tone something was wrong. She picked him up by his back legs and whirled him around her head almost taking me out.

'Whoa! What's going on?' I ducked out of the way. I'm sure the RSPCA would have something to say about this.

'He's not breathing,' she said, returning him to the straw and rubbing his chest. Like a switch being flicked to on, he seemed to jolt into life and Maggie moved him under his mother's nose.

Barbara started to wash her baby and it bleated. It was the cutest sound I'd ever heard.

'Aww.' My response was spontaneous. Maggie shot me a proud look so I didn't bother to change it into a coughing sound. She knew I was hooked.

She lifted the lamb's leg. 'Boy. I knew it,' she said. 'Right,' she added, rocking herself back and forth.

'You all right,' I asked, offering her a hand to help her up, which she accepted.

'I've been here since five o'clock this morning. I came to check on them and she was acting odd so I encouraged her up this end nearer the pens and kept an eye on her.'

'Explains the trendy outfit,' I said.

'Cheeky,' she said stretching out her spine. She picked up the lamb by its front legs, dangling it under its mother's nose and reverse-shuffled into one of the pens we'd made the other week. Barbara followed.

Maggie stepped out and closed the pen up again. 'Come on. Animal husbandry lesson number two.' She made two tentative steps, wincing hard with each one, before striding off towards the other sheep.

Nancy turned out to be a straightforward affair. Maggie showed me that the lamb was coming out front legs first with its head up, which apparently was exactly what you wanted. Minutes after we joined her out popped a lamb. Perfect and healthy. It was something special to witness.

'Right,' said Maggie. 'We need that sheep and lamb in a pen up there.' I looked back up the field. It was a long way. 'You saw what I did with Barbara's?'

'Yeah. You put it in the pen.'

'Yes, but she needs to come with it. I kept it in front of her the whole time. She needs to smell it. Here you go.' She wiped off the worst of the gunk and handed me the warm damp lamb. It bleated a protest and I felt it vibrate through my fingers. 'Off you go!' Maggie shooed me up the field. After a couple of steps Nancy followed us. Then she seemed to stop and lift her head.

'Keep the lamb lower. Lower!'

My back was killing me walking backwards at this strange angle. I dangled the lamb in front of its mother and like a dog sniffing a sausage she was back on the scent of the lamb and trotted towards it. Eventually I backed into the pen and put the lamb down and Nancy went back to washing her baby while I sneaked out.

'I think you've earned some breakfast,' said Maggie, tightening her dressing gown cord. 'Although I expect you've had yours.'

I'd only had a slice of toast. 'I could manage another one.'

'Right. I'm going for a shower first. You'll need to wash up too.'

I looked at my hands. Yep they definitely needed washing. 'Actually, I think I'll stay here for a few minutes.' There was something special about the lambs and I wanted to enjoy it a bit longer.

'Okay,' said Maggie, a knowing look in her eye. 'I'll give

you a shout when I'm serving up. Listen out.' She picked up her gardener's pad, got on the quad bike and headed back to the house.

I moved to stand between the two pens so I could watch both lambs. The first one was already on his feet and feeding from his mother. His tail was shaking like mad. Barbara had returned to chugging down grass and seemed oblivious. I glanced back at Nancy. She was having a lie-down. I didn't blame her after what she'd been through. The other lamb was almost all grey. It was a different sort of grey. I could see now why Maggie called them lavender lambs. I watched it feed for a bit and then noticed Nancy was tensing up, something was going on. I moved around the pen. Oh crap. No! There was another lamb coming out.

'Maggie!' I yelled in the general direction of the house. There was no way she was going to hear me if she was in the shower.

I dashed inside the pen to join Nancy. With any luck she'd pop this one out like she had the first. I took a deep breath and lifted up the tail. There was a head and there were legs. I looked again. There were three front legs. Three? Bloody hell.

20

MAGGIE

Maggie checked the tomatoes weren't overdone under the grill and gave the scrambled eggs another stir. She let out a huge yawn. If Tom hadn't been there she would have happily returned to her bed for a well-earned nap – she was knackered and her bones ached in protest at being out in the damp field for hours. But despite that she didn't want to miss a moment with Tom. He was like a blood transfusion. He gave her the pep she needed to go another week on her own. She wandered to the back door and stuck her head out.

'Tom! Breakfast!' she called. She was about to retreat when a distant but panicked reply reached her.

'Maggie! Help! Maggie!'

'Bugger,' said Maggie, under her breath. She dashed inside, switched off the cooker and marched out, swapping her slippers for wellies on the way.

When she reached the field she could see Nancy was

obviously in trouble and Tom looked like a stressed expectant father pacing and rubbing his hands together.

'It's got three front legs!' he said. He dropped to his knees as if he needed to have another look to be sure. His eyes darted from Maggie's face to Nancy's back end.

'Three front legs?' She couldn't stifle the laugh.

He glared at her. 'It has. Come round and look.' He was genuinely distressed.

'Or she's got two more lambs in there and they're trying to exit together.'

Tom frowned hard. 'Huh. Yeah… that makes more sense.' Nancy's breathing was off. 'She's not right,' said Tom, looking anxious.

'She's not,' agreed Maggie. She'd almost lost Nancy in a similar situation the year before and she doubted she could go through it again.

'Is she going to die?' Tom's face broke Maggie's heart. He looked up at her with pleading puppy dog eyes. The trouble was Maggie wasn't one for soft-soaping a situation.

'I don't know. We can only do our best for her. The rest is up to her.'

'You have to save her!' His voice was choked but at the same time vehement.

Maggie wondered what was driving that intensity. 'You can save her, Tom,' she said, her voice calm and assured.

'No. No I can't.' She noticed a shake in his hands. 'All yours,' he said, getting to his feet.

Maggie held the pen firmly shut, stopping him leaving. He gave it a shake in frustration. 'I'm all clean,' she said. 'Anyway this is a good learning experience for you.' Tom opened his mouth but Maggie didn't give him time to protest. 'We need to get the lambs out quickly. They've been stuck there too long as it is. Take hold of one leg.' She pulled a ball of binder twine from her pocket. 'Tie this on it.'

Tom looked at her for a moment before accepting his fate. He took the offered twine and knelt back down next to Nancy's tail. 'Follow that leg all the way up to the lamb's shoulder...'

Tom started to do as she instructed and then halted. 'The shoulder is inside the... the... inside Nancy.' He looked pleadingly at Maggie.

'Yep and that's exactly where your hand is going.' He shook his head but she noted he didn't let go of the lamb's front foot. 'Up to the shoulder,' she repeated.

Tom swallowed hard, fixed his focus on Maggie and slid his hand up the lamb's front leg and inside the sheep. His face crumpled in disgust. 'Got to the head yet?' she asked.

There was a pause and Tom's face was one of total concentration. 'Yeah. There's its head.'

'Great. Over the head to the other shoulder and then slide back down the other leg. And then keep a hold of it.'

Tom's hand reappeared and he gave a cursory glance at it. 'Eurgh.'

'Now you know that those two legs belong to the same lamb. Tie the other end of twine onto that leg and then push that third leg back inside out of the way. He'll have to wait his turn.'

This time Tom didn't protest and returned his hand to the sheep.

'You're a pro now,' said Maggie, watching progress

closely. 'That's it – pull the lamb out the same as you did with Barbara.'

Tom did as Maggie instructed and within minutes two more lambs had joined Nancy and baby number one in the pen. While Nancy washed the two new ones, the first one started to feed.

'Right, Tom. Here's the thing. One ewe, two teats to feed from and three lambs. You do the maths.'

'She can't feed three.'

'No. But Barbara here only has one lamb.'

Tom grinned. 'Great. We get Barbara to adopt one.'

'Not that easy. She needs to think it's hers.'

'How do we do that?'

Maggie pulled a face. 'You're not going to like it but it's for a good cause.'

Maggie explained to Tom that if he shoved his hand inside Barbara, made a fist and pulled it out there was a small chance she would believe she had given birth again and that the extra lamb was hers. After a small amount of protest Tom conceded defeat and got in the pen with Barbara. Maggie moved the hurdle up against Barbara to hem her in and kept her busy at her front end with a handful of sheep nuts while Tom braced himself for the job at the business end.

He closed his eyes, made some noises like a wrestler and thrust his hand where no hand should go. Maggie dashed around to the other pen, swiped Nancy's spare lamb and brushed him over with straw Barbara's lamb had been lying on before setting him down. Barbara was surprisingly unfazed by Tom's assault until he made a fist and pulled his hand back out when she bleated her displeasure. Maggie shifted the hurdle back to its original position, to give the sheep room to move. When Barbara turned around Nancy's lamb was lying in the straw behind her. Barbara dutifully went to it. She paused for a second to sniff it and Maggie and Tom held their breath until she began to wash it.

'Yes!' said Tom, punching the air.

'Well done, Tom,' said Maggie, letting him out of the pen. She was proud of how he'd galvanised himself and got on with the task. 'That isn't the nicest of jobs and to be honest it rarely works.' They watched the two ewes with their "twin" lambs.

'I don't know,' said Tom. 'Once you get over how gross it is, it's actually quite warm in there.' He looked surprised at his own words and they both laughed.

Back in the house Maggie directed Tom to the shower and left out clean towels and some clothes for him while she salvaged what she could of breakfast. He appeared in the kitchen adjusting a long-sleeved top with a fashion logo emblazoned across the chest.

'That fits you okay,' she said, putting the plates on the table.

'It's well nice,' said Tom. 'Were these your son's?' He put the rest of the clothes selection she'd left out for him on the spare kitchen chair.

Maggie seemed to baulk at the question. 'Ah. No, I got those for you.'

Tom looked puzzled as he sat down and reached for the ketchup. 'What, to keep?'

'I was in Leamington and they have the best-stocked charity shops there. Don't worry, I've washed it all. I wanted to replace the top you tore when you were mending the henhouse but I got a bit carried away. It was nice to have someone to buy for and at those prices…' Maggie was aware she was doing a justification dance so she stopped. 'Anyway, it's all yours if it fits.'

Tom eyed the stack of things he'd brought down. 'Even the Adidas sweats?'

'Yes, whatever they are,' said Maggie, with a chuckle. 'The lady behind the counter picked out things she said her grandson would wear. He's into labels.'

Tom's grin was fixed. 'Brilliant. Thanks, Maggie.' He paused between mouthfuls and a look passed between them.

'Come on, eat up before it gets cold,' said Maggie, breaking eye contact and marvelling at the warm glow inside her fuelled by Tom's gratitude.

While Tom's original clothes were in the washing machine Maggie set about making the cake she'd planned to bake before Tom arrived. 'What shall I do?' asked Tom, looking about as if seeking inspiration.

'I can show you how to make a lemon drizzle cake if you like?'

He snorted a laugh but on seeing Maggie's serious expression he pouted as he appeared to consider her offer. 'Sure, why not?'

She opened a drawer and handed him a clean apron, which she had to tie for him.

He looked down at the dancing sheep on the front. 'You must never ever tell anyone about this.'

She tried to keep a straight face. 'My lips are sealed.'

He was a good student and he listened while she walked him through the process. 'Why don't you have a recipe?'

'Don't need one,' said Maggie, tapping the side of her head and smearing flour on her temple.

Tom smiled at her. 'Can you write it out for me?'

Maggie gave him a sideways look. 'You're going to bake on your own at home?'

He shrugged. 'You never know. I might.' He gave the contents of the bowl a good beating as instructed.

Before long they were sat back with their respective drinks waiting for the kitchen timer to ping.

'You should be proud of what you did birthing those lambs this morning,' she said, taking a sip of the tea he'd made her.

'Nah. I panicked. I was useless until you came and told me what to do.'

'You'd have worked it out.'

'I doubt it. I was scared.' His head dropped to his chest and Maggie waited a moment. He was lost in the no man's land between the child he was and the man he so longed to be. There was something more than stuck lambs going on. If he wanted to tell her, he would. She'd not go forcing it out of him.

Tom sighed and poured himself another glass of Coke. 'You'll think it's daft,' he said with a self-deprecating smile.

'I'm sure I won't.'

Tom held his glass in two hands and turned it slowly, his eyes focused upon the liquid swirling gently inside. 'My mum died having a baby…'

'I'm sorry, Tom,' she said. It was all she could do not to scoop him into her arms and hold him. The poor mite, what must he have been through? The thought of it brought a lump to her throat.

He tipped his head back as if willing tears not to fall. 'The baby got stuck and she had some sort of fit.'

'Eclampsia?' offered Maggie.

'I dunno,' said Tom. He glanced at Maggie, his eyes brimming with unshed tears. 'I was at my grandparents' and Dad was at work.' Tom took his time. 'Dad should have been at home but he had taken some overtime. There was lots of whispering when Dad came to collect me. I remember being really excited because they'd promised me this Lego set when the baby arrived.' He turned to look at Maggie. 'Dad's face when he came in.' He shook his head as if trying to rid himself of the memory. 'He looked broken.'

'How awful.' Maggie's heart ached for both of them and what they had lost.

'When Dad told me about Mum and the baby I remember worrying that I might not get my Lego set. How twisted is that?' Tom's young face changed to resemble someone much older and more weather-beaten by life.

'We often think of the oddest, most irrelevant things, at difficult times. We seek out the little things we can cope with while we process the things we can't.'

'I guess,' he said.

They sat in silence for a while both lost in their own thoughts until the kitchen timer rang and brought them both back to the present.

21

TOM

The last two weeks have gone uber quick. I've been trying to revise but I don't think it's going into my thick head. GCSEs are only a couple of weeks away now and it all feels a bit real. Mr Thackery was telling us we needed to have a healthy meal and a good night's sleep before exams. Dad and I are still on the beans and fish fingers diet. Dad's quite happy. He's counting down to my last GCSE. He's more excited about me finishing my exams than I am. That's because he thinks I'm going to get an apprenticeship at the factory. I'm not but I've not managed to tell him yet. It's too hard.

'All right?' I said as I stuck my head around the living room door. The place remained a mess but the smell had improved.

'Fine,' he said. He'd got a bottle of whisky on the table. I left him to it. I got changed into one of the tops Maggie had got me. They all fitted, although a couple were a bit big. I don't usually change after school but then I don't usually have something worth changing into. It's a pale blue Superdry top and I can't stop looking at myself in the mirror. Glad nobody can see me. I might wear it for the next Save The Library meeting.

After some revision and a mild panic, because I realised I didn't know as much about World War One as I thought I did, I went downstairs to get a drink. I looked in on Dad. He hadn't moved from the sofa and was staring at the TV. For once the TV wasn't on.

'You sure you're okay?' I asked.

He turned slowly to look at me. 'The car's failed its MOT.'

'Right.' I wasn't sure what else to say.

'That's it. I can't afford to get it fixed. We have no car.'

I couldn't see how it was going to affect me so decided not to say anything about it. 'You want a coffee?'

Dad frowned. 'Is that another new top?'

'Yeah.' I stood up straight to show it off.

'Where from?'

'My mate's mum.' I'd not yet owned up about Maggie.

'She just gave them to you?'

'Yeah.'

Dad's expression changed from one of scrutiny to alarm. 'You know two people have been mugged?'

'Err. No.' I knew about Maggie, obviously, but I didn't know if she was one of the two he was talking about.

'Old ladies in the village just after it gets dark. Police are looking for a tall skinny youth.'

We looked at each other. I could feel my neck heating up. 'Did you want a coffee?'

'Hang on, Tom. What's going on? What are you not telling me?'

'Nothing.' I might have been too quick to respond but I didn't like the way he was looking at me. He knew I was hiding something.

'Bloody hell. It's you isn't it?'

'What?'

'The muggings. Oh, Tom. Why?'

'No, Dad!' What the hell? How had he jumped to that conclusion?

'Don't deny it. All the extra cash and now the new trendy clothes. Why you little…'

I dodged out of the way as he made a lunge. He'd clearly caught up on his drinking today. 'Dad. You've got this all wrong.' I backed away as he staggered to his feet. Anger and injustice bubbled in my gut.

'Don't LIE!' he shouted and spit flew in my direction. I was angry at being accused but he was in a proper rage.

'It wasn't me!' I yelled back at him. I grabbed my jacket and keys, stormed out of the house and slammed the door.

I was furious with him. When had I ever done anything out of line? Never. Okay, maybe a few things but nothing criminal. He didn't know me at all. I must have been walking fast because I was in the village in no time. I walked round to the library but I was too fuming to go in. I didn't want a dull natter with Christine. I wanted to rant and for someone to listen.

I spun around on the spot – I had nowhere to go. I strode off out of the village towards town. I figured eventually the temper would ease and I'd be able to slow down. I was quite a way before my legs started to return to a normal pace. As the anger ebbed away it was replaced with hurt. How could Dad think such a thing? Even after all that alcohol, surely he should know I'm not capable of mugging someone. And little old ladies too. Jeez.

As the fight went out of me, I wondered how long I could stay out. If Dad carried on drinking he'd pass out in a couple of hours. It was a long time to kill. I'd left my phone behind and I had no money. I was meant to be revising. Missing out on studying annoyed me more than I thought it would. I was turning into a proper geek. I needed to do well in my exams, I needed to show Dad I was better than the factory job. But I wouldn't be revising tonight because all my stuff was in my room. And now I'd walked in circles I was hungry too. This was a mess. I could feel tears behind my eyes so I clamped my jaw shut to try to keep them in check.

It started to rain. Bloody typical. Good job I'd got my jacket. Maybe I would go to the library after all. At least I'd be dry there even if I'd have to pretend to be interested in Christine. I could even google some stuff. I turned around sharply and almost knocked into someone coming out of their gate.

'Tom. Hi. I thought it was you,' said Farah, with her trademark smile. All feminine and alluring, with a hint of mischief – bloody hell, maybe I had been reading too much romance lately.

'Hey. You all right?' It was hard to make eye contact today. I was exhausted.

'Yeah. You?'

I nodded and then changed my mind. 'No. A bit crap actually.'

'I'm a good listener.' She tilted her head. 'If you wanted to chat.'

There was nothing I'd like more. 'But you're on your way out. I don't want to stop you if you've stuff to do.'

She checked her watch. 'Do you want to come in?' She tilted her head back up the path she'd walked down.

Did I want to go inside Farah's house? No-brainer. 'Err, yeah. Sure.' I tried to play it cool. I had to, otherwise I'd be jumping up and down and whooping like an idiot.

She led the way, unlocked the door and let me in. It was a large old house with a high-ceilinged hallway and a floor like a chessboard. 'Nice house,' I said, remembering one of the romance novel heroes had got brownie points for this.

'Thanks. My parents are decorating it bit by bit. Tea? Coffee? Lemonade?'

'Lemonade please.' I followed her through to the kitchen. 'Are your parents not home?' I wanted to be prepared for any encounters. Get my thoughts ordered in case they suddenly appeared.

'No, Mum's shoe shopping with my brother. For him not her, so they'll be hours. He hates it. Dad has some seminar… I think. Not sure. It's a work thing anyway. I was going to the library to revise. If I stay here alone I'll just watch TV and eat crisps.'

'Sounds idyllic.'

'Idyllic?' She smiled at me. 'Is that your idea of heaven, Tom Harris. TV and crisps?' She was teasing me but it was gentle and friendly.

'Pretty much. Add in some Coke and it's perfect.' Her eyebrows shot up. What had I said? Shiiiiit. 'Cola. I mean cola not cocaine. Bloody hell. Sorry.'

She started to laugh and I joined in. 'You're funny.'

Not intentionally. She took a large glass out of a cupboard.

The kitchen was all modern and fitted with shiny granite worktops and it was super clean and tidy. 'Ice?' she asked.

'Yeah. Please.'

She went to a large American-style fridge, pressed a button and ice clattered into the glass. This was a seriously nice place. I wished I'd not said that already. She poured the drinks and passed me mine. 'Thanks. Look, you might not believe me but I was going to the library too,' I said.

'Why wouldn't I believe you?'

Because I probably look like a stalker, I thought. Outwardly though, I shrugged. 'Because it's a bit of a coincidence. But it is true. I had a row with my dad and I can't go home yet.'

'You want to talk about it?'

'Not really…' She was still looking at me. 'He accused me of being the mugger.'

'No way!'

'I know. Right?' It was nice to see her disbelief at the injustice of Dad's accusation.

'I read about that in the paper. I think whoever it is they're targeting pensioners coming out of the post office because it's likely they've been to get cash out.'

It was a good theory. 'You know Maggie had her bag snatched?' I knew Farah wouldn't know this and relished being the one to tell her. Her reaction was exactly what I was hoping for.

'No way! That's awful. When was this?'

'A few weeks ago. I heard her shout and I…' What did I do exactly?

'You were there?' She was enthralled. It was great.

'Yeah. I ran to help her but I got punched in the face

and he made off with her bag.' At least my account was factually correct even if a little misleading.

Farah's hands shot to her face as she gasped. 'Tom. You could have been seriously hurt.'

I shrugged my shoulder and sipped my lemonade. It was the cloudy sort with a real lemon tang. No cheap stuff here. 'I wish I could have caught him, that's all.' Who was I kidding? Anyone could beat the crap out of me. Maggie did.

'Was Maggie okay?'

'Yeah. She was fine. She's tough.' We sipped our drinks and I marvelled at the looks she was giving me. I could tell she was impressed. This was awesome.

'When do you think you'll be able to go home?' she asked.

'Not for ages yet. We both need to calm down. But I should be revising.'

'Excellent!' She clapped her hands together. 'We can revise here together. It'll save us going to the library and getting wet.'

'Yeah. Okay.' My day just got a whole lot better.

I had the best time. We revised a bit. We chatted. Well, mainly Farah chatted and I listened, which was bliss because her voice is like discovering music for the first time. She made us ham and pineapple pizza for tea and served it with garlic bread, coleslaw and salad. Salad! Like a proper meal. Then we tested each other on our history and I did okay. She has some cool ways of remembering stuff. She even made me a couple of revision cards to bring home. They're in my pocket. I think I'll treasure them forever.

I took a breath before I unlocked my front door. The plan was to scoot straight upstairs and hope Dad was asleep somewhere but as I opened the door the smell hit me. Not the manky smell like before. This was sharp and pungent and made me gag – it was vomit. What happened next was a bit of a blur. I ran into the living room and there was Dad. He was lying on his back bubbling sick out of his mouth. He was unconscious and his face was a grey blue colour. I knew what was happening. I'd read about it – he was choking on his own vomit. Gross and fatal.

I dropped to my knees and with a few shoves turned him onto his side. I whacked his back to try to clear the blockage but nothing happened. I tried not to look as I stuck my finger in his mouth in an attempt to clear his airway – like I'd seen Maggie do with the newborn lamb. Nothing.

'Shit! Dad!' I shouted at him, partly in fear and desperation.

I gave him a mighty thump on the back and he vomited. Proper rocket blast chuck-up. It was disgusting and it was everywhere. But he started to cough and gasp for breath. He was alive.

22

MAGGIE

Maggie did her last check on the sheep and the new lambs were all feeding well. Two more ewes had produced two more lambs midmorning and both births had gone smoothly, which she was grateful for. She had three female lambs, which she'd keep and add to her flock but that would probably be as many as she'd be able to manage. She was still tired from the weekend and was planning on turning in shortly. Generally she tried to stay up until eleven o'clock. If she went to bed any earlier she usually woke up in the early hours and couldn't get back to sleep. It was a curse of being older, some afternoons she would be beyond tired but two in the morning she'd be bright as a button.

At this time of year she made sure she stayed up later because she liked to do a last check on the sheep and lambs before she turned in. Although she doubted she had any more who were pregnant. It was getting too late for any more lambs now. Colin was clearly a dud. No wonder the farmer who owned him wasn't in a rush to have him back. Useless article.

Maggie checked she was all locked up and took the keys out of the door so that if she died in the night Savage would be able to get in without breaking a window. She'd always assumed it would be Savage who would find her; he was the only person who had a key. But they weren't in any sort of regular contact so it could be anybody. She wondered how long it would be before anyone missed her. How long after that before someone could be bothered to go all the way out to Furrow's Cross to check? She reckoned about a month by which time all the animals would likely have died of dehydration. For that reason she tried hard not to dwell on it. She was actually in fine fettle. It wasn't like she was planning on turning up her toes anytime soon it was simply one of the odd things you considered when you spent too much time on your own.

She made herself a half-cup of tea – any more and she'd be up half the night pacing back and forth to the loo – and she treated herself to a digestive biscuit. She decided she'd read a bit more of her book and had just sat down when the phone rang. He didn't say much. She could tell he was crying, poor lad. He gave her his address and within a few minutes she was in a taxi.

She'd only got sketchy details from Tom. But from what she could make out his father had been taken ill and Tom had thought he was dead. Maggie's heart went out to Tom. She had grown incredibly fond of him. Losing someone you love was a terrible thing but to have lost a parent at such a young age cut a wound so deep it rarely healed.

Maggie could remember the last time she'd been driven

in a car. It was in the funeral car to her husband's funeral almost ten years ago. She remembered thinking that a hearse was most likely the poshest car most people would ever ride in and yet they'd not get any enjoyment out of it. The time before that she'd got a black cab across London when they'd gone to the theatre sometime in the 1990s. Now Maggie was more of a bus person. She liked the train but had no call to go further afield anymore. But she definitely wasn't a car person, she thought as she sat on the back seat of the cab. She always thought sitting in the back of a car on her own reminded her of how Hitler was chauffeured about – she wasn't sure why.

The taxi pulled up outside an ordinary terrace and she paid the driver. The small garden was part wobbly paving and part overgrown shrubbery. There was one light on at the front of the house and everything looked decidedly normal. Was this the right place? Why was there no ambulance? Maybe she was too late.

She walked up the path and the front door opened. A wretched-looking Tom was standing before her. He was wearing one of the tops she'd found for him and it was soaked in vomit. His eyes were red and puffy and he held his head low. He didn't speak, merely sniffed a bit.

'Did you call an ambulance like I said?' she asked, stepping inside and closing the door.

Tom shook his head. 'Dad said not to.'

If he was talking that was a good sign. Tom pointed into the living room and Maggie took a look. A man in his forties was sitting in a puddle of sick and leaning against a stained sofa with his head tilted back, eyes closed and breathing steady. The stench of whisky and vomit dominated the small room. The empty bottles and heavily fingered glass told their own tale.

She looked back at an ashen-faced Tom who appeared as if Death himself had cast its shadow over him. 'Are you all right?' she asked, trying to peek under his fringe. He nodded. 'What's your dad's name?'

'Paul.'

'Right, Tom. You go and get yourself showered and changed and I'll sort things out here.' She took off her coat and hung it over the newel post and watched Tom trudge upstairs. She took a deep breath. She'd dealt with worse.

'Paul? Can you hear me, Paul?' Tom's dad made an inaudible groan. He was sound asleep. That was fine, it would be easier to work around him. She was surprised Tom had managed to get a coherent sentence out of the man to be able to indicate he didn't want an ambulance called but she didn't doubt Tom's honesty.

Maggie relocated a pile of dishes in the kitchen to free up the washing-up bowl and set about clearing up the worst of the mess in the living room. She was cross at Paul for putting Tom through this but deep down she was also pleased to be able to help Tom. She took the covers off two cushions and slung them in the washing machine along with a random sock she found. She cleaned and tidied around the man and he barely moved, even despite the vigorous carpet scrubbing she did right next to him.

In her opinion Paul should be checked over by a paramedic but he was a grown man and she wasn't going to interfere. If he'd said he didn't want them called then that was his decision, however foolish. Her main concern was Tom and she wasn't sure on where social services would stand if they'd walked in with her earlier. The last thing she wanted was for Tom to get whisked into care. That wasn't a fate he deserved.

Maggie worked around Paul, who now appeared to be sleeping quite peacefully. It looked like the danger had passed. Given the state the carpet had been in she doubted there was anything else to come up. She moved behind the sofa and her foot hit something that made a telltale clinking noise. Underneath the sofa she found a stash of bottles – mostly empty and one full bottle of whisky. She hoicked them all out.

Maggie went on a brief treasure hunt checking the most unlikely places in search of alcohol where she unearthed two more almost-empty bottles and two half-full ones. She ferried them all to the kitchen and began pouring their contents down the sink. The bottles made a pleasant chink sound each time she popped them in the recycling box.

'Hey!' said the slurred voice behind her. 'Who the hell are you?'

'I'm Maggie. I'm a friend of Tom's.' She turned and smiled at Paul who blinked very slowly back, confusion distorting his features as he swayed in the doorway. It was good that he was on his feet.

'What?' He seemed to focus in on the contents of the last bottle being tipped into the sink. 'What the hell are you doing?'

'I'm doing you a favour,' said Maggie, rinsing the bottle out and adding it to the others.

Paul's eyes followed the bottle. When they alighted on the pile of empty whisky bottles in the crate he brought his hands up to his face. 'No!' He staggered across the kitchen holding onto the worktop for support. 'No, no, no...' he repeated his voice full of sorrow.

Tom appeared at the door. His hair wet and his face pale. 'You okay, Dad?'

'No! This. This woman,' spat Paul, jabbing a finger near to Maggie's face. She stepped back, keeping her eyes fixed firmly on him.

'That's Maggie. I rang her.'

'Why?' Paul looked genuinely confused.

Tom shook his head. 'Because... I didn't know what to do and you were...' His voice was choked up with emotion. Maggie wanted to wrap him in her arms and block out all his pain. No child should ever have to see a parent in the state Paul was in. Her blood started to boil on Tom's behalf.

'She! She...' Paul did more jabbing movements in Maggie's direction. 'Has tipped away my... MY... whisky!' He twisted around to face Maggie. She stood her ground. 'That's theft, that is!' His voice was getting louder and he was swaying dangerously.

'The last thing an alcoholic needs is a house full of alcohol,' said Maggie calmly, wiping her hands on a tea towel of dubious cleanliness – she'd wash them again when she got home.

'A what?' Paul uttered a strangled laugh. 'How dare you! You barge in here and you... hey... What are you doing?'

Maggie had moved to the fridge and she was taking out cans of lager. 'I told you. I'm helping you by getting rid of the alcohol. As long as it's here you'll drink it. And you can't get in that state again.' She glanced briefly at Tom, his brow furrowed, his eyes focused on his father.

Paul made a lunge for a can but Maggie was too quick

for him and spun around with the last lager, opened it in a flourish and tipped its contents away. Paul pulled at his hair and made a noise somewhere between a growl and a groan. He swayed a little until his eyes settled on a tall cupboard. He made his way over to it, opened it and rummaged behind the ironing board that was stored there, swearing when it toppled.

'Dad. What are you doing?' Tom was looking embarrassed, his eyes darting between his father and Maggie.

'None of your business,' barked Paul. Maggie had to bite her lip to stop herself giving the man a piece of her mind. She didn't want to embarrass Tom further.

'If you're looking for the two half-bottles of whisky, I found those first so they've gone down the drain with the rest,' said Maggie, matter-of-factly. 'Would you like a coffee or, better still, some water? Maybe wait until you've sobered up before you have a shower.'

'Why you...' Paul swung around, his clenched fist heading with force for Maggie's face.

'Maggie!' yelled Tom, his tone desperate. The sound rang in her ears.

23

TOM

I screamed at him. If he'd landed that punch he could have killed her. In a flash I had an image of me rolling up Maggie's body in a carpet. I dived forward but I was too late. It all happened too fast. As the punch came in, Maggie darted to one side and a lightning fast kick to the back of Dad's shin had him twisting in mid-air and he landed hard on the kitchen floor. He crumpled into a ball muttering swear words.

I dashed to Maggie's side. 'Maggie, are you all right?' I asked, as we both surveyed my father.

'I'm absolutely fine.' She held up her palms as if to prove it.

'I'm so sorry. I'm so sorry, Maggie.' I couldn't stop shaking my head. What the hell was happening? Nothing made sense tonight. My dad wasn't an alcoholic; he didn't go around hitting old ladies. Temper rushed through me and I clenched my fists. I wanted to lash out. To kick, to punch and break something. To hurt Dad how he'd hurt me. I knew inflicting physical pain wouldn't even come close but it would temporarily relieve my anger. I hated myself for even considering it.

I had to get out of there or I was going to do something I would always regret. I legged it out of the kitchen. I went to grab my jacket but Maggie's was on top of it and I had to wrestle it free. I yanked at the front door, tears blurring my vision and infuriating me further. I felt her hand land firmly on my shoulder.

'Tom.' Her voice was gentle. 'Please take a moment to stop and think.'

I froze. My pulse was racing. 'I've got to get away from him,' I said without turning around.

'Think about you and your future. Don't you have exams coming up?'

I took a deep breath and nodded. 'But I can't stay here with him.' My head dropped to my chest as my fury tailed off.

Maggie let go of my shoulder and I turned around. 'What's the alternative?' she asked.

'I dunno.' I had nobody else.

Maggie's expression changed from one of grave concern to unease. She took a deep breath. 'I suppose you could stay with me. Give him a chance to sober up and you to calm down. Do you think that would be all right with your dad?'

'Like he cares.' I looked back into the kitchen. Dad was still on the floor and had nodded off to sleep. He was a mess and I couldn't bear to see it.

Maggie followed my gaze. 'Okay. Just for the night.'

'Thanks.' I probably should have been more enthusiastic but I was out of energy.

'You'd best get your things together. Make sure you've got everything you need for school.'

I nodded and went upstairs. It didn't take long to chuck some stuff into my schoolbag and a couple of carriers. I brought my box of library books down too. I saw Maggie's lip twitch a smile when she saw them. She was waiting at the bottom of the stairs for me.

'A taxi's on its way,' she said, taking the carrier bags off me. 'I've left a note so your dad knows where you are.'

'No, I don't want him—'

She held up her hand to stop me. 'I've left my name and phone number. Not my address. I've explained the situation you found him in and that he is in no fit state to care for you right now and that my only other alternative was to call social services.' I felt my eyebrows rise. Maggie was not someone to mess with. 'When he wakes he needs to know you are safe but also how serious this is.'

A beep of a car horn told us the taxi had arrived. I took one last glance into the kitchen. Maggie had propped Dad up with some cushions and he was sleeping. His hair was greasy and he hadn't shaved. Vomit was stained all down his clothes. It was difficult to pin down how I felt at that moment – disgust, disappointment, hurt and anger were all vying for my attention. But I knew I didn't want to see him like this anymore. I followed Maggie outside and closed the door.

I woke up in Maggie's spare bedroom. We didn't speak at all in the taxi and only exchanged a few necessary words before she went to check the sheep and I went to bed.

Sunshine was overpowering the thin curtains and flooding the bedroom with light. The room was painted orange, which was a bit bright for first thing in the morning – a little like waking up in a volcano. But I had a double bed and I liked how the ceiling sloped down on one side.

I'd propped up Mum's photo on the bedside cabinet before I went to sleep. It was kind of nice to see it. Something familiar in an unfamiliar place.

Maggie had put my school uniform on a coat hanger after she'd ironed it late last night and it was hanging on the front of a large dark wood wardrobe. My uniform hadn't been ironed for months. I didn't want to go to school. I wanted to curl up and go back to sleep and stop thinking about Dad. I knew the change had been gradual but I guess I'd ignored it. It was like I only saw it for the first time last night and it had been like watching a stranger. I could see it play out in my mind and feel the helpless grip of fear when I thought he was dead, and the flash of fury when he was going to hurt Maggie.

'Tom?' There was a light tap on the door. 'Do you want your breakfast before or after you've had a shower?'

I gulped at how kind Maggie was. I didn't like to think about what I would have done without her last night.

'Tom? Are you okay?'

'Yeah. Just waking up. I'll shower first if that's okay?'

'Of course. Breakfast in twenty minutes. It's eggs and toast. Do you want fried, scrambled or poached?'

Having the conversation with her through the door made me smile despite everything. 'Scrambled please.'

'Right you are,' she said and I heard the creak of the stairs as she went back down. I stared at my uniform for a moment. The bit of yesterday with Farah had been sandwiched between my dad's outbursts and it had been great. Like the best home-made jam in a mouldy bread sandwich. A deep sigh escaped. Farah would be expecting me to be at school. I reached into my bag at the side of the bed and pulled out the revision cards she'd done for me. Her neat writing smiled back at me. I needed to have a shower and get ready.

Maggie's timing was perfect. As I walked into the kitchen she put a plate down on the table. Two slices of buttered toast with a mound of fluffy scrambled eggs on top. I was suddenly hungry. 'Thanks.'

'My pleasure. I've been thinking about getting you to school…' An image of me on the back of the quad bike shot into my mind. 'I've looked on the bus timetable,' she said and I was relieved, 'and as long as the buggers haven't changed it, the number nineteen bus should drop you quite close to your school. It leaves in…' She checked the kitchen clock and then her watch. 'Twenty minutes.'

'Okay.' I knew some people who got that bus.

She joined me at the table with a smaller version of my breakfast and a large mug of tea. 'Lambs were a bit lively this morning,' she said.

'How many now?'

'Six and there won't be any more. Colin's useless.'

We ate in silence. But it was all right. It's probably weird to compare silences but with Dad if he was silent it was like I was waiting for something to happen. For him to moan or shout or something. But with Maggie, it was just quiet. I liked that. I cleared the table and Maggie handed me a brown paper package. 'I didn't know what you did for lunch.'

'I usually just have a slice of pizza.'

'That's not much. Here's a cheese and pickle sandwich and a piece of fruit loaf. Is that enough?'

'Yeah.'

'Right. Now what happens after school today? Are you going home?'

I shook my head hard. The thought of it made my pulse race. 'I can't. Not yet.'

She nodded her understanding. 'Then a bus leaves from the stop by the school at half four. Here...' She handed me a ten-pound note. I hesitated. I'd not thought before but me staying here was going to cost money and it wasn't fair that Maggie should have to pay. 'Go on, take it. I don't want you being late.' I did as she asked and she guided me out of the kitchen.

'I'll pay you back.' I didn't know how.

'I've got a long list of jobs for you to do so I'll more than get my money back.' She opened the front door.

'Maggie...' How did I tell her how grateful I was? How I literally had nobody else but her. For no reason at all she was taking care of me. I swallowed hard. 'Thanks.' I kind of mumbled it because I was scared of crying.

'You're welcome. Now scoot or you'll miss that bus.'

I grabbed my bag and left.

It was a well weird day. It felt a bit like I was living someone else's life. The bus made a nice change from the cycle ride I usually had. I had time to look over my revision notes again. When I walked into school Farah was with a group of girls so I didn't stop but she ran after me.

'How'd it go with your dad?' she asked, her face full of concern.

How was I meant to answer that? I couldn't face lying to her and maybe I needed someone other than Maggie to know what was happening. And I was well pleased that she'd come over to ask me. 'Not great. I've moved out.'

'Tom? That's awful.' Awful was the last thing it was. I felt bad because I was glad to be away from him and it was great at Maggie's. It was a bit how I imagined a holiday in a bed and breakfast would be. But free and run by someone who actually cared about you.

'It is what it is. Thanks for your help yesterday.'

'No worries.' The other girls caught us up so I hurried off. I was doing better around Farah but a bunch of them was a whole different thing. As I turned a corner something struck me hard. I had my head down, as usual, so it hit my forehead and the top of my head. It bloody hurt but it could have been a lot worse. It knocked me off balance but I managed to stay upright and looked up to see Kemp holding up his rucksack. What the hell did he have in there? Bricks?

Kemp's grinning face loomed into mine. 'I told you to keep away from her.'

I rubbed my head. 'But you didn't tell her to keep away from me. She can't get enough, Kemp. That's not my fault.' I probably asked for the bag to get swung in my face a second time but at least I was expecting it and managed to knock it off course with my forearm. It probably wasn't smart but it felt good.

Kemp squared up to me. Shiiiiiit. I hadn't thought this through at all.

'Mr Thackery!' I called down the corridor at the teacher's back and Kemp scuttled out of sight. Only a temporary solution I feared.

There was no sign of Kemp after school, which was a relief. I did some revision in the school library until it was time to get the bus. It felt odd going back to Maggie's instead of home. For the first time in hours I wondered how Dad was. My phone had been in my locker all day but there were no messages from him. The bus passed the end of Maggie's track and I got a shot of happy through my veins. I wondered what was for dinner. The big breakfast, school lunch, sandwich and cake had kept me going all day but I was hungry now.

As I approached the house I could hear the faint bleating of the lambs in the field below and a hint of summer in the air. I loved it here – it was peaceful.

I tried the door and it was open. 'Hiya!' I called as I stepped inside.

'Hello, Tom,' called Maggie. 'I'm in the sitting room.'

I went through and came to a sudden halt. Maggie was upside down. She was balanced on her head and forearms with her legs tied in a knot above her. 'What the…?'

'Lotus headstand,' she said, before taking a slow deep breath.

'Right. Why?' I wasn't sure why you'd stand on your head voluntarily.

Maggie let out the breath and as if in slow motion she uncrossed her legs and returned them to the floor and then into a kneeling position. 'It's yoga. I'm focusing on building strength in my upper arms.'

'Right.' She was full of surprises.

'It's very good for you. It also stretches your muscles and reverses the flow of gravity. It stimulates the immune system and improves your circulation.'

'Gives you a different perspective too I guess.' She had looked funny on her head.

'Ha, ha,' said Maggie. 'Don't knock it before you've tried it.'

'Nah. You're all right.'

Maggie shifted into sitting with her legs crossed and tilted her head on one side. 'Join me.' I didn't know what to do. I was pleased I hadn't got PE while revision and exams were on the timetable; I wasn't expecting to have to do some here. 'Come on. Sitting on the floor is not taxing.'

Reluctantly I sat opposite her on the rug. It took three goes to cross my legs and she chuckled at me. 'My legs are longer than yours,' I said in my defence.

'And not half as flexible. At your age I could scratch my ears with my toes.'

'There's a useful skill.' I laughed at the thought.

'Close your eyes,' said Maggie. I closed one to start with but she was watching me so I did as I was told. She talked slowly and we went through some breathing exercises. If it hadn't been for the pins and needles in my foot it would have been quite relaxing.

'Okay. Open your eyes,' she said, eventually. 'How was your day?'

'All right.'

She gave a penetrating squint. 'I'm going to need more than that.' Her eyes were curious, interested.

I had a think. 'We're just going over stuff.' She motioned

with her hand for me to say more. 'We did a timed test in maths and I did better than I thought I would. We went through some complicated stuff that regularly comes up in chemistry. I'm not sure I'm ever going to get it. And some listening in French, which was even worse.' Her eyebrow twitched at this but she said nothing. 'But I got eighty per cent in the history test we did.'

She beamed at me and I wondered why. 'Tom, that's bloody marvellous! And a cause for celebration. I've made lemonade. Come on.' She was on her feet and out of the room while I was still untangling my legs.

In the kitchen she filled two glasses from a tall jug with lemon slices floating in it. The liquid was an odd colour and cloudy. I sipped it cautiously. There was no need though; it was delicious. I pushed my fringe out of my eyes and winced when I touched my forehead.

'You want to tell me about that?' Maggie fixed me with her stare.

She was like truth serum – I couldn't lie to her. 'Got whacked in the face. It's no biggie.'

'No biggie?'

'Just some beef this kid has with me.'

'Beef?'

'Why are you repeating what I say?'

'Because it's like a different language and I'm trying to learn it. So the kid you've got beef with, is he a bully by any chance?' She gave me a look that said she already knew the answer.

'Yeah. But it's no—'

'Biggie?'

'Exactly.' She was funny. I wished she was my gran. I'd love a cool grandmother like Maggie. But grans weren't cool. They did knitting and watched TV soaps, not yoga and riding quad bikes.

'You need to learn to block. Sharpen your reflexes. Learn some martial arts.'

'Yeah.' She was probably right but it was easier to keep out of Kemp's way. I'd probably make it worse if I stood up to him again.

'I know some moves.' She gave a shrug and carried on drinking her lemonade.

'Martial arts?' A snort of a laugh escaped but Maggie looked serious. 'What, like karate?'

'Quite a variety actually. I practise jujitsu, judo and some elements of aikido. All to a reasonable level.'

A few things slotted into place. 'That's how you dodged Dad when he was about to punch you.'

A smile tweaked at her lips.

'And the bag snatcher. Oh and when you thumped me.'

'I'm not apologising again. It was only a short jab.'

'But it was right on target. Bloody hell, you're the geriatric version of Bruce Lee!'

'Rude,' she said but she started to laugh.

This was brilliant. I've always wanted to be able to do something cool like martial arts but Dad never had the money for me to join clubs. 'Will you teach me some stuff?' I asked.

'I'd love to.' She took my glass off me and my first martial arts lesson began.

24

MAGGIE

Tom had taken an armful of wood down to Colin's gate in the hope of repairing it when the phone rang.

'Hello,' said Maggie, while juggling a tin of nails.

'Oh, uh. Hi, is Tom there?'

She knew instinctively who it was. 'Who's calling?' She sounded all prim even to herself.

'It's his dad.'

'Ah, Mr Harris. I was hoping you'd call,' said Maggie, pulling out a chair and getting herself comfortable. 'How are you feeling?'

There was a long pause. 'I'm fine, thanks. Can I just speak to Tom?'

'He's out at the moment but I wanted to assure you that he's fine.'

'I know he's fine,' said Paul, his words clipped.

'Well, you don't know he's fine because he's been staying here for the last two nights and this is the first time you've called.' She didn't want a row but she wasn't going to let him get away with washing over everything either. 'He was in a real state when he called me. You frightened the life out of the poor boy.' Paul went to interrupt but Maggie kept going. 'You have him to thank for saving your life. I hope you understand that if it wasn't for Tom you would be dead.'

'That's a bit dramatic,' he said with a half-laugh.

'Not in the least. It is pure and simple fact. You were choking. It took Tom a number of attempts to dislodge the blockage. You were unconscious and probably had minutes before you'd have suffocated. And your son witnessed that. Alone.' Maggie's grip on the phone had tightened and her pulse was rising. She didn't want to get cross with the man but it was hard not to when his irresponsible attitude had caused it all. She concentrated on her breathing and let the silence settle.

Paul cleared his throat. 'Okay. Well, I hadn't realised that.'

Maggie nodded to herself, happy that she'd got her point across. 'Tom is obviously concerned that this could happen again.'

'Can you ask him to call me when he's back?'

'I shall but of course it is up to him whether he does or not.'

'Now look here—'

'I'll pass the message on. Goodbye, Mr Harris.' It gave Maggie great satisfaction to put the phone down.

'Was that Dad?' Maggie spun around to see Tom was standing by the back door.

'Yes, it was. He wants you to call him back.'

Tom shook his head. 'I don't want to talk to him.'

Maggie's head bobbed in understanding. 'Of course. But you will need to speak to him at some point. My advice would be to not leave it too long.' She gathered the tin of nails and went to put her wellies on.

'I wouldn't know what to say to him anyway,' said Tom. He leaned against the doorframe looking solemn.

Maggie paused with one wellie on. 'Well. You need to be clear about what you want.'

Tom screwed his face up. 'Dad's not going to listen to a list of demands.'

'I don't mean like that. Surely you want your dad to make some changes?'

'I want him to stop drinking and stop going on about money and stop trying to force me to work at the factory.'

'Maybe one thing at a time,' said Maggie. 'There's lots of options for him to get help with the drinking. You could suggest some of those.'

'What like a threat? I won't come home unless you join Alcoholics Anonymous?' Tom seemed quite buoyed by the prospect.

'I wouldn't call it a threat. More you showing that things can't carry on as they are and that he needs to take some positive steps so you feel safe to come home.'

Tom nodded a lot. 'That's it. Hang on I'll tell him now.' He scooted back inside and picked up the phone.

Maggie only heard one side of the conversation. Tom spoke confidently and without making it sound like the ultimatum it was. She assumed Paul wasn't keen on the compromise because Tom's replies got shorter and shorter until he eventually fell silent. Maggie could hear Paul's raised voice.

At last Tom responded. 'You almost decked, Maggie!' There was a mumbled response.

'What do you care? You can't make me!' Tom slammed the phone down and stormed past Maggie and out across the yard. Maggie let out a slow breath as she watched him go. The teenage years were turbulent enough without having to wrestle with the worry of an alcoholic parent.

Tom made a good job of shoring up Colin's gate. He was a dab hand at hammering in nails now. Some of his temper had likely been released on the job. He was extra quiet and it pained her to see him troubled. She took the axe and showed him how to chop up the large sections of tree trunk into fire-sized pieces. Not that she needed any firewood this time of year but she'd put it away for winter and chopping wood was a wonderful stress reliever. She left him to it while she went to check on dinner.

They ate in relative silence until Tom put his cutlery down.

'Why won't he agree to stop drinking?'

Maggie took a sip of water. 'He needs to recognise for himself that he has a problem.'

'Nearly killing yourself is a problem. Nearly decking an old lady is a problem.' Tom was getting animated.

'But he probably can't remember any of it.'

Tom looked surprised. 'Really?'

'I doubt it.'

Tom leaned back in his chair. 'How do I make him see what he's doing?'

Maggie pondered the question. She knew too well that

right now Paul would be focused on all his other issues because for him drinking wasn't the problem. The alcohol provided his escape. 'I'm not sure you can.' She hadn't meant it to sound so final.

Tom gave her a brief nod before picking up his knife and fork and finishing his dinner in silence. 'That was really nice. My mum used to make cottage pie.'

'Shepherd's pie,' said Maggie. 'It was made with lamb. Cottage pie is with beef.'

'I didn't know that,' said Tom.

'They're easy to make.' Tom gave her a doubtful look. 'I can show you anytime.'

'Yeah, okay,' he said clearing the table.

Two nights turned into two weeks. They spent their time in a companionable silence reading their respective books. It was what they did after he'd done some revision – it was an easy routine they had slotted into. Reading with a brief interval for drinks, tea for her and Coke for him, and a discussion about the latest book club read that Maggie was enjoying. She studied the edge of the paperback. 'I'll have finished it by tomorrow. You can read it after me if you like?' suggested Maggie.

Tom was nearing the end of his latest romance. Maggie was enjoying sharing suggestions with him but even though he was branching out into other genres it was nice to see that he still had a soft spot for the romantic novels that had got him hooked on reading.

'I might,' he said with a sigh. He picked up his book and almost immediately put it down again. 'You don't read much about alcoholics,' he said. 'You know, in novels. Why do you think that is?'

'They don't make the best heroes.'

'I guess.' Tom picked his book back up.

She watched him for a moment. He was stretched out on the sofa, his head resting on the arm one end and his feet against the other. 'Nobody starts out intending to be an alcoholic, Tom. It's nobody's choice.'

There was a long delay before he replied. 'But he's choosing to be one now.'

Maybe she wasn't explaining it well enough. She didn't want to fall out with Tom over it. They resumed their reading; each delving into other worlds where they could switch off from being themselves and most importantly avoid the things in the real world they could do nothing to alter.

On Saturday they got the bus into Compton Mallow together and Tom seemed to be on red alert in case he saw his father. Maggie was ready for the man, having rehearsed her side of the conversation a number of times in her head, but there was no sign of him. He hadn't called again either. Maggie wasn't sure if this was a good thing or a bad one. Tom had no signal on his phone when he was at Providence Farm but he'd had no text messages either. She loved having Tom to stay but she knew deep down he should be with his father.

The library seemed different now – of course it wasn't at all. It had been the same way, pretty much, since it was built in the nineteenth century but the thought of losing it made Maggie pay more attention each time she was there. Nowadays she noticed the detail of the brickwork around the entrance. She saw the twentieth-century additions of metal brackets that supported the giant beams that criss-crossed their way above her head. The slight warp in the glass of the windows. It was like she was holding up a magnifying glass and the building was revealing its secrets.

Tom was comfortable here. She loved the sight of him talking to Farah. She was good for him. He managed to make eye contact with her now, which was a huge improvement. And she was sure he was standing straighter when he wore the clothes she'd got him.

This week Tom had read the book club offering and Maggie was delighted when he dragged over a chair and joined the group for the discussion. They had some other new members too and Christine had to pull up another table to accommodate everyone. The discussion was detailed and lively and, while he was quiet at first, Tom made a couple of insightful points about the plot.

After book club they convened the meeting. Christine hovered nervously nearby.

'Christine, you can sit down,' said Maggie pulling out a chair.

'No, I can't. They sent out another email to all the affected libraries. Instant dismissal if you're found to be colluding.'

'Okay,' said Maggie, rolling her eyes. 'How many signed the petition?'

'Forty-eight,' said Tom.

'How many do we need?' asked Farah.

'A thousand if it's to be taken seriously,' said Maggie. 'We'll have to go door-to-door.'

'Have we got people's email addresses?' asked Tom.

'I can't give you those,' said Christine, her voice hitting a new octave.

'Great idea,' said Farah and Tom straightened his shoulders. 'We'll send out the petition from my laptop,' she added.

'Ooh, I'm not sure about that.' Christine was fidgeting with her name badge.

'Nobody needs to know how we got the email addresses,' said Tom.

'Excellent,' said Maggie. 'How are the footfall numbers looking?'

'Twenty-one per cent increase,' said Christine.

'That's not enough. We need more people through the door,' said Maggie. 'Anything on the list, Farah, that could up our numbers?'

Farah consulted her notes and Tom gazed at her adoringly. 'Reading challenge but that's not until school holidays.'

'That'll be too late,' said Maggie. Christine blew her nose. She remained quite emotional about it all.

'The primary school are planning their visit. They need consent forms and it's taking a while to sort out,' said Farah. 'I guess we could ask local nurseries and toddler groups but they'd need an incentive.'

Tom pressed his lips into a flat line. 'How about we do a reward scheme?'

'No budget,' said Christine.

'Hear him out,' said Maggie, giving him a nod of encouragement to continue.

'Those little loyalty cards where you get a stamp each time you get a coffee and then after ten or something you get a free one.'

'But the books are already free,' pointed out Farah.

'I know. But we could give them something else.'

'Like?' asked Farah.

Tom's cheeks flushed. 'I dunno.'

'A bookmark?' said Christine, who was watching someone walk past outside. Her shoulders relaxed when they disappeared out of view. 'My sister makes birthday cards. I could get her to make some bookmarks.'

The mood went a bit flat. 'Stickers,' said Farah. 'Kids love stickers.'

'That's it,' said Maggie with gusto making Christine jump. 'We get a chart on the wall and for every ten books loaned they get a sticker. And with each sticker we get closer to the target of saving our library.'

Tom and Farah were nodding. 'But we can't put anything up in the library. The council won't allow it,' said Christine.

'Then we stage a sit-in!' said Maggie. Christine drew a sharp intake of breath.

25

TOM

I rang Dad yesterday because Maggie said he'd rung earlier but I'm not sure she was telling the truth. He didn't seem to know anything about it. Maybe he forgot. Or maybe Maggie thought it was time we spoke. He asked when I was coming home. I said when he gets help for the drinking. He called me ungrateful and a few other things before putting the phone down.

Maggie explained that drink changes people. She said I was to think of it as an illness. The alcoholism is making him this way and it's not entirely his fault. If it's not his fault then I don't know who's to blame. He buys the whisky, he drinks the whisky – I don't see anyone forcing him. Maggie says it's not that simple. She describes it like a corkscrew, a downward spiral and doubts he'll change until he reaches the bottom. She calls alcoholism a disease that haunts the soul. I think he's just a pisshead.

Today I decided I would call in on Dad. I'm not sure why – guilt, duty maybe. The niggling feeling that I should.

I walked there from school. It took ages but I'd only got enough money to get the bus back to Maggie's. I went on the pretext of needing more clothes. It was Tuesday and he was due at work that evening. I didn't know if he'd been going to work or not since that night. If he lost his job then he'd lose the house – I was starting to see how it was all connected.

As I turned the corner for home a strange sensation crept over me like a Dementor approaching. Home. It's a small word but means so much. It used to mean everything. My mother would say it at the end of a day out and it would make me want to cry because I didn't want the day to end. But I did love my home; I just liked the park better. It was a happy home because it was full of love. I remembered the time I was sick at school and she came to get me. "Let's get you home," she'd said. That home was warm, safe and exactly where I wanted to be. What did it mean now? A shabby place where I used to live with a drunk.

When I was faced with my old front door I freaked out. My neck went clammy and my heart was beating like it does when I do running at school. I kept imagining Dad was lying unconscious inside. His face blue, like it was when I found him. My palms were all sweaty and my pulse was racing. It felt like it was all happening again and the fear swamped me. It reminded me of playing a computer game when you know you're going to die and you can't stop it – only the sensation was a million times worse. To calm myself down I had to use some of the breathing exercises Maggie had taught me in our mini yoga sessions after school. I took a steadying breath and put the key in the lock. I'd have a quick check and then I'd go. I pushed on the door. It opened a crack. I sniffed the air. It didn't smell great but I couldn't smell vomit, so I went in.

'Dad?' There was no reply. I stood in the hall and looked around. The kitchen was a mess again. Plates were piled up in the sink and on the table. The cushions were still on the floor where Maggie had left them weeks ago.

There were three empty whisky bottles in the living room but no sign of Dad. I went upstairs. His bedroom door was shut. I got the few things of mine that I wanted and shoved them into my bag. I stopped outside his bedroom door and listened. Nothing. What if he was dead in there? If it happened again? If he choked and I wasn't there, he'd die. And it would be my fault. I could feel the panic rising again. I rushed to open the bedroom door. 'Dad!' I almost fell into the room.

'Holy crap!' Dad sat bolt upright. 'Bloody hell, Tom!' He looked awful. His hair was a mess; his eyes were dark and sunken against his deathly pale skin.

I was furious. I'd wound myself up into a frenzy. 'I thought you'd done it again! What's wrong with you?' I banged my fists down on the bed but the duvet cushioned them and it did little to release the tension that had built up inside me.

'I was asleep.'

'I thought you were dead. I thought you'd choked!' I couldn't stop the tears that streamed down my face. Partly relief but a whole lot of temper was coursing through me. How could he be like this? Where had my dad gone? I slumped to the floor and clutched at the duvet. I wanted my mum. I needed her. More than I ever had before. I hugged the duvet as if it were her. I wished it was. I needed to feel her hold me. To make me feel safe again. To sort everything out. But she wasn't coming. She was gone and she'd taken so much with her. It was like I was finding more and more things missing from my life. I'd lost my mother but I'd also lost my friend, my safe space, the person who comforted me and, worst of all, the feeling of being loved. I sobbed and I didn't care. I cried for her as well as for the mess my life had become without her.

'Tom?' His voice had softened dramatically. I couldn't speak. I felt him move down the bed and come and sit on the end by me. He put his hand on my head.

I lurched away. 'Get away from me!' I shouted at him through the sobs. 'You've ruined everything. You should have been there for Mum. You weren't there and she died. You should have been there. You could have saved her. This is all your fault.' I scrambled to my feet. My head was pounding and tears dripped off my chin. 'She's dead and it's *all* your fault!'

'Tom?' His face crumpled like he was going to cry too. 'Why are you being like this?'

It took a few breaths. I stopped shouting and stared at him. He was sitting on the end of the bed in a dirty T-shirt and old pants. I was calmer but my breathing was still erratic. 'I hate you.' I said it clearly and firmly so he knew I meant it.

'Tom?' I turned away from him and walked out, picking up my bag I'd dropped on the landing. I almost fell down the stairs in my rush to escape. I slammed the door as I left and went to get the bus back to Maggie's.

*

I had a key and I let myself in. I clicked Maggie's front door shut behind me. Something was cooking and it smelled good. I left my bag by the door, kicked off my shoes and went into the living room. Maggie wasn't there but I sat on the rug and crossed my legs anyway.

'Tom!' she called from the back of the house. I heard her footsteps approach. 'You're late. Is everything…' She didn't finish the sentence. I think she knew. Maggie came and joined me on the rug and started going through a few exercises. She spoke in that gentle lulling voice she always used for yoga. I tried to focus on her voice. I wanted to rub away the pain that was gnawing at my insides. I hated Dad for everything. He'd ruined it all and yet I felt like the worst person for telling him.

Maggie stopped speaking. I opened my eyes. Everything was blurring because of the tears. I couldn't stop them. Maggie was kneeling in front of me with her arms open wide. It wasn't a yoga position I recognised. I frowned at her.

'There's a hug here if you need it.'

I didn't need to think. I almost knocked her over as I dived forward. She wrapped her arms around me and held me tight. And I cried and cried. The more I sobbed the tighter she held me. I clung to her like a bear to a tree. So many tears. I couldn't stop them but I didn't care. I knew it wouldn't matter to Maggie; she never judged.

I don't know how long she held me, rocking me gently and humming. If I'd thought about it we must have looked like a pair of crazies but it was the nicest thing. Being held and comforted by someone. Someone who cared. I can't remember the last time anyone hugged me like that. I mean

Mum did but I can't remember the actual last time. I wish I could. If I'd known it was the last time with Mum I would have made an effort to remember it. To hold on to it. Save it as an image in my mind for me to return to whenever I needed. Maybe I'd save this hug instead.

Eventually I sat up and rubbed my wet face. 'Maggie…' I didn't know what to say. It was all a bit awkward once the tears had dried up.

She got up and stretched out her legs. 'I know it's a weeknight but I think we need pudding. How about jam roly-poly?'

Somehow she managed to make me laugh. 'Yeah. Great… and… thanks.'

'Anytime,' she said, wiping a tear off my chin as she passed.

We didn't mention the hug again but it was enough to know it was there if I needed it. We chatted over sausage casserole with heaps of creamy mash and loads of vegetables.

'How prepared do you feel for your exams?' Maggie asked, her eyes awaiting my response.

'Okay.' I shoved some food in but Maggie was after more.

'The revision is working then?' she asked.

I finished my mouthful. 'Yeah. It is. The flash-card approach that Farah showed me helps.'

'But it's you who's putting the effort in.' She looked stern but she was only trying to give me the credit. I'd been revising every evening and on the bus both ways as well as at school. I think it was starting to add up.

'Perhaps we could offer revision sessions at the library,' she said, watching me for a response.

'Maybe.'

'What else would be useful to kids your age? What things do they talk about in school?'

I scrunched up my face as I thought about the people in my year. Most of what was said was unrepeatable. 'The girls go on about revision timetables because they like to revise together. The boys don't. They chat about gaming and football.' She was waiting, so I had another think. 'Everyone is talking about what university they want to go to.'

'Hah!' said Maggie making me blink. 'That's a good one. We could look up information about which are the top universities. Best courses and top tips.'

I shrugged. 'I guess but they can find that online.'

'All in one place?'

'I dunno.' Maybe she had something. 'I think the girls would defo be interested.'

'And you should too,' she said. 'In fact, we need to do some research about which courses and universities you want to apply to. I could meet you at the library one day after school. Kill two birds with one stone.'

'If you like.' I don't know why I was being all casual because it was a good idea and I did need to start thinking about it. I knew what was stopping me. 'I need to get the grades in my GCSEs first or it's a waste of time.'

'You need to think positively, Tom. And if you're worried looking up universities will jinx things then tell yourself you're doing it for the library.'

'Do you really think they'll close down the library?'

'I'm afraid they will if they get half a chance. It's all about saving money short-term. Nobody looks to the future.'

I liked talking to Maggie. I didn't have to think first before I said something. With Dad it was easy to say the wrong thing and most of the time he didn't listen anyway. With Farah I had to vet everything first in case I made myself look like an idiot. But not with Maggie.

The jam roly-poly was awesome. I don't think I've ever had it before. Not that I can remember anyway. It was basically rolled up cake with custard on and I chugged it down. Dad and I don't usually do pudding unless there's ice cream on offer at the supermarket – he used to buy us that for a treat sometimes. Not recently though.

'You're a great cook, Maggie.' Dad said I was a bottomless pit but Maggie had filled me up. I felt loads better.

'Thanks,' she said. 'It's nice to have more than just me to cook for. Seems much less effort somehow. Never feels worth it for one person.'

'Your son was lucky growing up here.' It was a throwaway comment. A thought that popped into my head and straight out of my mouth but I knew the moment I'd said it that I'd said something wrong. Maggie went rigid like she'd walked into glass. She didn't say anything so I did. 'What's his name?'

There was something about her eyes that told me this was painful to discuss. I wondered why because she had his baby photo up in the other room so they couldn't have fallen out.

'River,' she said, at last.

I think I need to learn to control my automatic expressions. But it was hard not to react to a name like that.

Poor kid. Poor bloke. 'That's a bit unusual.' I was going for diplomatic but I think my grin betrayed me.

'It was the Sixties.'

'Right. The hippie thing,' I said. Then corrected myself. 'The flower thing.'

She sighed as if drifting away. 'It was a different time. A different me.'

There was something about her expression that bothered me. 'Does he visit much?'

'He can't,' she said. Her eyes fixed on mine. I recognised her expression now. Like seeing my own face reflected back at me. The look in her eyes was loss. Shit, she'd also lost someone close to her. Now I got why she understood how I felt about stuff. She'd been through it too.

'I'm sorry,' I said. It didn't feel like enough. There should be better words than sorry for when someone has been wrenched from your life.

She blinked and looked away. 'It's…' She fell silent.

I picked up the pudding bowls and stood up. I paused at her shoulder. 'I'm here too if you ever need a hug.' She looked up at me and smiled, her eyes brimming with tears. 'Anytime,' I said and took the dishes to the sink.

26

MAGGIE

Maggie didn't like deceiving Tom. He didn't deserve it. But she wasn't ready to tell anyone about her son. She doubted that she ever would be ready. It meant first facing her own demons and they were well buried with skyscrapers built upon them to ensure they could never rise. Although they did. Now like never before. All the things she did for Tom, all the care she showed him reminded her of what her son had missed out on. Of all the things she should have done. The more time she spent with Tom the more it was dwelling on her mind.

Maggie made two packed lunches – one for Tom and one for her.

'Here you go,' she said handing him his as he picked up his schoolbag. He'd been quiet over breakfast and she knew why. 'Good luck with your exam. It's the first one today, isn't it?'

Tom looked a little choked up and he swallowed hard. 'You remembered.'

'Of course. Now stay calm and if your mind goes blank do some of the yoga breathing exercises we've been doing.'

'Yeah, that won't get me beaten up.'

'I don't mean in a yoga pose, just sitting at your desk.'

He laughed and looked slightly less glum as he left.

She stuck her lunch into a bag with a flask of tea, hung it over the handlebar and set off on the quad bike. She loved being busy. It gave her such a buzz to have multiple things that needed her attention. Much better than conjuring up tasks for the sake of it.

Despite it being May it was a cloudy day with a keen wind whipping up the hill as she belted along the ridge. Since Tom had come into her life she'd been neglecting the woodland. It wasn't huge but it was something she cared about and the habitat it provided for local wildlife was essential. Each year she did a bit to keep it under control as it had run wild for many years. She'd found out about woodland management and a while ago had drawn up a five-year plan. It had taken her a couple of days to produce it, which had been a welcome distraction in her life at the time.

Bats, dormice and squirrels all made the woodland their home and many fungi and wildflowers thrived there. The deer and a number of birds were passing visitors who had a vested interest in it. There was a fascinating mix of trees, which puzzled Maggie. She loved the giant oaks that were dotted along the far edge as if they'd been planted as a border. There were other smaller oaks that had taken root naturally but too close to them and she was gradually felling them but it was hard work. There were clumps of elm, plenty of silver birch and a sprinkling of poplar, sycamore and hazel.

Maggie thought she caught a glimpse of a fox. She stood up on the quad bike for a better look but didn't slow it down by much. She didn't spot the blown-down tree branch, until it was too late. She twisted the handlebars but still hit the branch and the tyre burst. The bike halted almost instantly but Maggie didn't – the force propelling her off the bike at an odd angle. She landed badly on her left side, knocking the wind out of her.

The quad bike tipped onto its side and slid majestically down the slope. Slowing to a stop at the bottom in a nettle patch. Maggie waited. Pain blossomed along her left side. She took a moment to assess specifically where it hurt. Her ankle and her ribs. She tried to push herself upright but a sharp pain stopped her. A quick look around reminded her she was about as far from the farmhouse as she could be and still be on her own land. She craned her neck. The woodland sat between her and Savage's fields. The odds of him being in any of those within shouting distance were minuscule.

Maggie puffed out a breath. 'Bugger,' she said.

Injuring herself was a constant worry. Not the injury itself but the slow painful death that would likely follow because how long would it be before anyone missed her? Thank goodness Tom was staying with her. Although it was hours before he was due in from school.

She tried to stand but it was too painful. Her ankle had swollen and couldn't bear any weight. The pain in her side wouldn't allow her to hop either. She looked about her. A cluster of hazels was nearby, offering a little shade, so she set about wriggling her way across the path towards them, taking time every now and then to stop and catch her breath.

It took a while but she literally had all day. Once settled up against the trunk of the nearest hazel she made herself a fern bed to sit on in an attempt to save her backside from the damp woodland floor.

She shouted for help a few times. Some birds halted their calls momentarily but when she was done shouting they resumed. A soft pitter-patter of rain on leaves told her she'd not picked the best day for incapacitating herself – although when was a good day for that? Maggie used her good leg and both hands to drag over small sticks and branches, which she fashioned into a pile to rest her ankle on, raising it slightly.

Her lunch had gone down the slope with the quad bike, which was an inconvenience. There was little in the woodland this time of year that was edible. She watched the sun make its way across the sky as the hours drifted past her. It gave her time to think. And however hard she tried not to, her thoughts kept returning to her son, River. The memories were hazy, whittled away by time. And yet fleeting moments were concrete in her mind – him reaching for her, his giggle and those long eyelashes.

The rain picked up its pace and the wind whistled along the ridge. Maggie moved her fern bed around to the other side of the tree to try to avoid the worst of it. When the shivering started she knew she was in trouble. Having come out in a thin shirt, because she was planning on working up a sweat, she was wet through and icy cold.

From the position of the sun she knew time was creeping towards the evening and she began to worry. Perhaps Tom had gone to a friend's after school? He'd talked about revising with Farah again but he'd seemed too shy to ask the girl. Maybe he'd plucked up the courage. Perhaps his father had come to the school and insisted he return home – that was a scenario she had played out in her mind a number of times. She tried again to get up but she feared the ankle was going to give way and she'd end up in a worse pickle. For now all she could do was wait.

She was proud of herself for fashioning a leaf into a drinking vessel and managed to catch a thimble full of rainwater to drink. It didn't help her thirst but it briefly took her mind off the shivering. Every couple of minutes she patted herself down to keep the circulation going and to try to keep herself warm. She called out a few more times but there was no reply.

It was looking more and more likely that for whatever reason Tom wasn't coming back. She needed to get inside. Maggie scolded herself for not trying to get to the farmhouse sooner. It was going to take an age and the light was fading. She could try crawling but her dodgy knee would complain too much instead she settled for shuffling on her bum. She reluctantly left her fern bed and began to make her way back to the path. The rain had reduced to an annoying drizzle and she was grateful for it. She got a rhythm going – moving her hands behind her, lifting herself up and then pushing back with her good foot. It took a huge effort to move a few inches at a time.

She heard something on the breeze and she paused. Someone was calling. 'Help!' she hollered, but the pain in her side clipped her shout.

'Maggie!' Tom's desperate voice reached her. Joy coursed through her and for a moment the shivering abated.

'I'm here!' she called.

She heard his thumping feet pounding the ground behind her as he ran towards her. 'Maggie!'

She slapped a smile on her face. She didn't want to worry him. Poor lad had been worried enough of late.

'Hello,' she said, like she were meeting him in a tea shop, as he skidded to a halt next to her. She must have looked a fright.

'What the hell?' His eyes scanned her from head to toe and then fixed on her puffed-up ankle. She'd never felt quite so old and frail and she loathed it.

'Bloody quad bike tyre popped and it threw me off.'

'Where's the bike?' He stood up and looked about. The bike was barely visible at the bottom of the slope. 'Bloody hell! Did you fall down there?'

'No. I jumped off before it toppled. Can you help me up? My bum's gone numb.'

He shook his head. 'What hurts?'

'Left ankle and ribs but…' Before she could add anything else to the list Tom had crouched down and lifted her to her feet.

'Whoa! Ow!'

'You all right?' he asked, keeping her upright as she found her balance.

'Been better,' she said, choked by the care he was showing her.

'You're frozen,' said Tom. 'Put your arm around my neck and it'll be like the three-legged race.'

They both started to laugh and it seemed to propel them back to the farmhouse. The laughter dulled the pain of each step and Tom took her mind off it by updating her on his day.

Inside Maggie soon found herself wrapped in towels and hugging a mug of tea although the shivering hadn't stopped. She was overwhelmed by Tom's kindness. He'd got her settled, dug out some paracetamol, and now he was trying to get the fire going.

'Don't chuck the kindling in. Layer it up like that silly toppling-over game the kids play.'

'Jenga?'

'That's the one. Like that but with some gaps in. Ball up some newspaper and scatter it around and about too.'

'Yes, boss,' he said, with a salute. She liked how he'd got cheeky with her. The shy boy was almost a thing of the past, at least in her company. 'You sure you shouldn't get someone to look at your ankle tonight?'

'No we'll know in the morning if it's broken or not. The colour and the swelling will tell us that.'

He shook his head at her. 'You're a wise old owl.' He seemed to mutter it to himself as he arranged some logs on top of his Jenga masterpiece.

'And when you've done that please can you bring me the chopping board, a knife and an onion?' she asked. 'I need to get dinner on.'

'I reckon I can chop an onion. It can't be that hard.' Maggie gave him the look that said she knew better.

27

TOM

Maggie isn't a good patient. Patient being the key word – she has no patience with herself at all. It's odd because she's great with me. She takes her time to show me stuff and never loses her temper. But when it comes to herself she's really mean. Her ankle is sprained but she's treating it like it's nothing. She winces every time she moves and I reckon she's cracked a rib or two as well but she brushes it off when I mention it. She's trying to carry on as normal but I won't let her.

I've been at Maggie's for three weeks. I've learned how to iron jeans and T-shirts. It's as dull as. But like Maggie says if I get a job in an office I'll need to be able to iron my shirts so it's a good life skill. I have the radio on while I do the ironing. Maggie's never listened to Radio One she keeps going on about Radio Caroline and some pirate ship. When I get in from school she's changed it to Radio Two. I tut and shake my head but some of the stuff they play is all right.

She's taught me how to make spaghetti Bolognese. She

says it's basic but it's well nice. I think I'll probably live on it when I go to university. As well as pizza – I'll eat that too. Anything as long as it's not fish fingers.

I was in the school library revising English on my own when a text beeped and made me jump. It was Dad.

Hi, Are you in school today? Can we meet afterwards?

I'd not heard from him since I'd said I hated him and walked out in tears. I was embarrassed about it now. I didn't reply to his message. School finished ten minutes ago; he didn't even know that. It made me cross just thinking about my dad. I tried to carry on revising for my English exam but I couldn't concentrate because of Dad's text. Eventually I gave up on *The Tempest* and packed my stuff up. I wandered out of school, keeping an eye out for Kemp. I'd not seen much of him. Someone said he'd been grounded for turning up late to an exam but I don't know if that's true. Maggie has shown me a few defensive judo moves but it's tricky since she sprained her ankle and I don't know enough to stop him kicking the crap out of me.

I strolled out of the gates.

'Tom?' I turned to see Dad standing there. He looked worried, his shoulders hunched and his hands shoved in his trouser pockets.

I thought about stropping off but I'd have had to walk back for the bus.

'What do you want, Dad?' I adjusted my bag on my shoulder.

'I just wanted to talk… I've missed you. It's quiet at home without you.' His voice was subdued but not slurred, which was good.

Was I meant to say I'd missed him too? Had I missed him? Kind of. Not as much as I should have though. I didn't miss the stress or the constant worry of how I'd find him. I didn't miss the bloody fish fingers.

We looked at each other. I didn't know what to say. 'I'm listening.'

'I'm getting some help… for the drinking.' He didn't look at me as he said it. He was talking to his trainers. 'The doctor has signed me off work for a bit. I'll still get paid.' That was all he worried about. I shook my head. He faltered. 'It's not easy you know.' His voice was back to normal. Making me feel this was somehow my fault.

'I didn't say it was. It's not been easy for me either.'

He held his hands up in surrender. 'Sure.' There was a long awkward pause. 'I'm joining a group.'

'Little Mix?' I asked, surprised at my own attempt at humour in this situation.

Dad didn't seem to get it. 'Dunno. I've not been along yet. It's a local group for recovering alcoholics.'

'Isn't it a bit early for that?' It hadn't been long since there were three empty whisky bottles in the house. At what point did you stop being a drunk and start being a recovering one?

'I've got a counsellor too.'

'Great.' I know I sounded sarcastic but Dad seemed to

be acting like everything had changed and until I saw it for myself nothing had.

'I told Mr Gill you were looking after your gran so he's covering your paper round.'

'Thanks.' I briefly made eye contact.

'Have you been all right with…'

I waited to see if he'd fill in her name. I was insulted that he couldn't remember. 'Maggie. The seventy-two-year-old lady you almost knocked out!' I was getting cross. I unclenched my fist and focused on my breathing.

He seemed a little startled by my words. 'I'm sorry. I don't remember, son.'

'I do.' I was glaring so hard it made a muscle by my eye twitch.

He rubbed his hand over his chin. He'd shaved. 'She's looking after you all right.' It wasn't a question; he was looking me over. I'd had my hair cut, my clothes were ironed and Maggie had taken the hem down on my school trousers.

'I should get going.' In an odd way I'd liked Maggie hurting her ankle. It had given me a chance to do stuff for her. She'd done loads for me, and she had no obligation to do any of it. Dad, on the other hand, was meant to take care of me and he'd lost the plot.

'You'll soon be done with this place.' He pointed at the school behind me.

I turned to look; I don't know why. I'd seen it a million times before. Every weekday morning for the last five years. It was grey and uninspiring but I wasn't ready to leave. I looked back at Dad nodding away. He didn't get it. He'd never get it. 'Bye, Dad.' I strolled past him.

He gripped my shoulder and I stopped but didn't look up. 'I want you to come home, Tom.' I shrugged my shoulder out of his grip. 'When you're ready,' he added.

I didn't answer. I walked to the bus stop and put my earbuds in. I didn't want to hear any more and I didn't want to have to think about going back to live with Dad.

Maggie was manic when I got in. She'd been baking for the library sit-in. Goodness knows how many people she thought were coming but it looked good for my lunch for the rest of the week. I made her sit down while I made dinner. It was stir-fry and it was easy. Well, most things are if Maggie is giving me instructions and explaining it. I quite like cooking. Not as much as I like eating but that's kind of like the prize for having cooked. I've eaten things here that I'd have turned my nose up to at home but it's all been tasty.

Maggie chewed a mouthful with her eyes closed. She does this quite regularly. It's part of her meditation technique. It makes you focus on what you're eating. I used to bolt my food down but now I do the slow-eating thing too although not as obviously. You really get to taste the flavours. Maggie says it's the difference between taking on fuel and enjoying a meal.

'Very good, Tom. You've cooked that a treat. If you like you could add more ginger next time.'

'Dad was at the school gate.' It kinda burst out.

Maggie's eyes snapped open. 'How is he?'

I shook my head and her expression intensified. 'He's all right. He's tidied himself up a bit…'

'That's marvellous.'

'He said he's seen a doc and he's going to quit the booze but I'm not sure he can do it.'

'But that's a start. It's a huge thing for him to even admit he has a problem and then to realise that he needs help. It's a big step for him.' She nodded a lot and I stabbed at some noodles on my plate. 'He's making an effort, Tom. That's a really positive thing.'

'Mmm.'

'We need to make sure we support him,' she said and carried on with her meal. She'd always said my staying here was temporary. Was she thinking good, I'll get rid of him soon?

I was keen to change the subject even though it had been me who had raised it. I totted up the cake boxes – six. 'How many are you expecting tonight?'

'Difficult to say but most of the local businesses have had posters up for a week. We've had flyers in the post office and the pub and we're mini-bussing a few in from the nursing home.'

I laughed. 'Are you allowed to do that?'

'It's not against their will. Some of them don't get out much. Poor old souls spend all their time sitting doing nothing but staring at four walls.'

I didn't like to point out that most wouldn't be much older than her. 'So their trip out is to sit in the library and stare at—'

'Where they can read, chat and eat cake.' She tapped the top of the nearest cake tin.

'Is one of those lemon drizzle?' I could feel my mouth watering at the thought of it.

'It might be. Can you check on the lambs before we go?'

'Sure.' I took the things to the sink. Since Maggie had sprained her ankle I'd had a few more jobs come my way and the lambs was one of them. I didn't say but spending time with the lambs and watching them grow was the best. I'd discovered I liked doing stuff outside – who knew?

May was a changeable month weather-wise but it was still warm as I walked down to the sheep. The grass was lush and pretty much everything around me was green. The view across the fields and down to Furrow's Cross was something I could have looked at for hours. It made me understand why people liked looking at paintings, although I'd probably never totally get that. But with that view it made you want to stare at it. Each time I did I noticed something different. Maybe the way the fence was straight and then went all wobbly for a few sections and then back to straight again. How the trees at the bottom were in clumps of colours – dark greens, light greens and deep purply red. I should ask Maggie what sorts of trees they all are. She'd know for sure.

I reached the lambs. They're allowed in the field with their mothers and the other ewes now and they're hilarious to watch. One minute they're lying down; the next one of them will jump up and race across the field and they all follow. They run flat out until they reach the fence and then they stumble to a stop. I swear they're having races. It's hilarious to watch.

I rattled the gate and they charged towards it and stared at me like I'm the one who's behind a fence. They are so perfect and cute, like cuddly toys. I crouched and reached out to the smallest one, which I'd called Daenerys, and she

28

MAGGIE

Maggie had been fully occupied with plans for the library sit-in all day. But knowing Tom's father was getting help had spun her off course. She was pleased for Tom and relieved for Paul. But she was so very sorry for herself. Tom had no idea but he had changed everything. He had breathed purpose into her mundane life and now she could see that slipping away. The thought of him not walking through the door at five o'clock was like a physical pain in her gut – not dissimilar to her cracked rib, which still twinged from time to time.

They had sat in silence on the bus, both lost in their own thoughts. Today was potentially a big day for the library. Maggie had invited the local press and they'd sounded keen. She had also invited a representative from the council who seemed less so. Christine had rung four times in various stages of meltdown as she was terrified of being dismissed on the spot for aiding and abetting the anti-closure supporters. Maggie had explained countless times that if the library closed she was out of a job anyway but it didn't seem to land with Christine. She simply wasn't a risk taker.

Maggie and Tom walked through the alleyway from the bus stop. Maggie saw the hooded figure up ahead and signalled to Tom, with a quick flick of her hand. It was far too warm to be wearing something like that. Tom was carrying two large bags stacked with cake boxes so there wasn't much he could do. Maggie's ankle was improving gradually. She could walk on it with only a slight limp but it wasn't ready for any serious action.

Maggie was on red alert by the time they drew level with the hooded individual. She did a comedy double take. 'Blimey, Christine. I thought you were the bag snatcher.' Maggie shook her head.

Christine peeped from under her oversized hood. 'I can't risk being identified.' She looked about her agitatedly. 'Here are the keys.' She slipped them into Maggie's hand while scanning the alleyway. 'I'll be back later. But you haven't seen me.'

'Okay,' said Maggie, pressing her lips together to stop her breaking into a grin.

Christine slunk off. 'Come on,' said Maggie and she and Tom opened up and went inside. Farah and Betty soon joined them along with Betty's husband who was one of those people who nodded a lot but never actually spoke. Together they set up the drink and cake station.

Tom put out all the chairs and Farah had made more flyers which she scattered on the seats. 'Have you read *The Guernsey Literary and Potato Peel Pie Society*?' he asked her.

'Wow. That's some title. And no. Any good?'

'Yeah. It's all written in letters. There's stuff about the Second World War and… a bit of a romance.' Tom concentrated on straightening the chairs. 'I thought it might be your sort of read.'

'Sounds it. I'll check it out. Thanks.'

'Do you, um, like lambs at all?' he asked, scratching his head.

'What? To eat?'

'No. You know? To look at. In a field.'

'Umm.'

'I've got lambs,' said Maggie, sweeping past. 'You're welcome anytime to come and see them. Next farm along might even have one you can feed if you fancy it.'

'Oh, I see. Yeah. I'd like that,' said Farah, pushing her hair behind her ear.

'Cool,' said Tom and he went back to adjusting the seating.

The mini bus arrived earlier than planned but given some of the mobility issues it was a good thing as it allowed them to get all the nursing home residents inside and settled with drinks and cake. Alice was very excited to be there and kept telling everyone – repeatedly.

Tom, Farah and Betty set to their allocated task of asking people what they liked to read and recommending something. Farah struggled a bit and kept looking to Tom for suggestions, which he was happy to give. Betty recommended sagas to everyone regardless of what they said they liked.

Before long there was a steady stream of people through the door and the seats filled up quickly. More people arrived and it became difficult to move about, so Tom resorted to passing books around until someone kept hold of one they liked the look of.

'It's like pass the parcel,' said one elderly lady.

'Have you got any erotica,' asked the old man next to her and got a swift elbow in the ribs. Maggie handed him *Fifty Shades of Grey* as she passed and he beamed at her.

When everyone seemed settled, Maggie and the library supporters convened at the cakes. 'No sign of the reporter,' said Maggie running her bottom lip through her teeth. She'd been counting on some press coverage. 'And I don't know if the council representative is here or not.' They all scanned the room.

'What does a council representative look like?' asked Tom.

'Pompous, self-important, hates books,' suggested Maggie, still viewing the crowd.

Farah leaned in. 'Him,' she said, pointing at a balding gentleman at the back. He had a book open at the middle and was watching the people around him. 'There's no way he's read that much already.'

'Good spot,' said Maggie and she zoomed in on the man like a paparazzi lens on a celebrity.

'Uh-oh,' said Tom, watching her go.

'Good evening. Are you from the council?' asked Maggie. The man blinked a few times and then checked his watch. 'You are from the council aren't you?'

'Well. I'm not here officially.'

Maggie narrowed her eyes. 'Why not? Is this not worthy of an official council visit?' She was calm but forceful.

'I don't have the authority to discuss this with you.

Maybe I should go.' He put the book down and looked about as if assessing his best escape route.

'No, you need to stay. Would you like some cake?' Maggie pointed to the refreshments.

'No. I don't—'

'Farah. Could you bring this gentleman a coffee?'

'I really should be—'

'Or tea?' Maggie fixed him with a steely stare.

'Coffee,' he said, looking like he'd been snared.

'And what cake would you like? We have Victoria sponge, coffee and walnut or chocolate fudge left.'

He looked under duress. 'Victoria sponge.'

Maggie looked over her shoulder at Farah and she signalled that she'd got the order with a thumbs up.

'Now. Do you see the level of support we have here?' Maggie splayed her hand out and waved it in a circular motion and the man's eyes followed it. 'This library is the very heart of Compton Mallow. It is essential for the elderly.' She pointed at the nursing home residents and wished two of them hadn't fallen asleep. She quickly moved on. 'Some people don't see anyone from one week to the next apart from at the library. This is a lifeline for those people. It is vital for the young. An early love of reading has been proven to affect an individual's job prospects.' She had no idea if this was accurate but she knew the essence of it was true. 'Those on lower incomes rely on the library for their reading material. To deny them that is to deny them a basic human right. Whatever hurdle you put in our way we'll clear it. Whatever is on your agenda, we'll oppose it. In short this community needs this space and we're prepared to fight for it every step of the way.'

Farah appeared with the coffee and cake. 'Ooh, thank you,' said the man, his eyes widening at the large slice of cake.

Maggie stared at him, awaiting a response to her impassioned speech. He seemed to become suddenly aware of her gaze. 'Oh, I don't know,' he said.

'You don't know what?' asked Maggie, mild irritation obvious in her tone.

'I don't know that anything you do changes the plans.' He munched his cake. 'The closure date is set.'

Maggie was flummoxed. The library door opened and in walked a scruffy-looking man with hair that was once a comb-over but was now more like a cockerel's comb. He flattened it down. 'Press,' he said, checking three pockets before pulling out a credit-card-sized badge.

'Excellent!' said Maggie. 'Come and meet Mr…' She turned back to the man from the council who was looking more than uncomfortable.

'Tilley but I'm not here in an official capacity.'

'Mr Tilley is a council representative and I think it's fair to say he's surprised by the level of community support shown here this evening…' began Maggie. The reporter whipped out a notebook and started to scribble as the colour drained from Mr Tilley's face.

Maggie was thrilled with the success of the sit-in. She and Tom celebrated back at Providence Farm with cocoa and some leftover cake. The reporter had sensed a scoop and talked of tentative interest from the nationals. She suspected he'd hoped for interest from the nationals his whole career.

He'd taken photographs of the library, one of the protesters, and one of a startled-looking Mr Tilley, who kept repeating that they needed to refer to the council press office and website. She hadn't liked his insistence that the date was set for the library to close. She would challenge the council on that by phone tomorrow. But it wasn't enough; she needed to do more – a lot more.

'Do you think tonight did any good?' asked Tom.

Maggie pondered the question, scrunching up her eyes as she thought. 'I truly hope so. It was a good turnout, which was a relief. I just wish those people had used the library in the first place, then we wouldn't have to do all this.'

'That council bloke didn't seem hopeful though.'

'No, but people like that think their process is king and can't bear the thought of someone scuppering their plans. I think they've earmarked the building for something. Probably got a dodgy deal already in the offing. Bent buggers the lot of them.' She seemed to be talking more to herself than Tom.

'Your speech was good,' said Tom. 'That reporter seemed impressed with what you said. And I was too. I don't know how you do it. I'd like to be able to say stuff in a way that makes people listen.'

'It comes with age,' she said, wisely.

'I don't want to wait that long.' Maggie raised an eyebrow. 'Sorry, I'm not saying you're ancient or anything.' He flushed crimson.

'I know what you mean. You're a good lad,' she said briefly patting his forearm. 'Thanks for all you've done over the last few days. I really do appreciate it.'

'Do you still miss your son?' Tom's eyes were searching.

'Every day,' she said and he nodded his understanding. 'Losing someone special is like being given the perfect gift only to have it whisked away from you.'

Tom gave her a weak smile and turned to look out of the window.

Now that Paul seemed to be sorting himself out it wouldn't be long before Tom returned home and got on with his life. Saying goodbye to Tom, as she knew she must, would be almost as hard as saying goodbye to River, all those years ago. She knew now exactly what she had missed out on and it had been far more than even she had imagined. Watching the small changes in Tom, seeing him grow in confidence and simply spending time with him was a privilege and one she wished she'd been able to experience with River. She made a pledge to herself that she would find something to fill the void that Tom would leave but what or whom that would be she wasn't sure.

29

TOM

I know I did crap in my French reading exam. My mind went completely blank. I think I panicked a bit because my palms went sweaty and my heart went all thumpy. I had to do a bit of meditating to calm myself down. The invigilator came over to check on me and everybody looked, which did not help at all. But after a few minutes I was okay. Maggie had said all I can do is my best and she's right, so I looked at the words and they were kind of familiar but not enough that I could translate it completely. Instead I picked out the words I did know and made a few guesses.

I've never liked French. It's not like I'm going to visit France anytime soon. I might one day, when I've got a good job. Then I'd like to travel. I like the idea of a villa with its own pool. I've seen them on the adverts and they look impressive. I've never been on a plane. That's not strictly true. I did once go somewhere with Mum and Dad that had planes in a hangar and you could sit in them for a photo but that's not like getting on one to go on holiday. I don't remember where it was. That trip was when Mum's bump was huge, which couldn't have been long before she died. I wish I could remember more about it. I wish I wasn't forgetting her.

I know kids in my year who go on two foreign holidays a year. Two! And they talk about it like it's completely normal. This kid, Malachy, his parents have a holiday home in Spain and sometimes he goes just for the weekend – how mad is that? I even heard him moaning about it once because he was missing go-carting. I'd have liked to have had that call to make – go-carting or Spain? Actually it *was* a tough decision but I would definitely choose Spain.

Dad wasn't waiting for me after school. I'm more cautious now. I have a good check out of the window before I leave. I'm not sure how we've left things, me and Dad. It's all awkward like we're strangers but we're the only family we each have. Maggie said I should go and see him and give him some encouragement with the quitting the booze thing. I know she's right but I'm in the middle of my exams and I don't see him encouraging me. I said I might go after school on Friday. Maybe.

Maggie was back to the yoga. She reckoned it was helping her heal, and she was in a lotus headstand when I walked in. I sat down opposite her and crossed my legs. I can do that easily now – I'm getting more flexible. I think my arms are a bit more muscly because I chop the wood and carry the water buckets down to the animals. Not the same as if I'd been to the gym or anything but not as weedy as they were before.

'How was French?' she asked, her eyes popping open for a second but she held the pose.

'Cr... Rubbish.' I don't like swearing in front of her. It seems disrespectful. She's never said I can't or anything and she swears but somehow it feels wrong.

'Well, you don't need French for your A levels. So forget about it now. You can't do any more on that one.' Maggie had helped me work out what to focus on. She'd basically asked me what I was best at and what subjects I wanted to do at A level. Turns out they're the same thing. For my GCSEs I'm concentrating on English and maths because I have to have those plus my A level subjects: English literature, history and chemistry. Maggie thinks it's a good mix. 'What's next?' she asked.

'English lit.'

'Ah. Is that what Farah's coming round on Sunday to study?'

'Yeah.' I'm really looking forward to Farah coming over. I can't wait to show her the lambs.

'She's a lovely girl.'

'Yeah.'

Maggie's lips are curling at the edges like she's trying hard not to smile but can't stop herself. It looks weird when someone smiles and they're upside down. 'You like her don't you?'

'Yeah.' I smiled at my own limited vocabulary and at the thought of Farah. 'She's awesome.'

'You've got a good friend there,' said Maggie, and I felt the smile melt from my face. Friend. She was right. Farah was my friend but I didn't want it to stop there.

When I came down for breakfast on Friday morning the

kitchen smelled like heaven. Or at least what my heaven would smell like – cake with a hint of bacon. Not bacon cake – that would be gross. Maggie was grilling bacon and she had not long taken a cake out of the oven. I went over to investigate and have a better sniff.

'Hands off,' said Maggie, shooing me away from the cake and moving the bacon onto plates already laden with fluffy scrambled eggs. 'That cake's for your dad.'

'Why?' I took my plate from Maggie and joined her at the table.

'You said you were calling in on him after school and I thought he might like a lemon drizzle cake. And there's extra money for the bus to save you walking like last time.' She pushed a five-pound note across the table.

'I said I *might* call in.' I ran a finger over the money but didn't pick it up.

'Oh, well. It's up to you. The cake's there if you want to take it.' There was never any pressure from Maggie although she did know how to make me think about stuff. She'd gone to the trouble of making a cake, and getting the bus would be way easier than walking. I guess I could drop it round. I'd think about it. I took the money and shoved it in my trouser pocket and I could see her twitching a smile.

'Thanks for making the cake. I don't know if it'll survive a whole day in my bag.' I knew I wouldn't be able to resist picking bits off it. It would likely be a mass of crumbs by the time I got to Dad's, assuming I went at all.

'I made two. There's a good-sized slice with your packed lunch.' She knew me so well. 'I'm thinking of cooking lamb on Sunday.' She said it all casual and I dropped my knife in shock. It clattered against my plate.

'Which one?' I could barely squeak the words out.

Maggie started to laugh and I had to wait for her to catch her breath. It was horrible. I loved all the lambs. I could picture one of them being turned on a big spit over a fire like they used to do in Tudor times. I felt a bit sick.

'Not one of our lambs you daft ha'p'orth.' She was still chuckling. 'They're far too small. I've got some in the freezer. I'll roast a nice leg. All right?'

All right? I wasn't sure that I was. For the first time in my life I sort of wanted to be a vegetarian. I took a breath, looked back at the crispy bacon on my plate. I breathed in the smell. I picked my knife and fork back up and the thought of becoming a vegetarian vanished.

The curtains were open when I walked up the path at Dad's. I got my key out but the images of him unconscious rushed into my mind. I put the key away and knocked instead. We did have a doorbell but the batteries had run out ages ago and we hadn't replaced them.

Dad was frowning when he opened the door but it evaporated when he saw me. 'Tom. Great to see you. Come in,' he said, reversing out of the way. 'I'll put the kettle on.'

'I'm not stopping.'

'Oh, right. Well, come in anyway.' He went through to the kitchen. I followed but had a shufti into the living room as I passed. There were no empty bottles that I could see.

He leaned back against the worktop and looked at me. I put my bag down and stared at the floor. This was well weird. I was starting to heat up. The silence filled the room, sucking the air from it.

At last he spoke and I was so relieved. 'I've been to my first AA meeting,' he said. He sounded unsure.

'How was it?'

'Yeah. Okay. I don't know what I was expecting but they were all ordinary people. Nice people. We just chatted and listened. It was a bit strange at first but I'll go again.'

'That's good.' I wanted to ask if he'd stopped drinking but looking at him he seemed different. His skin was a normal colour and the dark rings under his eyes weren't as bad as before. His hair was washed and he was keeping up with the shaving.

'My counsellor suggested you and I have a chat about how you felt… you know. About my drinking.'

I didn't know what to say. I feared if I started to tell him, I'd end up shouting at him. I shrugged instead.

'How did it make you feel, Tom?'

One word shot into my mind. 'Shit.' I think that summed it up quite well.

'Right.' Dad nodded. He was no more equipped for this conversation than I was.

I remembered the cake and it felt like a lifeline. I hurriedly got it out of my bag. It was still intact. Maggie would be proud of me. 'Here. Maggie made it.' I handed it over.

Dad looked at the brown paper package like I'd handed him a hand grenade with no pin. 'Thanks, I guess.'

'You guess?' How rude was that? 'It's lemon drizzle cake.' The words sounded like an accusation. 'It's exactly like Mum used to make.' This was no good. I was getting cross. I was always going to be angry with him. I snatched up my bag. 'I have to go.'

'Why?'

I stopped and looked at him. He was clutching the cake and his face was a mix of sadness and confusion.

'Because there's stuff I have to do. There's lambs, sheep, chickens – they all need taking care of. And Maggie needs me.'

'Sounds like free labour to me.'

I steadied my breathing. 'I want to do it. And I'm staying there for free. So it's all fair.'

He nodded. 'Well, thank her for the cake.' He held it up. I nodded and turned to go. 'When will I see you next, Tom?'

I froze in the doorway. 'I dunno.' And I honestly didn't.

30

MAGGIE

Maggie held the letter in her hand. She'd written and rewritten it many times and still wasn't sure it was right but this felt like a now or never moment. She looked at the gaping mouth of the post box. Once she put it inside that was it. She was triggering something that couldn't be undone. Her hand hovered close to the slot. Could she post it? Should she? Out of the corner of her eye she spotted the local gossip striding her way and Maggie quickly posted the letter, feeling a flutter in her heart as she did so. That was it; there was no going back now.

Maggie walked back up the hill away from Furrow's Cross. She had an instant sense of remorse. Would she regret what she had just done? Or could it be a key turning point in her life? All she could do now was wait and see. It felt like she'd been waiting most of her life. Biding her time for when she had a chance to put things right. But whether she would ever get that opportunity did not rest in her hands.

Maggie was further up the hill when she spotted Tom's

bus and it lifted her mood. She watched Tom get off the bus, his posture giving away his mood as it frequently did. Slouched shoulders was not a good sign.

'Tom!' she called and he twisted in her direction, his features brightening momentarily.

'You all right?' he asked when she reached him.

'I'm fine. How about you?'

He puffed out a breath. 'I went to see Dad. He says thanks for the cake.'

'He's very welcome. And how is he?' she asked as they began the stroll up the track to Providence Farm.

'He's tidied himself up a bit and the house.'

'That's an excellent sign.'

Tom nodded but his pouting lips implied he wasn't that convinced. 'He asked me how I felt about it. His drinking.'

'Did you tell him how you felt?'

'Not really.' He gave a brief glance in her direction.

'And how do you feel, Tom?' she asked.

He lifted his head. 'I hate him when he drinks. I couldn't tell him that.'

'Maybe you should. If it's honestly how it made you feel.'

Tom's eyes widened. 'It's a bit brutal though.'

'Maybe. But if you're both honest with each other I think that's a very good place to start.' Maggie was preparing herself for a similar conversation in the future.

As they neared the house an estate car was coming down the track. The driver waved at Maggie and turned down the side of her house. 'Now what does he want?' said Maggie, under her breath.

'Who is it?' asked Tom.

'Local vet. Nice guy but usually costs me money when

I see him…' She turned her attention to the car's driver. 'Gregory. To what do I owe the pleasure?'

'Fraser Savage has been trying to get hold of you.'

Maggie spotted Savage's dog, Rusty, in the back of the car. 'What's wrong?'

'Difficult labour,' he said getting out of the car and walking around to the other side. 'She's lost a lot of blood. I'm taking her in to the surgery to put her on a drip and keep an eye on her for twenty-four hours.' He opened the passenger door and leaned in.

'Did she have the puppies yet?' asked Tom, peering into the back of the car.

'Only these two survived I'm afraid,' said Gregory, reversing out of the passenger side with a small crate. 'Savage is too busy with the lambs to take care of them so I was taking the pups in too but he was calling you to see if you'd be able to look after—'

'Ye-ah!' said Tom, racing around to join the vet. 'Of course we will. Won't we, Maggie?' His eyes were bigger than a pleading puppy's.

Maggie shook her head. 'They need feeding round the clock. Every four—'

'Two to three hours,' interrupted the vet.

'But that's not a problem.' Tom was already peeling back the jumper that was covering them. 'Oh wow. Maggie, you've got to see these. They're the cutest.' Tom's face was a picture. 'We'll help. Won't we?' There were the puppy dog eyes again.

'We'd need formula and puppy pads,' said Maggie.

'I've got enough formula for one feed in my bag but I can get one of the nurses to pop some more over on her way home tonight. As well as some puppy pads,' said the vet. Maggie pressed her lips together.

'Pleeeease,' said Tom, sounding a lot younger than his years.

It felt like a conspiracy to Maggie. 'Twenty-four hours only.' She pointed at Tom and then the vet, shook her head and went inside, leaving Tom to bring in the puppies and a bundle of things from the vet. She had spent her life trying to avoid getting attached to things and she wasn't about to start now, although looking at Tom she realised perhaps she was making that oath a fraction too late.

It wasn't cold but the puppies needed to be kept warm so Maggie made them a hot water bottle and dug out some old newspapers to put down.

'They need the fire on and something cosy like a blanket to lie on – not that,' said Tom, hugging the crate protectively.

'They're hours old, Tom. I thought a warm hot water bottle might be a bit more like being near their mother.'

'Okay. But newspaper.' He wrinkled his nose.

'All they're going to do is wee and poo and they're not doing it all over any blanket of mine. That old jumper of Savage's will do fine. Let's have a look at them.'

Tom gingerly handed over the crate. The puppies were like miniature versions of Rusty and Mac – one red merle and one black and white, both with pink noses. 'I bet Savage is sorry to have lost the others. They fetch a pretty penny these do.'

'How much?' asked Tom, going almost nose to nose with them.

'About a thousand pounds a pop I think.'

'Wow.' Tom whistled through his teeth and his shoulders

dropped. Maggie had feared he'd been harbouring thoughts of having one. What boy doesn't want a dog of his own?

'Dogs are a huge responsibility and a tie. Food and vet's bills are expensive. And you can't leave them for hours on end. They're a pack animal and they need other dogs or people. They need training and a border collie has to be kept busy and active. They're super intelligent and want a lot of exercise.' Maggie feared Tom's shoulders were drooping further. 'Still, they're your responsibility for the next twenty-four hours.' She handed back the crate.

'What? You're helping though? Right?'

'It's Saturday tomorrow; you've no school. I'm sure you'll be fine,' said Maggie. 'I'll get the dinner on.'

Tom ate his meal on a tray in the sitting room watching the puppies. He was nothing if not dedicated. Maggie saw it as a good opportunity for Tom. She was on hand if there were any issues but having responsibility for something so dependent would likely do him good. He followed the formula instructions meticulously, drew up the required amount into the syringe and promptly squirted half of it over the first pup.

'Crap!' said Tom. Maggie stifled a chuckle.

'You need to hold the puppy still.'

'He's too wriggly,' said Tom, trying to balance the puppy on his knee.

'Here,' said Maggie taking the syringe and refilling it. 'You hold the puppy and I'll show you how to gently squeeze the syringe.'

Tom cupped the black and white wriggling creature

carefully in his hands, his face full of awe as it fed. Tom swapped him for the other one after settling the first back in the jumper. 'I'll hold her. You do the feeding, this time,' instructed Maggie.

This one was a little more lively and whimpered the whole time she was feeding. Maggie suspected she was hungry. The puppy fought for the syringe and kicked her legs about. 'She's a little fighter, this one.' Smaller than the black and white but with beautiful markings, she warmed even Maggie's heart.

'Which would you have?' asked Tom.

'Neither,' said Maggie. 'Too much of a tie.' Although her main concern was that they would outlive her and end up in a rescue somewhere.

Tom screwed his face up. 'Not being funny or anything, but you don't go out much. Wouldn't a dog be good company?' Maggie opened her mouth to respond but Tom kept going. 'And a great burglar deterrent, living out here on your own.'

'I'm the only burglar deterrent I need. Well, me and my air rifle.'

Tom looked despondent. He kept the puppy on his lap and she fell asleep as he stroked her. 'I'd have this one. I've never seen a dog this colour before. Apart from her mum.'

'It is lovely, I agree.' Maggie would at least concede that.

Tom did a great job of feeding the puppies through the night and although Maggie was awake and listening out he didn't call for her help. She was proud of him for coping on his own. He cleared up their mess the next morning and put Savage's jumper in the washing machine without having to be told. They had a difficult discussion about him going to the library as he didn't want to be away from the puppies but as he'd promised Farah he'd be there for her first reading session, he couldn't let her down.

Maggie had reluctantly agreed to be temporary puppy nursemaid on the understanding he was only missing for one feed. It had been months since Maggie had missed a book club. It had been an important part of her week for such a long time and while she didn't like missing it she wasn't bereft. Tom was going to book club and would put her thoughts across as well as his own – or at least he had pledged to. She'd enjoyed the book and suspected most of the others would have too, which made for the least engaging kind of session.

Tom came rushing in a few hours after he'd left, bypassed Maggie and went straight to the puppies.

'Hi, Tom,' she said but got no reply so she continued the conversation on her own. 'Hi, Maggie. How did the puppy-sitting go? Okay, thanks…'

'Did you feed them?' asked Tom, marching into the kitchen.

'Yes. Savage rang. Gregory is bringing Rusty back after surgery closes tonight. She's doing fine.'

He pushed his hands deep into his jeans pockets. 'They'll be going back then?' His face was so glum.

'Actually. As Savage is busy right now and Mac is a bit boisterous I offered for Rusty to stay here for a few days.'

Tom almost fell over his own feet as he dashed forward and hugged Maggie. The spontaneous action caught her off guard and she swallowed hard. 'A few days,' she repeated, trying to keep the emotion out of her words. He let go and straightened himself out, looking suddenly self-conscious.

'Thanks, Maggie. You're the best.'

'Well that's as may be. Now fill me in on book group and all the library gossip. I'm desperate for an update on Audrey's swollen ankles.'

Tom made drinks and they adjourned to the sitting room where the puppies were wriggling around and getting ready for their next feed. 'Farah was awesome,' said Tom. His eyes fixed on the puppies. 'There were like eight kids and to start with they were all hyper and running around and stuff. But Farah kept telling them she knew a real fairy and a real dragon and if they sat down she'd tell them stories about them. Then she read this kids' story and she did the voices and stuff. The children loved it. I think the council bloke was impressed too.'

'Which council bloke, I mean, man?' asked Maggie.

'Not the one from before. This was someone Christine knew. Christine was in like proper meltdown mode. She didn't know he was coming. She wasn't that pleased that you weren't there for book club…' He cocked an eyebrow.

'And whose fault was that?' She pointed a finger at Tom and the puppies in turn.

'I said you had an emergency but there were ten people for book club so it was fine.' Tom picked up the red merle puppy and gently stroked her head.

'You mean they didn't miss me?'

'I didn't say that.'

'Anyway, this council person. Did you speak to him?'

'Yeah. I didn't want to, like, but Christine introduced me. I think she was trying to get the heat off her. I told him about the silver surfer classes and he asked if I'd do that at the library in town.'

'And what did you say?' Maggie leaned forward in her seat.

'I said he could do one.' Maggie tilted her head in a disbelieving fashion. 'All right. I said the village library was my priority until its future was secured.'

Maggie's mouth actually fell open. 'Well, that was the perfect thing to say, Tom.'

'Yeah. I thought so too.'

He really was full of surprises.

31

TOM

I didn't sleep that well on Saturday night. I kept coming down to check on Rusty and the puppies who were totally fine. Although the little brown spotted one kept blending in with Rusty's fur and I panicked because I thought she'd escaped. I ended up sleeping on the sofa, but I didn't mind. I could stare at those dogs for hours. Actually I did stare at them for hours. Who needs TV when you've got puppies?

Once I heard Maggie was awake I went and had a shower and put my best top on and clean jeans because Farah was coming for Sunday lunch. I know Maggie noticed because she smirked as I came in the kitchen. She thinks I fancy Farah, which I do. Who wouldn't? But I've been doing some serious thinking over the last few days. Maggie was right when she said Farah was a good friend. Maggie is usually right about most things.

Farah's dad dropped her off and he and Maggie had a chat at the door about the library and agreed that Farah would call on Maggie's phone when she was ready to be picked up. I took Farah on a guided tour of the farm. She'd brought her own wellies – pastel stripes. They were like the cutest boots ever. Her feet are tiny. I'd never noticed before.

'I'll be back in a sec,' I told her and I jogged off to the barn. She was looking at the view when I rode the quad bike across the yard and she turned around. I could see she was well impressed. Her mouth actually dropped open and she squealed. I knew exactly how she felt, I'd felt the same when Maggie had driven it out that first time. Farah got on and I gave her the tour of the land. She asked loads of questions and was seriously interested about Maggie's self-sustaining lifestyle – those were Farah's words not mine.

I stopped by the henhouse. 'Do you like eggs?'

'Yeah.'

I handed her the wicker basket. 'Then let's get you some fresh ones.'

I loved how much Farah was grinning. It reminded me how much I adored it at Maggie's. I opened one of the hatches on the henhouse and a chicken was sitting there roosting, which made the chicken cluck and Farah jumped backwards. It was real funny.

'How are things with your dad?' she asked, as we were dodging the chickens.

'All right.' She was watching me closely. 'Well. Not great.'

'You know you can share stuff. I won't blab.' She looked at me and waited.

'Yeah. I know that but…' What was I meant to say?

'I might be able to help. I'd like to if I can.' She was lovely – how could I not tell her?

I took a deep breath. 'He's an alcoholic.'

'Oh, Tom.' She looked shocked.

'He's getting some help now. Hopefully he'll be able to kick the booze.'

'And will you go back home then?'

I chewed my lip. 'I've gotta go back sometime. But look at this place. It's like being on holiday all the time.' I splayed my arms out and spun around. Farah laughed, so I did it some more but then I had to stop because it was making my head spin.

The lambs were on form and did a series of lamb races for her like they were showing off. Daenerys and Tyrion ate grass out of her hand and I swear if bluebirds had come and plaited her hair and squirrels had tied her laces she couldn't have looked more like Snow White. I retold the story of their birth, leaving out my screaming and retching and she looked suitably awed.

'I totally get why you love it here. And Maggie…' She looked back at the house. 'She's off the scale.'

'True dat.' We both nodded our agreement.

We called on Colin whose aggressive attitude I had bigged up but he stood there mildly chewing grass and looking calmer than a kitten. I swear he did it on purpose. At least I could show her the repairs I'd had to do to the gate. I think she believed me.

When we got back Maggie was putting in the Yorkshire puddings. I'd timed it perfectly, saving the best for last. We washed our hands and I took her through to the living room where Rusty came to meet us in the doorway and then went straight back to her pups.

'This is Rusty. She's staying with us for a while because she had a difficult birth. There were six puppies but she lost four.'

'Oh, you poor thing.' Farah knelt next to Rusty; the dog licked her hand and gave a thump of her tail. 'Can I touch the puppies?'

'Sure. Go ahead.'

'What are they called?'

'They don't have names. Do you want to name them?' It wouldn't do any harm. Maggie said they can't even hear until they're two weeks old. Farah beamed a smile back at me. 'The black and white one is a boy and this one's a girl.'

'How about Sheldon and Penny? I love *The Big Bang Theory*. Do you?'

'Oh yeah. I used to watch it, like, all the time.' Possible slight exaggeration but I have seen it. Farah eyed the black and white photo on the table.

'Is that Maggie?'

'Yeah. The baby she's holding, that's her son. He died.'

'That's so sad. How old was he?'

'I dunno. It's not something we've talked about.' There was a long pause where I didn't know what to say and I think Farah felt the same. She was petting the puppies when Maggie called us through for lunch.

Maggie's Sunday roast was ace as usual. Farah asked loads of questions about how she grew her own veg, which Maggie seemed pleased to answer. Apparently, we're eating seasonally – who knew? I don't have anything to do with the allotment or veg patch, as Maggie calls it, but now I think about it she must dig up quite a bit of stuff every week.

Maggie offered us Coke or apple juice and Farah went

into a bit of a speech about how bad Coke is for your teeth so we both had juice. I might cut down on the Coke.

After we'd wolfed down a rhubarb and strawberry crumble, which was without doubt the best crumble on the planet, I cleared the table and brought my schoolbooks down to the kitchen. Farah pulled out the latest iPad – it was my turn to be awed.

Then I remembered. 'Sorry, Farah, there's no Wi-Fi here.' I was a bit gutted.

'It's okay, it's got built-in 4G.'

'Mobile signal sucks too. Although I did once get one bar at the top of the stairs.'

'Can I try?' Farah looked at me.

'Yeah.' I pointed up the stairs like a goon.

The next hour was possibly the best I've ever spent. We sat side by side on the stairs looking up revision stuff on the internet with the occasional divergence into 'something she had to show me' which was generally some YouTuber doing something brainless.

'Right,' said Maggie from the bottom of the stairs. 'Will one of you show me how that tablet thingy works because I fancy getting myself one.'

'Of course,' said Farah. I moved up a step and Maggie took my place. I don't think Maggie realised how mega expensive they are but there was nothing stopping her having a go with Farah's. The three of us stayed sitting on the stairs while Farah walked Maggie through the basics and then handed it to her.

'Try Google Earth. It's brilliant,' I said hitting the app icon.

Maggie typed in her postcode and after three failed

attempts it zoomed in from the whole world to Furrow's Cross.

'Zoom in more, like Farah showed you,' I said. Maggie stabbed a finger at it. 'Two fingers,' I said.

'I'll give the bloody thing two fingers in a minute,' said Maggie, thrusting it back at Farah and we all belly laughed. Maggie left us and we went back to studying.

Farah's phone pinged and we both looked amazed that she'd received a text. We were sitting close enough for me to see who it was from when she pulled the phone out. Josh Kemp. Of all the people. What the hell was he doing texting her?

She fired off a quick reply and put her phone away but I was tense. 'Look, Farah. It's none of my business but Josh Kemp – he's not cool.'

She tipped her head at me. 'Are you warning me off him?'

I held up my hands. 'No way. You go out with whoever you like but…' Something struck me. Farah was way too good for Kemp. 'Actually yeah. I am warning you off him. He's a thug. You deserve way better than him.' The words just fell out.

'What, someone like you do you mean?' She was frowning.

'No. Not like me.' But it didn't matter what I said because the flush of colour to my cheeks was always going to give me away.

Farah didn't reply. She looked furious. She snatched up her things and tore downstairs. I almost fell after her in my panic.

'Farah. Look I'm sorry. I was out of order.'

She ignored me. 'Maggie, please can I ring my dad? I'm ready to go home now.'

Well done, Tom, you've ballsed your life up *again*.

32

MAGGIE

A couple of weeks later the ankle was almost fully mended and Maggie was able to focus more attention on her yoga. She had in mind that her own style of physiotherapy would strengthen her leg and enable her to pick back up her martial arts. And slowly she was building strength, which proved it was working. Tom was keen to learn more martial arts but there was a limit to how much instruction she could give from her armchair.

Tom's yoga had improved. They were meditating together daily and he was catching on with the different poses. His core strength was rubbish, which was odd because most men Maggie knew were adept at sucking their stomachs in, especially if a young female was in the vicinity. Maybe it was a skill that came later in life or with the advent of a paunch?

One evening she had spent hours trying to teach Tom how to do a headstand and after many failed attempts they had eventually achieved a wobbly version but they had laughed a lot on the way. It was lovely to hear him laugh. The first few days after the falling out with Farah he'd been quiet and she'd left the subject alone. Eventually he'd opened up about the quarrel.

It was hard for Maggie not to take sides but she did momentarily try to take an unbiased view. As a woman she could completely understand Farah's stance. On the other hand this Joshua Kemp sounded like a right little toerag and if Farah hadn't spotted this herself then a warning to the wise was to be praised. Sadly Farah had taken umbrage and was ignoring Tom at school and had not been to the library since. Both of these facts troubled Maggie. Tom was short of friends – something they'd had a long discussion about while in the plank pose.

'You'll meet people throughout your life, Tom, and some will become friends but most will not.'

'You must have loads then.'

'No. Not really. I've never been that good at… keeping in touch.' The truth was she always kept her distance. It was a conscious thing and a form of self-preservation but not one she would recommend.

'Aren't the people at book club your friends?' Tom relaxed his muscles and flopped onto his stomach.

'Hmm.' It was a reasonable assumption but while the book club ladies were lovely and a vital source of human contact she didn't know any of them well enough to invite them round for a coffee. 'There's nobody I particularly click with.'

'I know what you mean.' Tom sat up and crossed his legs. 'Sometimes you think you have loads of friends. I did when I was at primary school. I thought all the boys in my class were my friends. And then stuff happened and I realised they weren't friends, they were just boys in my class.' Tom's sad eyes stared unblinking at the window. It was one of the many moments she wished she could erase all of his pain. She came out of the plank and mirrored his position.

'Friends aren't merely the tumbleweed of faces that roll in and out of your life. Friends are the ones you connect with and who last a lifetime. You'll pass a million people on your path and just a few will be worth spending time with.'

'Choose wisely, says Yoda.' Tom gave a huge grin, but what he'd said was spot on.

Saturday morning had been a struggle to tear Tom away from the puppies and onto the bus. The trip to the library would do him good and he had a number of silver surfer sessions booked in so she wasn't going to let him wimp out. If Farah was there then it would also be a good opportunity for them to face each other. In Maggie's experience the sooner issues were tackled the better. Those left alone festered for a long time, sometimes even a lifetime.

'Do you think Penny's okay? I don't think her hearing's as good as Sheldon's.' Tom was looking longingly up the driveway as the bus pulled away.

'I think you're fussing over those pups. They're fine when you're at school all day. Their eyes have just opened and hearing is the last sense to fully develop so their ears are only now starting to work. She'll be fine.'

'Have you thought any more about keeping one?' he asked.

She didn't need to face him to know he was making eyes

bigger than the puppies did. 'I didn't think about it in the first place. I don't need a dog.'

Tom huffed and slumped against the window. Maggie quite liked it when he behaved like a teenager. He'd had to grow up too fast after losing his mum and everything that had happened recently with his dad, so it was good to see him acting his age.

He perked up when the bus pulled into Compton Mallow. His head was on a swivel. She knew who he was looking for, but there was no sign of Farah. Tom slunk inside the library and switched on the PCs.

'Is he all right?' asked Christine.

'Girl trouble. How are you?'

'I've been looking for new jobs.' Christine gave a weak smile.

'But we're fighting for your job here.' Maggie tried hard not to show her frustration.

'I know but I think I need to keep my options open. They're closing two other libraries in the area and both of their staff have already got other jobs.'

'That's playing into the council's hands.' Maggie straightened her shoulders. Sometimes it felt like she was fighting the closure single-handedly.

'Hmm,' was Christine's non-committal response. 'I've not applied yet but I've got all the forms. It's for an administration assistant at a company in town.'

'Right. Well, let's consider that your backup plan. Plan A is to save the library. Yes?'

'Oh, of course. I made more posters this week.'

Heaven preserve us, thought Maggie, as she feigned interest in the bland A4 sheets Christine waved excitedly under her nose. What they needed was something to grab the headlines. The piece in the local press had generated a couple of letters to the editor in support but had soon become lining for cat litter trays all over town, taking the local reporter's hopes of hitting the big time with them. Maggie needed to have a think.

The council had gone very quiet, which worried her. Her suspicious mind had conjured up all kinds of theories but she had no way of investigating if there was any dodgy dealing going on. That would be her prime angle to blow the whole thing open and save the library in the process. But that would only work if there was something juicier than the council trying to save money. She suspected they were simply biding their time until the twelve weeks were up and then they'd swoop in and close them down anyway. Well, not if she still had a breath in her body.

33

TOM

I sort of dipped in and out of the book club meeting. We'd read *Behind Closed Doors* by B A Paris and I'd liked it but it was the bit at the end of the session where people suggested books we should read next that I was interested in. I'd been thinking about it a lot and I wanted to share some of the books I'd enjoyed. It was a bit daunting because the other book club members were all quite opinionated and sometimes they talk over each other.

I had hoped Farah was going to be there but there was no sign of her by the time book club started. She had to come though because she was doing children's reading time, which was getting uber popular.

'Future reading suggestion,' said Betty but she didn't pause for breath or wait for anyone else to say anything. 'I'm thinking we should try some literary fiction.' There were mixed expressions around the table and not many of them looked positive. 'Well, I think we need to go more highbrow. Expand our reading choices – that's what a book club is all about. We hardly ever read literary novels.'

I cleared my throat. Not to get attention but because I didn't want my voice to do that awful croaky thing it does sometimes. They all looked my way. Crap, I had to say something now. Maggie smiled and nodded encouragingly at me. 'We don't read much romance either. I wondered if maybe we should. You know. If you like.' The faces seemed a lot happier about that, which made me feel good.

Betty didn't look impressed. 'I said highbrow, Tom.' She gave a tinkly laugh. She was taking the piss.

'Yeah. I know what that means. I just think something modern might be good too.' Maggie was giving me a look. I swear she would have done a round of applause if she could. I reached down and put a book on the table. '*The Flatshare* by Beth O'Leary. It's a romance but it's different.'

Maggie leaned forward and read the strapline. 'Tiffy and Leon share a flat. Tiffy and Leon share a bed. Tiffy and Leon have never met. Well I like the sound of that,' she said clapping her hands and there were nods of approval around the table. Betty huffed a bit but she said it could go on the list. I leaned back on my chair. I felt like I'd won a little victory.

The door opened and I twisted quickly to see who it was. It was Farah. My chair wobbled and I almost toppled backwards. I grabbed the table and righted myself but the jolt sent water skidding across the surface and spilling all over Betty's agenda.

By the time I'd apologised and mopped things up Farah was settled in the children's corner and out of sight. I'm such a dork.

My two new recruits turned up for my silver surfers lesson, which was good. Although one of them literally knew nothing about computers and I should have started with the bit where you switch it on.

'I've lost the flashy thing,' said Mr Mendle.

'The cursor,' I said. 'It's not lost, you just need to scroll down.' He looked at me blankly. I showed him again how to use the mouse to scroll but I don't think he was getting it. My other student was Alice who had been quite specific that she wanted help with online shopping, and she was having a great time on the Marks and Spencer website.

'Argh! I've lost it,' said Mr Mendle. His screen was blank.

'You're okay. Try not to panic. You've iconised the website that's all.' I showed him how to get it back.

'You are a marvel,' said Mr Mendle gripping the mouse tightly.

'Nah, it's just practice.'

'And he's modest too,' said Alice. 'If I want to look at bras I type bra in that box. Is that right?'

I was trying not to go pink when the door opened and my dad came in. I immediately looked over my shoulder and felt better that Maggie was watching – she was good backup.

'All right,' I said to him.

'We need to talk.' He looked serious.

'I'm busy right now.' I pointed at the sign over the computers advertising the silver surfer classes.

'I'm not taking no for an answer. You're my son.'

Alice was watching open-mouthed while Mr Mendle banged the mouse on the desk.

'You'll have to wait,' I told him.

'No. I'm fed up of you treating me like sh...' He seemed to sense that everyone was watching him. 'I'm just fed up with the way you're treating me that's all.'

I immediately saw red. 'You're fed up?'

'Yes.'

'What about me?' My voice was getting louder and was definitely too loud for the library. I sensed Maggie before I realised she was at my shoulder.

'Hi, Paul. I'm Maggie.' She held out her hand. He looked at it and then eventually shook it.

'He needs to come home,' said Dad.

'No way. You can't make me.' I was pissed with him for embarrassing me in the library.

'Actually, Paul,' said Maggie picking up her cardigan. 'I'd really like to have a chat with you. Shall we let Tom finish up here while we pop outside? We wouldn't want to make the lad feel uncomfortable, now would we?' She fixed him with one of her looks.

'I don't—'

'No, I'm sure you don't want to embarrass him,' she cut in. Although I'm pretty certain that wasn't what he was going to say. 'Let's go for a stroll.' She turned to me. 'You carry on. We'll be fine.'

She ushered him outside and people went back to their books. I glanced over at Farah and her expression was sympathetic but then she looked away and carried on reading to the kids.

'Now tell me, Tom,' said Alice. 'Would you buy these bras in pink or white?'

34

MAGGIE

Maggie decided a stroll to the church was probably a good option. Whether you were religious or not the church came with a certain aura and she hoped it would calm Paul down.

'He's a cracking lad is your Tom,' she said.

'I know,' said Paul. The hostility was evident in his voice. 'I want him to move back in. It's not right him staying with...' Maggie eyed him as he searched for the right words.

'An old woman,' she offered.

He nodded and then seemed to check himself. 'Someone who's not family,' he corrected.

'I completely agree,' she said and was pleased to see him look confused by her response.

'Right. Well. That's good then.' He shoved his hands in his jeans pockets, exactly how Tom did when he was uneasy.

They walked a bit further in silence. When they reached the churchyard gate Maggie opened it and stepped through. As she held it open for Paul she realised he wasn't following her.

'There's a bench with a nice view,' she said. 'I thought we could sit there while we wait for Tom to finish.

'I've not…' He tipped his head at the churchyard and realisation dawned on Maggie.

'Ah, I'm sorry. How thoughtless of me. We can go somewhere else.' She held the gate and waited.

'No it's all right.' He followed her through.

'I'm terribly sorry about your wife and your baby,' she said.

'He told you about that.' Paul was blinking fast.

'Yes. We talk quite a bit. It doesn't do to bottle things up.'

Paul snorted his derision. They followed the path to the bench and Maggie sat down. Paul hesitantly perched on the opposite end.

'You've not had it easy, have you, Paul?'

Another snort. 'I'm fine.'

'Oh, I know you are. I'm merely saying you've gone through a lot. Tom has too.'

'He's fine.'

She was starting to see a theme. 'No he's not, Paul. He's not fine at all. He is scared witless of losing you.'

Paul's mouth was already open to protest but her last sentence seemed to hit him like a sledgehammer. His eyes searched her face for a few moments. 'He's the one who left,' he said but the vehemence had gone from his words.

'That's not what I mean. He's terrified of you dying. Of you killing yourself with alcohol.'

'I've quit.' He said the words but his sheepish expression gave him away.

'It's not that easy, though is it, Paul?' She watched him closely and the intensity of her stare made him look away.

'People think all you have to do is stop drinking. Simple. But it's not. It's a part of you now. A way of life. An escape. It's a temporary relief from everyday stresses. Why would you want to stop that?' She paused. Paul was watching her closely but he didn't respond. 'I don't need to tell you how easy it is to convince yourself that you can handle it. That you're in control of the booze and not the other way around. That you can quit if you want to. But we both know you'd be lying to yourself.'

Paul took a deep breath and put his face in his hands. 'I don't know how I got here.'

Maggie heard the emotion in his voice. She reached out and patted his shoulder gently. 'It's where you go from here that matters. How you manage.'

'For a while I was managing. But it's in here.' He tapped his temple. 'You can't escape from everything in here. The sadness, the loneliness, the guilt. It swirls around all the time. And then there's bills, running a house, doing all the stuff a woman... my wife used to do. Looking after a kid.' He puffed out a breath. 'Having a drink helped. Stopped it all. Gave me a break.' He blinked slowly. 'And then the next day it's all back. I'm right in the middle of it all again. No escape. So I'd pick up another bottle. It's a cycle. There's no way out of it.'

'Finding your way out is what you have to concentrate on now. Not just for you but for Tom too. Living with an addict isn't easy.'

He looked up briefly. 'I hid most of it from Tom.'

'No, you didn't,' said Maggie. Her voice was kind. 'He saw it all. He's lived through it all.'

Paul wiped away a tear. 'Shit. I'm sorry.'

She handed him a tissue. 'Here. Have a cry – you'll feel better for it.'

Paul spluttered a laugh and took the tissue. 'That's not really my style.'

'Nobody minds here.' She waved a hand at the neat rows of gravestones.

His eyes seemed to follow her hand and fixed on the middle distance. 'I never come to the grave. It's too much. I can't think of her being here. Makes it all too real.' He sighed deeply. 'You know she... my wife... she'd do her nut if she saw me like this. Tell me what an idiot I am.'

'Would she? Or would she help you?'

Paul spluttered out a sob. 'Bloody hell. I'm sorry.' He blew his nose. 'I'm not usually soft like this.'

'It's not a weakness, Paul.'

He exhaled. 'There's plenty would disagree with you.'

'Well I'm used to that,' said Maggie with a wink. 'It's the wonder of getting older; you can say what you think and get away with it. On that note, I'll simply say, Tom is free to go home whenever he wants to but that's what is key. He needs to want to. I'm not going to force him and nor should you because he'll only fight it harder. And you have a lot to deal with at the moment. You need to focus on kicking your addiction. That's the best thing you can do for Tom right now.'

He nodded solemnly. 'I'm getting help.'

'That's brilliant. Take everything that's offered to you. In the meantime, Tom will be fine. I can promise you that.'

He balled up the tissue. 'Thanks.'

'You're welcome. I'm here if you want to talk more.'

He seemed to straighten his shoulders and slip back

into his previous dispassionate air. 'No you're all right.' He stuffed the used tissue in his pocket. 'We should be getting back,' he said.

'I think it's probably not a good idea to go head to head with Tom today.'

He appeared to consider this. 'If you think that's best.'

'I do.' Maggie stood up. 'I'll give you a few minutes with your wife,' she said giving his shoulder a brief squeeze before walking away.

35

TOM

'How are you?' asked Maggie, when I came in from school on the Monday and took a piece of cake from the cake tin. It had been that kind of day. I wasn't even in the mood for yoga or reading. 'Come on. Out with it.' She put her hands on her hips.

'I think I've stuffed up biology and Dad keeps texting me.' Rusty came to greet me, wagging her tail hard like she'd been waiting to see me all day. Dogs are awesome. They don't care if you're clever or not; they just like to hang out with you. I want my own dog.

'Right.' Maggie pulled out a chair and looked like she meant business. 'Biology. Is it one of your essential subjects for A level?' I opened my mouth but she replied for me so I carried on eating cake. 'No, it's not. Forget about it. But recognise how you feel right now about biology.' She left a pause. 'And think what you need to do so you don't feel like this about a subject that is essential for your A levels.'

'I guess.' She was right but what she was saying was that

I needed to revise more and I was sick of revision. It was all right revising with Farah but on my own it was tedious. 'But revision is sooooo boring and it doesn't matter how long I spend going over and over stuff it doesn't sink in.'

'What can I do to help?' she asked. I shrugged my shoulder and tidied up the crumbs I'd made on the table. 'Shall I test you? Don't look alarmed.'

'If you like but I don't know if it'll do any good.' I gave Rusty a fuss and she dropped her head in my lap. She was spending longer periods away from the puppies. I think she was getting a bit fed up with them.

'How's your dad?'

I couldn't help rolling my eyes at the mention of him. He was texting every day and it was doing my head in. I know he wants me to go home but badgering me all the time is not the way to go about it. 'He texted me four times today. Four!' I held up four fingers and Maggie smirked.

'Four's not exactly excessive.'

'But they're so long. One was all about his AA meeting. One about an appointment he's made with a debt counsellor, another about hoping to go back to work soon and the last one asking if I want to redecorate my bedroom because he knows some bloke who can get cheap paint.' I was bored just repeating it all.

'It sounds like he's missing you… very much.'

'I guess.' I rubbed Rusty's ears.

'And a new-look bedroom would be something nice to go home to.' Maggie went to check on dinner. I wish she'd say if I've been freeloading here too long. I felt bad that I didn't want to go home. But there was no amount of paint that was going to make Dad's place feel like Maggie's.

*

Maggie decided there was time for a martial arts class before I tackled more revision. We went around to the large lawn area at the side of the house and I reeled in the washing line so no one got strangled on it. She set out some rules that I was only to use what she taught me in self-defence or to gain spiritual enlightenment – whatever that is.

Maggie took up a boxer-like pose. 'Come on. Try to hit me.' She waved me forwards.

'No way.'

'You won't be able to land a punch. I guarantee it.'

I crossed my arms. 'But what if I do? What if I hit you and knock you out? I'll get arrested. Spend the rest of my life in jail or on the run.'

'What are you reading at the moment?'

'*Never Go Back* by Lee Child.' Book club had opened me up to a load of new stuff. And I was not reading as much romance since the whole beef with Farah who was still not speaking to me.

'Figures,' said Maggie. 'Just aim for my torso, then. Come on.'

There was no reasoning with her sometimes. Secretly I did want to have a go in a proper fight but not with Maggie. I slowly did a pretend jab at her middle and I'm not sure what happened next but in a heartbeat I faceplanted the grass. 'Oof.'

'You all right?' she asked offering a hand to help me up.

'Er. Yeah. Fine.' I got up and brushed myself down.

'Again?'

'Okay.' This time I decided I'd go in a bit harder. She

could clearly handle herself. I took a swing at her and my arm was up my back and I was eating grass faster than I could say sheep breath. She was super quick.

'How the he… heck did you do that?'

'Right. Watch, listen and learn. Do it again in slow motion and I'll walk you through your options.'

I did as I was told but with added comedy slow motion speaking. 'Dooon't huuuuuurt meeeee, Maaaaaggieeeee.'

She ignored me. 'Grab the wrist firmly, here…' She took hold of my wrist with a surprisingly firm grip. 'Twist your body around and force their wrist up and their shoulder down.' I'm eating grass again but in slow motion.

'Ow. Okay. Got it.' I'm not sure I have.

'Try it on me.'

'No way. I don't want to hurt you.'

She gave a smile that said she doubted I could. 'Then let's do a slow motion version. I come to punch you and you…'

I grasped her wrist and turned my body like she'd shown me and Maggie whipped her hand away and was gone. 'What the?'

'You gave me too much space and not a tight enough hold on the wrist. Try again.'

She was a hard taskmaster but before long I had her eating grass. Even if it had taken three attempts and lots of coaching.

'Hey! You!' came a shout from the driveway. Savage was jogging towards us. He looked like he was in slow motion. 'Stop!' he yelled, waving a fist.

'It's all right,' said Maggie, getting to her feet. I released her and held my hands up in surrender. 'I'm training him. It's fine.'

Savage finally reached us, wheezing heavily. 'I thought…' he paused for breath and waved for emphasis '…you were…' he put his hands on his knees while he took deep breaths '…being attacked.'

It was a good job she wasn't because this guy would have been useless. 'She's teaching me martial arts,' I said.

His expression changed and the belly laughs started. To be fair he did have the belly for it. He kept pointing at me and then Maggie and hooting with laughter. He handed Maggie a wrench, which she shoved into her pocket. 'That the size you needed?'

'Yes, thank you.' Her words were very precise. Savage carried on laughing as he meandered up the track. I'd have quite liked to make *him* eat grass.

36

MAGGIE

Maggie wasn't expecting to get a reply to the letter for ages yet so when she walked down to the front gate to collect the post she was bowled over to find a tell-tale brown envelope there. The sudden rush of excitement was short-lived as trepidation took over. She grasped the letter and stared at it. Was a quick reply good news or bad? She didn't know. She felt hot and cold like she was coming down with flu and her pulse had quickened. This was ridiculous.

A car turned into the driveway behind her. She folded the envelope carefully and popped it in her pocket.

'Maggie. How're the martial arts lessons going?' said Savage with a chuckle.

Maggie halted. 'Fraser, I'm busy. I'm sure you are too. Is there anything you want other than to make feeble jokes?'

He cleared his throat, suitably scolded. His face returned to its usual dour pose. 'How are the dogs doing?' he asked, leaning out of his mud-splattered Land Rover.

'They're all fine. Rusty's a good mother.' She slipped her hand into her jacket pocket to touch the envelope.

'Grand. The last of the cades will be out in the field any day so I can have the dogs back whenever. Your call.'

'Right. I'll keep hold of them for a few more days if that's okay. The pups are a bit more interesting now they've opened their eyes. And me laddo is rather fond.'

'Fine by me,' said Savage and his vehicle lurched off across the potholes.

A lift would have been nice, thought Maggie as she set off back to the house. It was going to be a wrench for Tom to let the puppies go. It was a shame Savage was by nature offhand or she'd have suggested Tom could occasionally go up to his farm to see them, but she knew the gruff farmer wouldn't be keen on that. The dogs had a purpose like everything on his farm – they either worked or made him money.

She put the kettle on and sat down at the kitchen table. Rusty came to check who it was, had a bit of a fuss and went back to the puppies. Maggie pulled the envelope out of her pocket and placed it reverently on the table. She wasn't sure how long she sat and stared at it. Myriad thoughts tumbled over in her mind. Spikes of panic littered her worried brain.

It was too much. She pushed the ominous envelope away and went to make herself a cup of tea. She stayed by the kettle to drink it and eyed the envelope from across the room. This was no good; she had to know. She grabbed a knife from the block, marched over to the table and in one slice she opened the envelope. Maggie pulled out the neatly folded white page inside and held her breath as she read it.

A trip to Leamington Spa on the tractor was probably an odd reaction, in hindsight, but she hadn't exactly been thinking straight. The breeze and the bumpy ride took her mind off the contents of the letter. It was all a bit overwhelming so it was best pushed to the back of her mind for now and she'd work out how to deal with it later. She needed to get the other tyre repaired for the quad, which was a good excuse to get out, and Tom could do with a few more things. Leamington Spa was her option of choice.

She dropped off the quad bike tyre, paid and collected the trailer tyre and ignored the jokes about having a season ticket. The tractor trundled into the town centre and she parked in the same place as her last visit, and went in search of the charity shops. It filled an hour and although she hadn't got as many logo-clad things for Tom as last time she was pleased with what she had found. It was always a bit of a lucky dip. She'd also got him some stuff he could wear around the farm and not bother about ruining. She splashed out on a new pair of wellingtons for him too. Her late husband's were too small. She'd seen him wince when he'd put them on the other day. Tom had really taken to life at the farm and worked hard. Giving him the right equipment was the least she could do.

The thought of Tom calmed her. But the sensation was fleeting. Should she tell Tom about the letter? But what to tell him? Without knowing it, Tom had taught her so much. He'd been the trigger that had made her write in the first place. He was a good lad. It was a shame his father didn't appreciate him. Didn't enjoy him as he should but how many parents were exactly the same? Too busy with their day-to-day lives to realise the most precious times would soon be a distant memory. Children were a gift but a transitory one. Mess things up and they were gone. Even if you did your job right you'd lose them in the end. Not quite so permanently but surely the measure of successful parenting was independent, happy offspring? Maggie figured either way the outcome was the same.

She checked the time. She needed to be heading back. Thankfully there was no traffic warden this time – only a few smartly dressed people shaking their heads at her tractor. She got in, waved theatrically at the bystanders and set off for home.

When Maggie walked in the kitchen she froze. Tom was standing by the table with the letter in his hands. For a moment she couldn't breathe. The look on his face was one of hatred and it cut through her.

'Tom…' Her voice didn't sound like her own. It sounded old and tired.

Tom's jaw was clenched. He narrowed his eyes. 'You lied to me. You lied. After everything…'

'Not exactly…' As soon as she'd said it she knew it was a pathetic response.

'You let me believe River was dead. But he's not. Is he? He's alive; he just doesn't want anything to do with you.' Maggie swallowed but couldn't muster a response. 'And why not?' He was almost shouting. He shook the letter. 'Because you're an alcoholic!' He was shaking his head.

She'd known she should have told Tom about her past but there had never been a good time. She'd seen his loathing and disgust for his father and she couldn't bear the thought of him lumping her in the same boat as him.

'I'm so very sorry.' She'd never been more sorry, except for the day she let them take River away.

'No wonder you knew what to do with Dad. That was you!' He looked horrified at his own words.

'It was a long time ago, Tom. And I'm proof that you can move on. Be a better person.'

'A better person?' he scoffed. 'I thought you knew what it was like to lose someone. I'd lost Mum and you'd lost your son. That's what you made me believe...' His voice cracked.

'I do know what it's like. My husband died and I did lose my son. He was five months old when social services took him away.'

'Because you were an unfit mother.' He shook the letter again. 'You gave him up for adoption. How could you do that?'

'I had no choice, Tom. It was the hardest thing I have ever had to do. At the time I truly believed it was the best thing for River.'

Tom threw his hands up, his face full of rage. 'Best for you more like. It's never going to be good to grow up without your mum. Never...' The temper seemed to diminish for a moment. 'I know.' He lowered his head, like the fight had gone out of him.

Rusty came through to see what the commotion was about and Tom sank to his knees to hug her. Maggie didn't need to see his tears to know they were there. It ripped at her heart to know she was breaking his. It was the most painful thing to witness. And worse still to know she'd caused it. Rusty rested her muzzle on his shoulder as if sensing his distress and trying to comfort him.

'Tom. Sit down. I'll put the kettle on.'

'No!' He lurched to his feet, his resentment almost palpable as he roughly wiped his sleeve across his tear-stained face. 'Tea won't solve this.' He slammed down the crumpled letter. 'I'm leaving.'

'Tom. Don't be hasty. Please.'

'I can't stay here.' He took the stairs two at a time. There was banging in the room above as he opened and closed drawers, each slam fuelled by his anger. Anger he was entitled to. She regretted not putting him straight when he'd assumed River was dead but she had somehow hoped there would be a right time to tell him what had happened. Now more than ever she realised he was just a boy. A lost child in a harsh world of continual change.

He thundered down the stairs and began his assault on the hallway. Maggie wandered through but kept her distance.

'Tom. Please can we talk? Find a way to fix things?'

'Nothing can fix this. You're not who I thought you were. I don't know you at all.' He lugged his schoolbag onto his shoulder while juggling two other bags and a box. 'You can bin the other stuff. It's only what you bought anyway.' With a slam of the front door he was gone.

37

TOM

By the time I'd got to the driveway I was a mess. Tears and snot everywhere. I slumped against the old gate and sobbed like a baby. I couldn't stop it and I didn't want to. It felt like it had to come out or I'd explode. I was grateful that Furrow's Cross was pretty deserted most of the time so there was nobody about to see me have a meltdown. Eventually the tears stopped and I rested my pounding head against the gate behind me.

How the hell could Maggie have deceived me like that? The one person I thought I could trust and rely on had massively let me down just like everyone else. All this time I'd admired her so much but she'd been lying to me all along. Maybe not the blatant sort of lies made to deceive but the effect had been the same – she wasn't who I thought she was. Maggie wasn't the rational caring old lady I'd believed her to be; she was an ex-alcoholic who'd given up her son.

There was literally no one I could depend on. Maybe nobody was who they seemed. Apart from the animals.

Rusty was beautiful inside and out; she was caring and loyal. Colin was literally the devil in sheep's clothing. But you knew where you were with animals – they weren't suddenly going to surprise you and tip your world upside down. They didn't pretend to be something they weren't and because of that they didn't let you down. Unlike people who did it all the time.

A few spots of rain landed on my jeans. Dark blue blotches bled across the fabric. I looked at my stuff on the ground beside me. I'd been hasty. Where the hell was I going to go and how on earth was I going to take all this with me? It was Friday night and I was running out of options.

I checked my pockets. I had enough money to get the bus into Dunchurch. I could walk home from there – it was only a couple more stops. I turned the coins over in my hand. Maggie had given me that money. She'd given me a lot. Why couldn't she be exactly as I'd believed? I sniffed back more tears. I really did need to man up. I was getting pissed off with all the crying.

I lugged my stuff down the driveway and across the road to wait for the bus. It felt as if everything had gone from being beyond brilliant to turning to crap super fast, like someone had flicked a switch. I had no choice but to go back to Dad's. I didn't want to. I looked longingly up the driveway in the hope Maggie would come marching down and persuade me to come back but she didn't. I'd probably outstayed my welcome anyway – not that she'd ever said. But she hadn't signed up for a full-time freeloader. I knew I was costing her money she didn't have. Maybe this was for the best for everyone. The bus came into view and I let out a sigh. My life was back to being crap again.

*

Things took another turn as I got off the bus. I was rearranging my stuff to make it easier to carry when someone whacked me in the back. I stumbled forwards, dropped the box but kept my balance. I think my core muscles are getting stronger. I twisted to see Kemp standing there laughing.

'You living rough now, Harris? You gyppo.' He snorted at his own joke and his minion Kyle Fletcher joined in. To be fair it was probably how I looked, carrying all my stuff about.

'Piss off, Kemp.'

'You gonna make me, hard man?'

I puffed out a breath. I was not in the mood for this. The crying had zapped all my energy and I felt shit. 'Nope. I'm going home.'

'Which doorway's that then?' He sniggered.

'Hilarious. You should do stand-up.' I started to walk away but he grabbed one of my bags from under my arm.

I knew I should fight back but I couldn't be arsed. 'Take it. It's dirty clothes.'

'Eurgh!' said Kemp chucking the bag at Fletcher who dodged it neatly and we all watched the clothes tumble out onto the pavement. Fletcher stamped on them, grinning at me the whole time.

'Pick 'em up, Harris,' said Kemp, squaring up to me.

'Nope. Keep 'em.'

'I. Said. Pick 'em up,' he growled in my face as he thumped my shoulder with each word. I grabbed his wrist and turned my body, like Maggie had taught me, but Fletcher shoved me and I wasn't strong enough to take them both on. They both started to whack me over the top of the head. We scrapped for a few moments until I heard someone shout and come running. 'Leg it!' yelled Kemp, giving me one final shove before he ran off.

It was utter shit to be back.

At least Dad was pleased to see me. I felt a bit bad letting him believe I'd come home because I wanted to but it seemed to make him happy, which was something. He'd gabbled on a lot about what he would have done if he'd known I was coming home today and slapped me on the shoulder, which I think was his best attempt at affection. It was beyond odd to be back in the house.

Dad made a big point of telling me he was still off the drink and that he'd restructured his borrowing, whatever that means, and now if he was careful we could keep the house and manage on his income. He can't afford to get the car repaired so it's gone for scrap and he's been using my bike instead. I nodded here and there and that seemed to please him.

My bedroom looked the same as before except it had a clean duvet cover and clean sheets on – I couldn't remember the last time they'd been changed. Maggie changed hers every other week. She dried them on the line at the side of the farmhouse and it made them smell different – like the outdoors had sneaked in. This bedroom smells different but not in a good way. I removed my *Call of Duty* posters from the wall, I'd moved on from all that, and took them downstairs to put in the recycling.

Dad had gone out. I checked the fridge. No beer – that

was something. There was a pasty, some cheese, milk and a new tub of margarine. The freezer contained four pizzas and lots of fish fingers. I looked in the cupboard. There were cereals, a couple of tins of curried chicken and an open bag of rice. Also some soup and lots of tins of beans. I sighed at the sight of the beans. No, correction, two of them were beans and sausages – it looked like Dad had been getting adventurous in my absence. I settled on pizza as being the best option.

While the oven heated up I got out some cutlery and laid the table, like I used to do at Maggie's. This table was way smaller but it would do the job. Maggie does things properly and eating on your lap is lazy.

I heard the front door open and Dad came in carrying a white paper bag, which he held up like a prize. 'I thought we'd have a treat. Fish and chips.'

He looked at the laid table. 'It's all right; we can eat them on our laps in front of the TV,' he said. 'I can't get over Maggie not having a telly.' He chuckled to himself.

I picked up the cutlery and went through to the living room. I had missed the TV. Especially when I'd first moved in to Maggie's but I'd quickly got used to not having one. Our evenings of reading, chatting and watching the puppies had become my normal.

Dad joined me and passed me my plate, which had a large piece of battered cod, with a lump of twisted chips on it – not a vegetable in sight.

'I bet you've missed this eh? Being out in the sticks. No telly. No shops.' He stuffed a chip in his mouth and made a murmur of pleasure. 'You can't beat proper chips.' He looked at me and paused. 'Well, get stuck in, Tom.'

I looked at my plate. The smell of grease was overpowering. 'At Maggie's we cooked fresh every day. Usually stuff she'd grown.'

'Right.' He looked deflated but only for a moment. 'Not fish and chips with your old dad, though is it?' He gave me a nudge and a wink.

'No. No, it's not.' I smiled at him. I knew this was him making an effort. But it was a bit depressing that this was his idea of living it up – having enough money left over to have fish and chips once a week.

Dad was back at work and he asked me if I was going out like he always used to do. It was as if I'd never been away – that was until the door shut and the house was silent. I sat on the stairs for a bit just thinking. I was alone. I guess I've been alone a lot since Mum died. I must have got used to it without even realising. Somehow being at Maggie's I've got un-used to it because now it didn't feel right. It felt completely alien.

Maybe it was the silence. But Maggie's had been quiet. I went and put the TV on and had a flick round the channels. *The Big Bang Theory* was on. I watched it for a bit wondering if Farah was watching it too. The key characters are Leonard, Sheldon and Penny. An image of the puppies popped into my mind. I really missed them. I missed the other animals too. But most of all I missed Maggie.

I read *Outlander* into the early hours, trying to get my mind to switch off. It kept replaying the argument with Maggie.

I could see the letter and feel the anguish. I must have fallen asleep eventually. When I woke up the book was on my pillow and I'd had a massive lie-in. I hadn't done that for weeks. The birds usually woke me up and if they didn't, I'd hear the lambs and that would.

I listened and all I could hear was the odd car going past, and Dad in the shower. This was my new routine – or more accurately, I was back to the old one. I could do what I liked. No animals demanding attention. No fencing to fix. No yoga. No martial arts training. No puppy duties. No Maggie. Not much of anything at all. Dad dropped something in the shower and swore. It was time for me to get up.

Dad was bouncing around the kitchen like Tigger on Red Bull. It was all a bit much.

'I got you some peanut butter. I know you like it,' said Dad, getting the jar from the cupboard and presenting it to me like I'd won a Brit Award.

I took the jar and studied the label. 'It's got palm oil in it.'

'Is that good?' he asked, leaning over my shoulder.

'Seriously? Don't you know how bad that is for the planet?'

'I thought you liked peanut butter. A thank you might be nice. Jeez.' The toast popped up and he passed me a slice. He was trying, I knew that, but right now it wasn't enough.

38

MAGGIE

Maggie was in a daze after the letter, the row with Tom and his subsequent departure. It was like having her heart broken twice over. Emotion had drained her of energy. She slumped into the chair at the kitchen table and reread the letter. Social services had pulled no punches. River had provided a response by email and it was detailed in the letter – *I do not wish to have any contact, now or in the future, with this woman. As an alcoholic and unfit mother she has no place in my life.*

It was hard to read but not unexpected. He had never tried to contact her. He'd had over fifty years to get in touch so the fact that he hadn't bothered spoke volumes. Perhaps she should have considered this before and left well alone. But, she reasoned, at least now she knew for certain. There would be no more imagined possibilities or fanciful musings. She knew there was no point in hoping, no point in wondering "what if?" All those questions had been answered. Sadly in the answering they had also destroyed the relationship she had managed to cultivate with Tom.

Maggie folded up the letter neatly and returned it to its brown envelope and placed it on the table in front of her. Silent tears blotted its surface. She wasn't sure if they were for River or Tom. The two had become inextricably linked for her. Without the connection she'd had with Tom she would likely never have had the renewed yearning to contact River. Had she thought for a moment that it could mean losing Tom she would have thought more carefully about it although deep down she knew she would still have gone ahead. She had foolishly not considered the impact on her relationship with Tom – she thought he'd be someone who would stay in her life. Not always living at the farm but she had hoped he would at least be part of her life in some small way even after he returned home, which she had always known he eventually would have to do. But that assumption had been wrong.

She replayed the scene in her head over and over – she could see and hear it vividly. It would take a long while to fade. If only she'd put the letter away before she'd rushed off. But having read it she had needed to get out and get out fast. It had been as if she had to distance herself from the truth. To clear her head and refill it with things that weren't River-related and in her rush to do so she had simply left it on the kitchen table.

The look of pain on Tom's face haunted her. He was the very last person she wanted to hurt. She hated that he'd assumed her son was dead but it had been much easier than to explain why River had been taken into care. She'd fought to keep her baby but at the time she was in no fit state to have parented him properly. It genuinely was his best option – hindsight had reassured her of that.

Maggie had been nineteen and living in a commune. Her alcohol and weed habits were nothing out of the ordinary and completely in step with those around her. It had been an exciting time of new opportunities and cultural revolution and Maggie had been carried along by it. Free love gave her the gift of a baby but she quickly learned that without an identifiable father and a steady income it was going to be a lot harder than she'd imagined. The rich kids of the commune got bored and moved out, taking their income with them, and Maggie got a job fruit picking. It was hard work and with a baby that didn't feed well and rarely slept she was at her wits' end.

It was many years later that she realised it must have been her pot habit and the alcohol affecting River. Sadly the worse he became the more she smoked and drank and the vicious circle had continued. Eventually social services came knocking and the baby was taken into care. The next few months were a blur of binges and arguments as she fought against the establishment, which ultimately won. Out of viable options she signed River over for adoption.

The months that followed were her darkest. Lost days. A pain so real it was as if she'd been cut open. Nothing took the edge off. The commune buildings were condemned and she found herself alone with nothing for comfort but cheap booze. A stomach pump and a stay in hospital had introduced her to an alcoholics' support group and she started a long and bumpy road to recovery. Staying in a woman's hostel she spent her days in the library and there she found solace. There were friends on the pages of the books. Their worlds whisked her away from the one she couldn't face. But by now what real life had taught her was that if she let people get close, she got hurt and after River she didn't feel that she deserved to feel love again on any level. She had set up robust barriers around her broken heart, promising herself she'd not let herself get hurt that way again, and moved forward.

She'd been inching through life ever since. Choosing men for their liquid assets rather than love. Her need for security stemming from the time she had nothing and nobody and the fear of ending up back in that dark place. She'd been lucky in her choices as her husband had been kind and amenable and while theirs hadn't been an epic love story she had cared for him deeply.

It had been him who had helped her stay off the alcohol permanently. He'd made her see it had to be completely erased from her life otherwise it would always be there waiting to tempt her when she hit a low point. He had been the calm to her storm. Someone she had expected to grow old with. But that wasn't to be. She saw losing her husband as Karma seeking balance. And yet something had brought Tom into her life and things had changed for a short period but now she was, once again, alone.

A whimper from the puppies brought her back to the present. She'd take them and Rusty back tonight. No need to keep them any longer with Tom gone. Savage would be looking to sell them as soon as he could. She just had one thing she needed to do first.

Maggie spent longer in the loft than she'd planned. Easily distracted by the past, she had lost most of the evening to old photographs and memories. But her search had been fruitful. She took the precious items downstairs, along with some tissue paper and a large envelope.

She laid out the tissue paper and carefully placed the items on it – River's baby booties, a silver spoon and a crocheted rabbit toy. The toy hadn't been his favourite. He'd taken that one with him; it had been the only thing that was permitted. She'd kept these things but rarely got them out because it was too upsetting to be reacquainted with what she'd lost. She popped in the few snapshots she had of him too and neatly wrapped up the parcel. She had her photograph in the frame that had pride of place in her sitting room and that was all she needed.

It seemed the right thing to do to send them to River now. She'd hoped one day to be able to sit down with him and share them and their stories but that was never going to happen. This was now the best solution. She took out a pen and paper and wrote the last letter she would ever send him. This time, unlike before, it was easy to write. This was goodbye. She'd been waiting to say this for such a long time and now that she could it was something of a release.

Over the years she'd often wondered about River's life and had frequently wished many things for him. Now she wished just one thing – that he was happy.

Maggie didn't go to the library on Saturday. Her day started like so many had. She took her cup of tea outside, sat on the bench and listened to the birds. She'd taken Rusty and her puppies home last night. Savage had thanked her and Mac had been overjoyed to have his partner in crime back although he was less than sure about the puppies who were overexcited at the change of scenery. Providence Farm was quiet without them. It was quieter still without Tom. She'd have to get used to that.

Maggie fed and watered all the animals but when she got to the lambs she felt a pang in her heart. One of the small males had been mauled in the night. It could have been a fox or a dog. A pretty brazen one too. The ewes must have seen it off or the lamb would be gone. He was lying down with his head bent low and his neck and back bloodied.

Maggie approached him cautiously. 'Hey there…' What was his name? She couldn't remember what Tom had called him. They'd all been given elaborate names from some book he'd read but she couldn't recall what this little chap was called. 'Right. Well, I'm afraid we'll have to contact deed poll because I'm changing your name to Tom.'

The lamb looked up and bleated but it was weak. Barbara wandered over but didn't intervene when Maggie scooped the lamb into her arms. 'I'll do what I can for him,' she promised Barbara and the sheep gave her a fixed expression while the other lambs frolicked about her like they were wired to the mains.

After a short ride on the quad bike Maggie gave the lamb a quick check over and washed him in warm water in the sink to establish how badly he was injured. Nothing broken, thankfully, but a number of puncture wounds around his neck and back. She dried him off, sprayed the cuts with antibacterial spray and gave him a quick squirt of the vitamin complex she gave newborn lambs. It wouldn't do him any harm and hopefully would give him a little boost.

Maggie popped an old tea towel in the bottom of the laundry basket and gently lifted him inside. He didn't object but nor did he settle down. He stood there with his head hanging forlornly. She had formula left over from when she'd had a couple of cade lambs the previous year so she made up a bottle and settled down to give the little lamb a feed.

He soon latched on and guzzled it down. He was weak from the attack and he'd likely not eaten for a few hours either. Now that he had a full tummy she settled him back in the basket, put the oven on low with the door open and the basket set down in front. She needed to make sure he was properly dried out and warm. The last thing he needed was to catch hypothermia. If Tom had been there he would have made some joke about slow-roasted lamb and it upset her to think of it.

She was washing her hands when the phone rang. She hesitated for a moment but then answered. 'Hello?'

'Maggie, it's Christine. Has something happened?'

'Ah, no. I wasn't feeling quite myself this morning. I thought I'd give book club a miss. That's all,' said Maggie.

'But we were going to have a Save the Library meeting and it's not just you. Tom and Farah are missing as well. There's only me and Betty and she's got a hair appointment at two.' Maggie heard Betty whisper 'ten past two' in the background.

'Right. Well, I don't know about Tom and Farah but I'm sorry I couldn't make it today. Hopefully next week.'

'Hopefully?' Christine's voice sounded strained.

Maggie let out a sigh. She knew she was letting Christine down but she had more important things on her mind than the library. 'I'll be sure to let you know if I won't be there, all right?'

There was a moment's silence. Christine lowered her voice. 'I didn't get an interview for that other job, the administration assistant.'

'I'm sorry to hear that.' And she was sorry but she couldn't solve everyone's problems for them. It turned out she couldn't even solve her own.

39

TOM

I'd made it through most of my exams and I'd surprised myself with how hard I'd worked. I'd got in a bit of a revision habit at Maggie's, which had been easy to carry on at home. Dad seemed puzzled by me revising loads but there wasn't a lot else to do on my own when he was out at work. There was the TV but I'd got picky with it since living away. I did watch it but only stuff I was really into. Before it was on all the time and I watched it constantly if I wasn't playing on my Xbox but not anymore. Apart from when Dad was home when it was on permanently. It was like he couldn't cope with silence.

We'd quickly slipped back into our routine but it was no longer a comfortable existence for me. Even when he was home we rarely spoke. There was stuff we should have probably talked about but we didn't. Everything that had happened before was a minefield that neither of us knew how to negotiate without someone blowing up and doing further damage so instead we didn't talk about it.

To be fair he did try to strike up conversations occasionally about his job and football but it's difficult to chat about stuff you're not interested in. I tried to talk to him about books but he looked like he'd fallen asleep with his eyes open. There was less time for us to speak anyway because he was home even less. He was out for a bit on a Saturday seeing his counsellor and again on a Monday evening at what he called "his group". We both knew it was Alcoholics Anonymous but I guess he was embarrassed to call it that.

I don't speak to anyone much at school either. Today I was alone in the school library and Farah walked in. She paused for a second and we both looked at each other. I don't know if I was meant to say something – maybe apologise again, I don't know – but she turned around and left. I don't think she knows I've moved back to Compton Mallow but as we're not talking I can't tell her. And what would be the point? She's not going to invite me round for pizza with salad and coleslaw ever again. I saw her talking to Kemp later. I wish I could lip-read. That would be an awesome skill. He seemed happy but she kind of didn't or I might have imagined that to make myself feel better.

When I came in from school Dad came downstairs and started making coffee. 'Pizza for tea?' he asked.

'Okay.' This was about the level of our discussions. A thought struck me. 'We could have coleslaw and salad with it.'

Dad looked up and grinned at me. 'Coleslaw?'

'Yeah. I like it. It goes really well with pizza. And we don't eat enough veg.' I actually missed the vegetables at Maggie's. I never thought I would but I do. It's a bit like I'm craving them.

He was shaking his head. 'Posh rubbish. You'll be eating olives and hummus next.' He laughed at his own joke.

'Maggie makes her own hummus. It's dead nice with carrots.'

'Right.' He gave me a weird look, like he didn't know if I was serious or not.

'Did you know carrots come in different colours other than orange?' It had blown me away when I'd seen all the different colours Maggie grew.

He blinked a couple of times. 'What like blue?'

He was taking the piss. 'No. Purple, yellow, white and a pinky red. They taste the same.'

He screwed his nose up. 'Never liked carrots much anyway, I can't imagine dyed ones taste any better.'

I opened my mouth to explain but he was stirring his coffee and it wasn't worth the effort. I missed having someone I could properly talk to.

After he'd gone to work I switched off the TV, pulled the curtains closed in the living room, moved the table out of the way and pushed back the sofa to make myself some space. I sat on the floor with my legs crossed, which seemed easy now. I liked doing yoga but I knew Dad would rip it out of me if he knew. He scoffed every time he saw me with a book so I figured the yoga would have tipped him over the edge. He was set in his ways and stuff like this would have weirded him out. I found it calming and after a day of full-on exam stress I needed to "chill out" as Maggie would have put it.

I did a few of the easier positions to warm up and

concentrated on my breathing. Maggie and I had a bit of a practised routine. I hadn't realised it at the time but doing yoga and talking about stuff at school made me relax. I don't feel relaxed here. I can't remember if I ever did. I did the plank for a long count until my arms started to shake. Maybe I could push myself a bit. Before I considered the pose I checked where I was in relation to the TV. If I fell on that and broke it Dad would have a blue hairy fit. The TV was his life.

I took my time to place my hands in the right position and feel where my weight was. I pushed myself up into a headstand. There was a brief wobble but I tightened my stomach muscles and it worked. I was stable. I was chuffed that I'd done it unaided and was holding the position. I let my mind drift.

The front door swung open and banged into the wall. 'Forgot my bloody pass card,' said Dad, looming in the doorway. For a millisecond I thought how odd he looked upside down. Then I realised the situation, lost concentration and toppled to the carpet in a semi-controlled way. 'What the hell?' said Dad.

I scrambled to my feet, embarrassment threatening to swallow me up. 'I… I… yoga.' Was all I could manage. I felt like a total idiot.

Dad looked embarrassed and shocked in equal measure. He waved his work key card at me and looked away. 'Right. I'd best get off.'

'Yeah. Bye.'

'Bye.'

I hoped this would be something else we'd never talk about.

*

I was having some toast for breakfast and a last-minute cram for my maths exam when Dad came in from work. He put his head around the kitchen door. 'Great, you're still here.' He pulled a tub of ice cream out of his jacket pocket and put it on the table in front of me. Salted Caramel Latte. Not my first choice but ice cream was ice cream. 'It's got no palm oil in it. I checked.'

'Ta,' I said.

'We're celebrating.' He clapped his hands together.

And I'd thought he was oblivious to my exams but apparently not. 'My last exam is next Friday,' I said, hoping we didn't have to wait until then to eat the ice cream.

'Right. Do you want to know what we're celebrating then?'

'Apparently not my exams.'

'Oh, yeah. That too. But something else…' I looked at him blankly for a moment and then gave up. I needed to get to school. 'I've got you an interview.'

I'd just put the last of my toast in my mouth, which was good because it stopped me from swearing. 'Is this the apprenticeship thing again?' I asked trying hard not to spit toast everywhere and stay calm.

'Yeah. Don't know exactly when the interview will be but you've got time to swot up.'

'I thought we were all right for money now.'

Dad's forehead filled with frown lines. 'We're managing but I'm not Steve Jobs.'

'He's dead.' I might have been missing the point.

'Is he?' I nodded. 'Anyway, some extra cash wouldn't go

amiss. What you pay me in board and lodging I could put some aside for a holiday.' He looked chuffed with himself. 'Actually, don't get too excited about a holiday because I need to check how much it is to stay in a caravan these days.'

'I need to go.' I hastily packed my books into my bag.

'Oh, yeah, 'course. We'll talk tonight. All right?'

I didn't answer. I put my bag on my back and left.

The cycle to school was usually a good opportunity to listen to music and empty my head but not today. It was as if he'd not listened at all the last time we'd had this discussion. It was like that old film *Groundhog Day*. Were we going to keep having the same conversation until I gave in and went to work at the dog food factory? My exams had been mixed. I reckon I'd done okay in some but others, like French, I knew I'd messed up. But like Maggie had said I needed to pass six overall and get good marks in the subjects I was considering for A levels and if I could do that I was staying on. Or at least that's what I'd been working towards. I realised all my conversations about my plans for my future had been with Maggie.

I pedalled faster and left the pavement without looking. My mind fully occupied. I saw a flash of white as the van turned into the road and then nothing.

40

MAGGIE

The vegetable patch was keeping Maggie busy. It had been a little neglected while Tom had been living at the farm but now she was distraction-free she could devote the hours it needed. Once again she had plenty of time to fill. She'd lost a few strawberries and raspberries to rabbits and birds but she repaired her netting and got back on top of picking the fruit and harvesting the vegetables in a timely manner. She'd made one batch of strawberry jam already and had plans for more but it would have to wait until after she'd taken her fleeces to the sale.

The shearing ring had visited, as they did every year, and had done the job in a blink of an eye. They were a group of Australian lads who stayed on a nearby farm and did the rounds of all the sheep farms in the area. They were quick and cheap and it provided a way for them to travel around Europe and amass some cash in the process. Maggie was always amazed by the speed they worked – a whole fleece clean off in under a minute. Sadly the downside of their speedy work meant they weren't there long enough to chat.

The fleece sale was an annual event and she cadged a lift with Savage every year. Savage was first and foremost a commercial sheep farmer but his family had always bred Jacobs, to keep their own pure bloodline for mixing with the commercials. She knew he had a soft spot for the breed but he'd never let on. His commercial fleeces didn't fetch much but the rare breeds fared slightly better and her lavenders better still. Savage always offered to take Maggie's for her, and she did trust him to get a fair price, but it was a day out and a change of scenery so despite the fact they barely spoke from the moment they left Furrow's Cross until they returned she nevertheless enjoyed it.

She was looking forward to it. The folk at the fleece sale were mainly crafters, as it was focused on rare breed fleeces, and there were often some commercial sellers but they were all sheep people and it was good to catch up with them. She only saw them once a year but the natter over a fleece and a cup of tea was always enjoyable.

Savage didn't like waiting around, therefore with ten minutes to spare, Maggie was already in the hallway with her keys in her hand. Her mind was somewhere else. The telephone startled her and she raced off to answer it, already cursing that if Savage turned up and she wasn't ready he'd be even grumpier than usual.

'Maggie?' It was a voice she didn't recognise.

'Yes, who is this?' She frantically checked her watch.

'Ah, well I'm Lyle and I've got your grandson here.'

The caller suddenly had all of her attention. 'I'm sorry. What did you say?'

'Tom. I've got your grandson, Tom, with me. He's had an accident…' Maggie couldn't help the gasp that escaped. 'He's okay… well, I knocked him off his bike.'

'Oh my goodness. Is he in hospital?'

'No, I offered to take him but he says he's all right.'

'Could I speak to him please?' Grandson, he'd said he was her grandson. Then she realised it was probably more about how embarrassed he would have been to say he was friends with a seventy-two-year-old woman. But still, grandson.

'Yep. Here you go.' There was a muffled exchange as the phone was passed on.

'I didn't know who to call,' came Tom's strained voice. 'The bike's knackered and Dad's going to kill me. He needs it for work tonight. I've got an exam and I don't know what to do.'

Maggie swept her emotions aside and went into efficient mode. 'Where does it hurt and how bad it is it?'

'My right side. My thigh. Kind of like the worst dead leg ever and it's throbbing but I can stand on it.'

'Excellent. Nothing broken then. What happened?'

'It was my fault. I wasn't looking. The bike's all buckled. Dad's going to kill me.'

'Don't worry about that right now. Where are you?'

'Not far from school.'

'Right. Can you—' She was interrupted by an impatient blast of a car horn. Savage would have to wait. 'Can you get to school do you think?'

There was another muffled conversation. 'The van driver says he can drop me at school.'

'And are you happy to get in a car with him?'

'Yeah, he's got logos for Taylor's Builders all over his van and he's given me his business card. I think he's legit.'

'Then you go with him. Leave the bike where it is. If it's damaged I doubt it will be stolen…'

'He says he can take the bike in the back of the van.'

'Can he bring it here?' Another longer blast of the car horn from Savage punctuated the conversation.

'Hang on.' She got part of the conversation at Tom's end. 'Furrow's Cross. Yeah. He says he will.'

'Excellent. Right, what time are you due to finish school today?'

'About three I think.'

'I'll try and get the bike fixed and back for then. Okay?'

'Yeah. Thanks, Maggie.'

She could hear the relief in his voice and it warmed her heart that it was her he had turned to. 'You're welcome. Now forget about this and focus on that exam.'

'Okay,' came his weak reply and the call ended. She was sorry that Tom had had an accident but the joy she felt at hearing his voice was immense. A hammering on the front door pulled her attention.

'Okay, I'm coming,' yelled Maggie, heading for the door. She opened it to a thunderous-looking Savage. She held her palms up. 'I'm sorry but Tom's had an accident, been knocked off his bike, poor lad.'

Savage's expression changed. 'Sorry to hear that.' He looked past Maggie and into the house. 'You not coming then?'

'No, I'm afraid I can't now. I've got to work out how to get a bike fixed.'

Savage seemed to misinterpret her thoughtful expression

as a plea for help. 'I need to get off now. But you're welcome to use my tool shed. And if you're not coming I'll likely be back within a couple of hours. I can give you a hand.'

'You know about bikes?'

'Yeah. I'm quite handy. When I was a nipper, I'd strip 'em down and build 'em back up again. Only transport we had as kids – that and Dad's Lamborghini…' Maggie's eyes widened. 'The tractor… that was made by Lamborghini.'

She chuckled and Savage's eyes crinkled at the edges. 'The fleeces are in the barn, if you're okay to take them?'

'No problem. I'd best get off but you've got a house key. Mac's in the yard and Rusty and the pups are in the back porch. Tool shed key is hung up in there.'

'Thank you. That's kind.'

The usual hard Savage façade came back down. 'Makes no odds to me.'

He reversed the Land Rover and trailer back up to the barn. She waited to wave him off but he drove past without a backward glance. It struck Maggie that Savage led a lonely existence. No wife, no family, just the farm. He'd lived there with his parents all his life, until they'd died a few years back. Set in his ways and with a job that kept him fairly remote he was probably facing the rest of his life alone.

When she thought about it, there were so many people who, for whatever reason, found themselves isolated. Maybe some were happy with that set-up, maybe even Savage was. They lived a stone's throw from each other but rarely interacted and then only on a superficial level. But perhaps interaction for interaction's sake was worse than being lonely. She and Savage were totally different people and would likely annoy each other beyond reason if they met on a regular basis. Yes, perhaps she was better keeping herself to herself. Especially now there was a glimmer of hope in Tom's phone call. Although she wasn't going to kid herself that his call had been forced by anything other than desperation.

She was shutting the door when she heard tyres on the gravel drive so she waited. The small white Taylor's Builders van trundled into view. She waved and he pulled in front of the house.

'You must be Lyle. I'm Maggie.'

'I'm really sorry about your grandson. He didn't look. He rode straight in front of the van. I didn't have a chance. Thank heavens I was slowing down for the corner.' He was young and gabbled a lot – like Tom.

'But he's not seriously hurt?'

'No. He was shaken up but I just sort of bumped the bike and it toppled over. I didn't actually run him over.' There was something mildly amusing about Lyle's intense need to reassure her.

'Well. Thank you for getting him to school. He's doing his GCSEs.'

'Yeah. He told me that. His bike's a bit of a mess.'

She followed him to the back of the van, where he lifted the old bike out. 'And the van?'

'A couple of scratches but some other guy had it before me and it already had a few bumps. It's fine, the gaffer won't even notice.'

They both studied the buckled frame of Tom's bike. Maybe her offer to fix it had been a bit premature.

41

TOM

I don't know exactly what I was expecting to see when I limped out of the school gate but Maggie on her tractor was definitely not on my list. I quickly looked over my shoulder to check nobody was watching. There were a few faces at the windows in the science wing but they looked like lower school so I might have got away with it. Most of those who were in my exam had business studies GCSE almost straight after and the few who didn't had all been picked up by parents. There was just me left.

I made my way to the tractor and looked in the trailer – no bike. Maggie twisted in her seat to look at me. It was odd to see her again. Seeing her stirred up stuff in my gut. I'd missed her but I'd had loads of imaginary arguments with her in my head and I still wasn't finished.

'Slight problem with the bike,' she said.

They were not the words I wanted to hear although I hadn't been looking forward to cycling home because my leg was killing me. I was getting grumpier by the second. 'Where is it?'

'Savage is working on it. He thinks he can fix it but it's taking him a while.'

'But I need the bike back.' I threw my arms up in frustration. This nightmare was getting worse.

'Sorry. It was beyond my bike-fixing ability.'

'You said you could fix it!' I was getting agitated. Dad was going to go mental.

Maggie gave me a look. 'I was trying to help.' She turned her head away, making me hobble around to the front of the tractor.

'Dad needs the bike to get to work. He doesn't have a car anymore. If he can't get to work he won't get paid and...' I could feel my pulse starting to race at the thought of the domino of events this could trigger. And worst of all that it might end up with Dad drinking again.

'Could he get a bus?'

'That costs money and the bus times are rubbish.'

'But it's an option.'

'No, it's not!' I was getting cross. I didn't want to have to tell Dad about any of this if I could get away with it. 'When will Savage finish the bike?'

Maggie tilted her head on one side. 'He reckoned he needed a couple more hours and that was about half an hour ago.'

I checked the time on my phone. 'As long as it's back before Dad wakes up we're good.' I took a deep steadying breath. This might actually work out okay.

'You all right now?' she asked.

'Yeah. Sorry.'

'Lift home or back to mine for cake while we wait for the bike?' She fired up the tractor.

I let out a sigh. I was still cross with Maggie about lying but my leg was hurting so there was no way I could walk home. With a lot of effort I hauled myself into the trailer. My phone rang and Maggie waited while I checked it. 'It's the library,' I said, before answering. 'Hello.'

'Tom, thank goodness. I can't get hold of anyone. Can you get to the library this evening? We need to have an urgent meeting of the Save the Library committee.'

'Uh, Christine. I don't know. I've had an accident and hurt my leg. So, no, I'm sorry but I don't think I can.'

'But we're losing momentum. I've had notice from the council that I'm losing my job.' Her voice went all weird and sounded like she was crying. It made me cringe. I hated stuff like that.

'You should speak to Maggie.' I went to give Maggie the phone but she shook her head and wouldn't take it from me. I mouthed "Speak to Christine" at her but she crossed her arms.

'I've tried calling Maggie but there's no answer,' said Christine, making me put the phone back to my ear.

'I think she's out.' I gave Maggie a look to say I wasn't impressed with her not speaking to Christine. I had enough problems without having to sort Christine's out as well. The library was now a long way down my list. 'How about Farah?'

'Her phone goes to voicemail and I've left two messages already.' She was starting to sound desperate. 'Don't you care about the library anymore?'

'Look, my lift's here. I've got to go. Sorry.' I ended the call. I felt bad but what else could I do?

The tractor lurched forward and began bouncing down the road. 'If you come back to mine you can take the bike home on the bus when it's ready. Or I can drop you home now and bring it back to yours on the tractor trailer later.' Maggie gave me a quick glance. 'But it's up to you.'

She'd got me. I didn't want her turning up outside mine on the tractor and she knew it. 'Yours then.'

I relaxed a little bit when we were away from school. 'You not going to the library anymore?' I asked.

'I've not been for a while, no. You?'

'Nah.' I realised I would have to go soon because I still had some books. I'd renewed them online using the computer at school but they'd have to go back eventually.

I was glad of the racket of the engine. The atmosphere between us was horrible. She used to be easy to talk to but everything had changed. I was regretting saying I'd come back to hers. What were we going to do for an hour? Sit and glare at each other? This was a bad idea.

Maggie stopped outside the farmhouse front door and handed me the door keys.

The log store was almost full up. 'Who chopped all that?' I asked.

'I did,' said Maggie. There was yet more uncomfortable silence while I processed what this meant – she could manage without me all along.

I didn't say anything. I got off the tractor and let myself in the house while she put it away. The smell inside enveloped me, like walking into a hug. It smelled of cooking and incense and it was like coming home. I shook the thought from my mind. What garbage was that? This wasn't my home. I lived with Dad. Who was Maggie anyway? Just some old lady from the library. She wasn't the person I thought I knew. I kicked my shoes off and went through to see the puppies.

I was standing in the living room doorway when Maggie came back in. 'Where are they?' I snapped at her.

She frowned for a second before realising who I meant. 'Oh, the pups are back at Savage's. Assuming he's not sold them.' My face must have looked startled because I was. I'd assumed they'd be here. I'd thought about them masses and every time I'd pictured them in Maggie's living room.

'But…'

'They are his dogs.' She seemed to have a hard edge to her now. Maybe it was always there and I just hadn't noticed.

'I know but…' I was interrupted by the loud bleat of a lamb and it wasn't in the field. I gave Maggie a questioning look.

'The small male of Barbara's. I can't remember his name—'

'Tyrion.'

'He got mauled by a fox so I'm hand-feeding him. I tried taking him back to Barbara but she was having none of it.'

'Not such a good mother after all.' The words were out before I could vet them. I could tell they had stung Maggie.

'I suppose not. But she's done her best.' I opened my mouth but managed to stop myself. We both knew we weren't talking about Barbara anymore. 'He's in the kitchen,' she said.

I walked off and tried to stop the bubbles of anger in my gut. In the kitchen Tyrion was standing in a crate like he was pleased to see me. It was painful to kneel down with my bruised leg but I managed it. Maggie passed me a seat cushion off one of the kitchen chairs for me to kneel on but neither of us said anything.

I fussed over the lamb while Maggie made herself a cup of tea and a bottle of formula for Tyrion. 'Come on. Out with it, Tom, it would be far better if you said what's on your mind. Let the anger out. It does no good to bottle things up.'

I looked up at her and she handed me the lamb's bottle. 'Thanks,' I said. She was right about me being angry, it was like that diagram on the indigestion advert having something acidic bubbling inside me all the time. But it was too awkward being instructed to have a go at someone especially when they were expecting it. I concentrated on the liquid in the bottle.

'I know I hurt you. And I'm truly sorry but I can't change what happened.'

Why was she always so reasonable? 'I assumed River was dead,' I said. Tyrion bleated for his bottle.

'I know. I wasn't sure how to tell you that he'd been taken away from me because I was an alcoholic.'

It was strange to hear her say that. I would never really be able to see her in the same group as my dad but she was. It seemed there was no particular type for who became addicted to stuff. 'You could have said. I wouldn't have minded.' She raised her eyebrows, which said plenty. 'Okay, maybe I would have minded but it would have been better than finding out like I did.' We both looked at the kitchen table like it was to blame.

'I know that must have been horrible for you. You see I wasn't thinking straight. The letter was a bit of a shock and I'd left in such a hurry.'

For the first time I thought what the letter had meant for Maggie. Her son didn't want to meet her. She'd reached out to him and he'd flatly refused. My anger disappeared like someone popping a balloon. I'd been too caught up in how I felt. Poor Maggie. Whatever she'd done, she was a good person and I didn't like to see the sadness in her eyes. You didn't get stories like this on that soppy Davina McCall programme. That was full of happy ever afters played out for the camera. This was real life, where real people hurt each other.

'It's a terrible thing to lose people you love from your life. The pain is the same however it happens and regardless of who is to blame,' she said.

She was right but, for me and Maggie, things weren't going to instantly go back to how they were. I tipped the bottle and Tyrion guzzled the formula down, his tail lashing about wildly. Maybe I'd stick to animals.

42

MAGGIE

Maggie had never been more grateful to an animal than she was to Tom the lamb, or Tyrion as he was originally called. He had provided some focus for the difficult hour and a half she'd spent with a subdued and morose teenage Tom. She hated herself for the damage she'd caused. Tom didn't deserve any further upset in his life, but what was done couldn't be undone. They had spent most of the time in silence taking it in turns to look at the clock whose hands seemed to move slower with every glance.

Inevitably Savage took longer than anticipated and when he finally banged on the front door the relief from both of them was palpable. Maggie rushed to answer it with a hobbling Tom close behind her. Savage held the bike up and then rested it against the house.

'Is it fixed?' asked Tom, craning to get a look at the bike.

'It's as good as I can get it,' said Savage. 'This modern stuff's not built to last.'

'But I can ride it. Right?'

'Yes. You can ride it.'

Tom's whole body appeared to loosen up. 'Brilliant. Thanks.' Savage nodded and made to leave. 'How are the puppies?' Tom sort of half shouted it at Savage's back.

Savage turned around and frowned so hard his flat cap moved down his forehead. 'Eating too much and making a mess. No takers as yet.' Savage lifted his chin. 'You know anyone who wants one?'

Tom shook his head, his face glum. 'No.'

'Do we owe you anything for fixing the bike?' asked Maggie.

'No,' said Savage, already walking away.

Tom and Maggie looked at each other. Tom started putting his shoes on. She didn't want to leave things like this but there was no more she could do.

Maggie's phone rang and she cursed it but went to answer it anyway. It was a brief call and had Maggie marching back up the hall. 'Get your shoes on. We're going to the library,' she said.

'I can't,' said Tom, already doing up his laces. 'I've got to get the bike back to Dad.'

'We'll drop that on the way. The library's been burgled and Christine's in a state.'

'What?' Tom looked surprised.

'I've no other details but we need to help Christine. I'll call a taxi.'

'Err. Okay.' He looked thrown by the change of plan. 'You'd better check it's big enough to take the bike.'

*

Tom left the bike in the passage at the side of the house, scribbled a quick note for his dad to say where he was going and got back in the taxi for the short trip to the library. There was no sign of anyone as Maggie paid the driver and Tom tried the library door.

The taxi pulled away and Maggie joined Tom who was peering through the glass. 'I thought the place would be swarming with police cars,' he said. Maggie rapped her knuckles on the door, making Tom pull his head back.

The blinds moved and drew their attention. 'Christine, it's us,' called Tom and he gave a wave at the now empty window.

They heard Christine undo the interior door before she appeared and let them in. 'How did they get in?' asked Tom, swooping inside.

'Are you all right?' asked Maggie, taking Christine by the arms and checking her over.

'Mmm. You'd better come in,' said Christine, locking up behind them and following them into the library.

Tom and Maggie scanned the room. 'What did they take?' asked Tom.

'Sit down,' said Christine, pulling out a chair. Tom and Maggie reluctantly sat down while Christine hovered behind a chair. A rap on the door had her apologising and scurrying off to answer it.

'What's going on?' whispered Tom to Maggie.

'Absolutely no idea,' she replied.

'Oh crap,' said Tom, spotting who was at the door.

Farah came hesitantly inside. 'Hi.' She gave an awkward wave to Maggie and Tom. 'I came as soon as I got the message.'

'I've got to go.' Tom limped for the door and Christine blocked his exit.

'What's wrong with your leg?' asked Farah, her brow puckered with concern.

'Got knocked off my bike,' said Tom.

Farah pulled her head back as if the words had punched her. 'Hell. Are you all right?'

'Massive bruise on my thigh. Bike got mangled...' He glanced at Maggie. 'But Maggie got it fixed for me.'

'You could have been seriously hurt,' said Farah.

'Yeah, well,' said Tom, putting his hands in his trouser pockets. He tilted his head towards the door. 'I should go.' He gave Farah a wistful look.

'Can I update everyone first?' said Christine, wringing her hands.

'Don't leave because of me, Tom,' said Farah. 'The library being vandalised affects us all.'

Tom spun around. 'Vandalised? I thought you said burgled.' He pointed at Maggie.

'Yes, Christine, said it had been burgled. Didn't you, Christine?' asked Maggie.

'I think you all need to sit down.' Christine tried to usher them onto chairs. Farah and Tom sat either side of Maggie. Everyone waited.

'What's going on?' asked Tom, scanning the room again. Maggie was thinking the same as him: she couldn't see any sign of a burglary or vandalism.

Christine slunk into a seat opposite the three of them making it look like she was being interviewed by a panel. 'Please let me explain.'

Christine put her hands together as if she were praying

and stared at her fingers as she spoke. 'I didn't know what else to say that would get you all to come tonight.' She looked up. 'I'm really sorry but now you're all here…' She gave a fleeting smile.

'What's going on?' said Tom, straightening his back. 'Was it all lies?'

Christine bit her lip. 'You've all stopped coming to the library.' She sniffed back tears. 'It feels like there's just me and—'

Maggie put her hand up to pause Christine. 'So you're all right and the library is okay?' Christine nodded and blew her nose.

'You lied about a burglary!' said Tom, getting to his feet. 'That's proper twisted.' He shook his head. 'I'm off.'

'Wait!' said Farah, making Tom do an emergency stop in front of her. 'I'm not saying what Christine's done is right but I know I feel bad about not coming to the library these last couple of weeks.' She leaned to the side to look around Tom at Christine. 'I'm sorry if you feel I've let you down, Christine.'

Maggie sighed. 'I agree. I'm sorry I've stopped coming too.'

All eyes fell on Tom. He shrugged his shoulders. 'I'm sure there was a better way to get us here. But… yeah, I feel bad about not supporting you.' He and Farah exchanged brief nods and he returned to his chair.

'Thank you,' said Christine. 'I am sorry for lying.'

'Right,' said Maggie, keen to not go around in circles. 'Where do we go from here?'

'That's my problem,' said Christine. 'I've had notice that I'm being made redundant because the library is definitely closing and I don't know what else I can do.'

'You're not on your own anymore,' said Farah. Christine looked grateful and inched her chair closer to the others.

'We need one last push. A big protest! Like a march that stops the traffic…' began Maggie.

'Not much traffic goes through Compton Mallow. It's not going to gridlock the Midlands,' said Tom.

Maggie continued regardless. '…Or a human barrier in front of the library when they come to shut it down,' she said.

'Bit late when they're actually closing it,' said Tom and the others glared at him. 'What? I'm just saying.'

'But a sit-in protest in the middle of the street might get the council's attention,' said Maggie.

'Will it, though?' asked Farah. 'I mean we did the sit-in inside and it's not changed anything. The council aren't taking any notice.'

They all went quiet and thought for a moment. Tom chewed on a thumbnail.

'We need an angle,' said Maggie. 'Something that makes people sit up and listen. Is the old school building listed?' She looked to Christine for a reply.

Tom sat up straight. 'This is the old school building on the green,' he said.

'Er, yeah,' said Farah slowly. 'That's what it's called.'

'This guy had that typed on a form,' said Tom, waving his hands as if trying to process his thoughts quickly. He turned to Maggie. 'The bloke who ran me over…'

'Lyle,' added Maggie.

'From that building company…' continued Tom.

'Taylor's Builders,' said Maggie.

'Yes.' Tom pointed at Maggie, like she'd answered a

question in a quiz show. 'He had a form on the front seat of his van and I had to move it to the floor. It had this address on it.' Tom was bobbing up and down in his seat.

'Tom, this could be important. What else did it say?' asked Maggie, leaning forward.

Tom closed his eyes for a moment. 'There were some numbers…'

'Excellent.' Maggie clapped her hands together. This was progress. 'It was probably a quote to do work. What else was on the form?'

Tom tipped his head up to the ceiling. 'I can't remember anything else.'

43

TOM

I felt like an idiot for not being able to remember anything else from the form I'd seen in the builder's van but I'd only glimpsed it for a moment. The large number at the bottom had made me gawp at that bit rather than the address. Maggie seemed to think it was a breakthrough but I wasn't so sure. It wasn't exactly concrete evidence that something dodgy was going on.

We needed to raise more awareness, get in people's faces. With Maggie directing everything we'd made some plans for a big Save The Library demonstration on Friday afternoon. Maggie thought if we caught the rush hour traffic – yeah, right, all four cars and a tractor – in Compton it would make more of an impact. She called it impact – pissing people off was what I'd call it but if it got us the attention we needed to save the library and Christine's job then I was up for it. We'd made a list of people to contact in the hope of stirring up some support from the locals and enough interest for the press and council to make sure they were there to see it.

I still think Christine was out of order telling us the library had been burgled but I get why she did it. We all do crazy stuff when we feel threatened. She was right that we've been distracted with other things. All being back together fired us up again. There is a special vibe about the library or maybe it's the people in it? We had a good discussion about what we needed to do and I think it got us refocused. We all had our instructions from Maggie – Christine was progressing from posters to placards, which was something. Farah was leading the leaflet drop. Maggie was contacting the press and the council and I was doing a social media blast. Basically we needed more signatures on our petition so I'd set us up a Twitter account and I planned to tweet loads of authors and ask for their support. I hoped it would work.

Being back in the library made me think about the place. I'd hate it to close down. If it wasn't for the library I'd never have met Maggie or got to know Farah – not that either of those relationships was going particularly well. There was also something else. The library had somehow renewed my connection to Mum. When I was there I got little slivers of memories of her. Sometimes it was the waft of the pages of a new book, not that I'm a book sniffer or anything but there's something about that smell that reminds me of Mum. I remember her reading to me here and being excited about the story but also feeling safe and cosseted. The library and reading had been our thing and now I was reconnecting with books I was kind of reconnected with her. Whatever it was it felt better and I didn't want to lose it.

Things were uncomfortable with Farah but at least we were talking again even if it wasn't like before. I was dying to know about her and Kemp but that was the last thing I could ask her. It bothered me more than I wanted to admit that she was hooking up with that goon but there was nothing I could do about it.

It took me a while to get all the tweets out. Maggie left to catch her bus but Christine waited and locked up after me. I had hoped Farah would wait too and walk back with me but she said she had to go. I walked home on my own. There weren't many people about – a few in the chippy and the pub. That was all. When I opened the front door I realised Dad hadn't left for work yet. I checked my watch. I should have hung around at the library for a few more minutes and I would have missed him. I wasn't being mean; I just didn't want to be here when he looked at the bike.

'Hiya,' he said. He was in the kitchen putting some things in his bag and he turned his back to me and hurried to complete the task. 'You all right?' he asked over one shoulder.

I stayed in the hallway. 'Um. Not really. I got knocked off my bike today.' It was still my bike even though we both used it.

He left the bag and came to the doorway. He looked concerned and I was pleased to see it. 'Are you hurt?'

'Bashed my leg up a bit but otherwise I'm okay.'

His concern deepened. 'And the bike?'

'I got it fixed.' The relief spread across his features. 'Well, Maggie got someone to fix it. It's not perfect but it's better than it was. I left you a message.' I pointed to the note on the hallstand where I'd left it.

'Sorry, I didn't see that.'

'Didn't you wonder where I was?' As far as he knew I was hours late in from school and I'd had no tea.

He shrugged and went back in to the kitchen to hastily zip up his bag. 'I figured you'd be out with your mates celebrating the end of the exams.' He heaved the bag onto his shoulder and came to face me in the hall. I was a fraction taller than him. I'm not sure when that happened.

'The exams don't finish until Friday morning.' And what mates were these? I wondered. He had no idea about my life but even now, after he was off the alcohol, he wasn't interested in finding out. I think that made it hurt a bit more. At least before he had an excuse.

'Oh. Right. Are you going out?' he asked.

'No.' I tried not to sound irritated but it was hard. 'I've just got in and I have no mates to go out with.'

'Right. Night then.' He put his head down and left me standing in the hall. I heard the click of the key in the lock and it made an odd sensation run through me. I hated being alone here at night. I'd never liked it but it was worse now, more obvious somehow. I took a deep breath and went to make myself some food and set about some final revision. My life was one big party.

I was having breakfast when Dad came in from work. 'There you go!' he said triumphantly plonking a typed letter down in front of me and patting it for emphasis.

'What's this?'

'Read it,' he said standing over me proudly. Why couldn't he just tell me?

I skim-read the first bit. The letter was addressed to me.

It was confirming my interview for an apprenticeship at the dog food factory. 'What the—?' I stared at it as something burned in my gut.

He slapped me on the back. 'You're welcome.'

How could he still be going on about this? 'But, Dad…'

'You said your last exam was Friday morning. This is for the afternoon. They had someone drop out.'

'I wonder why?'

'Dunno.' My sarcasm was lost on him. He scanned me up and down. 'You can wear your school uniform but maybe tidy yourself up.'

All kinds of alarm bells were echoing in my ears. 'Dad, look, I am grateful for you sorting this out but—'

'Don't mess it up.' He wagged a finger at me and looked slightly menacing for a second, which reminded me of when he was drinking. 'Don't look so worried. I'm joking. You'll be fine.'

Fine was the last thing I'd be with a life mapped out for me at the bastard dog food factory. I needed to get out of this. I stared at the letter: 5pm. 'Dad, I'm really sorry but I can't make it.'

'Why? What's more important than getting a job?' He was leaning over me.

'Err. Going to university. Saving the library.'

He snorted a laugh. 'You're joking, right?'

This was my chance to stand up for what I wanted. To explain what was important to me. To be my own man. But I bottled it. 'I need to go.' I picked up my toast and almost knocked my chair over in my rush to get away.

'See you later. Fish fingers for tea?'

'Err, yeah. If you like.' How the hell was I going to get out of this?

Wednesday I got in early from school because I only had one exam. I was quiet when I let myself in because I expected Dad to be in bed. I'd been distracted in my exam because all I could think about was the job at the factory. At one point I actually thought I could smell dog food but it must have been a waft of school dinners from the canteen – it was lasagne, which was a worry. I went to the kitchen to get a glass of water. Out of the window I saw Dad.

I watched him come out of the shed backwards with his work bag weighing heavy on his shoulder. He pocketed the shed key. He slunk down the side of the house and out of sight. A chill settled over me. We only went in the shed to get the lawnmower out but it couldn't be that because the grass hadn't been cut. He was hiding something and it didn't take a genius to work out what. I slumped back against the worktop like someone had punched the air from me. I instantly felt crap. I'd thought he was doing well. He'd kept all his appointments and I'm sure I would have smelled beer or whisky on him – maybe he'd changed to vodka. I don't think that has a smell.

I went out to the shed, checking over my shoulder in case Dad came back. The door was locked. Back in the kitchen I looked for the shed key but it was missing.

A wave of anxiety came crashing over me. I rang Farah – I needed to speak to someone and share the worries threatening to overspill. I couldn't go through it all again.

I thought it was going to go to voicemail when at last she

answered. 'Hi.' She sounded cautious. I didn't know what to say now I'd rung her. This was horrible. 'You okay?' she asked.

'No. Dad's acting all sus.'

'Drinking?'

I went to have another look out of the window but Dad was long gone. 'I dunno. Maybe. He's sneaking about and I can't think what else it could be.'

'Then you need to challenge him,' she said, forcefully.

I spun away from the window, the thought of calling Dad out on this was almost worse than the thought of seeing him mauled by booze again. 'I can't. What would I say?'

'That doesn't matter, Tom. You just need to stop him from relapsing.'

Easy for her to say. An image of Dad lying unconscious pierced my mind. She was right. I swallowed hard. 'Right I'm going after him.' I grasped my keys as I spoke.

'Do you want me to come too?'

'Yeah, that'd be good.'

'Meet you on the corner of my road in two minutes.'

I looked down the side of the house – he'd not taken my bike. Maybe there was a chance I could catch him up. I tried to run but my leg quickly reminded me that I couldn't. I hobbled as fast as I could, the whole time scanning up and down the roads I passed in case Dad was there. By the time I reached Farah's road my leg was throbbing and it had dawned on me what a total waste of time this was.

Within about a minute Farah appeared. 'Where is he?' she asked her eyes darting in all directions.

I scratched my ear. 'I don't know.'

She looked disappointed. 'What's the plan now?'

'I dunno.' I was hoping she was going to suggest we hang out. We stood in silence for a while, which was awful. The longer it went on the worse it was. I felt I had to say something. Anything. 'How's things with you and...' She glared at me. I shut up.

'I need to go over some revision notes,' she said pointing back at her house.

'Yeah. Of course. Me too.' I pointed in the direction of my house like a total idiot.

'See you at Friday's demo if I don't see you at school,' she said.

'Totally.'

She walked away. We were talking... kind of. That was progress. At least it hadn't been a complete waste of time. I limped home to do some cramming and worry about where the hell Dad had sneaked off to.

44

MAGGIE

Maggie was far more excited about library demo day than she should have been. Throwing herself back into the Save the Library plans had renewed her focus and pumped her full of energy. The snippet of information Tom had shared about the form in the builder's van had fuelled her determination. The form itself had been transformed with each conversation she'd had and by the time she got through to the local journalist it was now a bona fide quote to transform the library into a bar-cum-restaurant by a well-known chain, the name of which she dare not divulge, but its prices would put paid to a number of local businesses.

She'd said something similar to Bill from the pub and he was ready to take on anyone from the council. She'd managed to harness his anger into getting all the pub locals out in support. The local history group were up in arms at the thought of the old library building being raped and pillaged in the name of modernisation and the WI were fully on board – they didn't need an excuse to get baking.

Friday afternoon finally arrived and it was a sunny June day, which was perfect for an outdoor protest. Maggie trundled the tractor into Compton village centre and pulled up near to the library where a small crowd was waiting.

'Blimey,' said Bill rubbing his head as he looked in the trailer. 'I didn't think you meant we'd be building an actual wall.'

'It's the only thing that'll get their attention,' said Maggie proudly regarding the small mountain of straw bales. She'd loaned them from Savage for a small fee.

'Right, come on,' said Bill, to the group next to him. 'Let's get building.'

Maggie joined Tom, who was chewing what was left of his thumbnail and looking mightily perturbed. 'Exams all finished?'

'Yeah.' He seemed preoccupied.

'Well done. How's the leg?' she asked.

'Thanks. It's fine.' He pulled his phone from his pocket and checked it.

'Are you expecting a call?'

'No, just checking the time.' He shoved it back in his pocket.

'Okay, then. Let's get this protest started. We'll show them we mean business this time,' she said, taking off her jacket.

'You're not going to flash your boobs are you?' Tom looked horrified by his own words.

'That was only the one time and they provoked me.' He was still looking at her. 'No, I promise I won't do anything inappropriate.'

'Good. I'd better give Bill a hand,' he said and he began dragging a bale off the trailer.

Something was wrong with Tom but a full interrogation would have to wait. Right now Maggie had a protest to organise. Christine had done an excellent job with a number of very British slogans on placards including 'We are really rather cross' and 'I prefer books to people' as well as a bright array of more standard 'Save Our Library' ones. Maggie handed them out to the waiting crowd.

It didn't take long to turn the straw bales into a makeshift wall across the road and to line up the placard-waving protesters on either side. Almost instantly the cars started to back up. Farah and some girls of a similar age were quick to hand out flyers to the waiting motorists, explaining what was going on and why the library was so important to them. Maggie felt it was a stroke of genius using young women – they were far less likely to get shouted at than the likes of Bill or any of the ladies Maggie's age. She believed it wasn't sexist if the women were aware and in control of their own exploitation.

As the local businesses closed up for the day more people joined them and quite a crowd had gathered. The WI were dishing out tea, coffee and cake, which seemed to be an excellent incentive to come and stand in the road. Everyone was chatting and by the time the journalist arrived it was turning into quite the community social event. He shook hands with Maggie and a few others and then went to mingle and get some quotes. He was still talking about interest from the nationals but Maggie had heard that before.

Someone started a chant of 'We love Compton Mallow library' as some council officials arrived. Maggie joined in and shouted at the top of her voice. This was excellent fun. The officials went into a huddle as if choosing straws for who was going to approach the baying mob with their polite slogan placards and happy faces. Eventually a stout man strode over. 'Who's in charge here?'

'I am,' said Maggie stepping forward with a 'Libraries are brain food – don't let our children starve!' placard held aloft.

He took a backward step as if he suspected she was going to swipe him with it. 'You're breaking the law. We will call the police and we *will* have you all arrested.'

'Hang on, could you repeat that for the national press please?' she asked in her sweetest old lady voice. The newspaper correspondent stepped forward and the man's face went a strange colour.

A van pulled into the kerb and Maggie almost jumped with joy. It was the local television roving reporter. A two-man band of camera and newsperson piled out and headed their way. 'Ooh look, we're going to be on the news!' hollered Maggie and the council official retreated to the safety of his herd of suited men.

The next half an hour was bedlam as word got around the village that they were going to be on the news. Everyone turned out. Maggie was wise enough to know that they were only there to get their mugs on the telly but at this stage she didn't care what brought people there.

The party atmosphere grew until singing broke out, led by Alice from the care home. Farah tapped Maggie's arm and pulled her away from the noise. 'Christine's asking for you,' she said.

Maggie had almost forgotten about Christine. She was holed up in the library. Fearing the council might discover her involvement, she'd hidden herself away. 'Of course,' said Maggie, handing Farah her placard.

Christine was pacing the library when Maggie found her. 'Is it going well? Farah said it was.' Christine looked worried.

'Yes, yes. It's going very well. We've just been on the news.'

'Really?'

Maggie felt bad that Christine was missing out. 'Yes. Someone will have recorded it. I'm sure you'll be able to see it later. The chap from the council refused to speak to the television crew but they got him being driven away and hiding his face.'

Christine's lines deepened. 'He didn't say anything?'

'No. But that's good.'

'Is it?' Christine wrung her hands as she paced.

'Yes. Please sit down,' said Maggie and Christine paused for a moment and perched on the edge of a chair. 'He won't be able to authorise something just like that but he'll report back and those further up the tree will have to take notice now.'

Christine didn't look convinced. 'But will they? And even if they do will they still close the library and sack me anyway?'

Maggie took a moment to think. She'd been so caught up in the protest that the personal impact on Christine had escaped her a little. 'We've done all we can here tonight. Whatever happens we can say we gave it our all. And if it comes to it I'm sure you'll find another job.' She sat down on the chair next to Christine and looked around. How could one small building become so important? She thought about the people all those years ago who would have fought for it to become a library, who would have first stocked its shelves. Found sanctuary in the pages of its books. And all those it had brought joy and refuge to in its years as a library. There was a lot of history in its walls. 'We've put up a good fight.' She felt she was telling the library as much as Christine.

Christine gave an uncertain pout. 'I suppose so.'

'Now, give me ten minutes to thank everyone and get the bales moved and that will signal the end of the protest, then you can come out and have some cake and a cup of tea. All right?'

Christine looked downcast but nodded her agreement.

Back on the front line Tom was in full flow chanting away and waving his placard. Maggie was thrilled to see him come alive. The moment was short-lived as she spotted his father, a moment before he did, powering towards Tom like a Pendolino train at full tilt.

Maggie strode over and reached Tom at the same time Paul did. She stood to one side so Tom knew she was there if he needed her. 'What the bloody hell are you doing?' Paul shouted at Tom.

Tom lifted his chin. 'I'm saving our library.' Tom brought the placard down to rest on the ground and form a barrier between them.

Paul threw his hands up. 'You had an interview! What the hell are you playing at?'

'I'm sorry, Dad. I don't want to work there. I told you that,' said Tom, his voice calm and reasonable.

'No you didn't!'

'I did. You chose not to hear me.'

'Bloody hell, Tom! You need to grow up. You could have lost this job if I hadn't told them you were sick.'

'Dad. Please listen. I'm not going to work at the dog food factory. I'm going to university.'

Paul looked like he was going to explode. 'Not this again.'

'I've looked into university entry requirements and I've chosen what A level subjects I'm doing. I am staying on at school because I want to get a decent job…' Paul went to say something but Tom held his hand up to stop him. 'I know there are jobs at the factory and if all this comes to nothing then that's where I'll go, but at least let me try for a place at university. I think it's what Mum would have wanted.'

A heavy silence claimed the space between them. Paul's frown deepened.

'Can I get you some cake and a coffee?' said Maggie, touching his arm and drawing his attention away from Tom, who was sweating.

'What? No,' he said, doing a double take at Maggie. 'All right?'

'Yes, thanks,' she said, standing closer to Tom. 'Tom's worked incredibly hard on his GCSEs and here he is standing up for something he believes in. I know I have no right to be but I'm incredibly proud of the lad and you must be too.'

Paul opened and closed his mouth like someone had put him on mute. Tom turned and gave Maggie a smile. 'Thanks, Maggie.'

The continued silence from Paul was worrying. Maggie wasn't sure if he was going to lash out or stalk off. She felt for Tom. He had worked his socks off with his schoolwork and he'd helped get the petition trending on Twitter – whatever that was.

'Hello there, Paul,' said Bill, slapping him on the back and breaking the tension. 'I haven't seen you in ages. Have you come down to save the pub?' Bill caught Maggie's beady eye. 'I mean library but you know if the council get their way and turn that beautiful old building into a bar that could be the death of the Limping Fox.'

'Err. No. I came to see Tom, my son.' He nodded in Tom's direction.

'Well, I'll be,' said Bill. 'I had no idea he was your boy. He's a bloody star turn that one. He's worked like a Trojan doing the silver surfers sessions and getting this petition signed. He's even got me on Twitter. Now ain't that something?'

'Um. Yes.' Paul didn't sound too sure.

Someone called Bill's name and he waved back to them. 'I need to dash but look, don't be a stranger. We've got a craft ale in that you'd love,' said Bill.

Tom looked anxious as he waited for his father's response. 'You're all right, thanks, Bill. I'm not drinking at the moment,' said Paul. He paused to take a breath. 'Or going forward, actually. I've quit the booze.' He glanced at Tom. 'For good.'

The relief in Tom was almost palpable. There was a flicker of a smile on Tom's lips, which Paul mirrored.

'That's a bloody shame,' said Bill. He adjusted his trousers, gave Tom a high five and set to taking the straw bale wall down.

Tom and his father exchanged awkward looks. 'I need to give them a hand,' said Tom, laying down his placard on the pavement.

'Right.' Paul nodded. He fiddled with the collar on his polo shirt and walked off. Tom watched him go.

'You okay?' Maggie asked.

'Yeah. We'd better get this lot down,' he said, busying himself with dragging the bales down and hauling them over to the tractor.

Maggie started collecting in the placards. Out of the corner of her eye she saw Paul rush back across the road but she wasn't quick enough to intercept him. He marched up to Tom who had his back to him and was heaving the bales into the trailer.

'Tom!' Paul barked, making Tom spin around, his face wary. Paul made a movement like he was cracking his neck to release tension. His gaze dropped to the ground. 'I'm sorry.' He briefly gave Tom an awkward hug and stepped back. Neither seemed to know what to do as straw bales were moved around them. Tom nodded, Paul did the same then turned and strode off. Tom had a tear in his eye as he and Maggie watched his father go. They looked at each other and something passed between them.

Tom finished moving the bales and then helped take the table back to the library. He went to sort out the placards while Maggie had a final chat to Christine. She was walking back down the alleyway when she saw two figures jostling halfway down. One of them was Tom. She quickened her pace but made sure she was light on her feet so as not to alert them.

'I'm sick of telling you to keep away, Harris,' said the one on the right as he shoved Tom in the chest. She knew now how Colin felt when the rage consumed him. Within seconds she was between the two of them.

'Leave him alone,' she shouted.

The aggressor started to laugh. 'Shitting hell. Who's this? Super gran?'

'Leave her out of it, Kemp,' said Tom, before leaning into Maggie's ear. 'He's not worth it.'

'Oh, I know he's not,' she said. 'Get your phone out,' she added in a whisper. 'I know who you are,' she said to Kemp.

'Who's that then?' Kemp was still looking entertained.

'You're the scum who stole my bag.'

'What?' said Tom.

'Prove it, old woman,' said Kemp, no longer looking amused.

'I recognise your voice,' she said. 'I just need to call the police and—'

Kemp reared up over Maggie. 'You don't want to do that,' he said his voice almost a snarl.

'Why ever not?' asked Maggie, standing her ground, her shoulders back and her chin held high.

'Seriously. Leave it. You'll get hurt,' said Tom, fiddling with his phone.

'You should listen to Harris.'

'I was talking to you, Kemp,' said Tom.

'You've had fair warning,' said Maggie, raising a fist.

Kemp snorted a laugh. 'It will literally be the last thing you do,' he said reaching out and grabbing Maggie around the throat.

What happened next happened like it was on fast forward. Within seconds Kemp was lying on the ground clutching his ribs while blood poured from his nose.

Maggie leaned over Kemp's crumpled figure. 'And we got that on videotape. So unless you want the police to see you assaulting me or even better your cronies seeing me kick your backside, you need to straighten yourself out. Got it?'

'Harris! I want that deleted!' yelled Kemp.

'Don't you dare go after him,' snapped Maggie. 'Because if you do the rest of my family will beat you to a pulp. Got it?' Maggie's voice had an edge to it and her lie was convincing. Kemp swallowed hard. 'All we want is the muggings to stop. As long as there's no more, this video will never be released. One more mugging and...'

'Okay. I get it,' said Kemp, shuffling himself upright and inspecting the blood dripping down his clothes.

'Good. Come on, Tom, they'll be wondering where we've got to,' said Maggie her voice back to normal. Tom shrugged his shoulders at Kemp with an "I did warn you" look on his face and Maggie strode off like nothing had happened.

45

TOM

Dad's gone all quiet since the demo. Even quieter than usual, which means it's basically silent all the time. I don't know if that's worse than him ranting at me. I can tell he's disappointed that I chose to go to the demo rather than the interview and it's eating away at me like a zombie. If I don't get decent GCSE results then I'll have to retake them and he's gonna be all "I told you so" and "You could have been earning good money at the factory" and it's going to proper do my head in because worst of all he'll be right.

It was weird waking up and realising that there's no more GCSEs and no more school until September. I'm not sure what I'm going to do now. Some mates are doing National Citizen Service, which sounds cool but it costs fifty quid. With money tight there was no point asking Dad if I could do it. I'm back doing a weekday paper round but that doesn't pay much. I should probably get a job for the summer. I'll have a think about that but for today, at least, I'm going to chill out.

I heard Dad sneaking about. It was well early for him. My stomach clenched. What was he up to now? I'd had a good check around the house last night for any stashed booze and couldn't find any. I tried to look in the shed but it was locked up and the key wasn't in the drawer where we usually keep it. I tried looking through the shed window but all I could see was the lawnmower and spider's webs.

I crept out of bed, slung some clothes on and went downstairs. Maybe I should try talking to him. If he's having a relapse and he needs to get help, I could suggest that. I'd do pretty much anything to avoid him going back to how he was. I stuck my head around the living room door and then in the kitchen but there was no sign of him. He couldn't have vanished. I put my shoes on. If I left now I might be able to do a better job of following him. Last time Farah and I were useless. This time I needed to do better.

I opened the front door and then shut it quickly because Dad was going out through the gate. I counted to ten and opened the door again. He'd not seen me and he was now at the end of the road. I checked I'd got my keys and my phone and I followed him. Ours is a sleepy village and at that time on a Saturday morning there's nobody around making it hard to keep him in sight and not be seen. I kept dodging in and out of driveways and behind overgrown bushes like a rubbish spy.

He crossed the road by the shops and I hung back or he'd see me for sure. The bus pulled in and I used it as cover.

'Well, hello,' said Maggie, getting off the bus. 'To what do I owe this pleasure?'

What was she on about? I frowned at her. 'I'm not here to meet you. I'm following Dad.'

'Oh.' Her expression changed. 'That makes more sense. Look, Tom. I know I hurt you and—'

'It's okay.'

'But it's not. It's damaged our friendship and I'm truly sorry about that.'

I shrugged. 'I'm not mad at you anymore.' The truth was I missed her.

'Does that mean we can put it behind us?' she asked.

'Sure.' I wanted things to go back to how they had been too.

Maggie walked in step with me and we watched Dad cross the green. 'Mind me asking why he's under surveillance?'

'I think he's drinking again.'

'Ah. That's not good. He's gone past the pub though – that's a positive sign.'

'It's not open yet. Come on we're losing him.' I started to stride it out and Maggie kept up no problem. It was good to have her with me. If I ended up confronting him she was excellent backup. She was well early for book club but then old people hated being late for stuff.

After about five minutes we were heading out of the village and nearing the new estate. I say new because that's what everyone calls it but it's been there as long as I can remember. 'Have you any idea where he's going?' asked Maggie.

'Not a clue.' I'd been trying to think as we walked but he never came up here or at least I thought he didn't. I covered the area on my paper round and all that was there was houses. They were well nice houses, some with double garages and new cars outside.

'No friends up this way?'

'Nope.' Actually, now I thought about it, Dad didn't have any friends. Certainly none he mentioned. He didn't call or text anyone or meet people for a drink. It struck me that maybe he was as lonely as me. Poor Dad, we'd had more in common than I'd realised. I'd had my Xbox and he'd had his whisky. What a sad pair we'd been. I looked across at Maggie and she smiled warmly back at me. Meeting Maggie had changed things. Dad needed a friend like Maggie.

'Exam results end of August is it?' Maggie asked.

'Yeah. Third week of August.'

'Well, try to forget about them until then. You've worked hard and you can't do anything about them now.'

'But what if I've ballsed it right up?' I kept my eye on Dad as he turned a corner up ahead.

'Well, I doubt that you have, but you cross that bridge when you come to it.'

I knew she was right but it didn't stop it messing with my head. 'I think I might get a job just for the summer like.'

'Great idea. Doing what?'

Maggie had a knack of chucking spanners in. What sort of job could I do? Too young for bar work and not qualified for anything else. 'I dunno.'

'I could ask Savage if he needs a hand. If you're interested.'

'Ye-ah, that'd be awesome.'

'No guarantees and he's a tight old bugger who won't pay much but I know he had to hire in last year and he wasn't that impressed with them.'

'Will you do me a reference?' I took my eyes off Dad to look at her. Her face was warm and full of pride.

'It'd be my pleasure.' She patted me affectionately on the back. It let me know she cared and I'd missed that. We'd reached the corner where Dad had turned right. I slowed and we both looked down the road. It was completely empty apart from a few parked cars – but no sign of Dad.

'Where'd he go?' I said as I looked up and down the street like a crazy person. He'd vanished.

'He's either turned off further up or he's gone inside one of these houses,' said Maggie calmly. She leaned against the lamppost.

The next road was too far ahead for him to have made it that far. 'Why would he go inside?' So many questions were running through my mind. Did he have a girlfriend? I was disgusted at the thought of it. Or a drinking buddy? Or maybe it was a new friend from Alcoholics Anonymous. If it was a friend then why sneak about?

'I suggest we wait and see if he comes out.' She checked her watch and I leaned against the lamppost too.

'Thanks for coming with me,' I said.

'You couldn't have stopped me. I love a mystery.' Her eyes twinkled as she spoke and it made me smile. She was full of mischief. I'd really missed being around her.

'This job with Savage, would it be every day?'

'Yes, right through until autumn. There's loads to do on a farm this time of year.'

'Do you think he'd pay my bus fare on top?' I knew it was cheeky but if anyone had the balls to ask him it would be Maggie.

She laughed. 'No. But you can stay at mine. If it suits you.' She gave a nonchalant shrug.

I glanced up the road to see Dad reversing down a path and waving at someone. 'Look out he's leaving.'

We both reversed back around the corner. I was wishing

I'd worked out what I was going to say to him. I expected him to walk back towards us but instead he came out of one gate and went up the next path. 'What's he doing?'

'Come on,' said Maggie and she marched off towards Dad.

'Whoa!' But it was pointless. She was like a sniper's bullet – fixed on her target and there was no stopping her. I jogged to keep up. 'Let me handle this.' I sounded a lot more confident than I was.

Maggie let me go in front and I slowed down as I neared the house he'd just left. I could hear him talking. He was standing on the doorstep chatting to a woman. He sounded totally different. Not like Dad at all.

'Brilliant. Thanks. Should be next week but I've got your number if not. Bye then,' Dad said, in his fake cheery voice and he turned to leave. His face when he clocked me and Maggie standing on the pavement watching him was something I'll always remember. Rabbit in headlights was an understatement – more like rabbit facing a battalion of monster trucks.

He looked shifty as he dashed down the path and waved us back the way we'd come. 'What the hell are you doing here?' The penny seemed to drop before I had chance to answer. 'You're following me? Why the hell are you following me?' He was glaring at Maggie now.

'I asked her to come.' I didn't want him having a go at Maggie.

'Why?' he asked, sounding cross.

I was working out what to say when Maggie beat me to it. 'Because the poor lad thinks you're drinking again and he's worried sick about you,' said Maggie. 'Sorry, Tom,' she added in a soft voice. 'He needs to know.'

Dad's expression changed. 'Did ya really think that?' I nodded. 'I'm not, son. I promise.'

It was a relief to hear him say it. 'Then what are you doing?' I asked.

The front door of the house Dad had just visited reopened and a slim woman came out. 'Ooh, I'm glad I've caught you,' she said striding up to Dad. 'You know I will have that nude set, if you can add it to my order.'

Maggie and I looked at Dad as his face turned the colour of a ripe tomato. It was something I could relate to. He turned his back on us and spoke to the lady in his new cheery voice. 'Of course. One nude foundation palette. No problem. You won't regret it.' He pulled a form from his bag and scribbled something on it. He showed it to the woman who seemed very happy. She thanked him and went back inside. Maggie and I turned our questioning eyes back on Dad.

'What's going on?' I asked.

His shoulders slumped forward. 'I'm trying to make some extra cash.' He pulled a booklet from his bag and handed it to me without making eye contact.

I looked at the heavily made-up woman's face smiling back at me from the cover. 'Avon? Make-up, perfume and stuff?' I flicked through the brochure. 'You're the Avon lady?' I couldn't help the snort that came out. Maggie elbowed me in the ribs. She was probably right to. It must have been well embarrassing for Dad.

'I think seeking out additional ways to make money is most commendable,' said Maggie.

Dad turned his attention to her. 'It's a nice little earner to be honest with you. It's early days but the orders are coming in thick and fast.' Dad seemed really proud of himself. I couldn't ever remember him looking like that before.

'Well done, Dad.' I handed back the brochure.

'Thanks. Look I need to get round all of this estate so...'

'Of course,' said Maggie. 'We've got book club at the library.'

'Book club. You?' said Dad, pointing at me.

I stood up straight. 'Yeah. I like book club and if you don't take the... mickey out of it, I'll say nothing about you selling Avon.'

'Deal,' said Dad, thrusting out his hand and we shook on it.

46

MAGGIE

Maggie savoured how lovely it was to stroll back through Compton Mallow with Tom. He was chattier than he had been of late – the barriers between them were starting to dismantle and it warmed her heart. Although Tom hadn't said so he was obviously relieved that his dad hadn't relapsed. He found the Avon job far more entertaining than she did. So much for this generation and their liberal views, thought Maggie.

'This job with Savage,' said Tom.

'It's merely an idea. He might not need anyone.'

'Sure. But if he does, would it be like a proper job or is it like the stuff I did for you?' Maggie opened her mouth to protest but he waved it away like you would a wasp. 'I saw the log pile. And the animals are all fine. You don't need me. You don't need anyone.'

'That's where you're wrong, Tom. I *can* manage alone but I very much enjoyed not having to. And correct me if I'm wrong but I thought you got something out of it too.'

He gave her a shy smile. 'You know I love it at your place.'

'And I loved having you. You're welcome anytime.'

'That's nice of you, Maggie, but I know I cost money to feed.'

'That's not a problem. I'm not rich but I'm not short of a bob or two.' She gave a chuckle.

Tom gave her a sideways look. 'Huh? But you can't afford a car.'

She shook her head. 'Correction – I don't own a car.'

'You use your free bus pass.'

'Because I think cars are bad for the environment and running a tractor and the quad bike is more than my fair share of CO_2 emissions.'

Tom remained puzzled. 'You don't have credit cards.'

'Because they're made of plastic.'

Tom snorted a laugh. 'You're quality you are, Maggie.'

'Thank you,' she said, rather primly and slightly unsure as to whether it was a compliment or not. 'Why don't you get the bus back with me after book club and we'll tackle Savage about summer work at the farm?'

'Cool.'

There were more people in the library than usual. Perhaps the penny had finally dropped that locals needed to use it more if they wanted it to stay. There were some new members for book club and Tom was kept busy helping people get online. Christine was distracted and understandably so. She'd heard nothing from the council and there were only five days left until the library's official closing date. But despite this there was something different in the air. There was a buzz about the place and even if it was its last hurrah, Maggie was pleased to have witnessed it.

After a lively book club they'd said their goodbyes before Tom and Maggie caught the bus to Furrow's Cross. The rapport they'd once enjoyed was slowly returning as their relationship healed. They chatted on the way about everything and nothing as if racing to catch up on the time they'd lost. When they got off at their stop Maggie paused at the letterbox to collect her post and Savage's. From her letterbox she pulled out a leaflet about pizza delivery, a white envelope and an ominous-looking brown one. Maggie studied the latter for a second before plunging it into her pocket. Tom was asking about the merits of different sheep breeds and she tuned in and out as they walked up to Savage's, her mind distracted by the brown envelope.

'Right,' said Maggie, stopping Tom a few feet from the door. 'He's a grumpy old bugger. You'd best let me lead on this.'

'Actually,' said Tom, running his bottom lip through his teeth. 'Can I give it a go?'

Maggie lifted her chin. 'Of course you can. I'll be here if you need me.' She took a step back.

'Thanks.' Tom rapped on the door and it was answered with a flurry of barks and the sound of boots on stone floor.

The door opened and a harassed-looking Savage glared at Tom. 'Yes?'

'Hello, Mr Savage. I'm Tom. I wondered if you had any summer jobs available.'

'No, thank you,' said Savage and he went to shut the door.

Tom put his hand out to stop the door shutting. 'I did some work for Maggie and I think some sort of farm work might be what I want to do as a career…'

'Really?' asked Maggie butting in.

'Yeah. I love the outdoors and the animals and everything about it,' gushed Tom with a shy smile.

Maggie couldn't have been prouder. A cough from Savage reminded them he was there.

'Sorry, Fraser,' said Maggie. 'I can't recommend Tom here enough. He's a cracking little worker. He won't let you down. Not like last year's wastrels.' Savage made a series of noises that seemed to imply he agreed. 'But he'll want paying at the going rate,' added Maggie with a hard stare, which Savage returned. A frosty silence ensued. 'Well?'

Savage's badger-like eyebrows lumbered about his forehead. 'I'm not made of money.' Maggie tilted her head in a way that was oddly menacing for a woman of her years. 'Fine. I'll pay him what I paid them others.'

'Awesome. Thanks,' said Tom, shaking Savage's hand.

Maggie gave him a nod of approval. 'You'll not regret it,' she said.

Back at Maggie's they celebrated Tom's new job with a biscuit and a cup of tea for Maggie and a Coke for Tom – she'd got a couple of bottles in, just in case.

'Are you going to read it?' asked Tom.

'Sorry?' asked Maggie.

'The letter you got out of the box. It's another one about your son. Isn't it?' He leaned against the chair back and munched his biscuit.

Maggie pulled the crumpled brown envelope from her pocket and put it on the table. It looked so dull and uninteresting. But the sight of it filled her with trepidation.

'Why would they be writing to me again?' She spoke to the envelope. 'Surely everything has been said.' She looked up at Tom, tears welling in her eyes.

'Might be admin stuff.' He bent forward. 'You want me to read it?'

She thought for a moment. She was already afraid of what it might say. Although she couldn't think how things could get any worse. 'Please,' said Maggie, grateful she was sitting down, as her legs were feeling weak and her heart heavy.

Tom ripped the envelope open, and pulled out a typed page, which was wrapped around another envelope. The latter was made from thick cream paper and had already been opened, it had "Maggie" handwritten on the front in slanting writing. Tom laid out the typed sheet. 'Dear Mrs Mann, Enclosed is correspondence sent to us from Lisa,' read Tom. He looked at Maggie. 'Who's she?'

Maggie's head snapped up. 'I don't know.' She searched her mind but the name meant nothing to her.

Tom took out and unfolded the second letter. 'Dear Maggie, Thank you for sending the package of cherished baby items. It was very thoughtful of you and I felt they deserved a reply. You know my husband as River but his name was changed to Richard when he was adopted.' Tom paused. 'You can't blame them for that,' he said with a wonky smile.

Maggie wiped away a tear. 'Is there any more?'

'Yes. Sorry.' He returned to the letter. 'I feel I need to be honest so I'm afraid to say I don't know if Richard will reach a point where he will want to communicate with you. He knows I am writing to you and has reviewed this letter.

Richard had a happy upbringing with adoptive parents who love and support him in everything he does. His father was a dentist, now retired, and his mother was a…' Tom stopped and studied Maggie. 'Are you okay with this?'

Maggie nodded and waved for him to continue while she blew her nose.

He scanned the letter to find his place. 'His mother was a part-time music teacher. Richard is also a dentist and joined his father's dental practice from university and took over from his father eleven years ago. Richard and I met at university in Sheffield. We married in 1994 and have two children…' Maggie drew a sharp intake of breath but Tom continued. 'Rosie who is twenty-three and Oliver who is nineteen. We live in Kent with our two dogs and Rosie's horses.' Tom turned the page. 'I hope this letter has helped to fill in some blanks for you as your last letter did for Richard. With kindest regards, Lisa Haseley.'

Tom handed the letter to Maggie. She took it but the tears blurred her vision too much for her to read it. Tom's voice was swimming in her mind. Scores of questions she'd held for so long had been answered in a few sentences. The letter had given her much-longed-for information – he had a wife and children. She was a grandmother. And yet… What the letter hadn't told her, could never tell her, was what her son looked like. Other questions that had built up over the years seemed to breach the dam: Did his hair change from the baby blonde she remembered? What did his voice sound like? His laugh? Was he like her in any way?

'You okay?' asked Tom looking full of concern.

She didn't like being the one who made him look that way. 'I'm fine, really.' Maggie tried to pull herself together and blew her nose but the smile she pasted on was obviously fake. She stood up and hastily returned the letter to its envelope.

'You look like you need a hug,' said Tom. He didn't give her a chance to think about it or protest. He wrapped her in a tight embrace and held her. It was like something unravelled within her and she cried.

47

TOM

Maggie called a meeting the day before the library was due to close. It was a last chance to see if we could do anything. She invited the council to attend but she got no reply so we weren't expecting anyone. The newspaper article had stirred up tons of interest and support. They'd been careful about how they worded it but *information from an unnamed source about possible development plans* had certainly stirred things up. The builders had unintentionally helped as instead of denying any involvement they had responded saying they were unable to comment on individual projects, which was enough smoke for the newspaper to assume there was a flame somewhere. But the council had refused to comment about the building work and everything had gone quiet. I'd submitted our petition and heard nothing either.

Maggie had made cakes, including a lemon drizzle, and I was putting it onto plates when some more people arrived. Farah shut the door behind her. It was hard not to stare. I'd not seen her for ages – or at least it felt like it. Each time I saw her my stomach spun like the reels on a fruit machine. I concentrated on the lemon drizzle cake.

'Hi,' said Farah, coming to stand in front of me. 'This is it. D-Day.'

'I guess.' I didn't know what to say to her anymore. Things were still a bit awkward between us. And I had a gift for saying the wrong thing.

'I'm doing National Citizen Service. What are your plans for the summer?' she asked.

'I've got a job on a farm.'

'Maggie's?' she asked.

'No.' I was a bit hacked off with her assuming that. 'A farm in Furrow's Cross. Dipping the sheep. That sort of thing. It'll look good on my CV when I apply to universities.' Me and Maggie had been doing some investigation into agricultural courses and I was more fired up than ever.

'Cool,' she said. We looked anywhere but at each other. 'It's good to have a break from studying. I was fed up with it,' she added.

'Me too.' I nodded.

Farah tucked her hair behind her ears. 'Especially as I was baby-sitting Joshua Kemp,' she said.

Okay now she'd got my attention. 'How d'ya mean?' I asked.

'His mum knows my mum and they were worried he was falling behind so my mum volunteered me to help him revise. Total waste of time. The loser kept talking about how ace he was rather than studying. In the end I told my parents it was affecting my revision and that got me out of it.'

'So you and he…' I hardly dare ask the question.

'We weren't going out. We never were. You just jumped to the wrong conclusion.'

I tried not to grin but I was chuffed to hear this. 'Right. Sorry about that. Lemon drizzle cake?' In my excitement I almost shoved it up her nose.

We gathered around the table and Maggie called the meeting to order. The door opened and in walked the bloke from the council Maggie called the Bigwig. The guy was bald so I've no idea why she calls him that. Sarcasm maybe? Christine almost fell over in her haste to distance herself from the meeting and began reordering books on the shelf at high speed and most annoyingly in the wrong order.

'Christine, I need a word,' said the council Bigwig, taking Christine out the back. Which was a bit odd because it's basically a tiny kitchen and cupboard. Not the best place to have a meeting especially if he was about to confirm that she'd lost her job.

We all waited and watched the door until the moment the handle turned and then we all pretended to be doing something else. Christine came out first, her face covered by a giant tissue. Not a good sign but not exactly a surprise. Christine retook her seat next to Maggie but kept fidgeting like a kid does when they need a wee.

'I'll keep this brief,' said Mr Bigwig. 'Formal emails will be issued at three o'clock tomorrow but suffice to say Christine is being retained but will be splitting her time across three local libraries and overseeing the new mobile library.'

Christine started to cry as everyone congratulated her. I waved because I was on the other side of the table. Then I wished I hadn't because everyone looked my way.

'Congratulations,' I said in a squeaky voice that didn't sound like mine.

'What does that mean for Compton Mallow library exactly?' asked Maggie in her usual forceful way.

He seemed irritated. 'It means this library, along with Dunchurch and Harbury, will need additional volunteers to maintain the current opening hours. If they can't be found the library hours will be reduced, which may eventually lead to its closure.'

'It's a stay of execution,' said Maggie. 'Without volunteers it will inevitably be closed.'

'I'll volunteer,' I said. Farah smiled at me and I nearly lost my shit. It was like the sun finally coming out after a dystopian winter.

'Me too,' said Farah and there was an echo of the same from almost everyone there.

'Well,' he blustered. 'There's a formal process and you'll need to sign up with Christine.' He said some other stuff but I was more interested in Farah's excitement at us being library volunteers. Christine saw the council bloke out and as soon as the door clicked shut we all cheered. It was awesome. Lots of hugging and handshaking followed until I was face to face with Farah and we weren't sure what to do. We both flushed red and turned away.

It'd be beyond awkward if I asked Farah out and she said no. That would change things massively. I'd always feel like a loser and she'd think I was a bit of a creep for hitting on her. If we did go out, which is, like, a huge if – because Farah is way out of my league – but say we did. At some point we'd break up, which is always going to cause serious issues and then that'd be it. We'd never speak again and I can't afford to lose her. So friends it is. Unless of course she snogs my face off in which case I'd defo be up for it. Well, I'm only human.

Waiting for my GCSE results was torture but working on Savage's farm took my mind off things. I was outdoors all the time and mostly had one of the dogs with me. Rusty's puppies were both sold but at least I got to see Rusty most days. I loved the work. It was full-on and knackering but I was doing something useful and I was getting a tan. The money was all right and I'd been giving some to Dad and saving the rest. I tried paying Maggie some rent and she threatened to knock my block off so instead I thought I'd do something nice for her or get her something decent for Christmas.

Dad was okay about me living with Maggie in the week and coming home after I'd done my volunteer's shift at the library on a Saturday. Weekends with Dad were about watching telly and making up Avon orders but the atmosphere was more relaxed now that the drinking and finances were under control. At least we had something to talk about although he still wasn't great at conversation. I'd started cooking on a Saturday night. Maggie had been teaching me some simple stuff and a few trips on the bus to the charity shops in Leamington Spa have got both me and Dad looking half decent.

Living in two places probably sounds weird to other people but it suits me fine. I wasn't looking forward to going back to Dad's all the time when school restarted but I didn't have much choice. I'd talked to Maggie about it and she said I needed to tell Dad how I felt but I couldn't seem to work out how to say it without it sounding like I didn't want to live with him. He was okay now he was off the alcohol and I definitely didn't want to do anything that might set him back.

Results day was a Thursday and I decided to get the early bus down to be there when the results were handed out. Maggie asked if I wanted her to come with me. I kind of did but I knew some of the other kids wouldn't have their olds with them so I said no thanks.

There was already a crowd waiting when I got off the bus. Farah was with her mates. I lurked alone at the back. When they opened the school doors it was all quite organised but I bet everyone just wanted to charge in, grab their envelope and run out like Usain Bolt. I was queuing when I heard squeals and saw Farah jumping up and down with another girl. They both seemed happy. My stomach lurched. What if I'd messed it all up?

'Name?' asked the bored-looking lady who usually worked in the office. She didn't appear happy about having to come in to work today.

'Thomas Harris.'

'Like the author?' she asked.

A few months ago I wouldn't have a had a clue what she was talking about but now I was quite proud to share my name with one of the authors I enjoyed reading.

'Yeah. The same.'

She handed me an envelope. A brown envelope. I thought about the brown envelopes that came for Maggie from social services and I suddenly wished Maggie had come with me. I didn't want to open this alone. I wandered outside staring at my name on the envelope.

'Harris.' I looked up. It was Kemp.

'Kemp.'

He did the smallest possible movement of his head, so small you couldn't really call it a nod, and then he walked past me and joined the queue. It was the most civil conversation we'd ever shared.

'So?' Farah appeared at my shoulder. 'Haven't you opened it? Come on!' She was a bit hyper.

I couldn't *not* open it now. I ripped the envelope and I thought I was going to be sick. My gut churned like a turbo-charged cement mixer. I pulled out the white sheet of paper and looked at it. I stared at it but I couldn't take it in. It was like I'd lost the ability to read. I went over my name on the page about four times before I dare look at the grades. The numbers all swapped about.

'You got an eight in history. I'm claiming that!' said Farah. 'Gotta go – my parents are waiting in the car. See you at the library.'

I spun around but I was too late; she'd already run off. I watched her go out of the gate. I blinked a few times to check what I was seeing. Dad was standing just outside the railings watching me. He slowly raised his hand and I did the same like a slow motion mirror mime.

Dad came over and we stared at the sheet together. 'It was letters in my day. What do the numbers mean?' he asked.

'Grade four is a pass. But I need three at grade five and three at grade six – which is like an old B grade – or above to get into sixth form.'

He leaned forward. We both sort of realised at the same time. 'Apart from French they're all five or higher. Blimey.

Well done, son.' He slapped me on the shoulder but this time his hand stayed there. 'I'm proud of you, Tom.'

'Thanks.' We stayed staring at the results. I couldn't quite believe it. I'd got my best marks in the subjects I wanted to do at A level. That meant I'd definitely got a place in sixth form. I'd even scraped a five in biology. I let out a breath I hadn't realised I'd been holding in. I'd only actually gone and done it.

'You okay?' he asked.

'I'm surprised I guess.' I'd done way better than I thought I would.

'I'm not,' said Dad.

I looked at him. 'Why?'

'Because you're smart like your mum. And you've been swotting hard.' He held his palms up. 'That's not a criticism. I hadn't realised how serious you were about going to university until I saw you studying. And for what it's worth I think you were right to want more than the apprenticeship.'

'It's not that—'

'It's okay,' he said interrupting me. 'I'm proud of you for standing up to me. I mean I was pissed off at the time but you were right, you're worth more than the factory. This proves it.' He tapped the results. 'You should let Maggie know.'

I called Maggie to tell her and she nearly burst my eardrum with her shouting but I loved that she was so chuffed for me and not afraid to show it. She invited me and Dad over for a celebratory meal. I hovered for a second. I had her on loudspeaker and I wasn't sure if Dad would be up for it.

'You don't have to come,' I said quickly to him.

He smiled and nodded. 'If her cooking's anything like her cake then count me in,' he said.

⋆

When I opened the front door at Maggie's she must have been waiting in the hallway because she almost knocked me over with the force of her hug. 'You absolute bloomin' star!' she said, when she finally let me go. I didn't mind. I liked it really. I mean I made a big fuss of wiping her kiss off my cheek but that's expected. 'I knew you could do it. I never doubted you for a second,' she said. I knew every word was true and it was the best feeling.

'Thanks, Maggie. You know, for everything.' She batted my thanks away and turned to Dad.

'Hello, Paul,' she said. 'What about the boy then?'

'I'm very proud,' said Dad, following my lead and taking off his shoes.

'Right. Dinner is on. Fizzy elderflower is in the fridge to celebrate with but first I've got a little something for Tom. Well, more joint ownership really.' I had no idea what she was on about. Dad shrugged. 'I'll cover any costs,' she continued. 'But I'll be needing Tom here to do most of the work.' Maggie marched off to the living room.

'This is what she's like. You just need to go with it,' I whispered.

'Okay,' said Dad and he smiled.

'Are you two coming?' called Maggie.

I went through to the living room. Maggie was standing with her back to the door. When she turned around I thought I was going to spontaneously combust. She was cradling the red merle puppy in her arms.

'Penny!' I dashed forwards and she handed me the dog. Penny had grown loads since I'd last seen her. 'But I thought she'd been sold to some farmer up north?' That was what Savage had told me.

'I'm afraid you were right, Tom. She's deaf. Completely deaf in one ear and not great in the other one. She's no good as a sheepdog. Savage told me. Well, he was moaning that the farmer who bought her wanted his money back and that the dog was going to the rescue. I said I'd give him half what the farmer paid so here she is.'

'She's awesome.' I heard the wobble in my own voice. Penny was more beautiful than I remembered. Her blue eyes looked at me like I was the coolest person in the world. I turned to show her to Dad but it was tricky because she was licking my face. 'Isn't she gorgeous, Dad?'

Dad was frowning. 'And you get that she's living here?' he asked.

'Yes,' I said.

'But I'll need to keep the Monday to Friday arrangement with Tom for puppy training purposes, if that's okay with you both?' said Maggie, with a wink. What was going on? Had she already spoken to Dad about this? I was definitely missing something.

I froze. This was what I wanted more than anything. I loved my dad, of course I did, but I couldn't stand being in the house on my own. I hated being lonely. But I'd never told Dad and now I wished I had.

'Is this what you want?' Dad asked me.

I nodded. 'If it's all right with you.' I held my breath.

Dad's expression was hard to read. He looked from me to Maggie and then back again like he was weighing things up. 'Sure. Why not?'

'Excellent!' said Maggie clapping her hands together. 'It'll be hard work, mind. She'll take some training. She's not your run-of-the-mill dog. Not just because of the deafness but she's a bit quirky with a mind of her own.'

'I know,' I said. 'That's what I love most about her.' I put the puppy down and turned to Maggie. The sparkle in her eyes could attract a magpie. A chance encounter at the library had changed so many things. I was now a proper bookworm. I'd loved all the books I'd been lost in and all the characters I'd shared ups and downs with but what I'd got most from the library was my friendship with Maggie. She'd taught me loads about life, about myself and how to fight for what I wanted. She was my hero. 'Hug?' I said. 'You know. Only if you want to.'

I'd hardly finished the sentence before Maggie was pulling both me and my dad into her arms. At that moment we almost felt like a family – an odd, dysfunctional one, but it felt good all the same. 'Right,' she said, pulling away and briskly wiping under her eyes. 'Who wants something to eat?'

Epilogue

Five weeks later

Maggie and Christine had been planning a bit of a do. It was partly to show off the new mobile library van and partly to say thank you to everyone who had supported the efforts to save the library. It was the last Saturday in September and the sun was shining, which was causing an issue for the iced cakes the WI had made. Although given the hordes of people, they weren't going to need to last long. Maggie shooed a few of them into a more orderly tea queue.

Christine was looking smart in her new suit. She had taken it upon herself to adopt the title of senior librarian as she was by default the only full-time member of staff left in the area. It seemed to have given her a renewed enthusiasm for her job and she had taken on her new role with gusto. The library was thriving and the original Save the Library committee had morphed into an ongoing forum to keep the ideas fresh. Christine was very much leading it.

Maggie and Tom had settled into part-time volunteer

roles and were leading lights in the book club. Farah led the children's section and would be partly responsible for restocking the mobile library and managing orders that came in from its rounds.

'Where's the blooming van?' said Maggie. Tom looked nervously at his phone.

'It'll be here,' said Farah, eyeing them both. 'Wait till you see the paintwork; it's awesome.' Farah was rocking on her heels.

As if on cue a cheer went up from the crowd as the brightly painted van pulled up opposite. The van featured a beautiful design depicting books flying out of an open window like birds taking flight and it created a buzz in the crowd.

They all posed for photographs in front of the mobile library and the new venture was toasted with tea and cake and a lot of mutual congratulations. Inside it was just as impressive. Tom and Farah proudly showed off the romance section, which they had worked on together.

Once people had gathered outside Christine clapped her hands and everyone turned in her direction.

'I want…' Her voice was a bit squeaky. She cleared her throat and started again. 'I wanted to say thank you to everyone for all you did to save Compton Mallow library. You should all be proud and we hope to see you all on a regular basis so that we can stay open…' There were a few calls of hear, hear. 'And I wanted to say a special thank you to… well… someone very special for everything they did: Maggie Mann.'

'Oh, it was nothing,' said Maggie, but Christine beckoned her over to stand next to her.

'No, it wasn't,' said Christine. 'I would have given up if it hadn't been for you. So I... well *we*...' She turned to glance at Farah and Tom who were standing nearby looking shifty. 'We wanted to say a proper thank you for all your help in saving the library.'

Farah rummaged under the cake table behind her and produced a large basket of flowers and she and Tom handed them to Maggie. 'My goodness,' she said feeling touched by the thought. 'You didn't need to. I mean I love a good fight...'

'Don't I know it,' said Tom. He was getting cheekier by the day.

'Speech!' called out Bill.

Maggie addressed the crowd. 'This village library has always had a place in my heart. Books are such an underrated essential. Every book is a key that unlocks another world, leads us down the path of a different life and offers the chance to explore an unexpected adventure. Every one is a gift of either knowledge, entertainment or pure escapism and goodness knows we all need that from time to time. Like the rest of you, I always thought the library would be here. I never expected it to be under threat. It's a stark reminder to not take anything in life for granted. You only properly start fighting for something when you realise you're going to lose it.' She sighed thoughtfully. 'Anyway, if truth be told, I was saving the library for myself as much as the community. Quite selfish really.'

'Not at all. That's something you're not,' said Christine. 'Thank you, Maggie.'

The crowd applauded and there were air kisses and brief hugs. Maggie studied the basket of flowers. 'This is truly lovely. I've no idea how I'll get it home on the bus. But I love a challenge.'

When the excitement had died down and the cake had been eaten people started to make their farewells and disappear.

'Maggie?' said Tom, pulling her to one side.

'I suppose you were in on this,' she said pointing at the flowers.

'Er, yeah. And there's something else.' He bit his lip and the gesture made her instantly concerned. 'I did a bit of googling. And, well, there aren't many dentists in Kent called Haseley.'

'Tom...' Maggie swallowed hard. 'What have you done?'

'I sent an email,' he said. Maggie's shoulders dropped. 'I know it was none of my business but I figured if I told him what you'd done for me then maybe he'd get an idea of what a sound person you are and...' Tom was looking glassy-eyed.

'It's okay,' said Maggie, anticipating that he'd received a similar response to hers. 'I appreciate that you tried, Tom. That means a lot. But now we need to draw a line under it and move on.' She forced a smile. 'Okay?'

Tom's lips twitched. 'Thing is. I told him it'd be best to see for himself what other people thought of you.' Maggie's eyebrows knotted together. 'And I think he took me up on that.' Tom nodded over her shoulder.

Maggie turned slowly to follow Tom's gaze. Most of the villagers had dispersed leaving the WI ladies and a few stragglers. But standing by the mobile library van, talking to Farah, were four people: a man, a woman and two grown-up children. Tears instantly sprang to Maggie's eyes, blurring the sight she had longed to see. She couldn't say she would have recognised her son because sadly she knew she would have passed him in the street and not known who he was. In fact she was fairly sure she'd shooed him out of the way earlier. But now she watched him, talking and laughing, she knew in her heart it was him.

'River,' she said softly.

'Word of advice,' said Tom. 'You might not want to call him that.' He beamed a grin at her as she wiped away the tears, before giving him a friendly whack on the arm.

'Oh, Tom. I don't know what to say. Thank you.'

'The look on your face is all I wanted really. Come on, let's meet your son.'

Questions for your Book Club

- How significant is the library to the story?
- Why is the library so important to Tom and to Maggie?
- When Tom is first introduced to the reader he is described as invisible. What is your first impression of him?
- The story is told from two different character viewpoints: a seventy-two-year-old woman and a sixteen-year-old boy. Do you think their judgements are typical of the way the older and younger generations view each other?
- Both Tom and Maggie are lonely people and yet their lives are very different. Why do you think they are both lonely?
- You learn more about the characters' backgrounds as you read further into the novel. Did your opinion of any of them change? If so, how?
- Maggie has been keeping her secret for over fifty years. Should she have told Tom the truth? Is it ever good to hide the truth?
- Which character do you most admire, and why?
- What do you think Maggie learned from Tom and vice versa?
- What were some of the ways that they tried to save the library? What would you have done in Tom and Maggie's position?

Acknowledgements

A whole lot of people come together to get a book published and I am thankful to everyone who has had a hand in *The Library.* This started as a secret project when the characters popped into my head and were a world away from the romantic comedies I was used to writing. But their stories were so strong I couldn't ignore them so I wrote this book. At the time I didn't know if it would ever be published but I had to tell Tom and Maggie's story.

Huge thank you to my agent Kate Nash for not thinking I'd lost the plot when I presented her with my manuscript and for working so hard to find the right home for it. I will be forever grateful to Hannah Smith, Laura Palmer and the fabulous team at Aria for taking a chance on this project and making it the book it is today. Huge thanks also go to Lisa Brewster for the stunning cover.

Thank you to Alison May & Janet Gover for the March 2019 Writing Retreat that gave me reassurance that this was worth pursuing. Also thanks to Chris from that course for the two fingers comment. Thanks to my long-suffering writing friends who must have wondered if this book would ever see the light of day – I promise to shut up about it now.

Much love and thanks to David and Rosemary Boulton

for lovely discussions over lunch about life on a smallholding and for being fabulous early beta readers. Thanks to Ryan Nurse, another awesome early beta reader – you'll make an amazing editor one day very soon. Thanks to Emily Davis for answering my many questions about libraries and also doing a fabulous job as a beta reader.

I have to give a mention to Grandborough Farmer's Market which is just the loveliest community and to The Lost Farm, Grandborough for introducing me to Cym.

Huge heartfelt thanks to Cym Baseley for answering so very many questions and giving me a tour of her fabulous farm, introducing me to her sheep and for letting me witness the birth of a lamb. Any errors are entirely my own.

Thanks to the National Trust and Charlecote Park for keeping a herd of Jacob sheep which was a lovely excuse to visit and eat cake, all in the name of research.

I so hope this book will be enjoyed by reading groups and I must give a shout out to all my friends at Boozy Book Club for broadening my reading choices and expanding my knowledge of wine.

A huge thank you to library staff everywhere. You do an amazing job. And lovely readers please, please, please use your local library. They need your support now more than ever. Every time you borrow a book the author receives a few pennies from Public Lending Right, so you are supporting authors too.

And finally to the booksellers, book bloggers and especially to you the readers – thanks so much for letting me do the job that I love. And if you enjoyed reading this please tell your local book group and leave a review because it may help someone else find it and enjoy it too – Thank you.

About the Author

BELLA OSBORNE has been jotting down stories as far back as she can remember but decided that 2013 would be the year that she finished a full length novel. In 2016, her debut novel, *It Started at Sunset Cottage*, was shortlisted for the Contemporary Romantic Novel of the Year and RNA Joan Hessayon New Writers Award.

Bella's stories are about friendship, love and coping with what life throws at you. She likes to find the humour in the darker moments of life and weaves these into her stories.

Bella believes that writing your own story really is the best fun ever, closely followed by talking, eating chocolate, drinking fizz and planning holidays.

She lives in the Midlands, UK, with her lovely husband and wonderful daughter who thankfully both accept her as she is (with mad morning hair and a penchant for skipping).

Hello from Aria

We hope you enjoyed this book! If you did, let us know, we'd love to hear from you.

We are Aria, a dynamic fiction imprint from award-winning publishers Head of Zeus. At heart, we're committed to publishing fantastic commercial fiction – from romance to sagas to historical fiction.

Visit us online and discover a community of like-minded fiction fans.

You can find us at:

www.ariafiction.com
@Aria_fiction
@Ariafiction